ETERNAL
GRAFFITI

ETERNAL GRAFFITI

A Novel

Peter Marlton

The Story Plant
Studio Digital CT, LLC
P.O. Box 4331
Stamford, CT 06907

Story Plant paperback ISBN-13: 978-1-61188-332-9
Fiction Studio Books e-book ISBN-13: 978-1-945839-66-5

Visit our website at www.TheStoryPlant.com

First Story Plant Printing: September 2022

Printed in the United States of America
0 9 8 7 6 5 4 3 2 1

For all the friends who've gone too soon.

Poetry is eternal graffiti written
in the heart of everyone.
                    –Lawrence Ferlinghetti

Prologue

Montauk, New York, Fall 1980

I don't know if this is a confession or a purge, a scream or a lullaby. But I'm compelled to get it all down, and not for sentimental reasons, not to warm myself in the bittersweet glow of nostalgia. No, this sojourn into antiquity is a beginning, a becoming; I write out of necessity. My beloved ghosts are here with me. Sarah, the misfit and mystic, Shooky, the aspiring, drug-dealing Casanova, and my angel, Kiera. I failed them all, each in a different way, so I accept their scrutiny. I welcome it. As I begin to tell you our stories, they remind me that even under the most favorable conditions truth can be cagey, cunning, mercurial. Often it doesn't like being known, and when unwanted truths are about to emerge self-deception is its vengeance, its favorite trick. But it will be no match for me. I write in blood.

I chose to rent this little house on the outskirts of Montauk because it's perfect — battered but not broken, and close to the ocean, where I can walk away from this writing when I need to, and breathe. Yahweh, my tuxedo cat, is here with me too, taking this temporary move out here with me in stride, sitting behind my Remington as I type, following with bemused detachment the candle flames fluttering from a not-so-subtle entertainment of wind coming through a crack in the window. All day long I've watched the Halloween wind reshaping the dunes, making endless changes, corrections, revisions, the uncompromising architecture of sand resisting finality, refusing to be conquered, and the wind never satisfied. It's like watching an artist at work. I know that's what I'm facing, not that I'm an artist by any means. I'm just a twenty-eight-year-old itinerant man on the verge of losing my mind.

If I am to move on, to do more than survive, I have no choice but to reclaim the moments over the last ten years I care to hold on to and the wreckage from those years with which I will try to make peace. There is no place left to go, no place left to hide, no way to Houdini my way out of what all too often feels like the straitjacket of my past. I know I'm fucked unless I get through this. I'll make mistakes but they won't be of any consequence, no threat to your understanding, or perhaps even to your empathy. You may see that as a disclaimer and I wouldn't blame you. But I think of it this way: if my life were to be brought to light in a series of Impressionist paintings, not representing actual reality but rather new realities in themselves, this would be a walk in and around and through the stories each of them would tell.

Part One

November 1970 – June 1971

Here's to the few who forgive what you do,
and the fewer who don't even care.
— Leonard Cohen

Let me forget about today until tomorrow.
— Bob Dylan

One

On the Monday after the long Thanksgiving weekend in 1970, I came home for the last time to the little rented house my mother and I lived in. Two bedrooms, one bath, tiny living room, washer and dryer on the covered back porch. A typical low-rent box in Rockville Flats, California, an all but forgotten, end-of-the-road, jerkwater town on the southwest ass-cheek of the Mojave Desert. It's bordered in all directions by a barren landscape probably not so different from the one Christ wandered into as a would-be savior.

I remember walking into the house excited and a little afraid (which I never would have admitted at the time). My best friend Shooky and I were running away to Venice Beach early the next morning. It was something we'd been planning for months. Steven Gregory, our high school principal (at his core a simpleton, a gray suit with a head on it), told us earlier that day that because we were such fuck-ups we'd have to repeat our senior year. That sped up our departure date by months. No way were we going to stick around for that.

I found my mother sprawled out on the couch, unconscious. She worked the counter at Winchell's, selling donuts and coffee to truck drivers all night long on the graveyard shift. She must've traded with somebody to be home at that hour. I could smell the bourbon from ten feet away. I was probably as high as she was drunk. Shooky and I had been getting stoned for the last few hours. The hash had taken me to a magical place — an otherwise inaccessible neighborhood in my mind, one that was free of existential angst, uncontaminated by any form of law enforcement, where Rockville Flats' fossilized, infertile hills were uncharacteristically alive with the sound of music.

But there she was, my one and only mother, bringing me down again. She lay there in her white blouse, her nametag slightly askew (Janet), her black polyester slacks, and her fat little brown shoes rounding out an ensemble of hopelessness. Her whiskey-soaked brain was surely submerged somewhere on the edge of eternity, her *I've-smoked-for-twenty-years-and-I-ain't-quitting-now-and-you-can't-make-me* lungs sounding, as usual, like the tired engine of a battered old train desperate to make one last trip to Clarksville. I had grown so accustomed to seeing her in that condition that it hardly fazed me. I felt nothing. No, that's not true. I felt pity, which is worse than feeling nothing.

So it was another one of those days when everything in and around and about the house was redundant and stale, bereft of soul, devoid of hope. I wish now I had a happier memory of that last day with her, maybe just a tiny moment, maybe just her asking me to pass her the *TV Guide* so she could do her crossword puzzle and me saying OK, but then everything would have had to be so different. I was out of control back then and embraced it fully — the perpetually stoned-out peace-and-love poster-boy hippie kid who, underneath it all, was consumed with rage and hurt and resentment. Why that was will, I hope, become clear. No wonder my mom was a drunk. I stood and watched her wheezing, and chose not to think about the "good ol' days" when she and I got along. This time I was leaving. There was no point.

I grabbed a box of Cocoa Puffs, a carton of milk, a mixing bowl and a spoon, and took them into my room. I ate my chocolate breakfast food like I thought a gladiator would eat chocolate breakfast food, and felt like a Roman emperor when I was done.

I picked up the beautiful Gibson Hummingbird guitar I'd bought with drug money and practiced a few songs I'd written. I put the first stack of records on my little stereo, cleared off my "homework" table, set up my scale, took out the block of hash and the two pounds of weed I'd scored in Anaheim the day before and started to work. I had to weigh and cut as many grams of the hash as I could by the time Shooky came by to pick me up at five the next morning. Whatever I didn't finish I'd do in Venice. I didn't mind staying up. I loved the work; it took me out of myself. I bagged the thirty-two ounces of Michoacán first and set them aside to be ready for packing.

Two or three hours after starting in on the hash I realized that the last record had ended, and I heard nothing in the house except the mousy squeak of the dope scale. It must have been around midnight or later. Something was wrong. No wheezing. I walked out into the dark little hallway and looked into my mom's room. It smelled of stale cigarettes and dirty laundry. Piles of clothes were everywhere. Her bed was a sad, concave, spoon-like thing supporting a sheet-sculpture of the Alps. The bathroom was right across from my room. She wasn't in there either.

It was only three or four steps to the living room, which was still and dark, except for the slow sweep of a car's headlights moving across the walls and the cottage-cheese ceiling. I flipped on a light. Mom had not moved since I'd gotten home. She always screamed at me if I ever woke her, so I tiptoed up to the couch and leaned over to look at her face, which was turned inward toward the wall. I lifted her eyelids and saw a frightful mackerel stare. I put my head to her chest and couldn't hear a heartbeat. That was as close to her as I'd been since my father Harry left when I was eight. She'd clung to me for a short while after that.

Yelling her name, shaking her, slapping her, nothing had any effect. The fear I felt flipped my otherwise pleasant and mellow hash high for a loop. I wasn't sure what to do. I headed into the kitchen to get a pan full of water to throw on her, but then somehow I realized that the idea came out of anger rather than from an effort to try and save her (this had happened more than once before), so I decided I'd better call 9-1-1.

It seemed like the ambulance was there before I hung up the phone. The medics went to work. From my stoned-out perspective it looked like they were performing open-heart surgery. My mother moaned and threw up on the weird brown suburban shag carpet. Two cops parked outside and came sauntering in. I paid no attention to them. I was fixated on the unfolding drama. Mom passed out again. "Fuck!" one of the ambulance guys said quietly. They made their magic orange gurney spring to life. They flopped her onto it and then shot out the door as if she were a time bomb that might blow up the whole block.

I noticed then that one of the two cops was Officer Beatrice Walls, whose new blond bowl cut surprised me for its radical unattractiveness. We knew each other from a previous idiotic skirmish. Most of the cops in Rockville Flats knew me. I hated all of them. About a year before, Walls busted me for shoplifting. I'd stolen a *Penthouse* and dropped it accidentally on the way out of the store. I was the catch of the year for the store rent-a-cop, but a routine bust for Walls. This all happened while I was cutting school. The judge dismissed the charge if I agreed to do twenty hours of community service. So I spent a little time digging around in a county irrigation ditch for a couple of weekends. Big deal. The school suspended me for five days for truancy. Suspending a kid for cutting school is like punishing a masochist. I was thrilled.

I could feel Walls' eyes on me. She whispered something to her partner, an Officer Duke, a tall, tanned rookie trying very hard to look menacing. He nodded. She seemed to be his mentor. He stood by studying everything she did.

"Sorry about your mom, Owen."

Walls sounded like she was teetering on the edge of sincerity. I said nothing. I was trying to appear as though I wasn't high. We were standing by the open front door. The ambulance backed out of the driveway and screamed its way to the hospital. Walls' squad car was parked like nobody else would ever park, diagonally, on the *lawn*. The obnoxious, manic, red and blue twirling lights exacerbated my disorientation.

"I guess I have to go to the hospital?" I asked her.

"Sure," she said, closing the door. "But first I'd like to know what's gone on here tonight." She took out a flip notebook and a pen and stood there poised to write.

"Nothing has 'gone on' here tonight."

"Your mother just got hauled away in an ambulance."

"You're blaming me for this?"

"Well, what happened?"

"She doesn't need an excuse to get shitfaced, does she? She and Romeo have been having problems. Maybe that's what it's about this time."

"Romeo?"

"Her boyfriend."

Walls squinted. "Oh, come on!"

"Hey, it's not my fault that that's his stupid name."

She turned to Officer Duke. "See what I mean?" Then back to me. "What kind of problems have they been having?"

"They can't agree about where to retire on the French Riviera."

"Watch it, pal."

"I am watchin' it."

"What are your mother's drinking habits?"

What a stupid question! What an idiot! "You saw her just now. What's the mystery? She's a goddamn raging alcoholic. The whole police department knows that."

She scribbled all that while looking at me and not at the notebook, as if that were supposed to impress me.

"Where's the attitude comin' from, Owen?"

"East Berlin."

She snorted. "That's just dumb. That's it for now." She barked at the rookie: "Let's go."

"I gotta use the bathroom," he said.

I stared at the couch, which still retained a vague but discernible outline of my mother's body. I was thrown off-kilter by how rotten I felt after hating her for so long.

"Do you have any other family?" Walls asked.

"There's nobody else."

"What's your dad's name?"

"Harry Kilroy."

"Where is he?"

"Hey!" Officer Duke shouted. "You'd better come check this out!"

She made a serious tactical mistake by not keeping an eye on me — a fuck-up that maybe could have put her back on a motorcycle, standing on the street in ninety-eight-degree heat, pointing a ray gun at passing cars. I'll never know. All the stuff on her utility belt shook as she jogged toward my room. In my emotional hash-infused fog I'd completely forgotten that I'd left my door open — a fuck-up that was far worse than hers.

I took off running, winding my way around the black and white and off into the night. But there was nowhere to run. I knew I was finished. The cool desert night air was my last taste of freedom. Walls and Duke were chasing me now, demanding that I "halt." I asked myself, *for what?* To give myself up to whatever horrors were in store? Was Walls going to shoot me if I didn't stop? Part of me hoped so.

I ran so fast and so hard that she was forced to slow down — she was out of shape — and I didn't know where the hell to go at first. I thought about going to Shooky's but it would be a big mistake leading the cops there. I could hear sirens screaming.

A few houses were already decorated for Christmas, some festooned with bright, colorful outdoor lights. I'd seen them earlier, and on that sad night they looked more cheerful than ever. Santas, elves, sleighs, candy canes, and reindeer all congregated on the front lawns. Christmas trees decorated with more lights and glittery ornaments and topped by golden stars and golden angels stood in the windows of those houses. All this made the undecorated houses look like tombs.

I crossed Rockville Flats Boulevard and looked behind me and there was Duke, stopping, turning around and running at full speed toward the sound of the sirens. I couldn't figure out what the fuck that was about. He was running *away* from me. Walls was getting up off the ground.

I threw myself over the fence that separated the boulevard from the no-man's-land I'd spent so many afternoons and nights getting stoned in and headed to Manderley, a special little spot where Shooky and I always hung out. I took a second to rest and breathe. It was pitch dark. I could see flashlights, lifeless eyes not blinking, coming over the fence. I shimmied down a steep pitch into a ravine. It was even darker there, a pool of octopus ink. A minute later about a dozen of those dead flashlight eyes appeared around the perimeter. A cop shouted a blistering command to a police dog. It was Duke! So he was the K-9 cop. He'd gone for the dog. I was impressed. His command cut into the night air like a bayonet. I couldn't understand what he was yelling but there was no doubt it sounded like deep trouble. I was Lee Harvey Oswald. I decided that if those bloodthirsty bastards were going to catch me I was going to make them work for it. They were in my backyard. I ran west, toward the Pacific Ocean. I'd always wanted to live by the ocean. So what if it was more than a hundred miles away? I could hear the wind, my breath, my feet landing on the hard uneven ground, the crazy dog barking viciously.

Beatrice Walls shouted, "Owen, Owen!" in the loudest fake-friendly voice she could muster. "Everything is gonna be OK if you just stop running and show us your hands!"

No way out. No hope. I was the fun they were going to have that night. But I kept going. All the king's soldiers were relentless in their blitzkrieg, but they were taking the long way around because they knew nothing about where they were or what they were doing. The flashlights moved across the ravine, the beams getting bigger, brighter. I found myself in a large open area that a science teacher once said had been a lake in ancient times. My only hope was to get across the lake and climb up to a ridge that a million years ago probably served as a platform from which cave men practiced their swan dives. From there I might stay free a little longer. I scrambled up the hillside and after a few attempts I pulled myself up onto the ridge. But the not-very-well-regulated militia was closing in. They knew more about where we were than I thought. I started running and slipped and fell into a ditch, eating the dry dirt, scraping my hands on the little bastard rocks. I crawled like a wounded diamondback under a big gooseberry bush. The cops were converging on me now, no more than thirty feet away. I heard one set of footsteps approaching, crackling on the rocky ground.

Walls said, "Owen, we know you're under there. Show us your hands and come out! Unless you prefer to be dragged out by the dog." Another command from Duke and the dog went crazy, as if he hadn't been fed in weeks and wanted to crack my skull with his teeth.

I looked behind me and saw nothing but a cluster of flashlights and the ominous silhouettes of the Flatvillian soldiers behind them. Above me, through the branches of the bush, the spectacular panorama of useless stars. There was a sudden violent rustling sound. In what she probably thought was a career-restoring move, Beatrice Walls dived under the bush and pointed her deputy cowgirl six-gun an inch from my temple. I looked at her in shock — she knew me better than that — and then I turned to face the ground and waited to die.

"Don't be stupid," she said.

Two

If you've ever had a cop point a gun at your head you know how it feels to be made small, to be reduced to nothing but a body trembling with fear and outrage.

"Take that fucking gun away from my head, you pig bitch!"

Walls punched me in the ribs. I cried out, turned away from the posse, my head lying on the ground for a second, feeling like I'd been shot with a bazooka. How could she be *that* strong? I took in another dirt-breath, writhing in the hopelessness of the miserable Flatvillian night. She cuffed me tight and dragged me out and up on my feet. She put her gun away.

"Look at him," Hero Number One said from behind his flashlight. "A hippie faggot."

"With faggot hair," said Hero Number Two. (My hair was long, down to about the middle of my back. I was quite proud of it.) Some of his crime-fighting comrades chuckled. A few of them lit smokes, a brief glimpse of yellow flame illuminating their cop faces, and then the glowing red tips of the cigarettes appearing and disappearing behind the flashlights.

Hero Number One, trying to impress everybody, said, "I saw him selling his ass down in Hollywood last night."

Hero Number Three said, "He had to go that far to find a buyer!"

They all guffawed like it was the funniest thing they'd ever heard.

My ribs ached. It hurt when I tried to breathe. My stomach felt like searing-hot pinballs were bouncing around inside of it. I should have known to keep quiet, but I couldn't not say something back to that.

"I know why *you* were in Hollywood last night," I said, peering at Hero Number One behind his flashlight. I could feel the whole assemblage waiting to hear what I said next. "You were there for the same reason you always are — to suck your twelve-year-old boyfriend's little Oscar Mayer wiener. And guess what? While you were licking his come off your face, I was at your house fucking your wife in the ass."

The whole shooting match of crime fighters collectively went "Whoa!"

The would-be cuckold walked up and spit in my face.

"You puny little prick," he said. He whipped out *his* cowboy six-gun and placed it in my ear. "Take it back."

"Go ahead, pull the trigger, fucknut." I stood still, didn't move a muscle. Beatrice Walls' gun to my head was nothing compared to this. I was terrified, but I also wouldn't have minded if he shot me. It was turning into that kind of night.

"I said take it back, faggot!" The barrel of his gun seemed to be penetrating my skull.

He was such a pindick homophobe I couldn't keep myself from taunting him in front of his pals. I knew he might kill me and that scared me, but then what did I have to live for anyway at that point?

"Come on, creep! Kill me! Show your pals what kind of a he-man you are."

Walls said in a voice choking with tension, "Lloyd. Stop! He's a kid. Let him go. We've got him."

"I'm gonna kill this little fag unless he takes that back."

"Looks like I've hit a pretty sensitive nerve there, Lloyd." I turned as far as I could, which wasn't far, towards the increasingly tight cluster of crime busters. "What does *that* tell all you fuckers about him?"

"Owen, shut up!" Walls yelled.

Lloyd cocked the hammer on his gun. Pushed it further into my head. "You're dead. Say a prayer."

Some other cop said *"Lloyd"* the same way you'd say a dog's name when it's about to dig into the garbage.

Lloyd wasn't having any of that. He leaned closer to me and I could feel the spit hitting me as he yelled in my face. "Take it back or I'll blow your brains out!"

The barrel felt like it was at least an inch into my ear canal. Sound was muted.

"You're a weasel."

"Owen, are you *crazy*?" Walls yelled. "Just take it back and this will all be over."

"The loser's gonna have to kill me. That's how this is gonna have to go down."

"You think I won't?" Lloyd screamed.

He pushed the gun into my ear so hard it made my head bend the other way, so by the time my other ear just about kissed my shoulder the gun was vertical. Now I was bent all the way over to my left, my handcuffed hands dangling in a weird angle behind me. All the crime fighters were eerily silent now. You could hear the breeze teasing the bushes with cool, dry caresses. I wished one of the idiots would say something. The gun barrel pressing into my ear was cutting it up bad. Lloyd was trembling. I realized that the cops were just as scared shitless as I was. But then my mind suddenly became calm; a decision had somehow been made without me trying. I can't explain it. I just wanted out. I'd had it at that point. I was done with the whole thing.

"Get it over with," I said, my voice empty of malice, an unquestionable yearning taking its place. "Don't be the kind of pussy who doesn't. Be the kind of pussy who *really does* shoot the handcuffed kid."

I hoped when it happened it would be quick. I almost cried. The world was worthless, I was worthless. There was no hope. Everything had finally gone completely to hell.

Somebody *laughed*.

Lloyd punched me in the eye. I thought he might have broken my face. I fell backwards and hit the ground hard. My arms broke my fall a little but I thought I'd dislocated my shoulders. I was somewhat disappointed. Still alive.

He holstered his gun. "You're not worth another minute of my time."

The tension broken now, all the cops started laughing and talking shit to each other, like the whole homicidal-maniac scene had been nothing but a big joke. Walls, backed up by a couple of bruisers, stood over me. I watched Officer Duke walking away with Klaus the Destroyer.

Walls dragged me up off the ground for the second time. "You're on your way to a new life, Owen," Walls said. "Better get used to shutting the fuck up."

She led me up the hill. A circus of cop cars was parked askew on the edge of the ravine. We walked back to my house. There was a police van parked in the driveway. The door to the house was open and I saw a bunch of uniforms ripping the place apart.

"Do you think there's any way we could go in there and get my guitar?" I asked. "You kind of owe me, since you probably broke a few of my ribs."

Walls shook her head. "Holy shit, Owen. You're one crazy-ass kid. Now get in the car."

I slid onto the plastic cop-car seat in so much pain. I turned, slowly, slowly, so my back wouldn't crush my handcuffed hands. Walls got in, started the engine.

"You should have let that bastard kill me."

She held my gaze for a second and then picked up the microphone.

"Five-oh-eight."

"Five-oh-eight?"

"Suspect in custody. Heading to juvy."

"Ten-four, five-oh-eight. Juvy."

She put down the microphone and backed off the lawn and into the street. "Rockville Flats is finally rid of you, pal."

"Walls, as long as we've known each other I've wondered something. What's it like havin' to go through life being so fuckin' ugly?"

She stopped the car and threw it into park. I thought she was going to get out and come around my way and become violent again. But she turned around and said, "You know what, Owen? I know you've had a hard life. We all know that. It's pretty goddamned sad. But it's no excuse for being such a mean-spirited asshole."

"Yeah? And what was up with you tonight, Walls, pointing your fuckin' gun at me? Your shithead cop impression of a Christmas elf?"

§

I had three badly bruised ribs. One fractured. Most of the skin on my ear torn away. A black eye. Torn muscles in my shoulders. All of this was from a "fall" I took while I was running away from the cops. I would discover that nobody in court would believe my story. Cops would never pull a gun on an unarmed white kid. Everybody knows that.

§

My cell was the size of a grave, with green paint peeling off the walls, which were covered with scratched-in epitaphs: "Fuck the pigs" "Suck my dick" "Eat Shit " "Kill Warren" (a particularly sadistic guard), and so forth. Four feet above my cot a frosted rectangular window that didn't open let in a vague suggestion of light during the day. At night an invasive glare turned the cell gray because of floodlights.

Every time I closed my eyes I'd see my Sarah. Maybe it was the loneliness and isolation I felt that finally broke down the barriers between my memories of her and my determined efforts not to let them in. It had been four months.

She was one year behind Shooky and me in school. She was cute and small, maybe five-three or five-four, in bare feet most of the time, each toenail painted a different color. Her eyes were that stunning color of blue you see in pictures of coral reefs. The first time I saw her eyes, really saw them, not just when she walked by, I couldn't speak. It was like I'd had a stroke. She was coming out of detention — christened by the administration as the Cooling Off Room(!) — as I was going in, having just called my math teacher a fascist. We were two feet apart. We looked right at each other. I froze. She was annoyed but didn't say anything. I stepped aside and off she went. When I walked into the room, Ribs, the emaciated teacher's assistant whose job it was to lord over us, looked up at me, studied my face with uncharacteristic interest, and said, "Looks like *you* just met Sarah."

Her hair was very long, blonde sometimes, sometimes red, blue, or black, and she dressed like the freakiest of freaks: Catholic school girl with rainbow hair one day, fairy godmother the next, cowgirl in cowboy boots on still another, then Janis Joplin, then Blanche DuBois, then Elvira. Her notoriety was unmatched. She had a captivating smile that appeared often enough, but which emphasized a bit of an acne problem on her cheeks. Not long after she'd paralyzed me we became good friends.

I still remember so well how I believed she knew what a fraud I thought I was, what a phony loser. I was convinced she could see through me, detect or at least intuit all of my insecurities — what a shitty guitar player I secretly thought I was, my belief that I would never amount to anything, that I was worthless, ugly, stupid, and that now and in the end, I was, and always would be, alone. I told her all of this late one night on a camping trip when she and I were the only ones still awake. Everybody else had collapsed. We sat together under one cozy sleeping bag, my arm around her to keep her warm. She held my other hand. We were like two cats wrapped up in each other. Our faces were almost touching. We were being very quiet, which added to the intimacy. I could have kissed her but I didn't. I felt a deep, abiding, sublime sense of peace with her and I didn't want to do anything to fuck it up.

"I haven't seen any sign of your insecurities. You really hide them well," she said.

"Thanks. They're there, like broken glass at the bottom of a river. What about you? You seem like you don't have any, but you must, right?"

She laughed quietly, looked at the sky and said, "You know, right, that the light from those stars took tens of millions of years, maybe hundreds of millions, to get here, and a lot of them by now are already dead?"

"Yeah."

"I think I'm the light from one of those stars."

She was, most of the time, a compassionate and loving friend. Of all the people in our crowd, she would be the one who would remember good things that everyone else would forget, like which night would be the full moon. And if someone was freaking out on acid, she would always take charge, soothing them as best she could, trying to guide them into a better trip. She'd been there herself many times.

Not long after the camping trip, Shook and I took her to San Diego to see Taj Mahal and Country Joe and the Fish. Megan Marie Drysdale, Shooky's sometimes girlfriend, was supposed to come with us but for some reason she couldn't make it, so he was solo. By that time Sarah and I had naturally fallen deeper into each other's orbits. We held hands all night, kissed a lot, building up to a marathon make-out session during most of Country Joe, who, besides his *"One, two, three, what are we fightin' for? Don't ask me, I don't give a damn, Next stop is Vietnam,"* was kind of boring. On the way back to Flatville in Shooky's 1961 Citroen, Sarah and I made out intensely, even desperately, giving everything we had, like two drowning swimmers trying to make it to shore, trying to save each other's lives. A couple of kids with nothing left to believe in. We were in the back seat while Shooky drove. But just as things were really escalating she passed out. I knew she was very high, but I didn't know what she was on. She wasn't one of those people who'd announce it. Sarah wasn't known for taking downers. She was more of a speed-acid girl. We drove her to my house — my mom was working — and by dawn she was OK.

I didn't know Sarah for very long. She moved to Rockville Flats with her family just about a year before it all went to hell. She and I had given each other many "friendship" kisses before we went camping. That was nothing out of the ordinary among the people we hung around with. Even that camping night — again, the sweetest, most intimate time I'd ever had with anyone up to then — we'd kissed goodnight European style, just once on each cheek. We went to sleep cuddled together, her head on my shoulder, her hand in mine, my left arm falling asleep, my neck already stiffening up from an inability to move, and my never wanting the night to end. We were the talk of the morning when everybody got up. We went out of our way to assure them all that we were just friends. Nobody believed it, least of all me, but it didn't lead to anything, at least not until two weeks later at Country Joe.

I'd hoped the morning after the concert that Sarah would acknowledge that she was my girlfriend, that she would throw herself into my arms, kiss me, and tell me how happy she was. But she said she didn't remember anything about the ride home and yes, it was fun making out, but couldn't we please just be friends again?

One of the best and worst things about her was once she'd made up her mind about something you could do nothing to change it. One day in the Cooling Off Room she announced, inexplicably, to me and a few others, that "Mr. Sun, Mr. Moon" by Paul Revere and the Raiders would outlast "Voodoo Child" as a classic. She just blurted this out, out of nowhere. She caught all kinds of shit for it (and she probably said it just to provoke and enrage people), but no amount of terrorism or guerilla or psychological warfare had any impact, except perhaps to make her even more militant in expressing her point of view. So I had no hope trying to convince her that she should be my girlfriend. Whenever I tried to, she'd piss me off or try to make me laugh about it, depending on her mood. The message, however delivered, was always the same: I didn't have a chance. When we saw each other after that period we'd hug and kiss, but it was all awkward and sad. I'd tried much too hard, and yet I didn't try hard enough, or I didn't try in the right way, because I had no idea what that looked like. I was a neophyte at real love and she was a kaleidoscope of a girl.

But one summer night we went out to Manderley. We smoked a joint and drank Drambuie out of the bottle. I thought we were friends trying to figure out what that meant for us now. I think Sarah believed that too. But after we finished the joint we held each other for a long time without saying anything. And then we turned and looked at each other and kissed soft and long and full of hunger. Sarah said, "The moon's on the other side of the world tonight. No one's watching us."

We made love for the first and only time, with wild and tender and desperate passion, surpassing the intensity we'd found in ourselves in Shooky's car. Afterwards we were closer than we'd ever been, sitting naked, holding each other, the warmth of the night wrapped around us. We passed the Drambuie back and forth, smoked cigarettes and talked. The magic of that night became part of us forever, and yet even with its power it was unable to keep us from knowing, somehow, deep down, that it was all over. Before we left Manderley I told her I was sorry that I'd fucked it all up and she said no, she'd fucked it all up. We laughed. We were so completely *with* each other, without any self-consciousness or angst; I felt the moment would never come again. I couldn't leave anything left unsaid. We put our clothes on and stood there together, holding on, like we were waiting for something. In the next instant we'd be leaving Manderley, going back to that part of our lives we so badly wanted to escape from.

I looked into those sad, chameleon eyes. "I fuckin' *love* you, Sarah."

She gently put her arms around my neck and brought her face close to mine. I felt her warm breath on my lips. "You're an angel," she whispered. "I'm just really messed up, which is why I'm so sorry about everything. No matter what happens, never forget that this crazy girl loves you too." We kissed again for as long as we could before we let it go, and walked slowly, holding hands, back into our separate lives.

That we'd had a chance to live those hours, to say those sacred things, is to me, even now, proof that the universe very occasionally sheds its awful indifference. And I will always believe she was wrong. I fucked it up. Back then I had no capacity to do otherwise.

I saw her again not long after our night at Manderley. She'd just come back from her family's annual summer vacation. She said she was about to have a major breakdown and couldn't sleep, and asked me if I had any downers I could give her that would last her for a couple of weeks. I gave her all I had. Fourteen Nembutals in a little white envelope.

"I'll give you more when I can if you still need 'em," I said. "I know what it's like."

"You really are my salvation, Owen." She slid the envelope carefully into her back pocket. She looked at me for what seemed like a long time, perhaps reliving a little, our night at Manderley like I was. She hugged me tight — a long, deep, beautiful, I-need-you hug — and we kissed. I thought maybe we had a chance after all.

"You call me if you need to talk, OK?"

"OK."

"Promise? I don't like to think of you going through this shit alone. I mean, I know you have other friends and all, but, well, you know what I mean."

She nodded and shut her eyes and squeezed my hands and held on to them for as long as she could. I still remember watching her walk away. Her hair was blonde that day with black streaks. I thought it was very sexy. She was wearing a black T-shirt with Frank Zappa on the front, and a pair of cut-off jeans. It was too hot for bare feet, so she wore sandals. Just before she went around the corner she turned around and stopped. She looked at me and I looked back. We didn't say anything. I can still feel my heart break for her. She blew me a kiss, slowly and with finality. I did the same. Then she was gone.

That night she kissed her mom and dad goodnight, tucked in her little sister Penelope, kissed her, went into her room, and swallowed all fourteen pills. I heard from some-body that she'd left a note but the family never shared it with any of us. The next day I got a letter in the mail in a blue envelope. There was a little drawing of a shooting star where the return address would be.

> *July 23, 1970, 4:00 pm*
> *My dearest, sweetest, beloved Owen,*
> *Please please please forgive me. There was no other way. Be kind to yourself, and don't take any blame. I lied to you. I'm terrible but I had no choice. It's not your fault. You have a heart the size of the sun and I am lucky enough to have been in the bright light and loving warmth of it. That has been such a huge gift to me. Maybe next time around we can live happier lives? I'm so sorry, so very sorry, Owen. But you're gonna be rich and famous and your music is gonna bring so much happiness to people, as you have to me. Goodbye my dear friend and lover.*
> *Love always, Your Sarah.*

P.S. Please burn this as soon as you read it. If anyone should find it you'd be in trouble and that mustn't ever happen.

P.P.S. Voodoo Child is better. So I'll meet you in the next world, OK? Don't be late....

I never burned the letter. I took it home and hid it and brought it out again and again and wept over it and kissed it and tore myself apart over it. Sometimes when I held it I thought I could feel, or sense, her hand moving across the blue page, writing in silver glittery ink those awful, beautiful, unforgettable words, as if she had no hesitation or doubt about what she'd planned to do that night. A letter written with grace, love, and a chilling resolve. I'd still have that letter if my life hadn't turned into such a catastrophe.

I've asked myself a million times how I couldn't have known I was killing her. Part of me died with her that night. At the memorial party we threw for her I was trashed on Valium and hooch and so was everybody else. There was no other way. Shooky was the only one who knew I'd given her the Nembutal.

"It was an act of love, bro," he said after the party, trying his best to console me. "You had the best intentions. You were trying to help her out, ease her pain. She loved you for it. She's looking down on us tonight, right now, this second, blowing you more kisses."

I started crying so hard I couldn't speak.

"We're all crying about her, and we're all gonna stop one of these days. That's just how it is. For you, it'll just take longer."

§

I was convicted after a morning trial. I had no defense — I was a criminal after all. I had no expectations of anything good coming out of that whole mess. Officers Walls and

Duke testified about the dope and me resisting arrest, and that was that. My mother had survived her bout with alcohol poisoning and actually came to court on my sentencing day to tell the judge she wanted nothing to do with me. We'd been close once, like I mentioned earlier. But over those last hard years, when she started binge-drinking, hooking up with a parade of losers, I needed to get out of the house. I started cutting school, getting high, and staying out all night. Our relationship deteriorated. We'd finally become like two roommates who rarely spoke, coveting each other's silence and indifference, biding our time until we could get out of each other's way for good.

"The feeling's mutual," I told the judge. That didn't help. I was sentenced to thirteen months in a place called, believe it or not, the Wagon Train Ranch for Boys. I'd get out on my eighteenth birthday. I stood up and yelled at the judge as they were taking me out of the courtroom. *"Do I look like a fucking cowboy?"*

He ignored me. "It's lunch time," he said to the room.

Three

That night I paced around in my miserable little grave and tried to come to terms with how much I'd lost. There was the huge amount of weed worth several thousand bucks, probably my guitar, my friends in Rockville Flats, and especially Shooky.

Back then you couldn't help but like Shooky. He was fun and funny, smart, and had a magnetism and charm that girls loved. He was always reading books I had no interest in, like *Ivanhoe*. One of the things I admired about him was that he used to get so mad. A lot. He got mad and so I got mad with him. He was my friend, my drug-dealing partner, and a writer. We were gonna lead happy lives and anybody who told us we weren't could go fuck themselves. He loved his mother and his little sister Stacy, but "they live in a totally different universe, and I just can't relate," he told me. His dad left before he was born and his mother hooked up with another guy who left after Stacy was born. Life in Rockville Flats was like that.

Shook and I hated school, we hated being told who we were supposed to be, and were determined to be the opposite of what was expected, come what may. Anything, any sign, any law, anybody who said "no" to something that should've been "yes" was a target of Shooky's rage and ridicule. He so wanted the world to make sense. Before I knew him I didn't know that it didn't. To me it made plenty of sense: life was irrevocably fucked.

Just a few hours before my waltz with Beatrice Walls and my tango with Officer Lloyd, I'd gone to meet Shooky at Manderley, our little refuge out in the desert. He'd given it that name a year or two before when he was reading *Rebecca*. (The first line: "Last night I dreamt I went to Manderley again.") I didn't give a damn what we called it. I just loved being there.

Manderley was perched on a berm of Mesozoic granite that jutted out above the ravine I was in when Flatville's finest crime busters were after me. The surface, about ten or twelve square feet of rock, dirt, and shrubs, was uneven but for a couple of chairs carved out by a volcanic outburst about sixty-six million years ago in anticipation of Shooky and me needing a place to sit. From there we could easily spot intruders, in uniform or otherwise.

I saw him already sitting out there, looking like a Buddha the size of a dashboard saint. As always he wore shades, a red vest over a black T-shirt, Levi's, and let his long, Jimmy Page black hair speak for itself. We were ecstatic knowing we were dropping out of school and leaving the next morning for Venice Beach. We had money, a huge amount of reefer to sell, and looked forward to nothing but good times ahead. He turned around and waved and thrust a fist into the air like those black dudes did in the Olympics. "We're free, bro!!" he shouted. I did the same.

I sat down next to him and handed him a domino-sized piece of the hash that I'd scored in Anaheim the day before. There was no drug in the world that smelled as good. Turning his back to the wind Shooky fired it up in his favorite saxophone-shaped pipe, producing a plume of white, soul-preserving smoke that appeared to rise up out of his head. He took a deep toke, handed me the pipe and said, his voice climbing to a higher pitch, "Thanks to the Honorable Steven Gregory, principal extraordinaire, we're finally on our way, bro! Venice is gonna be like heaven! You're gonna play the Troubadour and be the next Bob Dylan, and I'm gonna write a novel about moving to Venice and getting laid all the time." He handed me the pipe. I took a good long hit and blew it out slowly.

"Not giving a shit about anything is liberating," I said.

"You're right, bro. It ain't apathy, it's freedom."

§

About a week after my trial word came down from probation that it was going to take them three more weeks to get their shit together and ship me off to the OK Corral. The guards assigned me a job mopping the unit floors, which included the A, B, and C hallways where the cells were, the bathroom, the chow hall, and the day room. I was indifferent at first but I ended up liking it. There was something Zen about sliding the mop from left to right, watching the dry dead floor suddenly shine under the warm Pine-Sol water. I took my time, did a good job. I worked seven days a week, always making it last as long as possible so I could be left alone with my thoughts while not stuck in the cell.

Days appeared and disappeared like the ideas you get on acid. When you come down you have a feeling there's something there to hold on to, but no, there's nothing. One morning I was just getting started on the day room, moving the plastic chairs aside, when I saw a book on the shelf above the TV. *From Here to Eternity*. With a title like that, I thought, it had to be something I'd like. I wasn't much of a book reader at the time. That was Shooky's thing. But having to fill so many hours day after day can pique your interest in things you'd otherwise pass up. I took the book — a monster tree-killer — to the guard station. One of the regular week-day-morning goons, a portly Chinese guy named Eric, looked up from a ledger he was working on. I kind of liked him.

"Aren't you supposed to be mopping, Kilroy?" The way he asked gave me the impression he didn't really give a damn one way or the other.

"Yeah. But I just saw this book on the shelf and I'm wondering if I can read it."

"I don't know. Can you read?"

"I read minds. And yours must be empty if you're asking me that."

"That's so funny I forgot to laugh. Lemme see it."

He took the book, fanned through the pages to check for contraband. He looked at the number on the last page. "Shit, man. It's longer than the goddamned Bible. You'll never finish it."

"I'll finish the fucking thing. What else am I gonna do in this shithole?"

He smiled, handed me the book, and said, "Mop."

§

I did finish it and it was one of the sublime pleasures of my life. I couldn't put the damn thing down. It took me so far away from that awful little cell! In spite of the fact that it made me more certain than ever that I would make sure I would avoid the draft — I could no more be a soldier than I could be a priest — I might as well have just floated out the jail door and flown over to Hawaii and merged my soul with Private Robert E. Lee Pruitt's. It saved me. I'd never known a book could do that.

§

I finally got out of juvy in January. I took a long, depressing drive through California with a man called Sergeant Bill. His full name was Jonathan Bill, but sadly for him he was forced to go through life as if he were a character from Mr. Roger's Neighborhood. This undermined his African-American ma-

37

cho lawman veneer. He was a decent enough guy though, kind of short, about fifty, a little overweight, with a cop mustache that looked like he'd installed a whisk broom under his nose. On our way out of jail I asked if we could go by my house and pick up my guitar.

"It means the world to me. I'm a songwriter. That's what I'm gonna do with my life. I *gotta* have that guitar! It's a Gibson Hummingbird!"

"Where do you live?"

"Rockville Flats."

"Well, shit. That's about twenty-five miles the wrong way. I can't do that."

"Don't you know anything about guitars?"

"I know they make a hell of a lot of racket."

"Mine doesn't. It's an acoustic. It's worth a *ton* of money. Like, a thousand bucks. I'll never have another guitar like that in my life, man."

Sgt. Bill gave me a suspicious look. "Now how is it that a kid like you can afford a guitar like that?"

"My grandfather bought it for me."

"Yeah? Well I flew in here yesterday from Timbuktu in a helicopter. Look, I know how you got the money. I read your police report. Sorry, son. You're just gonna have to let it go." He said that in a friendly way, a matter-of-fact statement. The all-too-predictable high-handed bullshit morality speech never came. As disappointed as I was, I appreciated that.

"Never mind. My mother probably sold it anyway."

I said nothing for the next couple of hours and stared out the window watching irrelevant civilian life go by, wondering what was going to happen to me. I wondered how things could get any worse. 1970 had been a horrible year for the world, and for me, by any measure. The Beatles broke up in April. In May, the National Guard shot thirteen students at Kent State University, killing four of them. The victims had been protesting Nixon's secret bombing of Cambodia. In July, Sarah. In mid-September, Jimi Hendrix OD'd in London. A couple of weeks after that, before any of us had a chance to really accept his death, Janis Joplin OD'd in a Hollywood motel. I thought about how that month in juvy had flipped my life into a tailspin I didn't think I'd ever get out of.

I remember lying awake in my cell on New Year's Eve, thinking of the people I loved who I'd never see again, as the boy in the other cot told me he'd murdered his father. You can't come back from something like that. I waited to speak until I was fairly sure he wouldn't hear any trace of shock in my voice. All I could come up with was, "I'm really sorry, man." It didn't matter to me whether what he'd said was true. He'd said it and cried.

§

I asked Sgt. Bill if they were going to shave my head at the cowboy ranch like they do in some prisons.

"Oh yeah, they do that to all you long-hairs just as soon as you get there. Then they take your hair down to Frisco and sell it for wigs."

"That's insane!"

He saw the terrified look on my face and chuckled. He even patted me on the shoulder. "Don't worry kid. I'm just pullin' your chain. You hungry?"

He bought us both Big Macs, fries, and chocolate milkshakes for lunch in Fresno. I had to eat mine with handcuffs on, but I managed.

Back in the car, freaking out about how far into fuck-knows-where we were going, I was once again mentally thrashing myself for not closing my bedroom door the night I got busted. Beating myself up every day. Who would think a simple thing like not closing a bedroom door could ruin your whole life? We were so close, Shooky and me, to the best life ever on Venice Beach — maybe only four or five hours away from freedom. I could picture him there, literally charming the pants off of beautiful girls.

We drove on. After seeing San Francisco Bay and the city, a place that held such fascination for me for all that had gone on there in recent years, there was nothing out there for me. After a while I started thinking about the kid who killed his father. He'd strangled him with a garden hose. "At least I'm not him," I said to myself. What must that have been like? Those last moments with his dad. And he was a nice kid too. We humans are a twisted bunch of freaks. My mind drifted to my last hour with Shooky. If you have a last hour with someone, you ought to be able to know that that's what's happening.

§

"Hey, man," he said that final day at Manderley, handing me the hash pipe. "I've been thinking about how many ways there are to die. I've decided I'd like to be fucked to death by a hot babe with great tits."

"That comes as no surprise to me, bro. There are worse ways to go, that's for sure. Choking on your own puke, like Hendrix."

"But that may not be my destiny. I'll probably end up getting eaten alive by piranhas. I've told you before how the Amazon beckons to me."

I laughed. "Do you think if reincarnation is real that you enter the next life in the exact same state of mind you're in when you die?"

"You mean like if you die laughing will you be born laughing in the next life?"

"Exactly."

"You'd be really lucky. What if you died wondering if reincarnation was real and *that* was your state of mind?"

It was common for us to have these kinds of discussions when we were stoned.

"I think Nixon's gonna start a nuclear war. I want to be on mushrooms for the mega-mushroom blast," I said with some enthusiasm. "That'd be a comparatively decent way to die under the circumstances."

"You know if you were to actually hide under your desk when the bomb hits, the tremendous amount of heat generated by the detonation would probably fuse the desk to your head."

"If you were unlucky enough to still have a head."

"What if the world doesn't end? It would be *worse*. We'd have no skin left. We'll be walking around in charred bodies. I guess the good thing is you'd be able to fire up a joint just by putting the tip of it against the back of your hand, like you do with a car lighter."

We cracked up about that one.

"That'd be a significant fringe benefit," I said, putting the pipe down on a rock.

Shooky suddenly stood up. "Hey, wow! Check out the sky, bro!"

Manderley had suddenly taken on the ambiance of a temple in the Burmese mountains. Colors I could not name began to sweep slowly across the sky like so many whispers of iridescent silk, weightless, luminous, turning the vast ocean of chaparral into wave after wave of chameleon sublimity. The wind was warm and soothing and carried with it the smells of the land and everything that grew on it, lived on it, preyed on it. Rockville Flats was the pit of human civilization, but that view was truly, spectacularly beautiful. I lit a cigarette and watched the sun dying by inches.

"You're thinking of Sarah?" Shooky asked after a while.

"Yeah. We're leaving. It feels weird."

"I know. I feel it too. But just think! Tomorrow we'll be bangin' beaver on the beach!"

"God bless that sick fuck, Steven Gregory!"

"God bless the bastard." We high-fived.

When it was almost time to go I said, "I'll have the hash cut and the weed bagged and ready. You're totally in, right? And you've got the money?"

"Of course I'm in! I'll pick you up at five a.m. on the dot. And yeah, we've got two thousand two hundred and thirty-eight bucks. That gives us each a thousand one hundred and nineteen. We kick ass, man!"

"We do! Far out! We're rich!"

"We're gonna make even bigger money in L.A. And I'm gonna write great novels. You're gonna make a bunch of million-selling records. What a life, man. We're gonna fuck millions of gorgeous chicks and live like rock stars."

"We're going to get out of this pre-historic Cro-Magnon town," I said. "Finally."

"Be ready at five. I don't want anything going wrong. What about your mom, man?"

"She'll be fine. She's like one of those non-stick pans."

I put one last chunk of hash in the pipe, ducked behind Shooky and lit it. We sat and smoked for a while longer, saying nothing, the sundown already nostalgia, the hash high deepening our resolve to be unlike the rest of the people in the world.

Four

Late afternoon. Sgt. Bill turned off Highway 101 at an exit that made you wonder why it was an exit. He drove deep into redneck territory, far, far away from anything resembling anything I could be interested in. About an hour later, at a bend on a long, lonely stretch of road, he turned into a gravel driveway and stopped at a rusted metal gate that was about twenty feet high. "Wagon Train Ranch for Boys" was stenciled midway up in small, faded white letters. He spoke to an intercom and the big gate swung open slowly. A guard waved him in.

He drove up a steep hill on an unpaved road with big ruts and potholes. The gate disappeared behind us as leafy tree branches, entangled like so many bony fingers reaching out to each other, choked the exit route. The access road eventually leveled off before climbing again, although not as steeply. To my left a cow pasture flared out across the hill, a few cows slumming in the high brown grass. Further up on my right we passed a lake about the size of a baseball field, with a flock of sheep clustered together on the far side, one big thatch of wool and dark faces. High on the rise above them, a tall fence topped by barbed wire reminded you of where you were. A dirt road off to the right wound around the downhill side of the lake. A thick grove of trees clung to the hillside, the tallest of them swaying in a high breeze. Sgt. Bill continued up through a couple of lazy turns, past a shed on the left with shovels, a wheelbarrow and other work-out-side tools, and finally reached the crest of the hill, where two large single-story barracks separated by a few burly shade trees and maybe two or three hundred feet of wide-open pathway looked out east over the cow pasture. Countless mountains and high hills floated their way west, falling, each in their own time, off the edge of the earth.

I could have screamed and nobody would hear me.

I made a friend that first day, Derrick, a kid from San Francisco with a giant afro, fantastic teeth that I still envy, and a calm demeanor that he said he'd managed to cultivate over the two years he'd been there. He was one of my room-mates. There weren't cells at the cowboy ranch. You slept in rooms with three or four others, and there was always a night guard outside in the hallway, reading or dozing off. A terrible job, sitting in a hallway all night.

"I used to get in trouble all the time," said Derrick. "I re-belled, man. It was a waste of energy. Now I keep to myself. I grew used to the solitude, the isolation, living in a popula-tion of idiots, morons, mouth-breathers. People who haven't a clue about anything. Granted, there've been exceptions. But still, I've had to tolerate the most extreme examples of human stupidity you can imagine. And then there are these guys to put up with," he said, nodding toward our fellow inmates.

I told him I was determined to escape. He shook his head, laughed, and invited me to get stoned later.

"That's all we do up here, man. We get high, and we wait until we turn eighteen. They know we get high but what are they gonna do? Empty the place out and bring in more dudes who get high? There's a reason why they put this place so far away from anything resembling civilization. It keeps us from escaping and it keeps the jailers from being under a micro-scope."

"I don't care." I looked around and felt like crying, but I turned that into anger so I wouldn't embarrass myself. "I'm getting the fuck out of here."

"Man, it's a seventy-three-mile drive to Highway 101. Everybody who lives on Gulch Hollow Road or anywhere close knows we're here, which means they know not to pick up hitchhikers. They sure 'n the fuck ain't gonna pick up anybody like you or me. So you have to either walk the road, which only a fool would try, or you go *that* way." He pointed to all those mountains and hills to the west. "If you try that they'll be coming after you from all sides with dogs. Then there's the food problem. Even if you manage a miracle and get out, what're you gonna eat? You're gonna scrounge for nuts and berries? If you make it to civilization you'll end up having to steal. Another big risk. Problems. Nothing but problems. Look, man. Just do your time. You've only got a year."

"Only?"

§

There's not much to tell. It was as dull and boring and un-imaginative a time as I'd ever spent — as dull and boring and unimaginative as the guards and the people running the place. A fight broke out every now and then; a guy got caught having sex with another guy. Two teachers came and tried to make it work for a while, but that didn't go anywhere.

There was only one classroom, and there weren't enough desks. If you were late you'd have to sit on the floor. All we ever did was doodle or daydream. The teachers came from outside in the real world. Young, conscientious, well-meaning people who were simply overmatched by the collective, rebellious disinterest, and the sad fact that even though we were all between thirteen and eighteen, there was a number of us who couldn't even read. In addition, the remaining inmates' disparate reading levels, not to mention the amount of barely repressed rage in the room, were such that the teachers were faced with an impossible task.

About a week after the second teacher quit, the third one showed up. His name was Ira. He was very thin, bookish, with granny glasses, a goatee and a mustache, and he wore faded blue overalls. He styled his jet-black hair in a ponytail that exploded from the top of his head like a newly discovered oil well.

He was hyper, beams of intense energy coming out of his eyes. He introduced himself. He spoke very fast. Maybe he was cranking on speed. He told us he'd lived all over the world with his parents and that he was in graduate school. You could tell he wanted to get all that intro stuff over with. He clearly had something else on his mind.

"I was gonna talk to you guys today about the importance of kindness — " Everybody groaned and cussed in disgust. "I know, I know. But instead," he held up a newspaper, "some *huge* news came out in yesterday's *New York Times*." He picked a bottle of some kind of earthy juice from a leather satchel and took a long drink, as if to fortify his commitment to tell us.

"How many of you are about to turn eighteen in the next year or so?"

About a third of us raised our hands.

"You're the kind of guys they draft and send to Vietnam," he said. "African-Americans, Hispanics, and poor white kids. Maybe your older brother or an older friend of yours is there or has been killed. If so, I'm very sorry. Military parasites are kidnapping guys like you off the streets every day and sending you off to kill and die. They call it patriotism. Well, guess what?" He held the newspaper higher. "The government has known for *years* that the war was a lost cause. And they've kept it a secret. The war was a sham from the start anyway. You've seen the protests over the last few years and maybe you've been out there yourselves."

He took another long drink of his earth juice and then began reading from the front page. You could see him consciously trying to slow himself down. He really wanted us to get it.

"In 1964 'President Johnson . . . intensified the covert war against North Vietnam' — that means it was a big lie

— '*a full year* before the government publicly revealed the depth of its involvement and *its fear of defeat*.' Do you guys hear that? They were already pulling this scam when you were in elementary school! This evidence is from the god-damned *Pentagon*. Information that was never supposed to come out, and the first of it is right here," he said, shaking the newspaper with vigor, "and I'm honored to share it with you.

"And I have to tell you something more about me. I'm the son of a diplomat. I'm a doctoral student at UC Berkeley. The parasites won't come after me because of my family's background and resources. I don't feel good about it. It's an outrage! I'm not proud of it. It's just my own story. And am I the kind of person with the strength of character to go fight in solidarity with you? No. I'm sorry, I'm not. But every one of you is living under the threat of a death sentence. You all know that, don't you?"

We all sat there saying nothing. I think we were all stunned that this was coming from a teacher.

"Well, don't you?"

"Fuck yeah," I finally said. Others responded with similar affirmations.

"But man, we don't wanna hear this shit," somebody said. "What the hell are we gonna do about it?"

"Not a fuckin' thing," somebody else said.

Ira emphatically shook his head no and wagged his finger in the air.

"That's where you're wrong, my friends. There is something you can do. And that's what I'm here to tell you about today. When you get your draft card, burn it. Don't wait. Burn 'em as soon as you guys get 'em. They're *lethal*."

Bradley Johnson stood up. He barely existed in my world. He was an athletic type, a jock, who still used Bryl-creem. I have no idea what he did to get in there.

"Fuck you," he yelled, pointing at Ira. "You're a *red*. A *commie*. It's our duty to fight if we're drafted. When I get out

I'm going to enlist! This is the greatest country on earth!" He started breathing rather heavily. "You're trying to convince us to shit on the American flag! And I can't *believe* you're feeding us this commie propaganda on Flag Day!"

"What the fuck is Flag Day, man?" I asked him.

"That just shows how stupid you are Kilroy. June fourteenth is Flag Day. Everybody knows that."

A whole bunch of guys responded: "I never heard of no Flag Day," "Why would there even *be* a Flag Day," "Fuck you and your Flag Day, Johnson."

"You've been brainwashed," Ira said. "First of all, this is not the greatest country on earth. We have more blood on our hands than — Look. Don't be stupid. You can't ignore mountains of evidence. Not only is the war a charade, we're machine-gunning entire villages, killing children, burning families alive. Your draft card is an invitation to a funeral. Probably yours. Just because you live in a Yankee Doodle fantasy world, and saying the Pledge of Allegiance makes you feel warm and fuzzy inside, doesn't mean you should risk your life so the stock prices for Boeing and General Dynamics go up. Your life is worth far more than that. And I'll tell you something." He waved the newspaper back and forth a time or two. "Knowing what we know now, my friend, if you enlist, you're signing up to commit mass murder in a puppet show."

"You're an *asshole* and a *commie* piece of *shit*." Johnson flipped him off and stormed out, knocking over his chair as he got up.

Ira was weird (what was with that hairdo?) but with a real passionate, righteous commitment to helping us. Johnson must have narced on him, because he was canned that afternoon for inducing us to commit a federal crime. Fired for trying to save our lives.

I remember saying to Shooky one time, "There's no way I'm going to let those Army freaks find me. They'd ship me off like a parcel of stale meat to the Mekong Delta or Khe Sanh, and I'd never come back. I *know* I'd never come back. Some-times I sit up late at night thinking about it, wondering what the first Viet Cong kid I'd be destined to murder is doing at that very same moment. Whether he would look me in the eyes when I killed him."

"Me too, bro. I wonder what the Viet Cong kid who's destined to murder *me* is doing. The kid our own age who's just as fuckin' scared of the war as we are."

Five

Wesley Adams arrived late in the afternoon the next day and was assigned to be one of my roommates. He was a short, fragile, waif-like creature with lifeless red hair that fell limply onto his pale possum-like face. He had tiny tombstone teeth with spaces between them like you would see in a military graveyard. Deep-set watery-brown eyes stared out at the world in anger. His head was a geometric oddity: flat on top, the sides descended by ninety-degree angles to just below his ears, and his jawline cut a diagonal that led to a pointed chin. Derrick said, "That kid's got a home plate head." It's hard to imagine there could be such a person but there you go.

I showed him around, told him what and who to avoid, and showed him where he'd sleep and store his stuff.

"I haven't given up on escaping," I said when he asked me if there was a way out. "But I haven't figured out how yet. Nobody has."

"*I* will," he said, as if we were all retards.

"What are you gonna do? Beam up? Don't be so sure of yourself, dude. You're gonna piss people off."

"Like I give a shit."

The next day — Wesley's first full day — he stood in the lunch line in front of me. The kitchen and the chow hall were in what everybody called Grandma's Barracks. "Grandma," the bitter, elephant-skinned old woman who cooked the slop for us, always wore a San Francisco Giants baseball hat pulled down over her long, silky, meticulously maintained gray hair. She ran that barracks like a drill sergeant. She slept there five nights a week and did the cooking for all twenty-six of us. I'd lived there the whole time. I'd heard the South Barracks was worse.

I only crossed her once. I used her private bathroom when the others were occupied. It was either that or piss in a jar. That's what I said to her when she yelled at me. She was in her bathrobe and appeared to be embarrassed to be seen without her hat. I looked more carefully and saw that she was balding.

"You'll wake up at six tomorrow and bring a wheelbarrow full of rocks from the pasture up to the back door of the kitchen by seven," she said, and shut the bathroom door.

"And then you'll put 'em back in your head?" I said quietly to myself as I walked away.

The next morning, exhausted after an hour of collecting the rocks and with blistered hands, I rolled the wheelbarrow up to door. She came out and lit a cigarette, took a long drag, blew it out, and looked at me for an extra beat. "Now go dump 'em back where you found 'em. You read me?"

"Yeah, I read you. I read that you've got one hell of a mean streak."

"You got that right, boy."

§

There was a Dutch door between the chow hall and the kitchen. We'd line up at noon every day and Grandma would hand out sandwiches for lunch. Always Jif peanut butter and Welch's grape jelly on Wonder Bread, which was the one meal everybody looked forward to. Even a moron can't ruin a sandwich like that. When it was your turn she'd plop one on a paper plate, usually without even looking at you, and you'd go sit down and eat it and drink your fill from one of the pitchers of Kool-Aid always on the table next to stacks of red plastic cups.

Wesley was agitated and had been since he walked in. He said to me, "I ain't eatin' no peanut butter and jelly."

"That's what she's serving, man," I whispered. "You eat what she gives you or you don't eat."

"I'm gonna tell her I'm *allergic* to peanuts. I'm gonna tell her that if I eat peanuts I could *die*."

"Is that true?"

"Fuck no. I just don't want peanut butter."

"You might wanna rethink this, bro."

"I'm Wesley Adams," he said to Grandma when he reached the front of the line. "You should have information about my food allergies. I can't eat eggs or peanut butter. If I eat a peanut butter sandwich I'll die."

She smiled. "I've seen your file. You're lying. I'll learn you this, boy: I don't suffer fussy eaters. You eat what you're given." She handed him his lunch. And without any hesitation *he smashed the sandwich in her face!* He spread it around clockwise and counter-clockwise with the same hand-wrist motion you'd use when cracking a safe.

It was, and still is, the most beautiful act of defiance I've ever witnessed. I can still see the splattered globs of congealed blue jelly sliding down her stunned and outraged face, dangling off her chin, mixed with the liberally distributed brown smears of peanut butter. Everybody cheered.

Wesley was dragged away and locked in a cell in the South Barracks by Bodean Gaff, a tall, lantern-jawed, balding-like-Grandma cowboy idiot, whose title was "Senior Rehabilitation Counselor." He spent every spare dollar he had sprucing up his 1968 Ford F-150 pickup truck. It was gorgeous. I hated him, but I had to admit that the truck was something else. When I'd showed Wesley around the day before, we saw Bodean come up the hill in the truck and watched him park it.

The ape got out and said to Wesley, "Hey newbie, this here's my honeybee. You stay out of trouble and I'll give you a ride in her someday."

Wesley said to me, "I'm gonna destroy that thing before I leave."

I thought he was joking.

§

The first explosion happened around midnight, followed by a second one a moment or two later. All hell broke loose. At first nobody knew what had exploded. They made everybody go to the parking lot. I was in the bathroom at the time and I hid for a minute until the place was empty, then peeked out and saw Bodean's truck in flames. Grandma and Bodean had already run out and I could hear them shouting instructions to everybody. Bodean was screaming crazy things. "Holy fuck! Who blew up my honeybee? I'll find you and I'll . . . I'll *kill* you! I'll rip your face off!"

I ran like hell into Grandma's room looking for cash. I found sixty-seven dollars in her purse. Bodean's room was next door. The room smelled terrible, like dirty socks and cheap liquor. There were porn magazines on his bed. I rifled through his dresser and found forty-one bucks in his sock drawer.

They'd have to open the gate when the fire trucks came. A couple of guys with hoses appeared and sprayed water at the truck. I made a run for it. I wondered where Wesley was and how he'd done it. I was proud of him. The little fucker!

I hauled ass down the hill through the cow pasture, careful to avoid the various piles of rocks people had dumped from Grandma's wheelbarrow punishment, which she grew fond of. I heard a walkie-talkie radio crackle. The guard at the gate answered.

"Griffin."

"Gaff is coming down. We need you up here," said a muffled voice.

Griffin said, "Copy that," and headed up the hill. I lay down as flat as I could until he passed.

I made it to the bottom and hid beneath the trees and bushes as close to the gate as I could. As soon as the fire trucks arrived I would be free. I watched as the South Barracks caught fire! It was a beautiful sight, a sacred vision on the hilltop. It burned so hot and so bright it must have been visible for miles. A 747 pilot coming in over the pole from London would see it as a beacon as he descended slowly into San Francisco.

I waited and waited, straining to hear the fire trucks' sirens, but they didn't come. I lay on the cold ground and waited some more. Gaff must have done a count because I heard him call out for me and Wesley. His silhouette was barely visible as he walked down the road. He was carrying a rifle. The smell of burning wood was comforting. I could hardly take my eyes away from the windswept changes in the shape and size and overall majesty of the fire. It was Biblical. It carried weight. It was the first pure, comforting light I had seen since that last sunset with Shooky.

I was worried about Wesley more than about Bodean, even though Bodean was armed. Nothing so saintly as to wonder whether Wesley was safe. No, I was concerned that when the trucks arrived he would get in my way.

Bodean was now close enough that I could hear him breathing. "Adams! Killjoy!" He always called me Killjoy. "I know you're out here. Come out and you won't get hurt. I'll get myself another truck and we'll just let bygones be bygones. Just come on out now. I may have to shoot if you don't come out and keep your hands up and identify yerselfs." He shot a couple rounds into the sky for dramatic effect. Bodean screamed my name and Wesley's name, the rising anger in his voice terrifying. A madman with a third-grade education carrying a loaded rifle. He got closer and closer. I heard his footsteps. I didn't want to look. I lay with my face in the dirt. He poked me in the side with the rifle. I looked up at him and he pointed the rifle at my forehead. I'd had quite a few run-ins with him and he hated me as much as I did him.

"You thought you had it bad before, shitface? You ain't seen nothing. Get your ass up."

At least the rifle wasn't in my ear. I said nothing. He moved a little and blocked my view of the fire. A fiery red glow appeared around him.

"Get *up*, Killjoy!"

I started to get up and he pushed me down on the ground, hard and fast, with his boot.

"I said get up!"

I started to get up again and he pushed me down again, harder.

"Motherfucker! I thought I told you to *get up!*"

I started to a third time and he pushed me down even harder.

"What's a matter with you? I *told* you to get up."

"Fuck you, you dumb shit Oakey." There I went again. What a fool I was.

He *rifle-butted* me! I bled from a cut above my left eye. It hurt like hell, but the sirens! I could hear the sirens!

Bodean leaned over me and with a great deal of rage in his voice, yelled, "Where's Adams?"

"I don't know."

He stood over me, thinking. He was going to have to open the gate for them. I pretended to pass out. He came over and kicked me hard in the ass. I didn't make a sound. Bodean yelled for Wesley and walked away.

The wild shriek and howl of the fire trucks cut into the night. They were honking outside the gate. The red and blue lights twirled and swam in the treetops, mingling in a tumult of color with the still-explosive flames from the top of the hill, turning the night sky into something you might see on a sublime acid trip.

Bodean activated the gate. I got up on my knees as he swung it open wide and to the left. When the first fire truck drove in it would be between him and me. He didn't think to move me over to his side to prevent that, but then who would? He thought he'd knocked me out. As the gate slowly opened it looked like I could probably *walk* out. But the first truck blasted through much quicker than I thought it would, with an ambulance coming right behind it and then a county sheriff. They climbed the hill as fast as they could. I was losing my chance. Bodean started closing the gate, but another fire truck was coming quickly. I ran to the opening as it roared through, the blood dripping in my eye partially blinding me. Bodean started to run in front of it to try to stop it. I could hear him yelling: "Escape! Escape!" The siren was still screaming and the driver couldn't hear him. I kept running. The truck made it through the gate and blasted up the hill. Wesley ran out from somewhere, heading for the opposite side of the entrance. "No!" I shouted to him. "This side!" Wesley did a pivot but it was too late. Bodean grabbed him. And then I was out! I ran like hell. The wildly flailing, crying, cussing, defeated Wesley Adams had saved me. Bodean saw me but there wasn't a thing he could do. I flipped him off and shouted insults at him. The bastard had no option. He had to drag Wesley in and close the gate. He had to be satisfied with catching just one of us.

I ran down the dark country road. I was exhilarated and terrified. They'd be coming after me any minute.

Headlights. A truck. I was in a panic. I rolled into a ditch, waited, head down in the dirt, but the truck didn't pass me. It screeched to a stop right above me. I turned my face away from the road and lay still. I heard a door open and a female voice from inside the cab.

"You from that jailhouse that's on fire up the hill?"

"No!"

"Yeah, you are. If you wanna get away you'd better get in here fast."

"I ain't from that place. Go on ahead, I'll be fine."

"Your face is in a ditch, man. This is your last chance. Get in or get busted."

"I don't know who you are."

"No wonder you got sent up here. You're stupid."

She closed the door and started on her way. It was then that I figured I could trust her. If she was a cop or some similar type of horrifying human being she wouldn't just drive away. I jumped up and waved and yelled at her as loud as I could. "OK! OK! OK!"

She stopped. "Get in!"

Before I had the door closed she took off. She had dark hair, wore a jean jacket and black jeans. She looked to be about thirty.

"You look familiar," I said. "Kind of."

"Your eye's bleeding." Steering with one hand, she leaned over and reached into the glove compartment, unselfconsciously resting her forearm on my knee. She gave me a little packet of Kleenex. "Here. Put some tissue on it."

"The goddamned thing hurts," I said. "Why'd you stop for me?"

"I know about that place. Everybody around here does. And now it's on fire. And you're diving into a ditch as I drive by." She gave me a quick glance. "It doesn't take Sherlock Holmes to figure that one out."

"Yeah, except I had nothing to do with the fire. I just ran the hell out of there when the fire trucks pulled in. Cops are going to be looking for me. So if you don't want to get busted for helping me, you ought to drop me off at the next hay stack, or the closest barn dance or whatever the fuck there is around here."

"None of them cowboys are gonna catch me. Don't worry. You wanna get out of here, don'tcha?"

"Yeah. I need to get down to Venice Beach. I'm sure my best friend is there. He has money."

"I hate those people. My brother died up there in that place. They said it was suicide, but I don't think so. They're evil people. I tried to get it closed down. You see how that turned out."

"Hey, I think I've seen you before. Did you flip off the guy who drove me up here? Standing outside your house in front of a tractor."

She laughed. "I might have. I do that sometimes when I see those creeps. But that's not my house, it's my uncle's. Mine isn't on that access road."

"Thank you so much for the rescue."

"Must be you got good karma."

"Marry me," I said. "Just marry me. I owe you everything."

"You're an idiot."

"So marry an idiot, then."

"You know what? Someday, with my luck, I probably will." She saw that the tissues were pretty well soaked in blood.

"Get some more tissue out of the glove. Take the whole thing out. I don't want you bleeding all over everything."

I applied more tissue to the wound. It stung when I put pressure on it, but I had to.

"How did you escape?"

"This goofy retarded sadistic moron cowboy mother-fucker couldn't catch me when he let the fire trucks in."

"You just described every man in this county."

"Ha! So we both need to get out. What's your name?"

"Lorelai. I'm not asking you yours. No offense. I don't wanna know. Let's get that eye fixed up. Tomorrow I'll drive you to San Francisco and you can catch a Greyhound down to L.A. How's that? I'm going to the city tomorrow night any-way. My sister's gonna have a baby any time now. She's a psy-chic, by the way. She told me something like this was gonna happen."

"Who *are* you really?"

"I'm the Good Samaritan in your story. Let's leave it at that."

And she was. She medicated the cut, she fed me, she made me take a shower. I slept on her couch. She gave me a beat-up old backpack and a sleeping bag.

"You need to get rid of those prison clothes," she said the next morning. "They smell and you need to get rid of 'em anyway. You're pretty scrawny but I can give you a pair of pants, socks, a shirt and a jacket that were Jack's. My brother's. They'll be good enough for now."

We went into a room where a cedar chest was set against a wall with a picture of the kid on it and a candle on either side. He looked like her. Dark hair. Handsome guy. I didn't feel weird putting on his clothes. I felt proud.

"We'll put you on the last bus tonight."

I'd give anything to see her again. This may be off-putting to say because of its obvious sentimentality and absurdity, but I hope she's living a kick-ass, happy life, and that nothing has ever gone wrong, and she's never felt any pain.

The Greyhound station in San Francisco seemed to be swarming with cops. We got there just before midnight. Lorelai saw me silently freaking.

"They're rent-a-cops. Mellow out."

She bought me a one-way bus ticket to L.A.

I asked for her full name and address so I could pay her back.

"That's very nice of you, but I don't want my information to be on you if you get busted."

"Lorelai's not your real name, is it?"

Her expression told me all I needed to know.

"OK. It doesn't matter. I love you, because for some crazy reason you care."

"This is in honor of my brother." She handed me fifty bucks even though I'd told her I'd stolen money from Grandma and Bodean. "Take good care of yourself."

"You're the coolest."

"Go get out of here. Be safe. Don't be stupid. You're gonna be one of a few thousand hippie kids running around Venice so you're not gonna have to worry too much. Cops down there get most of their thrills beating up blacks, Mexicans, and the homeless. You should be OK. You're a white male in America. That's not your fault."

"You take care of yourself too, OK? You're the best person in the world."

She kissed me on the cheek and walked away without looking back.

Part Two

June 1971 – October 1971

Where you come from is gone, where you thought you were going to never was there, and where you are is no good unless you can get away from it. Where is there a place for you to be? No place.
– Flannery O'Connor, *Wise Blood*

Six

I looked for a last glimpse of Lorelai from my seat on the bus but she was long gone. I felt happy and scared, melancholy and excited. The bus roared out of San Francisco like the driver was being chased by the FBI, but the ride to L.A. was quiet and uneventful. The next morning I stood in the bus station in a kind of daze. I watched dozens of people coming and going, some nearly broken by bus fatigue, others alert and with a great sense of purpose, still others sitting forlorn, bored, even indifferent, next to their luggage. Not one of them took a second look at me, not even with the bandage over my eye, which I found simultaneously unnerving and reassuring. A small group of Hare Krishnas boarded a bus to Las Vegas, ringing their finger-cymbals in repetitive triplicate rhythms, clutching copies of the Bhagavad Gita. I wondered what kind of trauma those people must have gone through to end up like that.

A couple of hours later I was on the beach. I stripped down to my shorts, put down my pack as close to the water as possible without risking getting it wet or stolen, ran into the ocean and dove in. The healing Southern California sun shined like divine light through the luminescent green-glass of the bending waves. The saltwater stung the hell out of the cut above my eye but I knew it was good for it. I dove in again and again, cleansing myself of my mother, and my father Harry, and Rockville Flats, the cops, Grandma, and Bodean.

I stayed in for a long time, feeling the waves wash over me, knocking me down from time to time, as if the ocean itself was reminding me that I wasn't in charge, but telling me that I was alive, that I was living the beginning of this, my new, happy life.

Venice looked to be in a state of decay and disrepair, so the run-down little beach town suited me perfectly. Everyone I saw made me think of people I'd known and liked. Life seemed easy and slow. I looked for Shooky but he wasn't around. A whole bunch of people had gathered on the boardwalk, forming a circle around five or six guys and a few women playing guitars, congas, bongos, a tambourine, a snare drum, sticks, and various other things that clicked and banged. And the girls all around me, the ones who stopped to listen and the ones walking by, made me crazy with desire. I hadn't seen girls in months and now they were everywhere.

I bought a couple of two-dollar shirts and a pair of used Levi's at a thrift store. Also underwear and socks. It set me back eight bucks. I walked around looking for Shooky. I came upon a bookshop half a block off the boardwalk with Buddha statues in the window. The woman behind the counter wore a peasant dress and a lot of sparkling bangles on her wrists. Long braided blond pigtails rested in the small of her back. They looked like ropes thick enough to keep a small yacht from drifting out to sea. She came around the counter carrying an armful of books, breezing by me. A patchouli world it was. She walked barefoot to a shelf and slid one of the books into its place. She looked pretty spacey, but in a sweet way. I liked her face. It was the face of someone who sees the good in everything and everybody.

"I'll be right there, my darling."

I felt sure that Shooky had been there. When the woman was done shelving she came over to me.

"Hi. Sorry to keep you waiting. What can I help you with?" She looked closer and saw Bodean's cut. "Oh! What happened to you?"

"Oh, yeah. I fell."

"That happened when you fell? Oh my!"

"I know, right? It was a long way down. I'm looking for a friend of mine. His name is Shooky — Jason Shook. He usually wears a red vest and sunglasses and has long wavy black hair like Jimmy Page. He's taller than me. If he was here he probably bought some corny classic."

"Hmm. Let me think a sec. I don't recall specifically. The thing is, a lot of guys around here fit a description like that, you know?"

"Yeah."

"Can I help you with a book?"

"I'm probably gonna have a lot of free time on my hands. Do you have something cheap?"

"What kind of book?"

"Will you pick something for me? Fiction, please. I can't think today."

She walked down an aisle and looked over a couple of shelves. She pulled a book out, opened it to look at the price and said, "This one's perfect."

Demian by Hermann Hesse.

"It will change your life," she said with glee. "And it's only a quarter 'cause it's used."

"Thanks for picking that out for me. That's really nice of you."

"If you don't like it you can bring it back. Do you live in the neighborhood?"

An amazing feeling came over me. Wow, I live in the *neighborhood!*

"Yeah, I do. Thanks again!"

"You're welcome." As she floated around to the cash register she said, "I'm Moonlight Wind."

"I'm Owen. Nice to meet you." I immediately regretted giving her my real name and promised myself I would never do that again.

"What does it mean?"

"What does what mean?"

"What does Owen mean?"

"Oh. I don't know." She handed me my change. "What does your name mean?"

"It means wind in the moonlight."

"That's far out."

"Thanks! Have a lovely afternoon," she said. "Enjoy the book! Come back."

"You too," I said over my shoulder. "I will."

Outside it took me no time at all to decide on a name. "Twenty Flight Rock" by Eddie Cochran and "Be-Bop-A-Lula" by Gene Vincent were two of my favorite songs. From then on I would be Eddie Vincent.

I walked up and down the boardwalk looking for Shooky. I was already sick of carrying my pack around. It made me look like I just got off the bus. But my mood was good. I was free. I was Eddie Vincent. I wanted to say my new name to somebody, anybody. I just wanted to hear it and feel it. Groups of friends carried on, joking and laughing with each other; roller skaters glided by; weightlifters lifted and pranced; and the endless murder of stunning girls continued to slay me. By the end of the day I wanted to walk back to the Buddha bookstore and tell Moonlight Wind my real name was actually Eddie Vincent. I went back down to the beach instead, to listen to the breakers, to watch the sunset and have a few moments of peace before night came. The sand still held some warmth from the afternoon sun, but it disappeared quickly. I watched the tide go out and the little sandpipers flitter around, running just a hair ahead of the waves as they washed up, then running back down to scarf on more food before having to run up the beach again. Soon Venus appeared. She looked like the tip of a sparkler held by a giant, invisible kid on a beach in Japan.

I ate a burrito and drank a root beer at a cheap Mexican restaurant and hung out as long as I could, until the cook shut the place down at eleven o'clock. I finally had to face the fact that I had nowhere to go. I couldn't spend any money on a motel. I would explore, see what my options were. I would have given anything for some speed to get me through the night. I wandered around becoming more and more desperate, and eventually found myself walking north on Lincoln Boulevard, trying to look as though I had a destination in mind. Every now and then a cop would drive by and I would feel my gut turning against itself.

A Denny's rose up a few blocks ahead like a mirage.

I sat in a booth at the rear and had a coffee, a hamburger, and piece of chocolate cream pie I intended to make last as long as possible. I wanted to look like I wasn't slumming in the booth. The waitress, an old woman named Gertrude, who appeared to be right where she wanted to be in life, kept my "bottomless cup of coffee" filled, calling me "Honey" every time she came by.

A pair of cops came in, which almost made me piss my pants, but they paid no attention to me. Instead they ate their graveyard-shift dinner quietly, maybe anticipating the sort of hell they might have to confront when they went back outside. The big question was, would they be humans or animals in the way they handled it?

"Don't you like the pie?" Gertrude asked. The cops were long gone. She'd brought the pie to me about four hours ago. It was as if she'd made it herself.

"It's delicious," I said. "I'm savoring it."

"Oh, good! Because I would've brought you something else."

"You're very nice. Thank you."

She paused, gave me a serious look, and said, "You be careful out there."

I left Denny's at sunrise, wondering how I was going to find Shooky and how long my money would last if I didn't.

The sun seemed to rise quickly, as if it was eager to climb out of the smog. I made it down to the beach in Santa Monica, found a quiet place under the pier and slept, one hand in my pocket guarding my money.

Seven

I woke up in the afternoon. After eating an ice cream cone I spent hours wandering around in a futile search for Shooky. Night came too soon. It came too soon for more than a week. To make my money last I ate only once a day, sometimes just an apple or a banana. I had no place to put the backpack so I had to carry it around. The longer I did that the more I looked like a runaway. Visions of Shooky handing me a thousand dollars kept me going. I didn't allow myself to doubt that he wasn't there somewhere. Not for very long anyway.

One night some old guy took my spot under the pier. Everywhere else was either too damp or too filthy. I walked the streets totally dejected, tired, and scared. A thick fog had drifted in from the ocean making the night feel sinister. After a couple of hours I came upon an empty two-story apartment building on Rialto Avenue that had been in a fire. A makeshift fence cordoned off the property. Two big signs covered the two downstairs windows: Condemned. No Trespassing. The front and the side of the building, visible from where I stood, showed black burn streaks climbing the walls like fingers trying to crawl out of a grave.

I didn't know what time it was, but by the bewildered expressions on the faces of the parked cars, who seemed to wonder what I had in mind standing around like I was, it must have been very late. I told them to go back to sleep. The fence had not been put up with any effort so I had no problem getting around it. I snuck alongside of the building in total darkness, hoping nothing terrible would happen. By the time I reached the back, my eyes had adjusted and I could see the back door was open.

I snuck in expecting to be murdered. The smell of the fire permeated the building. I knew the two apartments in front were damaged because the windows were gone. I stood still for what must have been a couple of minutes listening for any sign of trouble. Nothing on the radar. I very slowly pushed open the door of the first apartment I came to, careful to stop if it squeaked or made any kind of noise. When it was open far enough I stepped into a pond of water, feeling it ooze into my shoes and up to my ankles. Creeping, cold, dirty, black, fire water. My footsteps sounded like I was walking on sponges. I stood outside the apartment across the hall listening again. The building creaked and made me jump, and then a siren shrieked out on Venice Boulevard. But after a while the place felt about as safe as it could. If I were going to be robbed or stabbed or shot it would have happened by now.

I closed the door and took out a flashlight I'd bought after my first night on the beach and found the bathroom. I flushed the toilet out of habit, not thinking. In the silence of the night it sounded like the Grand Coulee Dam had busted open. I hid for a long time, but nothing. I checked to see if the hot water worked. No.

I took off my wet shoes and socks and looked for a place where they would likely dry the fastest. I chose the windowsill. The sun might dry them in the morning. I shook the sand out of my sleeping bag and lay down and stared into the dark.

§

When I woke up in the morning, light poured in through the naked window. Seeing the apartment for the first time in daylight I had to laugh. There was a lake of black water in the kitchen and charred beams were exposed in parts of the walls. The little spot I'd chosen to sleep, just under the window, was dry but ash dust was everywhere. I went out to the store and bought some soap and took a cold shower and was clean for the first time since I arrived in Venice. Up until then I would skinny dip in the ocean and that would be the way I'd keep myself from becoming too disgusting.

I spent all day every day looking for Shooky, walking all over hell. Sometimes I'd just sit and rest in places where I could be seen. The whole thing was physically exhausting, mentally draining, and totally depressing. After a while my money started getting dangerously low. I'd be out all day and get hungry and so I'd hit a McDonald's, the Mexican place on the boardwalk, or a number of other cheap places I'd come to know. Still, it was adding up. And I always had to have a stash of weed, which cost me too. When I was down to my last twenty I started hitchhiking around and eating in restaurants, running out on the bill. Or I'd go to Ralph's or Safeway when it was a busy time, usually around five or six in the afternoon, and pretend I was shopping like a housewife loading up to feed the family. I'd fill up the cart with something from every aisle while eating whatever I could get my hands on — usually crackers and sliced things in "easy-open" packaging like cheese, salami, and bologna. Bananas worked. Grapes too. Drinks were harder to manage. Once I opened a can of Pepsi and it exploded, the chemical contents staining the Safeway floor. That required a quick exit. But most of the time, when I'd eaten enough, I'd leave the shopping cart in an aisle at the back of the store and head out the door.

I had to find some money. My dad used to hang out at a bar called Felix's in Anaheim. He used to go there after working his shifts as Goofy in Disneyland. I knew Felix, having been in there quite a few times. I was sure he'd remember me.

"You want to talk to Felix, you say?" said the woman who answered the phone. Her voice was cheap whiskey, cigarettes, and jalapeños.

"Yeah. The short skinny guy with the big waxy mustache."

"I *know* who he is. Who's this?"

"Owen Kilroy. I've known Felix since I was a little kid. My dad, Harry Kilroy, would hang out there and I used to go in with him sometimes. Just say my name and Felix'll come to the phone."

I heard her take a drink and light a cigarette. "Son, Felix is dead." She said it the way she might say 'Son, Felix is in Santa Barbara.'

"He's dead? When?"

"About four or five months ago."

"What happened?"

"Selling guns to Mexicans. Things got bad."

"Holy Christ. Do you know if my dad was with him? Harry?"

"They only found one body in the dumpster."

"Wow, a dumpster. Goddamn, does *everybody* have to disappear?"

"What's that?"

"Nothing. I was talking to myself."

"Sorry to give you the bad news."

"In a way, it's no surprise."

"Keep on keepin' on, then," said the woman, and she hung up.

I slumped against the door of the phone booth and stared for a long time at the incomprehensible graffiti people had scrawled all over the glass. The effect was chaos.

§

Harry was never really a dad. It's true that he had a few good days, but that's what made the rest of them so empty. He lived in a musty hotel room in Anaheim. When I'd go visit we'd eat all kinds of crap, watch a lot of TV. Every night we'd go down to Felix's and he would get tanked. He'd routinely introduce me to the whores who pranced in there after dining out down the street at the Copper Penny, coming in for a drink before hittin' the grind. It was like he was introducing me to his family, women that would, in the real world, be my aunts or cousins. I remember their names were always Candy or Cinnamon or Sugar. Always something food-related. And their perfume smelled awful, like they'd sprayed themselves with Glade, or wore those little Christmas tree air fresheners under their clothes. But Harry loved all that shit. That's where he belonged. With those people.

Walking back to the Hotel Rialto after that phone call I looked at the No Trespassing sign and a verse in "This Land is Your Land" came to mind:

> *As I went walking I saw a sign there*
> *And on the sign it said "No Trespassing."*
> *But on the other side it didn't say nothing,*
> *That side was made for you and me.*

Harry played it for me one night. He could get through a song or two on his guitar. I'd heard it before but never the whole thing. "Nobody sings that verse," he said. "But on the other side it didn't say nothing!" He laughed. "It's my favorite." Handing me a guitar he laughed again and poured himself a drink. "Woody. What a guy."

The guitar was an old Yamaha acoustic.

"Happy birthday, kid." I had turned fourteen about a month before.

We were in his hotel room. Crappy lighting, a dilapidated old bed, disturbing stains on the paper-thin green carpet, and a bathroom down the hall. I slept on the floor in a sleeping bag. His window, dirty from neglect, looked out on an alley. Every time I was there I'd hear screams and laughter and pounding and moans — pain or pleasure or both — coming from rooms down the ragged hall. I liked all of it. It fit with my self-image as a different kind of kid.

I'd played guitar for about six months, borrowing one for weeks at a time from a guy who lived across the hall from Harry, a washed-up Navy retiree named Norman, who'd taken no interest in it. I'd take it home to Rockville Flats and bring it back whenever Harry decided he wanted to see me.

He taught me the chords to "This Land Is Your Land" and wrote out all the words so we could sing it together. There were three pages, and he set them down on the floor in front of me. He was so pleased with himself that he'd saved enough money on his lousy Goofy gig. But then for all I know one of the whores gave it to him. It doesn't matter. It was a fantastic present. He took the guitar from me and tuned it and handed it back with such heartbreaking pride. We played and sang together about four times that weekend. If I was allowed to keep only one memory of my father, it would be of the two of us playing that song together. As I snuck back into the building I wondered if he was still alive. I wondered if I would ever find out what happened to him. If he was dead, how did he die?

Eight

I took a newspaper into the little Mexican place on the boardwalk and looked for a job. I found only one thing that might be something. "Assistants needed. Some phone work involved. We prefer no experience so we can train you. Excellent pay. Come by 8:30 am any day. K & L International, Inc." The address was in Santa Monica. No phone number. I showed up on time the next day.

K & L International was located in a depressed block off Ocean Park Boulevard in a building that looked as if it had been shipped in pieces from Dresden in 1945 and then carelessly reassembled. Cracks split the stucco façade into provinces, and pieces of the pitched roof were missing. On the upper floor there was a broken window in the shape anger would look like if anger had a shape, and scattered pieces of broken glass sparkled on the ground. A black Porsche preened outside in the morning sun, as out of place as Grace Kelly would be in a back-alley Saigon whorehouse. I walked across the lot and into the building.

A directory on the wall listed Ningbo Xinxing Import Export Company on the first floor and K & L International upstairs. Climbing the creaky wooden staircase, I heard what sounded like a crowd yelling at a cockfight. The noise was coming from behind the door at the top of the stairs. The door opened onto a windowless room thick with smoke.

"Hey! Mott the Hoople! Close that fucking door!"

The voice was not unfriendly; it appealed to me in a strange, inexplicable way. I closed the door and looked around. In little makeshift cubicles six guys and a couple of women all talked or yelled into their phones, oblivious to my presence. Everybody was smoking. At the far end of the room a guy about thirty, with Elvis hair and Wayfarers, was on the phone, but not like the others. There was no tension emanating from him at all. He was the one who'd called me Mott the Hoople.

He hung up. "You're here for the job. Whatcher name, buddy?"

"Eddie Vincent."

"Lee Leland. Nice to meet you, Eddie." He reached out and we shook hands. "Congratulations. You're hired."

I didn't know what to say.

"You've never been hired just by walking into a room, have you? As soon as I saw you I said to myself, holy shit, Lee, there's a winner walking through your door! Welcome to K & L International."

"OK." I was thrilled. I had a job!

"These are your very busy co-workers." He pointed at each one in turn. Nobody paid any attention to us. "There's Donna Smith, Jimmy Wiggins, Paul Clark, Bruce Adams, Jane Clay, Mike Madison, Larry Jones, and Willie Keeler. Come on in here and I'll run it all down for you."

I followed him down a hallway into a room with a round table, a few mismatched chairs around it, and a small refrigerator that buzzed. He shut the door and the decibel level dropped about five points. You could hear the low hum of traffic on the boulevard through the broken window. Lee saw me looking at it.

"Air conditioning," he said.

"Yeah."

"You see that Porsche outside? Cost me $25,000. I paid *cash*, with money I made right there in that room. It took me less than a year, pal. I wouldn't lie to you."

I wondered when he might take off his sunglasses.

"What's your name again?"

"Eddie."

"Eddie, your path to riches is so beautifully simple you won't believe it. When you walk outta here with your first paycheck you'll ask yourself, how can making money be this easy? You'll work nine to one. You call companies in the Eastern and Central time zones. We focus on companies in the South because the people down there are easier to talk to. They're so polite it makes you cry. Now, here's what you do: you get the person on the phone who handles buying the paper and toner for the company. You know what toner is? It's the ink for copy machines. You pitch it the way I tell you to and you'll have 'em begging for it."

"Somebody's gonna beg me for *ink?*"

"Of course they're gonna beg you for ink, because you're gonna make 'em beg you for ink."

"OK. Um, I have a question. I need to be paid in cash. Is that OK?"

He belted out a laugh. "See! I *knew* you were a winner, you little tax-evading motherfucker! Yeah, I'll pay you in cash. But don't tell nobody else, kapeesh?"

I nodded.

"Now pick a name. I want you to pick something that will make people in Alabama think you're their incest twin."

"Man, I don't know how to do that."

"You're forcing me to consult the name bible, Eddie."

"Sorry."

He grabbed a book off a shelf called *America's Most Notorious Criminals.* He flipped through it, stopped on a page, looked at me, mumbled "no" to himself, then flipped around to a few other pages, and finally looked at me with a triumphant grin.

"Lester Gillis. It's Baby Face Nelson's real name. Perfect for you."

He closed the book, tossed it on the table, took out a cigarette case and offered me a smoke. He lit it for me with a lighter that looked like it was made of diamonds. Then he lit his own.

"You're not shackled to minimum wage here, Lester Gillis," he said, the cigarette in his teeth. "The job is pure commission. At first you'll get fifteen percent of every sale you make. After two weeks that doubles to thirty percent, after a month, forty percent, and if you're still here on New Year's, you'll get fifty percent and a hug from me."

"OK." I forced a laugh. No wonder everybody in there was yelling. If they didn't sell, they didn't eat.

He pulled a script out of a folder and handed me a copy. Its primary purpose was to show you how to handle objections like, "No, I don't want any, and I'll never want any." I went over it twice with him. I was terrible and he knew it. He took me back out into the phone room, the cockfight in kill-or-be-killed mode. He led me to a small cubicle which had just enough room for a phone, a phone book, and a space to take notes. Order slips were stacked next to a few old Bic pens without caps. Tacked crudely to the cubicle walls were pieces of white paper featuring various expressions of enthusiasm and encouragement: GET RICH! THE SCRIPT WILL SET YOU FREE! YOU'RE A WINNER! Comments such as "Go fuck yourself" and "Suck my ass" had been written in red ink on each one, reminding me of the walls of my jail cell. The cacophony in the room was remarkable. I heard a lot of things that weren't in the script, but Lee either didn't notice or didn't care. I later understood that if you were a real "winner" it didn't matter how you sold that stuff. You could threaten to kill a secretary's kid if that worked.

Lee handed me a phone book. "Biloxi, Mississippi, pal. To tell you the truth I don't know where it is and I hope I never go there. But we know it's Central Standard Time, which is all that matters. It's just after eleven o'clock there. Secretaries will be in a good mood because they get to go to lunch soon.

Turn to any page of the business section and start dialing, buddy. But don't call any attorneys. They're all cheap lying douchebags who can kiss my ass. Never call a motherfucking lawyer. You know what Shakespeare said about lawyers?"

"No."

"They can all sucketh my dicketh."

I laughed.

"And remember Rule No. 1."

"What's that again?"

He just looked at me as if to say, "You're kidding."

"Oh, yeah. I'm Lester Gillis."

"Exactly. Never give your real name, Lester Gillis. You might come to regret that, kapeesh?"

"Kapeesh."

"OK. Go kill 'em, buddy." He patted me hard on the back and went to sit at the desk he'd sat in when I arrived.

Half an hour later a young guy who looked like he might one day be a game show host — perfect haircut and a bland, handsome face — slammed his phone down and yelled, "Yeah baby!!!"

Lee echoed him. "Yeah baby!!" He rang the hotel bell on his desk a few times. You're a *beast*, Jimmy Wiggins! How much?"

"Ten reams and two toner!"

"Haha! That's my man!" Then he played "We're in the Money" on the kazoo.

After being shut down all morning I managed to get the secretary of Kirk Newman Insurance to transfer the call to a Mrs. Flint, the office manager. It was my first transferred call. I was nervous and excited.

"Hello there, Mrs. Flint, my name is Lester Gillis."

"Not interested. I apologize for having to hang up on you." Click.

I looked over at Lee, who'd been listening on his extension.

"Great effort, Lester! Don't worry, nobody makes a sale the first day. And that Mrs. Flint? A total bitch! Now look at my finger." He manically dialed an imaginary phone. "Keep calling and calling and calling. Never put that phone down."

I didn't sell anything that day. I remember feeling like I was going to starve to death or end up back in jail by doing whatever was necessary to get money to eat. I was jonesing for a joint. As Lee drove off in the gleaming black Porsche, I lit the last one I had and headed for the beach. The beach was free. That was only thing I could count on.

"Hey, you gonna share that?"

It was "Jane Clay." She'd rung up a sale that morning.

"Sure." I passed the joint.

"My name's Greta." She was taller than me, with long dark brown hair with bangs and round glasses tinted blue, each lens the size of a poker chip. She wore a tie-dye dress that fell to just above the knees and a Levi jacket.

"Hi. I'm Eddie."

"Hi. Jesus Christ, what a shitty-ass job!"

"Yeah. Terrible. How long have you been doing it?"

"A while. I've made a little money, but I hate it."

"It's pretty crazy in there. Lee's something else."

"Lee's a pathological liar, but he's got a great sense of humor."

"He's a pathological liar?"

"Oh yeah." Greta gave me a look as if to say, 'Are you that gullible?' "Did he give you that line of bullshit about paying for the Porsche by selling this garbage?"

"Yeah, a couple of times."

"The Porsche belongs to his stepmother. She's a big shot over at United Artists. Did he tell you he'd pay you in cash?"

"I asked him to and he said he would, but not to tell anybody."

"See what I mean? He pays everybody in cash!"

"That's pretty amusing, actually."

It felt so good to be having a conversation with someone. It seemed like it had been weeks. She was so relaxed and so easy to talk to. I couldn't help smiling.

"What?"

"It's nothing. I've been kind of, I guess you could say, isolated for the past little while. It's really cool to be talking to you."

"It's cool to be talking to you too. Thanks for sharing your joint."

"Yeah, yeah." I gestured back behind us. "This is all beginning to make sense to me. Buying a Porsche from selling toner? That would be one hell of a lot of toner."

"It'd be a Nile River of toner."

"Yeah. A Black Sea of toner. An Old Faithful of toner."

"OK, enough. How old are you anyway?"

"Eighteen."

"You're pretty darn cute, if a little on the urchin side. You wanna come over to my place and ball?"

She handed me the joint. I held it, unable to speak. I stopped walking. I watched as her smile faded. "Hey, if you have to think about it that hard, never mind."

"No! No, it's not that. I'm just surprised. Nobody's ever asked me that before."

"I don't ask it very often. Every now and then when I'm feeling like I want some company and I meet someone with a good vibe, I open up the doors to see what my karma's bringing me. Sometimes it's something good. My boyfriend's in Vietnam. It's been eight months and he's not coming back anytime soon. He might never come back. I have to face that."

"Yeah, that fucking war."

"A girl needs some comfort, but if you're not into it . . . ."

I was nervous, excited, and dumbfounded all at once. "I'm into it."

"OK. But I have to get to know you first. Don't think we're just going right over to my apartment and, you know, fuck."

Nine

What happened after that was one continuous blur. We headed down Ocean Park to the beach, which was about two miles. She asked me lots of questions. I told her I was looking for Shooky and gave her a description but she hadn't seen him. She asked me where I was staying. Oh, this place I found. It's a building that burned down. I found a way into an apartment that isn't too bad. They didn't turn off the water yet. The shower works! That sounds awful. Now I'm not sure I can have you over because if I do I won't have the heart to let you leave knowing you're going back to that place. Oh, don't worry about me. I call it the Hotel Rialto because it's over on Rialto Avenue. I'd invite you over but the place is a mess. I made her laugh. She asked me if I had the munchies. Yeah! The best hot dogs in the world are on the Santa Monica Pier. It was my turn to ask questions. She was from Salt Lake City. She grew up in a strict Mormon family that she said had suffocated her. I knew I had to get out. It took forever to get to eighteen. I graduated from high school in June 1967. I left for San Francisco the next day. Holy shit! You were in San Francisco in the summer of '67? Yeah. It was incredible. Talk about women's liberation. Lots of sex. Lots of drugs. And music! There was music everywhere. I shared a house with a bunch of people. We were like a family. That sounds so cool. My whole life has been about music. Really? Yeah. I'm a guitar player. A songwriter. Yeah? Are you any good? I'm OK. I'll get better. That's what I'm gonna do with my life. She smiled. Did you live in the Haight? No, I lived in a post-apocalyptic commune in Marin County, near Fairfax. We had one TV that was often used as a kind of drug. It was my job to watch the news on Monday nights and write down everything I saw that had to do with Vietnam. That was the work. We usually used the TV as a sedative. What do you mean? If anyone got really angry we'd give them peyote and let them watch afternoon cartoons. It would invariably calm people down. What was it like living there? We did some heroin. We were nude all the time. There were thirteen of us. We never had an even number because we had to eliminate tie votes on things. It was pretty wild. Everybody had sex with everybody else. I liked the feeling that gave me, not just the sexual feeling necessarily, but more so the feeling of freedom, of leaving my god-awful Mormon prison life behind. That's part of why sex to me is just something people do. I'm not hung up about it. But I fell into this major jealousy thing with a guy and finally split and came down to Venice. Now here I am selling garbage over the phone. Man, I've gotta do something to change my life. We had our hot dogs and watched tourists go by for a while. By that time I was really horny and couldn't wait to fuck her. I did my best to play it cool. I asked her more questions about the summer of '67. She was there in the park the day George Harrison came to check it out. She was on acid. George looked like a raccoon, she said. Rocky Raccoon? No, that's the White Album. It wasn't out yet. Oh, really? You're not even eighteen are you? Yeah I am. You're even cuter when you lie. And you've been lying the whole time, right? No I haven't. I don't know why you say that. You're what? Sixteen? Seventeen? (She was so *in control*. I didn't want to tell her anything, but then I thought if I didn't she'd change her mind.) Ok, shit. You can't tell *anybody* this. I'm seventeen. I'm on the run from a juvy prison. Oh, well, don't worry about the cops down here. There are too many blacks and Mexicans for them to fuck with. Jesus Christ, please don't tell anybody. The fact is, the cops *are* after me, at least up north of Frisco they are. Oooh, you know I *like* the idea of balling a fugitive. Really? Hell yeah. You're a teenage rebel outlaw. How cool is that? You'll be all right if you stay in Venice. Hey, now that we've traded secrets, I gotta make a quick phone call and then let's walk to my place along the beach. She went to a pay phone and had a short animated conversation. About half an hour later we walked into an old building on Horizon Avenue, a block from the boardwalk. She checked her mailbox but there was nothing. She stood looking at it for a few seconds and then slammed it shut. Her apartment was on the third floor, just one room with a mattress facing a very small kitchen against the wall by the door. A sink, a tiny refrigerator, and a hot plate. A small closet next to the bathroom. The one window faced east and looked out over the backyards of houses. She'd decorated the place nicely, with milk crates as little tables, covered by silky fabric. A little stereo was on the floor across from the foot of the bed. There were a few posters on the wall: the iconic one of Dennis Hopper and Peter Fonda in *Easy Rider*, a concert poster of Cream, and Jimi Hendrix at the Berkeley Community Theater. Candles were everywhere, and she began lighting them. I was so horny I thought I was going to come in my pants. As she was lighting the candles she said, Will you put some music on? Sure, what do you wanna hear? You pick. I already picked today and I picked *you*. Her record collection was pretty amazing for someone who seemed to be so broke. I was nervous trying to decide. What would she think good sex music would be? I must have taken quite a long time because she took off her dress and said put on whatever you want, I can get it on to anything. I looked at the Cream poster and then put on *Disraeli Gears*. Perfect! Turn it up loud! I did. Louder! OK. She was spread-eagled on the bed, masturbating. Now get your goddamn clothes off and come play with me. I jumped down next to her and kissed her. She grabbed my hand and very aggressively slapped it onto her pussy. I'm so wet. Finger-fuck me. I did. We laughed a lot. She pulled and stretched and pinched one of her nipples with one hand, and spit on the palm of the other a couple of times, and slathered the spit all over my cock and began stroking me. It was all happening very fast. I came all over the place. She laughed with delight. Well, look at you! Yeah, I haven't been laid in months. But don't worry, I've got plenty more where that came from. I caught my breath and went down on her. What a very considerate young man you are! she said, as if she were a British matron. She came quickly and fifteen minutes later I was ready to go again. There was a knock at the door. She jumped up immediately. Oh good! They're here! She ran naked to the door and let in two guys, one with a Super-8 movie camera at the ready and the other guy with a rack of klieg lights. This is Ray — the camera guy waved at me — and that's Keith. I hope you don't mind, Eddie. They're gonna film us. We're gonna get paid. I sat on the bed, my seven-teen-year-old woody standing up again, introducing himself in spite of my fear, clearly enjoying the bizarre, unexpected delights of this strange afternoon. I was speechless, scared. I didn't know what to do. The klieg lights went on and the camera started running. Greta jumped on the bed and whis-pered to me. Just do everything I tell you and this will be good. Eat my pussy again, slowly, while fucking me with this. She handed me a blue dolphin dildo. While you're doing that I'll blow you. Let me know if you think you're gonna come. We'll either stop and let you rest, or we'll tell Ray and I'll tell you where to come on me. OK? And so it began. She per-formed as if there was something crucial at stake. Ray was eagerly getting all of it with his camera, cheering us on, while Keith followed him around with the klieg lights. About every fifteen minutes Ray had to change the reel of film and we had to stop and wait for him. The whole thing was a wild turn-on for me, in the most primitive, depraved way. That surprised me. I came twice all over Greta, as per her instructions. When we were done Ray gave Greta fifty bucks and tossed a twenty at me and said that was good, see you two again, and left. The room was quiet. I felt like I was coming down from some kind of insane sexual acid trip. That's the wildest sex ever. Greta smiled. You're good! I do a little film for Ray every now and then, but never with anyone I don't like. Really? Hey, you should've told me first, you know. If I had told you, you would've said no and man, I need that fifty bucks. Nobody can survive on that goddamned toner job. And you were good. Ray was pleased. We should do another one. That creepy-ass bastard should be giving you a lot more money. You're like a top-rate porn star. Well, I have to throw myself

completely into it. I have to access the whore in me, otherwise I can't do it. That's not a bad thing, at least not to me. I
just wish I could do it all with somebody I love. We used to,
Aaron and I. What we had was beyond words. But he's not
around. I'm sorry. That's OK, at least I'm here in Venice. You
can't imagine what it was like to grow up a Mormon. It was
like growing up in a prison cell made of signs that said "NO."
I mean, listen. Before my first high school dance — which I
didn't want to go to anyway — the adults made an announcement to everybody about us not getting too close to each
other. Our instructions were: "Leave room for the holy spirit.
Bible width between." They walked around the dance floor all
night and called that out between every song: "Leave room
for the holy spirit. Bible width between." You see how I live
now. You see what kind of shit I have to do to survive. No offense. I really enjoyed that today. But I'd rather live another
life. She bought me dinner and paid with the fifty-dollar bill.
Afterwards I said goodnight and walked out. We didn't kiss.
It wasn't like that, not at all. She said see you tomorrow? I
said I guess without turning around. She caught up with me.
Hey, I really did pick *you*, you know. It couldn't have been just
anybody. You're cute, you're good-looking enough in an off-
beat sort of way, and it's no coincidence that you came walking into Lee's circus *today*. Will you at least think about doing
another one with me? You need the money. Lord knows *I*
need the money. And it was fun, wasn't it? Yeah, I guess I had
an OK time. That made both of us laugh. I walked away feeling good in that after-lots-of-good-sex kind of way, but even
more I was in shock, confused, depressed, dispirited. I headed through the dark, empty streets to the Hotel Rialto under
an almost impenetrable fog. I had nothing left in me but
loneliness and heartache for what might have been if everything had been something else. And, like Greta, a longing for
another, better life.

Ten

My dreams that night were the kind with funhouse mirrors and Super-8 cameras and annoying, blinding lights, and at other times, cold dark rooms with Greta leading me through them by candlelight. I woke to the sound of water dripping into a puddle outside the window. Summer rain. The sun hadn't risen yet and so I lay there staring at nothing, my thoughts wandering erratically. I wondered who'd lived in that apartment and where they were now. I wondered where my parents were at that moment. And then I wondered why I wondered.

The Hotel Rialto was like a crypt that morning.

After work Greta and I walked out together. I was in a better mood because I'd actually made a small sale. One ream of paper and one toner cartridge to a two-man accounting office in Birmingham. The rain had stopped and there were patches of blue overhead that looked like they might triumph over a few petulant, tear-filled clouds that hovered a mile or so away. She asked me how I was doing.

"I slept like I was dead but I woke up too early. How about you?"

"Yeah, the same. I'm a little sore. You fucked me to death."

"I'm awful damn sorry about that. But not that sorry!"

She laughed. "You're a nut. But don't worry. If I'm gonna be sore, I want it to be because of *that* rather than some mundane reason, like spraining my ankle slipping on beach slime." She ran her fingers through my hair. "Where'd you get this haircut?"

"Prison. The barber was blind."

"You know what? For a fugitive you're pretty sweet. A street urchin but mostly a 'sweet urchin'. You wanna go to the Pier for a hot dog?"

"Yeah, but I'm buying."

"Oh, I see. Big shot salesman."

"Actually it's porn boy."

The ocean was alive and in a dark mood. A wind blew in from the north and the surf was forced to come in sideways and didn't seem too happy about it. The Pier wasn't crowded. The rain had kept people away so there weren't many tourists to gawk at. But the hot dog was delicious in the way that only hot dogs at the beach can be. After we ate we sat and smoked. The whole afternoon was ahead of us. I was weary of looking for Shooky and didn't know what to do with the rest of the day. I'd been in Venice for weeks. Greta seemed relaxed. She hadn't sold anything but it didn't bother her, or if it did she didn't show it. I was getting very horny for her again.

"I got nothin' to do today," I said.

"Me neither. You want to go to my place?" She said this while taking off her glasses and cleaning them with her T-shirt. "Salt air always does this," she said, showing me tiny sand particles on the lenses.

"Yeah, it might rain again."

"No sex. But we can hang out if you want. You can play my guitar."

We bought a bottle of Old English 800 and a "Family Size" bag of Lay's potato chips. When we got to her place she ripped the potato chip bag open so hard that a few of them went flying across the room like skeets. We laughed. She pointed to the closet with a palm-sized chip in her hand.

"The guitar's in there. Play me something."

The closet was as disorganized as the rest of her place was orderly. In the back, behind a black dress and a long red coat hanging on a weak metal hanger, scrunched into a corner by a big box full of old clothes, her guitar case woke up and looked at me wide-eyed, as if it were a dog and I might have food. I brought it out into the daylight. Clumps of dust clung to the case like little gray barnacles. I opened it slowly. The strings looked like they'd been there since Elvis was a baby, but the guitar was a good one.

"This is a Yamaha. Like the one my dad gave me once. Where did you get it?"

"I found it. Well, no. I'll be honest. I *stole* it. A couple of years ago in San Francisco. It was in the back seat of an Oldsmobile parked in front of a house on Belvedere Street. Middle of the day. I opened the door, grabbed it, and carried it away like it was mine, like I could play it, like I was Joan Baez. I walked down to Haight Street and there was this girl busking. She was wearing one of those old lady dresses and playing something kind of hokey, like "Where Have All the Flowers Gone." Her hair was blowing in a breeze coming from Golden Gate Park. She was kind of beautiful. Her voice wasn't that good but it didn't matter. She was out there, doing it, you know? It's more than I ever did. I thought, 'Shit, maybe I just stole her *other* guitar.' But then she didn't look like someone who'd drive an Oldsmobile, or even own a car, you know? I thought of bringing it back but that didn't seem like a good idea. What if somebody saw me? I felt bad about it, but what could I do?"

"You must have been desperate."

"But that's just it. I wasn't. I just out-and-out stole it. I still don't know why. I can't play it. I don't even want it."

"I used to write songs in my backyard because it was so hot in Rockville Flats. I had the most gorgeous guitar. A Gibson Hummingbird. Man, the sound I could get out of that beauty."

"It has a beautiful name."

I tuned her guitar and played a song I wrote. I don't remember which one. I hadn't played in months, so it must have been an easy one. The ancient strings were cutting into my fingers and they hurt. I had no calluses.

"Wow, you're pretty darn good."

"This is a decent guitar."

"Now it's yours. I can see it belongs with you."

"Mine?"

"I've been waiting for the right time to give it away. This may sound like bullshit, but it isn't. I feel a sense of responsibility to the person I stole it from. I've wanted to do the right thing by him or her by doing the right thing with the guitar. Once I walked away with it there was no way back. It wasn't ever going to work, me playing it. So I stashed it away. Until now. It's been waiting for you all this time, Eddie."

"Really?"

"Really."

"Thank you! I can make some money on the boardwalk with this. With the first five bucks they throw at me I'll take you out for burritos."

"You got a deal." She leaned over and kissed me on the cheek. "Will you play me something else?"

I kissed her again, felt a stir in my pants, and put down the guitar.

"No sex. I told you that. Play me another song."

"Well, OK. Since you're breakin' my heart I'll play you a song called 'Heart Breakin' Mama.' It's by Skeets McDonald, a country singer, but it's a rockabilly song. Eddie Cochran plays guitar on the record."

I played it for her. And she clapped a little.

"Eddie, you know I'm not your girl, right?"

That stung, even though I hadn't thought of her that way. "Yeah, I know. Why do you say that? I don't even want a girlfriend."

"Because you sang that song."

"It's just a song. A funny little ditty."

"Yeah, but you could have played anything. 'Johnny B. Goode.' 'All Along the Watchtower.' I assume you know both of 'em. Everybody does. And you said I was breaking your heart."

"Oh, I just said that because I thought it was funny."

She got up off the bed and took the empty beer bottle and put it on her kitchen counter. She lit a cigarette and leaned against the sink.

"Eddie, I have a boyfriend. And I really do like you. And yeah, until Aaron gets back from Nam, *if* he gets back, I'm happy to fool around with you when I'm in the mood and make a movie or two. I really hope we *can* make another movie because I need the money."

"I think we should rehearse first and see how it goes."

"Hahaha. Like we really need rehearsing! But yeah, I'll 'rehearse' if you'll commit."

"Yeah, let's go ahead with it. I need the bread. It's just that thinking of some dude watching us and jacking off makes me feel weirded out."

"If you focus on me it'll be less weird."

She called Ray and set us up for four-thirty the day after tomorrow.

"So we're gonna rehearse tomorrow then, right?" I asked.

"Four-thirty, you horny little fugitive."

"That's me! Anyway, look," I said, "I'm sorry your boyfriend is in Vietnam. I don't even know if there's a word for how bad it must be over there. I had a friend, Kyle. He was kind of a friend anyway. He used to buy liquor for me and my friends. He went to Nam and lost his mind."

"What are you telling me *that* for?"

"I'm sorry. I was trying to be understanding."

"That's like me telling you I have a headache and you telling me about your little brother Billy who died of a brain tumor."

"I'm sorry. I'm stupid. Does he write to you?"

"The last letter I got was three months ago and it took a month to get here."

"What is he? What rank I mean? Sergeant? Corporal? General?"

"Yeah, Eddie. He's a general." She rolled her eyes. "No, he was drafted. That means he's nothing."

She started to cry. I got up, lit a cigarette, and threw the match out her window. Now we were both standing. I wanted to comfort her, but I didn't want her to think that a hug meant I wanted her to be my girlfriend.

"I'm lucky I'm on the run," I said. "The bastards can't get me."

"This is *not* about you, Eddie."

"I know. I'm sorry. I'm an idiot. What's his name again?"

"Aaron. He might already be dead. I have no way of knowing. His family knows nothing about me. They're in Laredo. I met him in line at a Johnny Winter concert. We spent two weeks together. I know that's a short time, but we're soulmates. What we had was inexpressible in language. It was spiritual as much as it was sexual." She broke down again. "And I'm thinking bad thoughts, Eddie. I'm ashamed of myself. Like sometimes I think I'd rather find out he's dead than find out he's just stopped writing to me. Isn't that awful?"

I walked over and hugged her. She cried a while longer before I told her I was heading down to the boardwalk to try and make some money.

"Maybe I'll come down. If not, I'll see you tomorrow."

Eleven

I walked to the boardwalk and staked out a spot near the patio of a Hawaiian restaurant, but just as I started playing "Heart Breakin' Mama" (it felt safe since I'd just played it for Greta) Don Ho drowned me out over the restaurant's sound system, singing "Tiny Bubbles." I moved a couple of blocks down to what looked like a good spot outside a little NYC-style bodega. Within minutes a tall, emaciated, wearing-a-stupid-red-handkerchief-on-his-head hippie dude with a dulcimer walked up to me.

"Hey, my enlightened bro. This is *my* stage. You're gonna have to split the scene, amigo."

He really did say "my enlightened bro."

As I walked away I heard him playing a terrible version of "Like a Rolling Stone," one that in an enlightened world he would have been arrested for. His dulcimer sounded like a fucking door chime in a yarn store.

I played for an hour and didn't make anything. I was awful. Everybody seemed suddenly busy, rushing around, hell-bent on getting away from whatever awful jobs they had, heading straight into whatever calamities they were doomed to face at home.

When I got back to the Hotel Rialto that night there was a tractor parked in front, and half the building was a pile of rubble. The walls of my apartment were gone and so were my backpack and my sleeping bag. I thought about spending the night there anyway and prepared something of a horizontal space comprised of various non-deadly detritus. But when a rat scrambled across my chest, I headed out to find somewhere to sleep on the beach, defeated, demoralized, and thinking Shooky must be dead.

That night I dreamt I went to Manderley again.

And there I was at Manderley on that last day with Shooky, the two of us smoking the exquisite Lebanese hash, looking ahead to our emancipation from Flatvillian misery. He took the pipe from me, gave it a look, and said, "You found us some fine hash, bro. We're gonna make a ton from this. Bummer you didn't find your dad too when you were in Anaheim."

"I didn't really want to find Harry anyway. I went by all the seedy places he used to take me. It all just reminded me of what a low-life he was. It was weird. I aborted the mission pretty quickly."

The dream switched to Harry wearing his Goofy costume, drinking from a tall can of Coors while walking through Tomorrowland. He chug-a-lugged the rest of it and tossed it away, throwing it back over his head into the middle of the street. He pulled another one out and did the same thing. Now two cans in the street. I heard a kid say to his mother, "What's Goofy doing in Tomorrowland and why is he throwing those beer cans away like that?" The mom said, "Goofy's a visionary, honey. He knows things the rest of us don't."

Just as quickly the dream returned to Manderley. I took a hit from the pipe. Got a major head rush. I couldn't think for a second. My brain went into a slow orbit around the inner vacuum. A minute later, as I started coming out of it, I took a moment to look at my hand. It was fascinating, then not.

Shooky said, "Hey, pass the pipe, bro! Don't Bogart!"

I woke up remembering that conversation, which we had on that last day, and it made me miss Shooky more than I wanted to.

"I'm not Bogarting, I'm spacing out. And look who's talking. You Bogarted about two *lids* of Megan's weed during Pentalust. You were a massive dope hoarder."

"Pentalust" was what we named the weekend when Katie Wayne, a foxy overachiever I fooled around with now and then, was house-sitting for a family of Pentecostal Christians. They were going on a pilgrimage to Bedford, Texas, to play with snakes, speak in tongues, and generally raise Pentecostal Cain. Katie and Megan Marie Drysdale, who was always Shooky's favorite (he never had just one girlfriend), invited us over for two nights and two days of all-out debauchery.

"I want us to 'sin' in every room in their house," Katie had said when she told me about the opportunity. We were making out in her Corvette. She was from another world, bound for glory in whatever work she decided to do. She was so *driven*. Of course, she knew as I did what life had in store for her — a useless advanced degree in comparative literature from an elite college, marriage to a squeaky-clean New England rich boy incapable of expressing his feelings, foreign-made station wagons with leather seats, beds with cozy down comforters, Mary Poppins-type nannies, catered dinner parties, two well-behaved children who wildly succeed in life, and one antisocial misfit who ends up in drug rehab. Katie wanted to take advantage of every chance she had to live as if there were no tomorrow. That's why she hung out with me. Back then I knew no limits. But our fling didn't last very long. She didn't have the necessary stamina to keep up with me. Or maybe it's more accurate to say she got tired of me. If you're not a real stoner, the initial charm of being with one can lose its luster pretty quickly.

"'Massive dope hoarder?" Shooky laughed. "That's bullshit! And Pentalust was about a *year* ago, man. How many more times are you gonna bring this up?"

"It wasn't a year ago. It was the weekend before Easter. I remember because Katie and I fed each other a whole family of chocolate Easter bunnies."

"Well anyway, Megan didn't even *have* two lids. And that Saturday I was on *acid*. 'Massive dope hoarder'! I'm gonna call Megan and ask her."

"Good idea. We were all talking about it. That's all I'm saying, bro."

"She would have said something."

"She *did* say something. Just not to you."

§

I called Greta first thing the next morning and said I was gonna spend the day looking for Shooky. I told her I was starting to hate him for not being around. I didn't tell her I had no place to stay anymore.

"It looks like he ran out on you, man. Sorry. Hey, I gotta go to work."

"Tell Lee I'm sick, OK?"

"You *are* sick. That's what I love about you. How'd it go?"

"I didn't make anything. I was really rusty. I'll be better today. So we're still on for our so-called rehearsal later, right?"

"Yep. Don't worry about the busking. You're gonna do well. You're good."

"Thanks. Hey, I'll need to take a shower first. Is that OK?"

"I would appreciate that."

§

It seemed like I had every palm leaf in Venice memorized by then and Shooky wasn't underneath any of them. Toward the end of the afternoon I went to the boardwalk. I played guitar by the bodega, keeping an eye out for Dulcimer Boy. I felt a lot more confident even though I still had tender virgin fingers. I was actually enjoying myself in a way I hadn't in months. Only music could do that for me. I imagine it must be like surfing is for a surfer. Nothing else can get you to that place.

I made a buck ninety in about an hour and a half. More than minimum wage. I went into the bodega and bought a Dr. Pepper, drank it, and saw the clock. Ten to six! Damn! I headed out for Greta's walking as fast as I could. Just as I was about to make the turn onto Horizon Avenue I heard a girl's voice coming from inside Shark Attack, a funky surfboard shop I'd walked past a hundred times. I'd never heard her before. I stopped. I *had* to listen. It was as if I had no control, no agency. I felt it in my whole body.

She was saying to someone, "And if a shark bites you *and* the board, and you survive, we'll replace the board free of charge. You just have to be sure to show us the bite marks." She laughed. "Now if you'll excuse me for a minute, I'll be right back. I want to show you something."

She sounded Irish. Or maybe British. I couldn't tell. But it was more than the accent. She could have been speaking French and I still would have understood that something had just happened to me. I darted into the shop to see her but she'd gone. Somebody looked at me and narrowed his eyes and I realized then that I was filthy. If I'd have let her see me in that condition it would've ruined everything.

§

"You're late. What happened to you? You smell like a beached whale!" said Greta, letting me in. She stepped away as far as she could.

"The Hotel Rialto was demolished yesterday. I had to sleep on the beach."

"Oh no! Eddie, that's terrible. I'm so sorry. But now go take a shower. You're gonna contaminate my whole place."

"That sounds like a fabulous idea. Then we'll rehearse for tomorrow!"

"Sorry, my friend. You're out of luck. That was our appointed hour. I have to go."

"Well, well, well." I still had that girl surfing around in my head so I didn't care much about the rehearsal.

"I agree. Now go on, go clean up. Wait a minute. Where's your stuff?"

"Gone. My apartment doesn't exist anymore."

"So the only clothes you have are what you're wearing?"

"I hadn't thought about that, but yeah. I didn't have much else anyway."

Greta lit a cigarette, stood against her kitchen counter shaking her head. "My little outlaw."

"Yeah." I started for the bathroom.

"You can stay here tonight. I'll put your clothes in the washer downstairs on my way out. I won't be back until the morning, so you'll have the place to yourself. Make sure you're on time to put 'em in the dryer or somebody'll Shanghai 'em."

"How much time?"

"Half an hour."

"Where's the washer and what am I gonna wear down there?"

She took a slinky robe out of the closet. It looked like red silk, with frayed edges and a few little holes in it.

"Holy Mormon horror."

"You'll survive."

She told me how to find the laundry room and handed me a spare key. I tried to kiss her.

"Are you nuts? You're like a swamp zombie!"

She left.

Taking a shower, washing my clothes, getting dressed, listening to Van Morrison, I kept hearing that voice. But what would she want to do with me? After all, who was I? About midnight I walked down to the boardwalk. The fog was in, the air a salt-laced bracing spin of promise. Nobody was out except for a few scruffy people wandering around. I stood outside Shark Attack, closed up behind its rusting armor, a corrugated metal gate, wondering what she looked like. It didn't matter. I smoked half a joint, and when I started back to Greta's I gave the other half to a kid like me who looked lost and confused, like he'd just gotten off the bus.

Twelve

"**R**ay had to reschedule to tomorrow," said Greta. We were in McCabe's music store after work. I was there to buy a new set of strings and try out a few guitars just for fun. "Someday I'm gonna come back here and buy another Hummingbird," I said, looking at one hanging high up on the wall.

"Did you hear me? Ray had to reschedule to tomorrow."

I hadn't heard her. "OK. But I might not be clean tomorrow unless I can come over early and take another shower."

Greta grabbed me by the hand. "Hey, look at me."

"I am looking at you."

"No. Really look at me."

"I *am*."

"Do I look like a person who would let you sleep on the beach again?"

"Yes."

"Very funny. You can stay with me until you get your shit together. Just don't ask me what I'm doing. I'm not your girlfriend, and even if I was, what I do without you would be none of your business."

"Wow, thank you so much! You're saving my life. Someday I swear I'll do something wonderful for you."

"I hope so."

When we got outside I said, "And I know you're not my girlfriend. Jesus. Why do you keep saying that? It's funny you bring it up again, because I want you to come with me. Do you know Shark Attack?"

"Of course. Everybody does."

"I fell in love with a girl who works there. I need you to go there with me so I don't look like a fool."

"How am I supposed to keep *that* from happening?"

"I don't know. Just come with me."

We hopped on a bus back down to Venice.

When we were walking on the boardwalk I said, "Act like the reason we're there isn't because of her."

"How did you meet her?"

"I haven't. I just heard her voice."

Greta laughed. "*What? Are you in junior high school?*"

"She's Irish or Scottish or British or something. I haven't actually seen her."

"And that makes her invisible?"

"Maybe she is invisible. We have to go see."

"Or *not* see."

"Right."

"Sorry, I've been in a mood today, in case you haven't noticed. I keep reminding myself that I shouldn't be happy while Aaron is in Vietnam. Not that I *am* happy. But even when I'm having a pretty good day I tell myself I should focus on how fucked up my life is. I try to convince myself to complain even when I don't feel like complaining. And then it's the opposite. I think I owe it to Aaron to be happy. I mean, how can I complain about anything when he's over there going through fuck knows what kind of nightmares? I should be running through the daisy patch singing, 'Feelin' Groovy.' I don't know how to *be*, Eddie."

"I don't know. I'd say trust yourself. You're afraid that you're betraying him as if you don't care, but you do. You're in a sad-ass situation that'd be hard for anybody."

"Listen to you." She kissed me on the cheek. "Thank you."

"Talk to me about it anytime. I'll listen and you'll feel better. And when you're happy, I'm happy. So there's that. I know how rotten life can be."

"I can tell."

"How?"

"Because you're just as damaged as me."

We laughed about that one.

About fifty feet from Shark Attack I started to freak out.

"Greta, let's forget about this stupid idea. I don't wanna meet this girl. I just wanna go to your place and fool around."

"Hold on, Don Juan. You're gonna chicken out?"

"This whole idea is dumb. Like I said, I've never even seen her. Come on!"

She laughed and grabbed my arm and pulled me in the direction of my impending humiliation. "You told me you fell in love with her!"

"That was a huuuuuuge exaggeration. For all I know she looks like Quasimodo."

"Let's go find out."

"No. Will you let me go and leave me the fuck alone about this? I never should have told you." I wrestled out of her grip and started walking away. "Let's go fool around."

She grabbed me again. "No looky, no nooky!"

"Oh, fuck the fuck off," I said, pushing her away.

She laughed and took my hand and walked me to a spot just across from Shark Attack. I told her I had to have a smoke first. I fired one up for both of us.

"Fine. Stall."

I remember how it felt standing there with her that day, with the sun grudgingly and slowly setting, the moon hanging above us like an afterthought, imperceptibly moving the tides, something the whole world takes for granted. The girl who was about to change my life forever didn't matter to me anymore. My fear of meeting her convinced me that I wasn't interested.

I said to Greta, "This is stupid. I don't have time for this."

"Yeah. Right. You're so busy." She pushed me into the store. It was bigger than it looked. It wasn't very wide and maybe a hundred feet deep. Closest to the entrance a couple of racks of surfer shirts, tank tops, etc., provided a gateway into the cornucopia of surfboards that lined the walls. They stood looking straight ahead like a platoon of weird board-game soldiers in a dazzling array of colors. Some were for rent, some for sale. A few hung suspended from the ceiling. Those had a bunch of autographs on them.

"Signed by sharks," I said, trying to pretend I wasn't nervous.

"Loan sharks," Greta said. "They're probably repossessed."

A few customers strolled around as — and I remember this as if it were yesterday — "Here Comes the Sun" was on. It was like a movie soundtrack. Greta scanned the room like a poacher. "Where's your paramour?"

"Quit being so obvious." I took another quick look around. "She's not here. Let's go."

"I wanna look at some surfboards."

"No you don't."

She walked over and began inspecting the soldiers. A central casting surfer kid, blond, handsome, tanned, appeared and asked Greta if she needed help.

Looking at me and trying her best to annoy me, she asked him, "How do these float?"

Exasperated, I walked over and told her I had to go and that I'd see her at the apartment.

"Don't you wanna know how these float?" she asked me, smiling ridiculously.

"No."

"It's basic Newtonian physics," the kid said to her.

"Mmm," Greta hummed, leaning in with feigned interest.

I started heading out of the store when Kiera appeared as a silhouette, all the light of the late afternoon sun behind her. I saw nothing but the shape of her body, and for a second it was like I could dream what she looked like, impose whatever image I wanted to, a kind of *tabula rasa* of a person. You can believe that she was far more beautiful to me than anything I could have conjured up. She came in quickly, carrying a box, breezing right by me and heading to the back. Now I could see her fully. She was a little shorter than me. Her long, dark brown hair was in a ponytail, falling gently between her shoulder blades. She wore a jean skirt, red low-top Converse All-Stars, and a red Shark Attack T-shirt. The multi-colored logo was a huge shark on a huge surfboard cruising effortlessly in the curl of a huge wave, chomping down with his huge teeth on a screaming, bleeding surfer hanging halfway out of its mouth.

As she walked by the blond kid she said, "Sorry I'm a little late, Warren. I ran into Crazy Hazel and had to stop and buy her a sandwich."

"You can't save the world, you know," he said, not looking her way, pulling out a surfboard for Greta, who seemed to be having the time of her life. She looked at Kiera, then at me, and with no attempt at subtlety nodded her approval. I made a face, as if to say "Stop doing that!"

"Right," Kiera said to Warren. "But I can make sure she doesn't go hungry now and then, can't I, Mr. Cheap?"

"She takes advantage of you."

"No, I take advantage of her. She's my good-karma bank."

"Keep it up, one day you'll be out there yourself. "

She laughed. She replaced a roll of paper in the cash register and came back into the main part of the store. Everything about her made me tremble. I had never in my life been so happy to be clean. Before she had a chance to talk to anybody else I walked up to her and smiled.

"Hi." Petrified as I was, I will never know how I managed that. Perhaps fate pushed me like Greta had.

"Hi!"

"Um. I have a question about a surfboard?"

"Well, good. What can I help you with?"

I had to come up with a question. I had to come up with a surfboard too. I walked over to one of them, took a quick glance at Greta, who wasn't looking at us, and said, "How does this float?"

"Well, first of all, this is much too small for you. You're thin and it looks like you don't weigh much. You need one that's about eight feet long. It won't fit in your car, that's the main drawback. You attach it to the roof. But it will suffice on white water and bigger waves. And by bigger I don't mean giant Hawaiian waves. Five-, six-footers. You're a beginner?"

"Yes. How can you tell?"

"Well," she said, smiling. She tilted her head to the side in a comical way, to communicate that it was obvious. "How often do you plan on surfing?"

"A lot."

"Meaning?"

"Oh, I don't know. A couple of times a week maybe." I was starting to believe it myself. And I wanted her to never stop talking to me.

"We'll pick out a longer foam board for you with lots of volume. So not this one."

"What's volume?"

"Lots of volume means you won't sink and die a horrifying death paddling out to a wave."

She was so cute I couldn't speak. She passed by me and strolled down the row and I strolled after her. I inhaled quietly as she went by. She smelled like everything beautiful in the world. Flowers. Salt air. A dash of her sweat. Spices. A summer night. She picked out a board. It was blue with racy red and white stripes. Turning around to gauge how close Warren was and then turning back to me, she said with a quiet laugh, "Look how hard he's trying."

"She's really got him goin' doesn't she?"

"Yeah. He cracks me up. He's nice, but a little conservative. No doubt he'll be a successful businessman someday. Selling eggs to hospitals."

"Why eggs to hospitals?"

"I don't know. It's just what came out of my mouth." She laughed and said this as if it were just as much a curiosity to her. "Anyway, I'm telling you about volume, right?"

"Right."

"It's the ratio between your weight and the cubic liters of the board. We have a scale in back. It actually belongs to Warren. He's a bit of a control freak, so he's the only one who weighs people. I think it's absurd. Anyway, if you'd like he can —"

"No, no, no! That's OK. To be honest, I don't really care." I felt so stupid saying that.

"Oh yes? Well."

"Where are you from? I love your accent."

"Thank you. Ireland. Where are you from, fledgling surfer?"

"Oh, everywhere and nowhere."

"I see. A man of mystery."

I laughed and made a face as if I were indeed a man of mystery, which made her laugh with me. "Where in Ireland are you from?"

"A village called Drumcliff. Well actually, Dublin, but I think of myself as being from Drumcliff. I was actually born in Sligo, a town nearby. You've been to Ireland?"

"I've never been anywhere."

"Oh. I thought you, when you asked me what part, I thought —"

"Yeah, I know. It's just something I said. Kind of dumb."

"No, I do that too. I once asked a customer who told me he'd surfed in the Strait of Magellan if he'd surfed the whole thing or just the straight part. I was high."

I laughed yet again, not only because the joke was funny but also as a joyous response to what was happening.

"How is it you're in Venice?"

"I'm at UCLA."

"Majoring in surfing?"

"Haha! Film and Literature."

She was out of my league.

"Drumcliff, eh? It sounds dangerous. It has the word 'cliff' in it."

"No, it's not dangerous. Are you afraid of heights?"

"No. Yes."

"Well, don't worry. It's a village. Quite lovely. Yeats is buried in the church cemetery there."

I didn't know who he was. "You mean Billy Joe Yeats, the blind Appalachian banjo player?"

She laughed. "Is there such a person?"

"Probably not. Who's Crazy Hazel?"

A customer was standing down by the cash register, waiting, holding a red boogie board. Warren heard Kiera laugh.

"Hey, can you ring that gentleman up please?"

"Are you actually interested in the surfboard today?"

"I'll have to think about it."

"OK. I'm here every day."

I had a moment of panic. I had to say something else before she took off.

"I'm Eddie. I like that you're Irish."

"I do too. I'm Kiera. Nice meeting you." She gestured toward the customer. "I have to skedaddle."

I like that you're Irish? What a moronic thing to say. I watched her walk away, wishing she'd walk in slow motion, wanting to draw the moment out as long as time would allow. As soon as she got to the register I went over and told Greta I would see her at the apartment, and without waiting for an answer I walked out, my head spinning.

Thirteen

I went back to Shark Attack the next day but this time I didn't have to be convinced.

"Don't forget to be here by four-thirty for our frolic with Ray," Greta said as I was on my way out.

"Don't worry, I need the money too."

I was a nobody, no past worth falling back on, no future worth betting on, and I'd only met Kiera the day before. But I *knew*. I walked into the store, found her at the cash register flipping through a pile of receipts. She wore a white skirt that day with a white Shark Attack T-shirt. The grisly logo was in color. Her hair was in a long braid, with little multi-colored beads woven through it.

I went straight to her, my nerves like sparklers. I forgot to say hello. "Will you come take a walk with me?"

She looked up, didn't flinch, took what felt like a rather excruciating pause, and said, "Hi."

I exhaled more dramatically than I wanted to and I didn't want to be dramatic at all. "Oh yeah, hi." I chuckled self-consciously. "So I'm here because I haven't thought of anything else but you since yesterday. I probably shouldn't say more or I'll make a bigger fool of myself than I already am. You're gorgeous and cute and smart and I would like to get to know you. Will you take a walk with me?"

She gave me the once-over, her expression one of surprise and curiosity. "I'm guessing you aren't known for your subtlety?"

"I'm as honest as you are beautiful."

That hit home. "Thank you." She smiled demurely.

Warren called to her. "Kiera, there's a phone call for you." This annoyed the hell out of me. I wished one of those surfboards on the ceiling would fall and crush him.

"OK, it'll be just a second," she said to Warren.

I was deeply discouraged. "Sorry, it looks like you have to take that."

"I will. It's OK. I told you, he's a control freak." She shifted her position, her weight on the opposite leg. "So what do you imagine you'll do if I say no?"

God knows how this came out of me, but I heard myself say, "I'll come back tomorrow and ask you again. And tomorrow after that if I have to."

"I see." She nodded toward my shirt. "Tell me honestly, is that an actual tank top or did some wild circus animal rip out the sleeves?"

I laughed. "If you promise to take a walk with me I'll tell you," I said with what I thought to be a winning smile. I stood there on the edge of a razor blade.

Warren called to her again in a singsong voice: "Phone please!"

She turned to the phone behind the counter and started to pick it up, turned back to me and said with a wry smile, "Promise you? I don't think so. But I will *agree*. I have a break at four-thirty. Meet me outside?"

I left in a state of rapture. OK, I thought, so I'll be just a little late getting back to Greta's. I walked down to the water and watched the waves come in. I couldn't sit still or stand still, so I walked down to the Santa Monica Pier. By the time I got there and back it would be just around the time to meet her. Each moment was a clusterfuck of thoughts and emotions, "clusterfuck" being a positive word in this case. That lovely girl liked me! How could that be possible? Love at first sight. *"Yes, I'm certain that it happens all the time."* If John and Paul said it, it must be true.

I got to the Pier and tried to buy a Coke. I'd already opened the goddamned thing before finding my pockets empty. I'd left my money on Greta's kitchen counter. There I was with the open Coke in my hand, unable to pay the guy. I apologized. I really felt bad. It was the same hotdog stand that Greta and I always went to and the guy had always been nice to us. He was a short, muscular man of about fifty, wearing a bandana that kept his long curly black hair out of his eyes. He was the kind of guy who could kill me with his thoughts.

"OK," he said. "You come pay me tomorrow."

I said I would. I started to ask him for another one so I had something to bring to Kiera. He saw me thinking. "Whatever you have in mind, my friend, the answer is no."

On the way back I was mulling over the being-late-to-Greta's scenario. I decided I'd meet Kiera and tell her I'd forgotten an appointment and ask if I could meet her tomorrow. That plan went straight to hell the minute I saw her. She came out of Shark Attack at the same time I arrived. Seeing her outside for the first time, her smile, those freckles, her lovely hands, incredible legs, the sun seeming to glow brighter on her than on anyone else I'd ever seen — I couldn't walk away. I was *incapable* of walking away.

"You look beautiful."

"Thank you. You look like an enterprising young man," she said ironically. "Now what's the story with the shirt?"

"You were right about the wild circus animal. I applied for a part-time job as a lion tamer. The interview didn't go well."

She laughed. "Let's go that way." She pointed to the water. "I always go down to the beach on my break."

"Sounds perfect."

She looked at me with curiosity as we walked on the sand, maybe trying to sort out why she had agreed to this. I was mesmerized. The light on her face. Her hair in the breeze coming off the water. Her dark brown eyes.

"Jesus. You're gorgeous."

"You're very sweet. I heard you playing guitar on the boardwalk."

"Oh god I hope I didn't embarrass myself."

"If you had I wouldn't be here." She smiled at me and I nearly had a stroke. "I love what I heard, I just couldn't stop. I was late for work and I was broke anyway."

We talked non-stop after that, walking along the water's edge. We took off our shoes. The foamy waves washed over our feet. Hers were pretty. She told me a little about school, that she lived nearby with a roommate, and more about Ireland. I kept asking her questions so she wouldn't ask me any, but she wasn't putting up with any of that.

"You're in a bit of trouble, aren't you?"

"How can you tell?"

She shrugged. "I just can."

I stopped and thought and watched the waves and the light changing in the sky above the mountains out at Malibu. She let me think.

"Do you really wanna hear this? It's a long story," I said.

"I love long stories."

We started walking again. Every now and then we'd stop and watch a dog leaping for a Frisbee or a flock of birds flying over the water, that kind of thing.

"Well, for starters, I have no place to live. I'm staying with a friend for now."

"Is that the girl you were with yesterday?"

"Yeah. That's Greta."

"She looks cool. I love those wild glasses, man. Far out!"

"She's great."

I lit us a couple of cigarettes and when I handed her hers she gave me a look, then took a deep drag. "That's a movie star move. Lighting my cigarette like that and handing it to me."

"I'm glad you smoke. We can die together."

She laughed. "So you were saying?"

"Well, I might as well tell you that I'm running from the cops."

"You were in jail, or you're trying to stay out of jail?"

"Both. But I never murdered anybody. Drug charges."

"Oh my god that so exciting!" She clapped!

"That's the first time anybody ever applauded me for anything!"

"What was it like, being locked up? You have to tell me *everything*. I want to hear all the stories about you being on the chain gang, and playing sad, lonely harmonica songs late at night in your cell, and singing 'Nobody Knows the Trouble I Seen.'"

"You're hilarious!"

We both cracked up.

"How much time do we have?"

"Oh, shit. I've got to get back soon, you're right," she said with a sigh. She walked to the water's edge and let the waves wash over her feet. I stood back a ways, just taking her in. I can still see her standing there, her back to me, a warm breeze fluttering her white skirt around, both her hands gently keeping her hair out of her eyes. As I think about it now, maybe she needed a moment to let herself wonder what this extraordinary thing was that was already happening to us.

"I brought something for you," she said, walking back to me. She pulled a keychain out of her pocket and gave it to me. It was a perfect little wooden surfboard, a lot like the one she'd shown me yesterday, with a silver chain looped through the back end. I was speechless.

"Do you like it? If you take the chain out it floats."

"I love it. Wow. I really love it. Thank you. But you know what's funny? I don't have any keys!"

"What's that song? 'I'm a man of means, by no means'? Is that you?"

"'King of the Road' by Roger Miller," I said laughing. "How is it that an Irish girl like you knows that one?"

"I wasn't raised in the fuckin' *Congo*, man! I've even heard of Elvis. Imagine that."

"I'm trying not to."

She laughed.

I had nothing to give her. I was about to apologize when I saw a piece of driftwood about six inches long, with a knot and a bend in the middle. Dark wood polished by god knows how many endless days on the ocean. I went over, picked it up, cleaned off a few clinging pieces of kelp, and brought it to her.

"I got this for you."

She took it into her hands gently, as if it were something fragile and precious. "Oh, you shouldn't have. It must have been so expensive."

"I bought it on layaway. Do you like it?"

"I love it. You are the most generous guy I've ever met."

"I know."

She laughed.

"I love your name. Kiera. It's beautiful."

"It means 'dark hair and brown eyes.' I guess that's me, right?"

"That's you. Foxy, hot, beautiful you. And I really like your ring." It was on the ring finger of her right hand.

"Hmm, you noticed it. Wow. It's very special to me," she said, holding out her fingers and looking at it. "My mother gave it to me, and I never take it off. She died when I was eight. I can tell you about that next time. There is gonna be a next time, isn't there?"

"Yes."

"Yes."

Looking at the ring again she said, "Take a closer look. It's an antique. The stone is called black onyx, but you can see if you look closely how it's really a very dark brown. I love how it's held by the silver, and how beautifully the filigree was done. It looks not like a ring, really, but like beautiful rounded strings of little silver beads and lace holding and embracing the spirit of my mother." She looked up at me. "You see?"

I nodded, almost unable to speak. She was beyond lovely. "It's perfect on you. I'm really sorry about your mother."

"Thank you."

We were silent for a bit, not sure how to move on to the next moment.

I almost kissed her. But like that night with Sarah, I didn't. Instead, I kissed the keychain and put it in my pocket. She very lightly kissed the driftwood. As we walked up the little hill where the sand starts to get softer, I asked, "Do you think there are things out there in this world that defy explanation?"

"You mean like the crazy wars in Vietnam and Ireland?"

"Yes, exactly. But I also mean spirits. Like maybe you and I knew each other before. It feels like that to me. It feels like we're picking up where we left off at some point."

"Yeah, it does now, doesn't it? Where I come from people like me believe, to some degree anyway, in Celtic mysticism — ancient spiritual beliefs about things that can't be explained empirically. Mysteries. Coincidence or fate? That sort of thing. In Ireland there are ghosts and spirits. We call them faeries. Not in a derogatory way, you know what I mean? Yeats wrote a lot about them."

"Who is this Yeats character?"

"One of Ireland's greatest poets. Maybe the greatest. His grave is about a mile from my house."

The closer we got to Shark Attack the more nervous I became. I didn't know how to say goodbye.

"Uh oh." Kiera took hold of my arm. Her touch electrified me. "There's Warren." She pointed to him stepping out of the store, looking around. "But you know what? It's just a job."

"What a drag. I'm sorry if you're in trouble."

"I'm not. I had the best time."

"Let's do something tomorrow."

"I can't. My sister's coming in tomorrow and we're going to San Francisco and then up to Napa for a week. I am *not* looking forward to it. She's a bitch. She thinks she's my mother, but I love her anyway. But yes, when I get back I'd love to. You know the Buddha bookstore?"

"Yeah."

"Meet me there a week from the day after tomorrow at noon. That's a week from Saturday, right?"

"Yes! A week from Saturday at noon. I'll be there. Good-bye, and have a great trip somehow."

"I gotta run. See you then. Bye Eddie! Thank you for the lovely driftwood."

"Thank you for this," I said, holding up the keychain. "Good luck!"

I was elated, but as I watched her running on the sand and turning around one last time to wave at me, I waved back feeling guilty that I hadn't told her my real name. Off she went. And then panic set in.

Fourteen

With every step up to the apartment I felt the tension in the air getting thicker.

"Where's Ray?" I asked, pretending I thought he'd still be there. Greta was smoking and pacing.

"He left. You're forty-five minutes late, Eddie. What am I supposed to do now? You cost me fifty fucking dollars!"

"I was with Kiera and I just lost track. I'm so sorry. Shit!"

"I needed that money, Eddie. And so did you, you fucking idiot."

It was awful seeing her so distraught. I picked up the guitar and headed for the door. "I'm so sorry. I'll get out of your life. I'm fine on my own."

"Where are you going?"

"You don't want me staying here anymore. I'm really sorry I fucked everything up." I walked out and started down the stairs. She came running out.

"Eddie, get your stupid ass back in here. You can't sleep out there. Come on back. And anyway, we've gotta get Ray on the phone and set this whole thing up again. We're gonna make this happen, OK? Please?"

When Kiera told me that she was going to San Francisco I was disappointed, but now I felt relieved. I had time to get this done, once and for all.

"OK. We're gonna make it happen," I said. "I'll fuck your brains out and we'll make everybody happy. But this has to be the last time."

"I agree. I'm sick of it."

She got Ray on the phone and we were set for late Sunday morning, this time on somebody's boat in the harbor at Marina del Rey. I spent Saturday looking all over hell for Shooky. I felt like I was searching for my lost child. You can't give up on something like that, especially when there's a thousand dollars waiting for you if you finally succeed. By the end of the day I gave up and played cover songs outside the bodega. Dulcimer Boy had finished. I was getting better. I made a little money, enough for a burrito. I retreated back to Greta's.

"Doing this tomorrow is not the end of the world," she said. "We both need the money."

"Ray's a creep."

"Yep."

"How did you meet him?"

She was standing at the window, smoking. It was hot in the apartment.

"I knew him in Marin. He was one of the guys I lived with in the commune. He moved down here before I did and he was my only friend here for a while. Then he got into making money from these movies and one thing led to another."

"How many have you made?"

"I don't know. Not that many. Maybe four or five. He hasn't been doing 'em that long. He's helped keep me off the streets. God knows why — I'm not attractive and I know it — but there's something about me he likes. I need to stop this before Aaron gets back from that motherfucking war. I don't want him to know about it. Ever."

"I don't want Kiera to know about it either. And shut up. You're very attractive."

"You're a sweet guy. How'd it go, anyway?"

"It was magic, man. She's going to San Francisco for a week with her sister, but we're gonna get together when she gets back. I'm crazy about her, Greta. She's the love of my life."

"That's cool, but hey, you just met her."

"I get that. But sometimes you just *know* things."

"Yeah. Like I know I'll kill you if you fuck up like this again."

"I said I'm sorry."

"Look, Aaron would have done the same thing."

"Really?"

"Well, it's true. I believe in true love."

"You know what? Before this afternoon, I'd forgotten what it was like to hope. Isn't that weird?"

"It's not weird," she said, coming over and putting her hand on my shoulder. She squeezed it and then sat down on the bed and propped herself up with a pillow. "It's sad and happy at the same time."

Fifteen

Kiera and I didn't waste any time when she got back from San Francisco. We met in the Buddha bookstore as planned. When I got there the door of the store was propped open. I walked in and nobody was there, nobody at the counter. I went back outside where a bookcase stood in the sun working on a tan, offering great reads for a dime. Kiera appeared. She was radiant, wearing a sleeveless sundress with wildflowers blooming all over it. Her hair was in a high ponytail because it was already hot that morning. She carried a large canvas bag.

"Kiera! Hi!" I kissed her hello. Our first.

"Lunch," she said, nodding to the bag.

"Far out!" I took it from her to carry.

Moonlight Wind came out and said hi to us. She wore a yellow dress with peace signs all over it, sandals, and a choker made from weeds or something. Her hair was in a ponytail, too.

"Hey, I remember you," she said to me. "You were here a long time ago. You bought that Hermann Hesse novel. *Demian*. What did you think? Did it change your life?" She said to Kiera, "I think I told him it would change his life."

"I wish it would have told him to change his clothes," said Kiera, putting her arm around me.

I laughed and said to Moonlight Wind, "You remember me? Wow. That was a long time ago. I'm Eddie. And you're . . . *Moon*-something? Sorry, I don't remember exactly."

"That's OK. I'm Moonlight Wind. So nice to see you. And . . . Eddie? That's not what I remember."

"It was a while ago," I said as casually as I could. "How have you been?"

"Wonderful. I just came back from a month in Nepal. Trekking in the Himalayas. I'm mentally and spiritually clear for a while. Who knows how long it will last? But I know I'm going back. Not sure when yet, but definitely."

"You climb mountains?" Kiera asked.

"No, no! Trekking has nothing to do with climbing. No, it's walking, or hiking, on trails. It's really no different than, say, hiking in Yosemite. Except, well, the big difference is you're at a much higher altitude. The air is thin, but pure. I say pure instead of clean because you're at the top of the world, away from anything that can contaminate it. The altitude slows you down, gives you an opportunity to think. Or not think, depending on where your head's at when you get up there."

"God, that sounds incredible," Kiera said.

"Where is Nepal anyway?" I asked.

"It borders India to the south. Tibet to the north. It sounds far away and it is, but once you get there everything is unbelievably cheap. On the trek you sleep in little huts, always owned by a family, for the equivalent of about ten cents a night. Food costs maybe twenty cents more."

Kiera and I both said "wow" at the same time.

"Someday," she said, looking at me, then at Moonlight Wind.

"I remember you had that bloody bandage over your eye," said Moonlight Wind. She took a step toward me and put her hand on my forehead. "It healed, but it left a scar."

"Yeah."

Kiera did the same thing. She softly placed her hand on my forehead and looked at my scar. Her touch made me feel lightheaded. And her face was so close to mine.

"Oh no," she said. "How did that happen?"

"It's a long story."

"I like long stories." She softly kissed the scar.

I felt like I would never be unhappy again.

"So, did you like the novel?" Moonlight Wind asked.

"I never finished it. In my life I never had anything close to a paradise, let alone a lost one, you know what I mean? I was raised by wolves. I just couldn't relate. And to be honest I thought Emil Sinclair was kind of a pussy."

Moonlight Wind said, "That's one way to read it." She laughed. "Come on in, I've got another idea."

She disappeared into the bookshelves. As soon as she was gone Kiera and I kissed again, softly, and then we really kissed.

"I knew you were lovers the minute I saw you together," Moonlight Wind said when she returned. "And in the end, the love you take is equal to the love you make. So make love a lot you two."

Kiera and I looked at each other, curiosity aflame. How would this little moment play out?

I put my arm around her, pulled her close to me, and said with a quiet little laugh, "Why don't we do it in the road?"

She responded with a mischievous smile. "I'll let you be in my dreams if I can be in yours."

We laughed. Perfect.

"You know," Moonlight Wind said, "they say the greatest story ever told is the Bible. They even made a movie called that, which was a piece of shit. But the *real* greatest story ever told is the story of the Beatles."

"I agree," said Kiera.

Moonlight Wind handed me the now-famous Hunter Davies' biography. "If you haven't read this you are destined to. I've seen you play on the boardwalk."

"Oh, great! Thank you." I started digging in my pocket for change.

"No, no. This is a gift from me, as I am a part of your Universe and you guys are a part of mine. Enjoy. Besides, it's only fifteen cents."

"Wow! Thank you again, Moonlight Wind. I can't wait to read it."

"I'll read it too," said Kiera. "Thank you. You're a lovely person. I've seen you around, and it's so nice to actually meet you. I'm Kiera. I work at Shark Attack. Look for me if you ever need anything."

"I'm absolutely charmed, Kiera." She kissed her on both cheeks.

We said our goodbyes and out we went.

"That woman is either crazy or she smokes the best dope in the world," I said, "but I do want to read this book."

"She's a sweet, gentle soul," Kiera said. "I don't think there's anything more to it."

"You're right. I was trying to be funny and I bombed."

"Well, now we have reason to celebrate if somehow, by some miracle, you end up making me laugh again this afternoon."

"I think we're in for a pretty grim day."

"Me too."

We headed to the beach, holding hands.

"I had a much better time with Nora than I expected," she said. "You might think me a terrible person, but the reason things went so well is that she's all fucked up. For once, I was playing the role of the one who has her shit together. She just broke up with her husband and is getting a divorce. I never liked the guy. I thought he was a smarmy bastard. He sold insurance, so that's not a stretch. Did you ever see *Double Indemnity?*"

"No, I haven't."

"Oh, you have to see it. It'll come around to the Nuart or the Fox Venice one of these days. This smarmy insurance salesman played by Fred McMurray helps Barbara Stanwyck kill her husband for insurance money. Nora's husband was just like that."

"She's better off then."

"I have to admit, it was quite nice to feel superior to her and know that it was true, if you know what I mean. Nora's been mostly a bitch to me ever since our mum died, so you can imagine."

"I'm so sorry about your mom. What happened?"

"Pancreatic cancer. It's one of the worst kinds. But I suppose you can see it as one of the best kinds in a way, because it kills you quicker and you suffer less. She died four months after she was diagnosed."

"That's terrible. That must have been so hard for you."

"It was. But my father was so strong through it all. He was losing the love of his life but he never stopped taking care of Nora and me. Never for a moment did I ever feel like he wasn't there for me. I got very lucky having a father like my da. After Mum passed he'd leave little notes around for me to find, like inside a schoolbook, or under my pillow. 'When I count my blessings I count you twice.' Stuff like that. Not just for me, but for Nora too. We all missed my mum terribly. I still do. What about your parents?"

"Harry. That's my dad's name. Crazy guy. Divorced my mom when I was about eight. He got fired from his job at Disneyland for drinking. He worked part time as Goofy for minimum wage. The worst part of the job was the Goofy head. It was huge! It weighed about fifteen pounds. And it was like a steam bath in there and he'd sweat like crazy on hot days. But the best part of the job, I heard him tell Felix, his bartender friend, was when he bent down to shake a kid's hand he'd really be ogling the mom's tits. So he was a paid tit-ogler four days a week."

She laughed. "I think if my da was Goofy he'd ignore the kid and look directly at the tits with no pretext."

"Your dad is my kinda guy. Anyway, after Harry got fired he disappeared. I haven't seen him in a long time."

"Oh, I'm so sorry he's gone away somewhere."

"Yeah. Thanks."

"And what about your mom?"

"She's a sad, ruined alcoholic, out of touch with the real world."

"Do you talk to her?"

"Nope."

"Wow, that's so awful. You're like an orphan. Geez. I'm sorry."

The tide was coming in. We walked barefoot, holding hands, not talking for a few minutes, waves crashing into our calves and ankles, making the walk even more fun. A couple of times we had to keep each other from falling in. The beach was crowded. Lots of kids playing in the sand, tons of people walking their dogs, groups of friends hanging out, and lots of surfers and body surfers in the ocean. We spread a blanket Kiera brought, as far from other people as we could.

"So do you want to tell me what happened?"

"OK. And I want to hear yours too."

"You first. I'm excited to hear about you being a delinquent."

"Well good." I kissed her then, a sweet, gentle kiss that blossomed into something quite a bit more. When we stopped she said, "That's the best kiss I ever had."

"Me too." We looked into each other's eyes and studied each other's faces and caressed them with barely perceptible touches and then made out for about half an hour. We were in a movie, the surf pounding, gulls laughing, the sand giving way under the blanket to every move we made. We didn't give a damn who saw us.

She asked me if I was hungry.

"I am for you." I gazed at her without blinking, as if she'd hypnotized me.

"Ground Control to Major Tom!"

I kept staring. She grabbed my hand and bit my finger.

"Ouch! I am catatonically in love."

"Settle down now, baby. I'm talking about lunch." She handed me a ham and cheese sandwich and opened a bottle of wine.

"Thanks. Where'd you get the wine?"

"The guy at the bodega sells it to me and Emily, my housemate. We flirt with him and it makes him want to please us."

"You mean the bodega with the old man, the Indian guy in the turban?"

"Yep. Isn't that cool?" She took out a sandwich, took a drink of wine from the bottle, and handed it to me.

"Cheers," I said, tipping the bottle in her direction, taking a big swig.

"Cheers!" She held up her sandwich. "OK, now you're on the air."

I told her the whole sordid story. When I got to the part about Lorelai, my Good Samaritan, Kiera said, "I love her. I do, Eddie. I love her."

It was like being stabbed with a dull blade, her calling me Eddie.

"I do too," I said. "I believe in angels. She was one, and so are you."

"You're such a charmer, young man." She kissed me. "And what's with the cops and their homophobia?"

"They're terrified of homosexuals. Me? I have no problem with it. I'm not a cave man."

"I know that."

We kissed again for a long while.

"So how do we keep you safe?" she asked when we surfaced.

"I just have to be careful not to light any police cars on fire or rob any banks."

"Will that be hard for you?"

"Yes."

"Well then I'm leaving." She pretended to get up and I wrestled her back to earth.

I looked into her eyes as she lay there beneath me. "Guess what? My name isn't really Eddie Vincent."

She smiled. "After all you've told me, I guess I'm not surprised. What is it? Frankenstein?"

"Haha! No, nothing as cool as that. It's Owen. Owen Kilroy."

"Oh, I love it!"

"Really?"

"Yeah. You know, Eddie Vincent sounds like some guy who wears white shoes and an ugly plaid jacket and hangs out smoking stogies at the dog races."

"That's hilarious!"

"Owen Kilroy is more you."

"And you would know that now, wouldn't you?"

"Yes, I would."

§

Late in the afternoon we packed up our things and walked back across the warm sand to the boardwalk, where the usual carnival was in full swing. After we threw our garbage away Kiera put her arm around me and said, in a proud, happy voice, "I live on a walk-street called Breeze Avenue. Walk-streets are people only. No cars. You'll love it."

Sixteen

The house on Breeze Avenue was a block from the board-walk, five minutes from Shark Attack. It was a funky, one-story blue bungalow with a little cement yard, a couple of chairs and a table under a teenage Jacaranda tree, and a gate that couldn't keep anybody or anything in or out. The house had a wonderful smell, a warm, welcoming mixture of marijuana, vanilla, and traces of sandalwood incense.

"I'll give you the tour. I live with my best friend Emily — oh, I told you that. There's a bathroom, laundry in the back, and *this*," she said, waving her arm around as if she were waving a wand, showing me the spartan living room. The star was a big couch, upholstered in what looked like long-faded red velvet.

"That was salvaged from the lobby of an old 1930s movie palace in Pasadena. I just love it. We got it at the Salvation Army for only twenty-eight bucks!"

"Wow, I love it!"

"Me too. You can almost *feel* all those old movies tucked away in it."

Across from the couch was an overstuffed chair that Churchill might have favored if someone had given him a chance to sit in it. At some point it must have been a much lighter color. Lots of stuffing was missing from the arms.

"Maxwell, my cat, owns that and likes to ruin it."

"He's very good at it."

"By the way, he insists on being called Maxwell. Never Max."

"He's royalty?"

She shook her head. "He's gay."

I laughed.

There were a couple of milk crate tables just like Greta's, one in front of the couch. A stereo and an abundance of records sat atop a white wooden table against the opposite wall. The living room walls were painted red and purple and there were all sorts of things hanging from them, like beaded necklaces and balloons. There was a small table with two chairs in the kitchen. Posters of The Beatles, Joni Mitchell, Hendrix, Linda Ronstadt, Dylan, and a few people in photographs I didn't recognize looked down upon us with cool detachment.

"Who are they?"

"French writers. Anaïs Nin, Colette, Marguerite Duras, and François Sagan. Emily's getting a Ph.D. in Comparative Lit. She's writing about them. She speaks fluent French. I love them all, especially Colette. She's very sexy."

"Far out! Have you been to France?"

"Not yet."

She led me down a little hallway and knocked on a door. Nobody answered. We looked in. "This is Emily's room. She smokes a ton of weed. I smoke, but not nearly as much as she does. My ex-boyfriend gave her a whole bunch, like a couple of *ounces*, right after we broke up. He hit on her, standing right here. Can you imagine?"

"What a creep."

"Exactly."

Emily's room: lots of clothes on the floor, and books and binders and papers and a desk lamp that had red lace fabric over it. Quite a few of the books were in French. An ashtray full of butts tattooed with lipstick. A closet partially open, with not very many clothes on the hangers. Behind a blackout curtain, a window. A bong that had seen a lot of use was close to the head of the bed, like an oxygen tank would be for someone with emphysema.

"I love her," Kiera said. "Best roommate ever. She's got about twenty-nine million years of school left."

Next was the bathroom, which was a woman's bathroom in every way you can think of. Nothing to read. Candles on all four corners of the bathtub. Hair dryer, clean everything.

"A candlelight bath. Wow."

"Mm-hmm. One of my favorite things."

Further down the hallway, which had concert posters on the walls, we came to her bedroom. It was inviting and looked so comfortable, with a double bed covered by a brown and black bedspread, fluffy pillows, a nightstand with a book on it, and a little reading lamp. Next to a big window she'd put a desk and a small bookcase full of more books than it could handle. Several framed photographs lined the top of the bookcase. She picked one up. "This is my father and me in Mullaghmore, walking on the road around the village. It's tiny, on the ocean near Drumcliff. I told you about Drumcliff, didn't I?"

"You told me you're from there."

"Yes. We go there as often as we can."

Behind Kiera and her father, green pastures with sheep and cows, and the magnificent, strange mountain, Ben Bulbin, dominating half of the sky. I was to come to know and love Mullaghmore. We would walk that same road together many times. In the picture, a sense of peace, safety, and well-being.

"Wow, that's so amazing."

"It is, isn't it? My favorite place ever."

She put the frame down and gestured to the next picture. "And that's my sister Nora, with whom I have a love-hate relationship as I told you. That's in front of the Anne Frank House in Amsterdam."

"Did you take it?"

"No, that was taken by Theodore, her sleazy insurance salesman husband. I've never been there, but it's also on my list."

She picked up the last of them. "And this is my mum. Her name was, in an English pronunciation, Aiveen. It's an Irish name. You'll laugh at how it's spelled."

"I've never heard that before. It's not A-i-v-e-e-n ?"

"Hang on a sec, I'll write it down. It's better that way. A greater impact is what I'm after, you see?"

"I'll brace myself."

As she wrote the letters down she said, "It's A-o-i-b-h-e-a-n-n." She held up the paper. "Isn't that cool?"

"Yeah, how could *that* spell Aiveen? The Irish mind. Geez."

"You can see a bit of her in me, can't you?"

Her mum was playing a piano, looking into the camera with a big smile. "You could be her twin sister. She was one foxy babe."

She laughed and we kissed and fell over onto the bed and made out for a while.

§

Kiera whipped us up some dinner. I set the table. We ate macaroni and cheese and cinnamon toast on two Flintstone plates.

"I got those for a *dime* at a thrift store!" she said when I took them out of the cabinet.

"Each?"

"No! For both of them!"

When we sat down to eat she said, "I'm sorry I forgot to ask if you've been OK this last week. Please tell me you've been safe and warm at night. Where are you staying?"

"I'm still there. At Greta's. She lives on Horizon, a block from Shark Attack. And she's been so generous. Incredible."

"Is she just your friend?"

"We've had sex a few times, but just for fun. We are definitely not a couple."

"I'm glad to hear that. I mean, I'm not exactly thrilled to hear you've slept with her, but I'm happy to know it's not anything serious."

"She's become a good friend. Her boyfriend is in Vietnam. She hasn't heard from him in a long time and doesn't know if he'll ever come back. So after work one day she invited me over."

"I see. Well."

"That's all over though. We've agreed we're just friends. Living together as friends in a small room is sort of workable. Sex would fuck it all up."

It was true, Greta and I had had a talk after that last afternoon on Ray's friends' boat. She knew that night I'd be back out on the streets. "You can stay until you find something, but no sex! At all. We'll find a mattress for you. Agree?" I did.

"What about you? You must have guys hitting on you all the time at UCLA. And at Shark Attack."

"I do, but I've never been too impressed. I hate to say it, but American boys really don't interest me. You're not like them. There's something very different about you. The same was true of the asshole. In a lot of ways you guys are alike. But I soon figured out he was a liar and a cheater and I dumped him as soon as I found out. It was an experience. He wasn't all bad. I just have no patience for that kind of bullshit."

"How long were you guys together?"

"About six weeks." She laughed. "It's not exactly gonna be the first sentence of my obituary, you know what I mean?"

I laughed. "Yeah. I know exactly what you mean."

"With you, though, it feels different than anything else I've known. There's a lot of electricity and mystery between us. There's the promise of *discovery*. There's no mystery with these American guys. The only thing there is to discover is that most of them have the maturity of a ten-year-old."

A short movie clip suddenly sprang to mind of Shooky and me at Manderley about a year ago, making up raunchy, depraved lyrics about fucking Ginger and Mary Ann on Gilligan's Island, sung to the tune of what we called, "The Star-Spangled Bang Her." I said to Kiera, "Um, yeah. Wow. Lucky for you that ain't me."

When we finished dinner we decided to go out and see if we could find somebody to buy us a bottle of wine. The bodega guy never worked past seven. Just as we were on our way out we heard a key in the door. Kiera opened it and Emily fell forward, but didn't fall over, and there were a few seconds of hilarity. She was almost as tall as Kiera, with long red hair in a ponytail and glasses and huge hoop earrings that came down almost to her shoulders. She was wearing a white blouse with her name embroidered on it in red script. *Emily S.* She carried a heavy shoulder bag. Even with that, she brought a burst of kinetic energy into the room.

"Hey, honey," she said to Kiera, throwing the bag on the couch.

"Hi, cutie!"

They kissed on both cheeks.

"Emily, this is Owen."

We shook hands and told each other how nice it was to meet.

She said, "You guys wanna smoke a joint? I need to get high. I need it *bad.*"

"Sure," I said. "You had a rough day?"

"Yeah. Work. Ugh."

"I didn't tell you," Kiera said, "Em is a tour guide. What a crack-up. She takes people on bus tours of the stars' homes. She points out Cary Grant's fence, or Mickey Rooney's hedges, or Jimmy Stewart's chimney. Then there are people like Ed McMahon, and Em, who's that guy on 'Let's Make a Deal'?"

"Monty Hall."

"People like that," Kiera said. "Not exactly Marlon Brando."

Emily laughed. "The tourists love that shit. They'd piss their pants for the Tidy-Bowl Man."

"Do you drive the bus?"

"No way."

"It would be the last ride for those people," said Kiera. "Hey," she said to Emily, "we were just on the way out to see if we can score some vino."

"Look no further, my dear." She took a bottle of red wine out of the bag.

"You're a walking talking miracle," said Kiera.

She headed down the hall. "I'll be right back."

Kiera opened the bottle. A twist cap. "Can you get us glasses, love?"

I brought them out as Emily returned with a couple of joints. She put one on the table in front of the couch and lit the other. Kiera poured the wine. Then she went to the stereo and put on *Led Zeppelin I*. I plopped down on the couch and she came and sat on my lap. We passed the joint around and drank our wine.

"I saw that fuckhead Shooky today," Emily said.

A shock went through me. *Shooky?*

"That must have been a major drag," Kiera said, groaning. "God, I hate that fucker. Well, I don't *hate* him, but, you know...."

"It was weird. Of course he asked about you. He said he still wants you back."

If it was *my* Shooky, I thought, and he was going out with Kiera, I would have seen him around by now.

Kiera rolled her eyes. "The asshole just doesn't let up! I hope you told him to fuck off." To me she said, "That creep of an ex-boyfriend I told you about."

"Uh huh." Reality was creeping up on me.

"I did," said Emily.

"Your ex-boyfriend's name is *Shooky?*" I asked, lighting a cigarette to give myself something casual to do.

"Not as funny as Eddie Vincent, but still."

"Who's Eddie Vincent?" Emily asked.

I put the cigarette down and leaned forward with my hands on my cheeks — I knew the answer to the next question. "Is he tall, with long wavy black hair and always wears a red vest?"

Kiera nodded. "Oh god. How do you know him?"

I felt like I'd been kicked in the chest. "He's my best friend. Holy shit. Holy fuck. I can't believe this." I had to force myself to breathe.

"Oh boy," said Emily.

Kiera took my hand in hers and said, "Owen, are you OK? Because I'm not."

"I've been looking all over the place for him since I got to Venice. He has a thousand dollars for me. Do you guys know how to find him? I *have* to find him!"

"Oh my god," said Kiera. "Owen, I'm not going anywhere *near* him."

"*He's* the creep?" I laughed mirthlessly. "That's terrible! Fucking awful!"

"I ran into him in Hollywood," said Emily sheepishly. "I've got his number. I kept it as a major emergency backup if I couldn't score anywhere else."

"Emily! Fuck." Keira shot her a what-were-you-thinking look.

"I know. I never would have called him, I swear. Anyway, he said he was headed out to Malibu. I got the impression he lives out there. I'm sorry to ask, Owen, but why is *that* prick your best friend?"

"Yes, *why?*" said Kiera.

I couldn't tell if she was accusing me of something.

"We were dealers in high school, working hard to save enough money to come to Venice and lead these amazing lives. Then I got busted and everything went to shit. When I knew him he was cool."

"I think we all need more wine," Emily said after a significant pause in the proceedings. She gave us all a refill. "Here's to the bizarre." We clinked glasses.

"When I got busted Shooky had two thousand dollars in cash and half of that is mine. This is gonna save me! I'll be able to move out of Greta's."

"How do you know he's even gonna have the money?" Kiera asked. "He's a liar and a cheat."

"He'll have it. He won't fuck me over. I know he won't."

The record stopped and we all sat in silence again. I stood up and started walking around the room, thinking that maybe she'd want to end it with me now. "Hey," I said to her, "If this means things aren't gonna go any further with us, that's cool. I get it. I'll just take off."

Kiera held out her hand to me. "Come and sit and don't be silly."

I held her hand and sat back down on the couch and we snuggled up. From utter despair to relief and elation in seconds.

Kiera laughed, then groaned. "I can't believe this is happening."

I asked her how she met Shooky.

"Through me," Emily said. "I bought a lot of weed from him."

"I didn't really mind when I thought it was just weed," Kiera said, "but it turned out he was selling heroin too. And the bastard cheated on me. The last time, I caught him with some little beach bitch in his apartment."

"I have to say, the beach bitch doesn't surprise me. But *heroin?* Really?"

"Yep."

"The last time he was here," said Emily, "he *begged* Kiera to take him back. He'd been calling here every day —"

"— about sixty million times," said Kiera.

"And leaving notes and flowers."

"How long ago was that?"

"A couple of months ago."

"That's about right when I got here."

Kiera said, "So one day I was reading on the porch and he walked up. I told him in a very polite but firm voice to stay out of my life. I said we're *done* and that's all there is to it. Please leave. He asked if he could come in and use the bathroom, so I let him."

"And then he comes to my room and hits on me," said Emily. "He threw two lids of Colombian on my bed and said, 'We both know it's about you and me now'."

Kiera laughed. "And Em told him, 'Get a fuckin' life. And if you're not out of this house in ten seconds . . .'" — Kiera and Emily joyfully completed the sentence in unison — "that crazy Irish bitch will kill you!"

They laughed and laughed and I tried to but I was too stoned and too confused. Trying to picture him in Kiera's house, playing out that scene, was leaving me speechless.

"Are you all right, O?" she asked with sincere concern. It was the first time she called me O. She was so high she had her face about two inches from mine. It was too funny.

"Jesus Christ. Are all Irish girls this cute?"

She kissed my eyes and my nose and my cheeks and my lips. "Nope."

"Get a room, you two. Oh wait, you already have one."

Kiera whispered to me, "I want to take this slowly, OK?"

"OK."

"I don't want you to leave yet, but when you do I want you to come back for breakfast if you want."

We spent the rest of the night talking, the three of us, until Emily went to bed. It was quiet then, the music had stopped. We were so high and so drunk. I faded, then slipped away for a short while.

Kiera woke me with kisses. "Come to bed."

"OK," I whispered, slipping my hand under all the wildflowers in that sundress.

"No, baby," she said, gently but firmly removing my hand "Come to bed to *sleep*. It's too late for you to leave now."

Seventeen

I can still feel the softness of the sheets and the way the bed held us together, and the blissful sweetness of her body next to mine. We didn't make love that night, no, we just floated there, content to let the wine and the weed and the sense of belonging we felt take us into sleep together. When we woke up and saw each other's sleepy smiling faces glowing in the early morning sunlight, we kissed and wrapped ourselves into and around each other and made love. Aside from pure physical pleasure, the only time I'd felt anything having sex was that incredible night with Sarah at Manderley. That was love too, but of a very different kind, a beautiful but heartbreaking goodbye.

Consistent with our belief that somehow, some way, we'd known each other before, Kiera and I had the unique experience when we made love during those early days, of simultaneously discovering what was new about each other, and celebrating what was so familiar. We talked about that many times, always in a state of astonishment. Are we *really* this lucky? we would ask, always answering that with an emphatic yes, followed by gleeful laughter. Kiera changed my way of thinking about the nature of my existence. Prior to being with her, my life had been focused almost exclusively on avoiding and minimizing pain.

That first morning we lay tangled together, spent and silent, softly caressing each other. Maxwell jumped on the bed and walked up to Kiera, purring in high gear.

"Maxwell, this is Owen," she said. She leaned close to him pretending he was whispering in her ear. She looked at him and asked, "What's that you said?" Then she listened closer and nodded.

"He wants you to pet him."

I reached over her and pet him and he seemed to like it.

"Where was he last night?"

"Out whoring around with his boys, as usual."

"Do you speak kitty or do you just understand it?"

"I taught *him* how to speak kitty."

"Well, then tell him I absolutely adore you."

She whispered in his ear and listened to him for a few seconds.

"He says he can tell that I absolutely adore you too. And he knows me better than anybody."

§

Emily had already gone to work by the time we got up. She'd left a note on the kitchen table.

Hi Owen! Fun, weird night! Here's Shooky's number. 213-741-2329. Call at your own peril.
XoXo, Em P.S. It was sooo great to meet you!

"I can't believe this," Kiera said, picking up the note. "I wish your best friend was someone else. Sorry for saying that, but I think you know what I mean."

I poured oatmeal into a pot of boiling water. "I don't understand something."

"And what might that be Mr. Eddie 'White Shoes' Vincent?"

I finished stirring the oatmeal in, covered the pot, and turned down the heat. "Shooky and I are a lot alike, which is why we're best friends. And it's not surprising that he would be into you, because we've always liked the same chicks — but any dude with half a brain and a pulse would be into you, so, you know, duh. But we're not *that* alike. He's better looking than me, he's smarter than me, and he's taller than me. So I can see how you'd be attracted to him, but I'm not sure how you could be — well, let me put it this way: is *he* your type and I'm an exception, or the other way around?"

She grabbed two Tom and Jerry bowls from the cabinet and placed them on the counter next to me. In one bowl Tom stood at the bottom, waving at me, and Jerry was in the other, doing the same thing.

"The only thing you said that's right is that he's taller. The rest, you're just wrong about. You're just as smart — and a lot smarter emotionally. And you're quite the handsome young man. Anyway, I don't have a type. I'm nineteen. I'm a modern woman. I like who I like and I like you best. You're funny and kind and sexy, and I think we knew each other before, and I don't care about anything else." She kissed me. "So don't be a sillyhead."

"Sillyhead is my middle name."

She laughed and pointed to the bowls. "I got these at the same time I got those Flintstone plates."

"Thank you for explaining that to me," I said, and then nodded to the bowls. "Those set you back another dime?"

"I think these were a little more. Maybe fifteen cents. I mean, they're *Tom and Jerry*."

"You knew of them in Dublin?"

"Of course! Ireland isn't fuckin' Bangladesh, man!"

"It isn't?"

"Hahaha. Now serve up those oats."

"One advantage to growing up basically parentless is that you learn to cook a little," I said. "It took me twenty-three years to master oatmeal, so you're lucky."

"That's impressive, considering you're seventeen," she said, laughing a little.

"Oh. Right."

She took the milk out of the refrigerator. "Do you *really* think Shooky will have your money?"

"I have no doubt. He may have turned into an asshole when it comes to lying to girls and his insanely high libido, but he'll have it. Maybe I'm naïve, but I trust him. I mean, he kept two thousand dollars of our money at his house. He could have split any time with it."

"I don't think you're naïve. What do you know about his libido?"

"All teenage guys know everything about their friends' libidos."

"Hmm. I didn't know that."

"It's a universal truth, babe. The twelve apostles all knew which one of them was getting laid the most: Simon the Zealot."

She laughed and then said, "So guys are just like girls. They tell each other everything."

"Yep. Like Shooky is — I don't know if you want to hear this."

"Sure, why not? He's your friend and I dated him, so."

"He's by far the horniest guy I've ever met. His passions were sex and literature. Mainly sex."

"I know."

"He can't keep his dick in his pants. Being faithful to someone is totally beyond his capability. So if you have even a tiny molecule of a notion that what he did was intended to hurt you — *you personally* — you can erase it. He would do that to anybody. He doesn't understand monogamy. That doesn't mean it's OK, don't get me wrong."

"That makes me feel even worse. It makes me sick. How does it end up that he's your best friend?"

"He was my *brother*. I met him not long after my mom moved us to Rockville Flats from Plainview. Shooky and I spent all our time together. We were part of a very tiny minority of actual thinking humans in Rockville Flats. I can't remember if I told you that the night I got busted Shooky and I were supposed to leave for Venice the next morning. Just like I figured, he came here by himself. He's a good person."

"He's selling heroin, man. People die from overdoses all the time." She paused and studied the topography of the oatmeal for a second or two. "Did you ever sell heroin in Fuckhead Flats? I'm calling it that from now on, by the way."

The question carried a lot of weight and I was glad to be able to say no.

"Thank you for making us this magnificent, mind-blowing breakfast. Is it about ready?"

"Yep. You'll never have a better one."

"If that's true, that's kind of sad."

After we ate, we kissed a kiss that was to be just a kiss, but things took off quickly to the point that we literally *ran* back to the bedroom. When we were completely satiated we lay there in each other's arms again, in a daze.

"Wow," she said. "We're pretty fuckin' nasty. I love that. I love talking dirty."

"Yeah. Wow. Me too. It's fun."

"*You're* the best breakfast I ever had," she said.

"You are for me!"

We lay there quietly for a minute or two feeling each other's slowly decelerating heartbeats and our breathing returning to normal. We fell asleep.

§

"Look, I'm sorry to break the mood," she said when we woke up and regained lucidity.

"What do you mean?"

"I know Shooky's your best friend and everything, but I have to be honest. I can't ever see him again. He wants me back, remember? Remember he told Em that just *yesterday*. We broke up *two months* ago and he still won't let go. If he finds out we're together it'll get bad real fast."

"Maybe not if it's from me."

"Oh god, please. You don't understand. You *can't* tell him about us."

"What's not to understand?"

"Trust me. It won't be good. He's obsessed."

"Don't worry, I can manage it." I said that with a confidence I wasn't sure I really felt.

She sighed heavily as if to say, 'You have no idea.' "You'll call him after I leave?"

"You don't mind me being here while you guys are gone?"

"Mi casa, su casa, señor."

"Muchas gracias, mi amor."

"Do you feel at home with me?" She put her hand in mine.

"I feel more at home with you than anyplace I've ever been."

"I want you to stay with me. I want us to live together. Unless you think it's too soon. It may be crazy to you, but it's not crazy to me. This is what love at first sight looks like, don't you think? I mean, what *else* would it be like? John and Yoko knew each other for ten minutes and have been together ever since."

"Let's make a record and be nude on the cover!"

"Ha! Yeah. But seriously, my mum died when she was thirty-two. Life is short. Carpe diem and all that."

"What's carpe diem?"

"Seize the day. That's what we have to do. Does the thought of moving in with me scare you?"

"To be honest, I'm afraid you'll get tired of me. I'm not kidding. You're older and more sophisticated."

"Oh yeah, I'm sooo old, and sooo sophisticated!"

"You're going to UCLA. I dropped out of high school." I heard my voice rise with tension. "I have zero education. All my life people have left. They've either died or disappeared. That's my fear. That the same will happen with you."

"You know I'm so sorry about all that. And we can talk about it whenever you need to. But if you start whining about *us*, about me and whether I'll stick around, I *will* get tired of you. We have no time for that. If you settle down and let things go, you'll have free access to *all* of me." She kissed me hard and then jumped up and started looking for what to wear.

I said, "I've been imagining this since you tried to sell me that surfboard."

"I wasn't trying to sell it to you, sir, I was only giving you the information you asked for."

"Well, you were good because you made me want to buy it."

"But did I make you want to *surf?* That's the question."

"You made me want to surf your body."

"Well, you were definitely riding the curl just now."

We looked at each other and laughed.

"You know what?" I asked, taking a lot of pleasure in watching her.

"What?"

"I've loved you since the moment I first heard your voice."

"Mmmm. That's sweet."

"The day before I met you, I was passing by outside and I heard you tell somebody you'd give him a replacement board if he ever survived a shark attack."

"Yeah, we *do* give anybody who's survived a shark attack a new board. It's a gimmick, but I think everybody likes it because it's so dumb and improbable. I mean, if you get attacked by a shark you're probably going to be bitten in half or something, and if somehow you survive you're probably gonna live the rest of your life on a skateboard."

"I've always been afraid I'll end up like that. Living on a skateboard. Maybe not so bad. At least you've got wheels."

"Haha! You know when it happened for me? Well, two things actually. First, when you asked me where in Ireland I was from and I told you, and then I asked if you'd been there, and you said you'd never been anywhere. You were sweet and vulnerable. And then when you said that thing about Billy Joe Yeats, the blind Appalachian banjo player, it cracked me up."

"Oh good. I thought that was so dumb."

"And you're such a great guitar player. I want you to play for me every day. And I want to take care of you, Owen. You've never been cared for the way you deserve to be, and I'm the one that is going to be that person. You're finally gonna know what it's like to be really loved."

"You're an angel."

"You are too."

"What'll Emily think about me living here?"

"Oh, Em won't mind. She likes you. And her rent will go down to a third instead of a half because we'll be paying two thirds. Think it over. Ask Eddie Vincent what *he* thinks."

She sneezed and when she put her hand to her face she said, "Oh, shit! I smell like us! I have to take a shower! My mind is a wee bit discombobulated." She bolted down the hallway to the bathroom. I followed her.

"I don't need to think about it. I don't care if it's crazy or stupid or reckless. That's the story of my whole life. Why would I stop now?"

"Yay!" She got into the shower. When she came out I was making the bed.

"Do you need any help getting your stuff?"

"Thanks, but I own nothing but the guitar Greta gave me. Moving is just a matter of me going to get it. But hey, I *am* pretty embarrassed to tell you that the only clothes I have are the ones I'm wearing. The clothes I got at the thrift store are gone." I told her the Hotel Rialto story.

"Good god, Owen. Your life has been so awful. I'm sorry I made that joke at the bookstore. I was just kidding."

"What joke?"

"Never mind. It was nothing. When do you get paid?"

"In a couple of days. Tuesday. But if I see Shooky I'll have a thousand bucks!"

"Yeah, well. If that doesn't work out, we'll go back to the thrift store and get you a few things. In the meantime, you can wash your clothes here. The washing machine is in the back."

"OK."

She gave me that look of hers, the look I would come to know so well, the one that meant *I can read your mind.* "You're a bit overwhelmed, aren't you?"

"No I'm not."

"Yes you are. How could you not be after what you've been through, not only in your life but in the last few weeks? It's all gonna work out whether you get the money or not. This is what's supposed to happen. We're us. That's all that matters. Trust me. See you later, love!" She kissed me and ran out.

Part Three

October 1971 – August 1973

Be slow to fall into friendship, but when you are in,
continue firm and constant.
– Socrates

Eighteen

I walked around the house, taking it all in. I walked outside and sat in the sun and got up and walked around the yard some more. I walked around the block. I was excited and stunned that I was moving in with Kiera. Moving in with her *that day*. Where did this luck come from? Back inside the house I lay on her bed for a while (*our* bed now?) and asked myself, how did I get *here?* And the Shooky-Kiera situation? It was simple, really. Just not tell him anything about her and keep them apart.

I dialed his number.

"This is William Burroughs," Shooky said. "Why do you think you'll benefit by calling me?"

"Shooky! It's Owen!"

"Owen? Holy Christ! You crazy bastard!! Where *are* you?"

"I'm in Venice. I escaped! Man, I've been looking all over the place for you. Where are *you?*"

"You escaped! How cool is that? I was so worried about you, bro. You couldn't find me because I'm not in Venice. I moved out to Malibu a couple of months ago. I'm renting a little guest house. Not on the beach. I didn't make it *that* big. Up the mountain in this dude's backyard, or compound, or whatever you call it. The guy's house is huge. I had some problems with this chick and needed to relocate. It's great here. How the hell did you get my number?"

I hadn't thought of that. "My girlfriend, Greta. She's been here forever and knows everybody. She put the word out that I was looking for a guy named Shooky. Somebody finally came through, I don't know who. Major stroke of luck, man."

"Outta sight. In a weird way L.A. is a small town. Things circle around. Do you have a car?"

"I've been sleeping on the beach a few times, man. I've got nothing."

"Fuck me, Jesus. Well I've got a grand for you, bro. Actually one thousand a hundred and nineteen to be exact. Your half of what we had. Give me your address, man. I'll come pick you up."

"I knew you'd have it! Thanks so much, bro. I've dreamed of that money, man. I've been running out on restaurant bills, stealing food from supermarkets. It's been a real drag." I gave him Greta's address. "I thought you might have fucking died, man."

"Talk about a drag. Things were getting a little out of hand in Venice." I heard the click of a Zippo. He took a breath and I heard him exhale. "I've got a room all set up for you."

He sounded so excited and optimistic. And so *innocent*.

"Wow. I've got to get a couple of things done before you come down."

"I've got a few errands to run. I have to be in Westwood around three. That'll take a few. I'll see you at four. I can't wait to see you, my brother."

"Me too, bro."

I had not known before then the degree to which you can feel two completely opposing emotions at the same time: terrible, black-edged, life-sucking anxiety, and the all-consuming happiness of being in love.

§

Greta was in the shower.

"Hey, it's me!" I yelled through the bathroom door.

"Come in! I want you to tell me everything!"

I went in and sat on the toilet seat and watched her through the shower curtain. She was washing her very long hair. It was quite the undertaking.

"Bald people have it easy," I said.

"Hey, there's a razor in the cabinet. I forgot it. Can you hand it to me please?"

I found the razor and handed it to her. She was all soaped up. "You're very cute with all of those white puffs on your body."

"Shut up. So you spent the night! How was love sex?" She peeked out at me from behind the curtain, eyes bright and cheerful. She was genuinely happy for me. "Did it change your life?"

"Love sex was incredible. Twice this morning!"

She started shaving her legs. "It's a different universe, isn't it? Aaron and I used to levitate."

"Wow! Hey, so guess what?"

"What?"

"She asked me to move in with her."

She peeked around the curtain. "Are you bullshitting me?"

"No!"

"I can have my place all to myself again?" She ducked her head back in, then back out. "You *are* moving in with her, right?"

"I love that girl."

"This is so great! For both of us."

A few minutes later we were sitting on her bed while I told her the whole Kiera-Shooky story.

"Well, that's one dose of wild, fucked-up karma! Who were you in your last life? Hitler's father?"

"I think that explains it. Listen, I need to ask your advice."

"I left my crystal ball in San Francisco. But what's the question?" She stood up and lit a smoke and stood up against the kitchen counter like she always did, her hair all piled up in a purple towel.

"Kiera and Shooky both invited me to move in."

"So you're asking me to help you decide who you want to live with? That's kind of weird, man."

"No, not at all. I'm gonna live with Kiera. I'm not a spazz."

"Well then I don't know what you want advice about, my dear confused one."

"You know what? I don't either."

"Well at least we're on the same page."

"You know how I'm a fugitive?"

"That's a pretty dramatic way of putting it, but yeah, you told me the day we met."

"I changed my name to Eddie Vincent when I got here. My name is really Owen Kilroy. You're only the second person who knows that."

"Kiera being the first."

"Yeah."

"I'm not surprised. You know I kinda like Eddie Vincent better."

"Really? Kiera said it sounded like I was the kind of skeezy guy that hangs around the dog races, wearing white shoes and a plaid jacket."

Greta laughed. "Exactly! I think that's why I like it."

"So here's the thing. I have to lie to him and keep him away from Kiera."

"Why? What's he gonna do, kidnap her?"

"She is adamant about it. She says he's obsessed. He didn't sound that way on the phone with me. He sounded the opposite, like he split to Malibu because it ended."

"Maybe your new little sweetie is a bit of a drama queen."

"Shit. I hope not."

"I just don't understand why this is such a big deal."

"Well, it is. I have to take her word for it, don't I?"

"I guess so."

"So will you help me?"

"I don't know. What do you want me to do?"

"The first step is making Shooky believe you're my girl-friend and that I live here. You won't ever have to meet him. But I'd like to give him your phone number."

"And what do I do? Just keep saying you're not here?"

"If you don't mind. It's just for a while until I can get this sorted out. Or no, what would be better is if you could call me at Kiera's and give me the message."

"If you think you can turn me into your secretary just because we're friends and you've got some kind of *Days of Our Lives* bullshit going on, you're crazy."

"I know. I'm sorry. I just don't know what to do. I've never been in this situation before."

"I don't know anybody who has."

"Hey, what about if I paid you? Shooky's got a thousand dollars for me. I'll give you ten dollars a day."

She looked surprised and hurt. She came over and took the towel off her head and started brushing her hair. "Why would you think I'd do that for money? I can't take money from you for that. I'll take care of it. But you better wiggle your way out of this. It's too twisted."

Nineteen

I ran down to Shark Attack and waited for Kiera to finish with a customer. I liked the way she looked at me from the other side of the store. It was like two lovers making eye contact across the room at a party while they both talk to other people. I wondered when this was all gonna blow up in my face.

She was able to get away for her lunch break. We walked down to the beach. The day was slightly overcast, and fewer people were out than usual. There were surfers, as always, black seal-like wet suits tempting predators. We sat down in the sand just up the beach from the store.

"So you talked to Shooky?" she asked nervously.

"Yeah. It was great! He's got my thousand dollars! I told you he'd come through! I'm gonna pick up the money today. But the situation is complicated."

"Really? Gee, I'm stunned."

"Yeah, I know. He's assuming that I'm gonna live in Malibu with him. He's got a room set up for me and everything."

"This is so weird."

"My life is *always* weird."

"So is mine, but in a different way. Here I am with two guys in this *Jules and Jim* scenario. Well, not quite. (It's a movie, of course.) All my life growing up I was the good girl. The book reader, the perfect grades, the good daughter — or actually the 'better' daughter, which Nora made easy for me because she was always such a cunt — and throughout all of it I had this vague feeling that I was living somebody else's life. I always had this feeling I couldn't define, except to the extent that I knew I wasn't really that girl. Not that I thought I was Lizzie Borden or something, but you know, I wasn't a fucking *saint*. This all really started when my mother died. My da was so brokenhearted, I promised myself that I'd be nothing but good for him. I felt I had to be.

"Moving to L.A. is the best thing that's ever happened to me. I'm learning to be myself. Da's paying my rent, so I guess I'm not totally the liberated woman, but I couldn't make it otherwise. Shark Attack pays for everything else. I love school, and I love my life for the first time since I was eight. And now I have you, my vagabond, guitar-playing hoodlum."

"If you were a saint I'd have so much fun corrupting you."

She thought about this for a second. "Ummmmm. That *would* be fun. Let's pretend I am. A chaste, virgin saint who resists being corrupted but finally gives in," she said, looking at me mischievously. "But not until this shit gets resolved."

I laughed with pagan delight and said, "Houston, the Eagle has landed!"

"You're an adorable nut," she laughed.

The ocean breeze was blowing her hair in her face like always and she swept some of it back behind her ear, revealing a lovely silver teardrop earring. She picked up a handful of sand and poured it on my leg and kept doing that. We didn't have much time and I had to get serious again.

"I need you to please tell me why you're so freaked out about this before I go lying to my best friend."

Kiera stopped with the sand and said, "This is not going to end well, O. I haven't really told you the whole story."

"Uh oh." I felt an electric shock go through me. "What don't I know?"

"About a month before I went to San Francisco I met him again. We drove up to Malibu."

"Oh god."

"It was idiotic. I didn't even tell Emily this. She thinks I haven't seen him since we broke up. We ended up — things got out of hand and went a little too far."

"How far?" Now I grabbed a handful of sand.

"We had sex in his car. I knew I'd made a huge mistake. I was horny and we always had good sex, you know? But when he said, 'I'm so glad we're back together,' I had to say, no, we weren't. It got pretty ugly."

My whole body seized up, tension everywhere. Even in my eyes. I felt rage. Rage! I had never felt jealous over a girl before. I knew it was absurd. How could I be jealous about something she did before she met me? But I was. It was confusing. "I don't know what you guys said before that happened, but no matter what it was, you gave him every fucking reason in the world to think you wanted him back. Anybody would think that. Especially Shooky."

"Please don't be mad at me. That's not helpful."

"Sorry, it's just. Whatever."

"I know. He said, 'You've forgiven me.' I said, yeah, I have. 'But don't read anything into it'."

"How the fuck was he not supposed to read anything into it?"

"OK, OK, OK, I was a stupid idiot. I get it. Can we move on please?"

"What happened when he cheated on you?"

"It wasn't only once. I'd say it was probably about one a week. There are hordes of beautiful girls in Venice."

"I know."

"He couldn't keep his hands off them."

"That's Shooky. And I bet in a moment when he was trying to purify his soul or something, he told you about 'em, right?"

"Yes. You know him pretty well. I can be the dumbest person. You'll see."

"You're not dumb, you're Irish."

"Same thing."

I laughed, and she said more seriously, "He's not leaving me alone, O. It's getting really scary. He writes me letters addressed to Shark Attack. That way he knows Emily won't see them."

"When was the last time?"

"I got one this morning."

"Oh, fuck me in the eye."

She pulled it out of her back pocket and gave it to me. She hadn't opened it. In a sudden burst of wind it almost flew out of my hand. "Do you want me to read it aloud or should we read it together?"

"Read it aloud."

Dear Kiera, My Foxy Babe-o'-the-Universe,

My bounty is as boundless as the sea, my love as deep. The more I give to thee, the more I have, for both are infinite. I am waiting patiently for you, my darling, but I can only betray my passion for you for so long. Time is running out. I won't be able to contain my love for you much longer. I know you'll love me forever. And forever I'll love you. I refuse to turn away from the truth. I'll never give up on us. My heart isn't breaking, because I know you really want me back too.

I love you with all my heart and soul.

Jason Arden Shook (aka your Shooky)

Kiera and I looked at each other and said, in unison, "Oh my god."

"That's the worst one yet." She started crying. "And now you're going up to meet up with him and you're best friends, and fuck knows how this is gonna end."

"Don't worry." I held her and soothed her and promised I would take care of it and told her it would all be OK.

"I believe you," she said. "Kind of."

"So, here's what's up. Shooky's picking me up in front of Greta's at four. I'm gonna tell him she's my girlfriend and that

I'm living there. When he calls me there, she's gonna take a message and then call over to your place so I'll know that he called."

"That's so nice of her."

"I'll call you as soon as I can. If not tonight, then tomorrow for sure."

"OK."

"So what's all this 'my bounty is as boundless as the sea' stuff?"

"It's from *Romeo and Juliet*," she said, drying her eyes and laughing a little. "The thing is, it's Juliet who says it. I guess he got a little mixed up."

We sat for a few minutes, watching the waves, saying nothing, holding onto each other as if to keep ourselves from sinking.

Twenty

Shooky pulled up in front of Greta's building in his Mustang. "Hey, you crazy bastard! Hop in, bro, and let's move!"

I got in and we hugged. He handed me a joint that he'd just fired up.

"It is so great to see you, man," he said as he tore out of there. He looked the same, except his hair was longer and both his ears were pierced.

§

Shooky's place was a small Spanish-style bungalow on Malibu Crest Drive, tucked into a cluster of palm, eucalyptus, and laurel trees about two or three hundred feet from the main house, which was undergoing what looked like major renovations. Everywhere you looked you saw signs of wholesale destruction, and nearby, piles of wood and metal and wiring for rebuilding. A couple of small yellow tractors were incidentals in the big open space. A mini-mountain range made up of piles of black dirt and sand marked the perimeter of the property.

"The owner isn't living here right now, obviously," Shooky said. "He lived here by himself for months after his wife left him. He decided he needed to get the fuck out and redo the whole place. We're on three and a half acres; the house is twelve-thousand square feet. Imagine living here all broken hearted, by yourself. I can't tell you who he is, but it wouldn't take very long to find out if you wanted to. I keep him supplied in cocaine and that pays my rent."

"That's a great deal, man. That view of the ocean is blowing my mind."

"Famous people live up here, man," he said as we got out of the car. "There was a rumor going around that Ringo bought a house somewhere around here. He's in Hollywood a lot. In the clubs on the Strip. The Roxy and The Rainbow. I see these people all the time, man. And when I say I see them, I don't mean I just run into them down at the little market on Pac Highway, although that happens too. The elite music people in L.A. come to *me* for their dope, man! I don't know if I'm their first choice, but it doesn't matter. They come. Fuckin' actors too. We've hit the jackpot, bro! It's *unreal*. Let me show you my digs."

We walked up a short little path beneath those trees to the bungalow. Two padded chairs waited for us on the porch, a small table between them.

"We'll sit out there and smoke a bowl or two in a minute," Shooky said.

The first thing I saw when we got inside were the bookcases. They were empty, but books were piled high in front of each one.

"I moved in a while ago and I've never gotten around to this shit," he said. "Nothing in here is mine except the books."

There were a few pieces of furniture in the living room, a couch, a couple of modern, uncomfortable-looking chairs, and a glass table in the kitchen. Nothing on the walls. Looking around, you wouldn't think anybody lived there.

"I'll show you your room."

We walked down a hallway to a good-sized empty room with a window open. I could smell the trees, the earth, and feel the coolness of the shade coming through. There was a bathroom and a shower. It was a very nice, cozy room.

"Whaddya think, amigo? We'll get you some furniture, don't worry about that. I'm loaded."

"It's amazing, man. I'm speechless."

"I'll show you my room. Sorry, it's a little bigger."

It was down a short hallway. "Plenty of privacy when we're playing around with the lovelies." His room had two windows facing east toward the hills, a bigger bathroom with a deep tub, a walk-in closet, and a king-sized bed.

"Now, for the big splash. This will just take a second."

He went into the walk-in closet and came out and handed me eleven one-hundred-dollar bills and a twenty. "Here you go, brother. It's good to have you back."

"I can't believe it!" I said, taking the cash. "Thank you, brother. I don't know what to say."

"Let's grab some beers and smoke a couple of joints. I want to hear everything that happened after that last day at Manderley. And then I'll tell you how I got the hell out of hell."

It was early in the evening when I finished the long story. The sun had gone down — a spectacular sunset featuring multi-colored, wispy clouds above the horizon — and we were very stoned.

"You know who the most intriguing person is to me in your whole crazy-ass story?" Shooky asked.

"Who?"

"That chick who picked you up on the road the night you escaped. What was her name?"

"Lorelai. It wasn't her real name."

"We should drive up there and try to find her. Give her a pound of Hawaiian or something. You owe her your life, man."

"I don't think I could find her. Besides, I'm not going anywhere near there."

"Did she let you bang her a couple of times?"

"It wasn't like that."

"Missed opportunity, man."

"No it wasn't. She was just helping me because of her brother."

"Look, man. Any chick who picks a guy up on a deserted country road in the middle of the night would *have* to be a mind-blowing fuck. That kind of recklessness *translates*."

I let that go.

"So what happened the night I got busted?"

"I heard the sirens. I knew it was about you. I don't know why. A feeling in my gut. I hopped in the car and drove by your place and saw the pig car on your lawn and a fuckload of 'em around the ravine. I hauled ass back home, grabbed the money and the dope I had — unfortunately just a fraction of what we lost at your house — and drove straight-the-fuck to Venice."

"Wow. Good move, man."

"Yeah, man. I left *that minute*. My mom and Stacey were asleep."

"We lost so much money that night. It was my fault. I left the door to my room open."

"Dude, you thought your mom was dead. Anyway, I've made it all back, bro, and then some."

"Do they know where you are? Your mom and Stacey?"

"I send my mom cash. I have a friend who goes to Hawaii every month on business and I give him five hundred in an envelope and he mails it from there so they can't trace it back to me here. He's a competitor but a friend too.

"I tried to find out where you were but there was no way to do that without drawing attention to myself. I figured you'd get here eventually. Things came together pretty quickly after I got here. Not that quickly. It was rough in the beginning, but it all worked out exceedingly well."

§

We drove into Hollywood manic with the munchies and ate a huge dinner at a Chinese restaurant on Hollywood Boulevard. Afterward, Shooky said, "Let's go see Bogart's shoe prints." We headed toward Grauman's Chinese Theater. The famous corner of Hollywood and Vine was bereft of glamour. There were more than a few derelicts wandering around, probably once-upon-a-time wannabe stars and starlets the movie business had kicked in the teeth and forgotten. Outside a hotdog stand across from a bar called Diamond Jim's, two transvestite whores were beating each other up with their purses.

"Cheap entertainment," Shooky said with a laugh. "Hey, I wanna show you what my novel's gonna be about. It might be the saddest thing you'll ever see." We walked a couple of blocks north off the Boulevard and turned a corner. "Baby whores," he said.

There they were. Kids like the one I'd taunted Officer Lloyd about were lurking on corners, in doorways, alone or two or three together. Two very young girls dressed as Girl Scouts, but in skirts that no Girl Scout would ever wear like that, were talking to a sleazebag through the passenger window of his pick-up truck. After a moment the two kids looked at each other, shrugged, laughed, and got in. Off they went.

A blond boy dressed in tight jeans and a black T-shirt, probably no older than twelve or thirteen, was hanging out in a doorway smoking a cigarette, looking tragically seductive while the trolling perverts driving by sized him up. In another world he'd be the star of the middle school musical. A bald, fatheaded scumbag with three chins pulled up to the curb in a big black Mercedes 600, his gaze fixed on the kid.

"Check out this sick fuck," Shooky said.

We were close enough to hear the buzz of the electric passenger window opening.

"Hey, beautiful," said the creep in a breathy voice just loud enough for us to hear.

The kid didn't move. He didn't even look at the car. He showed a total lack of respect, almost contempt. The slimeball might as well have been a flea or a cockroach. After what must have seemed like an eternity to him, the old bastard finally conceded the power play and called to the kid again.

"Hey, beautiful!"

The kid raised his head slowly and looked at him with a surly twist of his lips. "What?"

The skunk waved him over with a depraved smile. But the kid waited, took a long, slow hit off his smoke, then another. This was no rookie we were watching. He knew there was money in that car and he knew how to drive the fucker crazy. He took a leisurely look around for cops, snapped his cigarette about twenty feet into the street and sauntered over, moving his hips in an alarmingly provocative way for someone his age. He leaned in the window. They spoke in low voices. We couldn't hear what was said, but the kid shook his head no, no, no. A little more talk, another no, then a third, more emphatic no. The kid backed up and started walking away.

"OK, OK!" the old man said loud enough for everybody on the block to hear.

The kid walked back to the car. Still more talk. Finally he nodded, got in, and the scuzzbag drove off with him.

"I'm gonna call my book *Baby Whores*," said Shooky. "I discovered this was going on a while ago. It's fascinating in a dark, fucked-up way. Normally, these kids are so desperate they go right up to the car, no messing around. The reason why that kid could pull all that shit off was what the guy said and the way he said it: 'Hey, beautiful.' The kid knew as soon as the motherfucker spoke that he had him. 'Hey, beautiful.' Jesus Christ. And then the Mercedes, of course. Imagine a kid that young, that smart, ending up like this. His parents ought to be executed. This world is a disaster. But at least he's probably making himself a couple of hundred instead of twenty or thirty. He can quit early tonight."

We headed back to the Boulevard.

"I fucked a few of the better-looking whores in Hollywood when I first got here," Shooky said. "Not kids, obviously.

Babes in massage parlors. Not anymore though. I don't need to."

At Grauman's we walked around looking at the hand-prints, footprints, and cement signatures of the Hollywood giants.

"It makes me feel better that most of them live — or lived — incredibly tragic lives," said Shooky.

"Like who?"

"Judy Garland? Drunk. Veronica Lake? Drunk. Elizabeth Taylor? Drunk. Marilyn Monroe? Pill freak. Need I say more? Anybody who's lucky in this world and doesn't know it, in the end, isn't."

§

When we got home Shook went into the kitchen. Without a word he opened a drawer and took out a syringe, a spoon, a box of matches, and a small bag of what I knew to be heroin.

"Don't worry, bro. I'm not a junkie. You want a hit?"

"No. Thanks." I sat at the table watching him cooking it up, pretending this was the most normal thing one would do after coming home from a Chinese restaurant. I made myself watch him cook the smack, suck it into the narrow syringe, tie off his bicep, tap a bulging vein in his forearm, slide in the needle, draw blood back into the syringe to mix it with the smack, and then slowly inject himself. It was horrifying and fascinating at the same time. He immediately closed his eyes and his head fell backwards and then forward until he opened his eyes again.

"You should try it, man. There's nothing better."

"You're just asking for it, man."

"For what?"

"Death."

"I like death. It suits me. And don't fuck up my high with your fears, bro." He started nodding out and there was nothing left in him that night as far as I was concerned.

163

I lay on his couch for a long time trying to stay awake, fighting my body's insistence on sleep. I wanted to think about Kiera. I wanted to know what it felt like to ache for her.

§

I was due at K & L at nine and barely woke up in time to call in sick. Lee wasn't happy. "Mott the Hoople, you're an ace, buddy. I need all my aces here, on the phones, making me money, making you money. Let's be here tomorrow, OK, buddy?"

"I have a wide variety of cereal," Shooky said when I walked into the kitchen. He took several boxes down from a cabinet and placed them on the kitchen table with a half-gallon of milk, two mixing bowls from the dish drain, and two large spoons. I faced a difficult choice: Cap'n Crunch with Crunchberries, Fruity Pebbles, Cocoa Puffs, or Trix. I mixed Cocoa Puffs and Cap'n Crunch and was delighted. Shooky praised my choice and did the same.

"Shit. It's time for the Beverly Hillbillies," he said. He turned on a small TV at the far end of the long table. "Almost forgot."

After breakfast we sat out on the porch and smoked a joint.

"So business is good, eh?" I asked.

"Yeah, man. The weed is lucrative, the coke even more so, but the fuckin' heroin is what's really gonna make us rich."

"Shooky, you're not just doing smack, you're dealing it too? You get caught, man, you're in prison for, like, thirty years."

"It's big, big money. It's a fuckin' bonanza. You're gonna be swimming in cash, bro. In the *deep* end of the pool."

"I'm freaked out that you're doing it yourself."

"Leave me alone about that, bro. It's not like I'm addicted. And even if I was, I don't I have to go out and mug people to get my next fix. I'm buried in the stuff."

There was no point taking it further.

"You're gonna be rich, Owen."

"How much money are we talking about?" I was curious, not interested.

"I've got sixteen thousand dollars in a safe. I'm clearing five grand a month and it's only going to get better."

"Sixteen thousand bucks? Jesus Christ!"

I had one of those moments when your body tells you what you're feeling even when you think you're feeling something else. When you want to be feeling something else.

"And half of the next sixteen grand will be yours, amigo!"

"Yeah, but what if I get busted?" I pictured good old Lloyd holding his gun to my head. I felt a phantom pain in my ribs and the taste of Flatvillian dirt in my mouth.

"You won't. If you do I'll bail you out."

"Oh good. Then it'll all be OK," I said sarcastically. "Fuckin' ridiculous."

"I heard you call in sick. Whatever that job is, quit it! We're on a one-way trip to heaven on the gravy train."

"Gravy Train is dog food, man."

"What's the job?"

"Selling paper and toner over the phone."

"What the fuck is toner?"

I told him and he chastised me. "What *are* you, dude? What *happened* to you? You'd rather do that for whatever pittance you're making instead of getting rich with me?"

"Shook, I am one hundred percent spooked about getting busted. I don't think you realize how bad it was for me, man. The risk you're taking is huge. Being busted as a kid is nothing compared to what happens once you turn eighteen. Like I said last night, you go to prison for about thirty years dealing smack. Selling to the stoners in Rockville Flats was one thing. This scares the hell out of me."

"You're seventeen. What are you worried about?"

I was annoyed and he knew it. I lit a cigarette, blew a smoke ring and watched it float away.

"I'll be right back," he said, and went into the house.

I was analyzing what I was saying while I was saying it. It was all true, the fear of arrest, prison, a ruined life. But all the same, I knew I'd never have any part of it. I had no idea how I was going to tell him about Kiera and me. I heard his footsteps coming and then there he was holding a framed picture.

"The love of my life," he said. "Kiera Anne O'Kernaghan."

"Huh?"

"She's the one on the left."

He proudly handed me the picture. Kiera was outside Shark Attack, laughing at something that was really hilarious. Emily was next to her, laughing too, long blond hair in her face. I guessed Shooky must've taken the picture. They were all having such a great time.

"What a babe, huh?"

"Wow, she's . . . she's . . . a fox." I could hardly get the words out.

"The blonde's her roommate, Emily. Another babe I'd like to take to Bang-cock."

"Yeah, I know what you mean."

"Kiera's not as hot as Megan Marie, but dude, I don't care! Not only is she smarter than Megan, but she's funnier too. And she's Irish, so there's that exotic thing going on. I can see you're wondering about the sex. Bro, she slut-fucks! You know what I mean? She'll do *anything*, like a goddamned Tijuana whore! The most uninhibited chick I've ever been with. Megan Marie, who's a goddamn *wild cat* as you know — well, compared to Kiera, she's like the corpse of a fuckin' Mennonite."

I must have looked like I'd had a seizure.

"I know, right? I'm just as much in awe as you are."

"Wow," I whispered with what I felt might be my last breath. Now I wasn't bothered at all by my lying. I wanted to kill him.

"*Look* at her amigo and just *imagine*."

I thought I was going to pass out. I wanted to bash his head in for saying those terrible things about her. The images of the two of them together were flipping through my mind like I was peering into a Mutoscope, unable to stop myself from cranking the pictures, backwards and forwards, backwards and forwards, and it was torture and I was sure some part of me would never recover.

"Hey, are you OK?"

"I'm doing just what you said — imagining it," I said, choking out the words.

He reached over and took the picture. "Yeah. I hit the jackpot."

"I need to go get a glass of water, man. I'm suddenly really thirsty."

He followed me into the kitchen. "There's a water pitcher in the fridge. I've got cucumber slices in it. I learned that from this sophisticated chick who runs an upscale dog-shampoo-glamour-make-over pet shop thing in Beverly Hills. She buys a lot of coke. It'll do the trick."

I poured myself a glass, drank it, and poured another.

"I can't live without her, man. And listen — this is really important. I need you to help me get her back. You gotta help me."

I thought I was going to explode. "What? Jesus Christ, how the fuck am I supposed to do *that?*"

"Whoa, take it easy, man."

"How in hell am I supposed to help you get her back? Call her up? 'Hi this is Owen. My friend Shooky loves you. He's a really cool heroin dealer. Will you take him back, please?'"

"What the fuck is the matter with you?"

I started to shake. I thought I was going to throw up. I sat down on the kitchen floor. I should have told him right then about Kiera and me. I should have ended the whole charade right there. But no. I decided to go along with it until I got home. *Home.* With Kiera. Who I was already thinking of differently now.

"Dude, you're sick. What's going on, man?"

"I'm sorry, man. I apologize. I think it's the Chinese food or maybe too much sugar for breakfast. Let's go back to the porch."

We sat down outside.

"It's simple. Just take over the business for a little while so I'll be freed up to fix it with her. I'm too busy now. I need to hang out in Venice with her and get her to admit that she loves me. Because she does love me, man. It's just a matter of time before she comes around."

It was all getting worse by the minute and I didn't know what to do. I told him I'd be right back, and went into the bathroom. I was losing it and had to put a stop to it and get my shit together. I took some deep breaths and reminded myself of all the horrors I'd been through in life. "I'll get through this too," I said to myself.

"Are you sure you're OK, man?" Shooky asked when I made it back to the porch. He held a leather satchel on his lap.

"I'm just feeling a little weird. Like I said, I think it's the food combo. Makes me a little crazy, but I think I'll be OK."

"Yeah, you don't look too good. I totally get that you're scared of getting busted. I don't want to talk you into anything you don't want to do. But I think you'd be crazy to walk away from eight thousand dollars." He took sixteen stacks of hundreds held intact by rubber bands out of the bag and laid them on the table between us.

"That's sixteen thousand dollars. Take a minute to *absorb*."

"Oh my fucking god, Shooky."

"Oh my fucking god is right. That's what freedom looks like, bro."

I thought, that *is* what freedom looks like.

"Check this out: no matter how long it takes — and this is true if it takes me an hour or a year to get her back — when you're done helping me I'll give you half of that, plus half of the profits we make while you're working. I mean, eight thousand of that," he said with emphasis, "was gonna be yours anyway if you were here."

"Man. Wow. I'm overwhelmed. I don't know. It's a huge risk."

"What else can I do to entice you? What else do I have to offer? I *need* her, man. My life means nothing anymore without her."

"What?"

"My life, man. It means nothing without her."

"Why do you say that?"

"Just take my word for it, she's gonna be my wife someday. Sooner rather than later. So I've arranged for you to get two fake IDs and a fake draft card. One for you as a seventeen-year-old and the other as a twenty-one-year old with a draft card. Don't worry, I've already paid for them. You'll be safe. There's a guy in Venice who does this. He calls himself 'The Scribe.' You can get 'em as Eddie whatever if you want."

"Eddie Vincent. Thanks, man. That's great. Why two of 'em?"

"You want to be seventeen if you get busted. So when you're out and about making deliveries you carry the younger one. And you'll want to be twenty-one to buy booze, and you'll have to have a draft card. It's illegal not to have one on you. The military maniacs are serious, man. When do you turn eighteen?"

"October 9th. If I get busted after that I'm fucked for life. So . . . ."

"Shit, man. That's like only a month from now. If you're only gonna do this before you turn eighteen I'll need to speed this up."

"I didn't say I would, man. Don't push me into this. I know what it's like to be locked up. You don't. This is a bigger deal than you think."

"I understand. But I need your help, man."

§

We cruised down the hill in what I'd come to think of as the-car-that-Kiera-fucked-him-in. The traffic on Pac Highway was ridiculous. We were practically at a standstill.

"Bro, I need to ask you something," I said. "How much thought have you given to how many people die from OD-ing on smack?"

"Excellent question. People die in car accidents all the time, right?"

"Yeah. So?"

"How many people per 100,000 in the United States died of a heroin overdose in 1968?"

"Why would I know that?"

"You wouldn't, but I do. I'm not an amoral psychopath, bro. When the opportunity came for me to deal smack I had the same concerns. So I went to the library and checked it out. 1968 is the most recent statistic I could find. And the answer is one. For every 100,000 people in this country, *one person* OD'd on smack and died."

"OK."

"OK. Now tell me how many people per 100,000 died in car crashes in 1968?"

"You know I don't know that either."

"No, you don't. Well I do. *Twenty-six.* So if it's so terrible to sell smack because of the death rate, why isn't it twenty-six times more terrible to sell cars?"

"I don't know how to answer that, bro."

"Nobody does. Kiera didn't."

"What happened? How did that end, anyway?"

"It didn't end. We're just on hiatus. The gist of it is I made a few small mistakes and she's way too judgmental."

§

When we got to Venice, Shooky said, "Consider this too. Most of what you'd be selling is no different than what we did in Flatville. Not everybody buys smack, but the profit margin is higher. So I don't see that there's that much for you to think about, bro."

"I'll talk to Greta and see what she thinks about everything. She used to do smack all the time in San Francisco."

"You gotta introduce me."

"Hey, I forgot to ask, how's the writing coming now, by the way? You said you were gonna write a novel about those baby whore kids. Anything happening now?" It was a huge strain to try and act normal.

"Writing's on the back burner for now. But yeah, I'm gonna do that, and I've got a lot of other ideas. Kiera comes first though. So look, call me tonight. Time's a-ticking away."

He pulled over and pointed down an alley off of Market Street . "You'll find The Scribe halfway down there on the left. Knock on the garage door that has a "condemned due to rodent infestation" sign on it. Don't worry, it's just to keep people from breaking in."

I got out of the car. "OK, man. Thanks. I'll call you."

"And hey, bro?" He slid his sunglasses down his nose so I could see his eyes. "I need you to do this for me. I wouldn't be pressing you if it wasn't a matter of life and death. If we could jump into a time machine and go back to last summer, I would do *anything* to help you and Sarah stay together. She'd probably be alive today. She'd probably be here with you now."

"Wow, man. You're bringing up Sarah to get me to sell heroin for you?"

"Yep. Because it's true."

I didn't think I could ever forgive him for that. He waved and whipped the car around and drove off.

Twenty-One

Ipulled myself together for my meeting with The Scribe. I thought he would probably be a man in monk robes, with sunken eyes and a magnifying glass, but he turned out to be a short young Jewish guy with a serious face, wearing a tie-dyed yarmulke and suspenders that held up a pair of green old-man pants. His white shirt was stained with blotches of black ink. The Scribe's lair was a darkroom with some sort of sophisticated printing machine filling most of the space. The air was saturated with the smell of chemicals and thick ink. There was hardly enough room to turn around. The Scribe had expected me and already assigned me number 239 on my draft card.

"There'd have to be a World War III for them to get you with 239," he said.

"I need to take your pictures for the driver's licenses. I'm gonna have to light you with more shadows than I'd like to. I've gotta make you look older. You wanna buy booze, right?"

"Definitely."

He took the picture. "What name do you want?"

"Eddie Vincent."

He wrote it down. "V-i-n-c-e-n-t, right?" I nodded. "Come back tomorrow between four and five. No earlier, no later."

I thanked him and headed over to Greta's. I was emotionally exhausted. Jealousy was breathing down my neck.

I wanted to bang my head against her building to get the Shooky and Kiera Show out of it once and for all.

§

I went upstairs and tried to play guitar. I tried to read. I paced around. Greta finally came home and put a few things down on the kitchen counter, saying, "Nothing from Aaron today. But I got a coupon for pizza." She looked at me. "What's the matter with you?"

"Kiera and Shooky."

She threw her purse on the bed, pulled out a pack of Marlboros, tapped one out and lit it. "What's going on?"

"Shooky went out with Kiera, right?"

"Yeah, I know. So?"

"He said she would 'slut-fuck' him. He compared her to a Tijuana whore. I know Shooky. That means there's nothing she wouldn't do with him."

"Don't worry, man. Whatever she did with him she'll do with you. Why? Do you think she won't?"

"That's not what I'm worried about."

"Then I'm not understanding the problem."

"It makes me crazy to imagine them together like that!"

"Like what?

"Anything means everything."

"So? You didn't even know her."

"It makes me see her differently."

"Differently how? Wait. Oh my god! Now I get it. You are *such* a fucking hypocrite!"

She started pacing, but it was more like she kept walking towards me and then away, as if she couldn't decide whether to hit me.

"We've fucked in front of Ray," she said, "and that Neanderthal Keith. *On camera!* And I'd say we were pretty, um, versatile. What does that say about how you think of me? I'm a cheap Tijuana whore too?"

"No, no! You're my *friend*. It's different."

"Why? No it isn't."

"I'm not in love with you."

"So when you fucked her did she just lie there like a piece of plywood, or did she show some signs of life?"

"Let me put it this way. It's by far the best sex I ever had. No offense."

Greta laughed. "None taken. Do you hear yourself? The best sex of your life? What are you *talking* about then? Who cares what she did with Shooky. You are *so* young and *so* stupid. You're acting like just because you're in love with her she's supposed to be some pure little Irish flower, a little virgin spring daisy, waiting for you to pop her innocent little Irish cherry. I can't believe it. You fuck me every which way in front of Ray and Keith — *for money* — and at the same time you want her to be Snow White. You insult me with your hypocrisy! If you can't handle her being a real woman with a real sex life, if you can't handle that she's fucked other guys before you with passion and lust and imagination, then you'd better move to Salt Lake City and become a friggin' Mormon. You'll find plenty of your kind of women there."

I was speechless.

She mumbled to herself and then said, "Wow. Just like a dude, man. Double-standard city."

"No, no. That's not it."

"Well what is it then? You're lucky to have a passionate woman like that in love with you. The two of you have all the pyrotechnics you need, with true love added to the mix. If you don't fuck it up you're gonna experience something very rare and very special. That comes along maybe only once in life if you're lucky. Most people probably never experience it. Or if they do, the guy goes away and dies in *fucking Vietnam!*"

She started crying. I sat next to her and put my arm around her while she wept.

"I miss him, Owen. I'm afraid he's dead and I'll never know for sure."

"I'm so sorry. This waiting, I know it's so hard. I'm sorry, Greta. And please know, I don't think anything but good things about you."

In a few minutes she blew her nose and got herself together and looked at me with traces of anger and envy in her eyes.

"You better get your shit together, Eddie Owen Vincent Kilroy." Then she slapped my cheek. "You're a lucky boy. Don't be a fucking idiot."

"You're ferocious when you're mad."

"I take nothing back. For once in my life I know everything I just said is right on."

I was afraid to speak. After a while she said, "Why don't you play me something? Sitting here like this sucks. Play me something new."

"What do you mean new?"

"New as in a song that came out in the last two years."

I played "If Not For You" as a ballad, more to make it easier to sing, but it worked pretty well that way anyway. "That's how I feel about you."

"Thank you, that was sweet."

I told her that Shooky had given me the money and I wanted to do something with her, something fun.

"Thank you. To be honest, while I'd love to go out and do something, and maybe we can, maybe you and me and your sweetie — if you can manage to get over your little tantrum — the best thing you can do for me is help me pay the rent this month. It's seventy-five dollars. That would be huge."

"Here," I said, peeling off a couple of hundred dollar bills and handing them to her. In a very bad impression of Dog Race Eddie, I said, "Now go buy yourself something special."

"Generous, wonderful, wack-a-doodle Eddie! I love you too. You're growing up fast, kid. Now go get your girlfriend. And let this whole sex thing go. It's dumb. And she's *lovely*."

§

I felt a little better on the short walk to Shark Attack. But I knew that as soon as I saw Kiera, pictures would pop into my mind in spite of all my efforts to erase them. I hated feeling jealous. I hated thinking of her in any way that didn't make me feel good about things. I waited outside the store for her. When she came out she ran to me and threw herself in my arms and kissed me. "Oh, I missed you," she said. I felt nothing but joy in that moment, an all-encompassing joy and surprise that this amazing woman loved me. I took her hands in mine and I told her how much I'd missed her too. We walked back, slowly, even languidly, to her house. She asked me how it went with Shooky. That's when the feeling ended. An untethered voice in my head said, *I could ask you the same thing.* I willed whoever that was away. I put my arm around her and kissed her cheek as we walked. "We have a lot to talk about. Things are gonna get crazy. Shooky wants me to help him get you back." Kiera moaned and put her head on my shoulder. "This is a catastrophe," she said.

Twenty-Two

We finished the macaroni and hot dogs I'd made for dinner and were sitting on the couch drinking wine. "Something more's the matter," Kiera said. "You're not all here. We're not getting anywhere with this crazy problem. Tell me what's going on."

"Nothing's the matter. I'm just freaked out. There's no good answer to this."

"People change. Maybe we should see how things go for a while, let him down easy. I don't want to start a war."

I forced myself to focus, which meant I had to stare at my hands. "No. But we can't let him think for a second that his plan to get you back is gonna work. That would be cruel, don't you think?"

"Yes."

"Unless you're considering taking him back," I said, looking at her.

"So *that's* it! That's what's been going on all night. What are you *talking* about?"

"I think you're maybe having second thoughts about not being with him because you guys had such great sex. And you just said, people change."

"What on earth did he tell you? But wait. You know what? It doesn't matter what he said. I've asked you to *move in* with me and you're doubting me? Wow, what a fool I am."

Emily came in from work, vivacious and in a great mood.

"Hi guys!"

"Hiya, sweetie," Kiera said. She got up and bolted down the hall to her room.

"What's going on?" Emily asked.

"Shooky wants me to help him get Kiera back."

"Oh shit!" She dropped her stuff right where she was standing, went into Kiera's room, and shut the door.

I stayed on the couch without moving, feeling like a creep. Maxwell was asleep on top of the couch, but now he woke up, took one look at me, jumped to the floor, walked down the hall to Kiera's door, and meowed. He tapped on it with one paw and it opened. Emily said, "Come in, kitty." He did. The door closed again.

I had blown it badly. Finally Emily came out to the living room and said that Kiera wanted to see me.

"Don't be an asshole," Emily said.

"I won't."

"Hi," I said. She was in bed, petting Maxwell, who was lying blissfully next to her.

"I need to know why you said that. I've opened up to you. I've made myself vulnerable to you. I thought we had something different and special. I've said things to you I've never said to anyone. And you just threw it all back in my face."

I sat down on the bed feeling like I weighed about nine hundred pounds. "We do have something different and special."

"Do we? Then where did that come from?"

I knew this was a now-or-never moment and I'm a lousy liar.

"Remember how I told you that guys always know who's horny and all that?"

"Yes."

I reached for a part of the top sheet and began twisting it in my fingers.

"You're very nervous, aren't you?"

"Yeah."

"Just fucking say it."

I made myself look at her. "Shooky told me that you guys had, like, mind-blowing sex. He said that you were open to do anything. Which explains why you had sex with him in his car out at Malibu, even though it was supposedly over between you. It's made me insanely jealous. I can't get the two of you out of my mind. And I'm having trouble dealing with it because never in my life have I ever been jealous."

She sat up slowly. The way she looked at me made me feel like I was a reptile staring back at her from inside an aquarium.

"You should be happy that I'm 'open to do anything' as you say. You get to share the benefits of that. Or are you afraid of me now?"

"No, are you kidding? But still —"

"— And yes, he and I, we had super-great sex. He's very good at it. Big deal. But you think that's why I might be going back with him."

"I can think of worse reasons."

"What the hell do you think of me? That I'm some kind of vapid chick with no sense? The sex was fun and because of that I'm suddenly going to dump you? How asinine is that? What would I be doing with you in the first place if that were true? I'm sure he told you about it in a way that was degrading to me. Kiera the slut. I bet he used that word. And then he bragged to you about it all as if he'd won a Gold Medal at the Sex Olympics. The incredible irony here — wow! As if I needed any more reason to never want to see him again. I'll be right back. I'm getting a cigarette."

She brought me one. That gave me a little hope.

"Do you have a lot of sexual hang-ups, Owen?"

"Is jealousy a hang-up?"

"I don't know. You tell me. You're the one who thinks I'm a slut."

"I do not! Maybe it's better we talk tomorrow." I stood up.

She bolted up on her knees. "We damn well better talk now."

"I just don't want this to get out of hand."

"I don't know where you're from, but my arguments don't get out of hand. Never have."

My experience with arguments was that they either exploded, or threatened to explode, but I was afraid to tell her that. I didn't say anything. She was livid and I went from feeling like a reptile to feeling like a gnat, which puts the reptile on a pedestal by comparison. I sat back down.

"I don't like being judged," said Kiera. "You don't even know me, man. We've known each other for, like, half an hour. And we're living together because we both believe in something we can't completely explain. And now on our first night living together we're talking about how I went about fucking Shooky!" She made a remarkably effective frustration noise. "Shall I ask you about all the sex you've had? Should we go down that road?"

Of course there was no way I would ever tell her about what I'd done with Greta.

"No, we don't need to go through all that."

Maxwell sat in her lap. He purred and purred. I pet him a couple of times.

"I'm sorry. I'll let it go. It's just a momentary loss of sanity. It's all gonna be OK."

"Maybe it will. If you don't judge me and make me feel like I'm a whore or something. Because I'm not. And I can't *believe* I just felt like I needed to say that. I'm not sure this is gonna work."

"You *didn't* need to say that."

"You really hurt me, you know," she said, wiping some kitty drool from her hand. "This is not a good start to us living together. It's not a good start under any circumstances. I need to know, are you actually a prude?"

"I didn't mean to hurt you."

"Yes you did. That's what people do."

"I'm not a prude. I hate that word. It's so insulting."

"It's only insulting if deep down in your heart you don't want to be one, but you're too chickenshit to be anything else. You know what? The word 'prude' was originally a Victorian word in French that meant 'an honorable woman.' Emily told me that once and I told you she studies French. We were having a conversation about — well that doesn't matter. Anyway, if you know you're a prude and you accept that about yourself, you don't mind being called one because it's honorable."

"You've obviously given this a lot of thought."

I glanced up at the pictures on the bookcase and saw her family glaring at me.

"I grew up in Ireland," she said. She was pissed off again. "Where sex is bad. Pleasure is bad. I've had to free myself of that. Sometimes freeing myself has been a whole fuck of a lot of fun. I don't think I should be crucified for that."

"I'm not crucifying you. I was just jealous."

"Look. With you or without you, I wouldn't go back to Shooky in eighty million years. Which is why this whole thing is so blown out of proportion it totally freaks me out about you."

"Don't be. I'm fine. I'm OK."

"How long do you think it will take you to get over this, *for real?*"

"Don't worry about me."

"Do you wish I was a virgin?"

"No, of course not."

"Because all this jealousy weirdness makes me wonder."

"Well, I just learned today that I *can* be jealous. The truth is, I am afraid of losing you, Kiera. That's what this is really all about. I've only loved one other person on this planet before I met you, and I killed her."

Kiera stopped petting Maxwell. "What? What do you mean you *killed* her?"

"Her name was Sarah. We had something really special together. Not like us, but I loved her. No one meant more to me. She was having a very tough time and asked me to give her something to help her sleep. I gave her a bunch of Nembutals — extremely powerful barbiturates (downers) — because she said she was gonna have some kind of a breakdown if she didn't get to sleep. That same night she took them all and committed suicide." I immediately got choked up.

Kiera put her arms around me. "Owen, I'm so sorry. That's so awful. That poor girl. But you didn't *kill* her and you have to stop thinking that you did."

"I did too. I should've known better. I was a fucking fool."

"When did this happen?"

"The summer last year. July 23rd."

"See, now *I'm* jealous," Kiera said, lying back down and resuming her affection for the kitty. "Jealous of a poor dead girl. That makes me wackier than you, which isn't easy."

"No, it isn't."

"Be careful with me, O," Kiera said in a strong, firm voice. "I'm a sensitive soul. I may not seem that way, but I am. I hope knowing you can hurt me like this will make you think twice next time we have a problem."

"I promise I'll be careful. And anyway, there won't be a next time."

"Thinking there won't be a next time is not being careful. Not realistic. You know what I mean?"

"Yeah, I do." I kissed her. "And since you said you're jealous of Sarah I feel less bad, if that makes any sense."

We shared Maxwell for a while, both of us petting him and not talking. I never knew I could feel that much gratitude for a cat.

"Shooky shot up when I was there. Heroin," I said. "It freaked me out."

"He's doing *it* now too? This is a disaster waiting to happen, O."

"I know."

"He's clearly unstable. He's obsessed with me and I'm scared. You don't think he has guns, do you? Drug dealers carry guns, don't they?"

"Not Shooky."

"How do you know?"

"Well, I guess I don't, do I? But no. There's no way he'd have a gun."

"He could come here," Kiera said. "And if he sees you here it'll send him over the edge."

"We have to remember he's not a violent person, OK? Now can we change the subject? I want to show you something fabulous."

She sat up. I told her to close her eyes. I put the eight hundred-dollar bills in her hands.

"Open your eyes, love."

She looked at the money and whispered, "Oh my god, O. It happened. Why didn't you tell me right away?"

"I knew he'd come through. I wanted to wait until the right moment. In case I had to bribe you to stay with me."

"That's not funny." She turned my palm over and felt along the lines, which made me look down at them too. "This would be so much easier if he wasn't sort of a good person."

Twenty-Three

"He'll come down here," said Emily later that night. "He'll break into the house and kill us."

She and Kiera and I were sitting on the couch smoking cigarettes and finishing off a bottle of wine.

"No he won't," I said. "Let's just understand something, OK? Shooky's got a huge heart. Yeah, he's gone off the deep end over Kiera, and yeah, he cheated on her, and I know he hit on you Emily, and yeah he's into heroin now, but I knew him long before he came to Venice, and he's an amazing guy."

Emily chuckled derisively. "Wow, man. Do you get how that sounds? He's dangerous. I bet Charlie Starkweather was an amazing guy too."

"Who's Charlie Starkweather?" Kiera asked.

"A mass murderer." To Emily I said, "Please."

"Starkweather killed more people than Manson," Em said to Kiera. "Just shot people at random for the thrill of it."

"Well, Shooky's not a lunatic," I said.

"How do you *know?*" Emily asked. "You weren't here when he hit on me. There was *all kinds of crazy* in his eyes."

Kiera said, "I guess I need to be here when he comes and make sure he knows it's over for good. If I'm not he'll keep after me. I'll tell Warren I have an emergency. That way there won't be a scene at work."

"Fuck, fuck, fuck," said Emily.

"I'm exhausted," Kiera said. "Let's go to bed, O. Good night, Em."

Emily stood up and hugged her, and then she hugged me too. "Good night, you guys. Owen, I'm sorry about Shooky. I didn't mean to rag on him to you." She squeezed me lightly on the arm and headed for her room.

§

I called Shooky about noon. Kiera sat next to me, listening as best she could.

"Hey man," he said, sounding disappointed. "I called last night but nobody picked up."

"Yeah, sorry. Things got a little crazy. How's it going?"

"Great. I hooked up with this foxy babe who used to be a nanny for Engelbert Humperdinck's kid. She spoke Russian. Probably a spy."

"Wow. How'd you meet her?" I exchanged pained glances with Kiera.

"I was so high I don't remember, to tell you the truth." He laughed. "So hey, we need to talk, dude. I wanna nail down this plan."

Kiera grimaced and nodded, encouraging me to take the plunge.

"Shooky, I need to talk to you, man."

"Dude, don't say no yet! Give me a chance to convince you. Eight thousand dollars is yours. It should be yours anyway, like I said. I need you, bro. I *need* to convince Kiera that she loves me."

"Listen, man. Please just listen, OK?"

"Yeah, sure. Go ahead. What's up?"

"I'm sorry, man. Life is full of weird coincidences."

"What does that mean?"

"I'm so fucking sorry I didn't tell you yesterday. I just didn't know how. I actually met Kiera. We're living together. I love her, man. So I can't help you try to get her back, man. That's why I looked so sick yesterday. I didn't know how to tell you."

Kiera grimaced again and put her arm around me. She leaned in closer to the phone. We waited. And waited.

"Shooky?" No response. "Shook, are you there, man?" The line was silent.

"Holy shit," said Kiera. "He's gonna come here."

"Shit. I have to go pick up my ID and draft card from The Scribe between three and four!"

"If he doesn't come by then we'll go together and I'll leave a note for Em."

§

It was about six in the evening when there was an urgent, aggressive knock on the door. Kiera and I went together to answer it. Shooky was standing on the porch, trembling. His eyes were heroin-pins. The look on his face was scary. His speech was slurred.

"Hey, bro. If you're really still my brother, you have to step aside. Kiera is *mine*. I told you that yesterday and you didn't say a fucking word. Time to step aside, bro. I was here first."

"I'm not *yours*," Kiera said. "I'm not anybody's. I'm not to be possessed. And it's over, Shooky. I've told you that sixty billion times."

"You're fuckin' delusional, baby. You *know* you love me."

"Man, you're on smack," I said. "You're stoned out of your mind. And you're not thinking straight."

"I feel fucking wonderful, Owen. Can't you tell? Now don't change the subject. Are you gonna bow out and give me a chance to work things out with my woman or not?"

Kiera said, "I'm not your woman! *It's over.* Over. It's final. Please, Shooky. There's no going back. I just want to be friends. Why can't you accept that?"

"Why can't *you* accept that we belong together? I know that it's hard for you to admit it, but I forgive you for that, baby. I really do. Now can I come in?"

"I don't think it's a good idea for you to come in." She held her hand up as if to make him stop if he tried. "You're not acting rational."

"Owen? You gonna invite me in?"

"Man, it's Kiera's house."

"Yeah, but you said you're living here. Are you the *man* of the house or a pussy-whipped motherfucker?"

"It's Kiera's house. I don't have a say here." It was killing me, all of this.

Shooky stood, slightly off balance, five feet away from me, dying. "I offered you *eight thousand dollars* to help me, man, and you stab me in the back now? Fuck you, man. How long have you two known each other? You were cheating on me all this time, Kiera? You two-timing bitch!"

"Man, don't insult her like that."

"You don't have to answer for me," Kiera said. "I never cheated on you, Shooky. You cheated on me all the time, but I don't give a damn about that anymore. I'm *really* sorry it's turned out like this. If you want, come back when you're not so high and we can talk about it. But right now, you have to leave."

"You both can go fuck yourselves. I never want to see either of you ever, ever, ever again. Bro, you just stabbed me in the back. I was true to you. I kept your money safe. I always kept you in mind. I got a two-bedroom house because I knew you'd show up sooner or later. And now this little Irish cunt comes around and you throw away our friendship?"

"You're making yourself look pretty fucking bad, bro. Seriously."

"Fuck you every day for the rest of your life, you back-stabbing bastard. After all we've been through! Now I see the real you and it's disgusting. Repulsive. And Kiera, I'm sorry for what I just said. You're a jewel, a diamond, a shining light in a dark, fucked-up world. But you can fuck off too."

"I wish we could have been friends."

"And I wish I was Hemingway or Shakespeare. So there you go." He walked to the gate, flipping us off without turning around to look.

I followed him. "Shooky. It doesn't have to be like this, man."

"It doesn't?" He spun around and almost fell over. "YOU WOULDN'T EVEN LET ME INTO THE FUCKING HOUSE!"

He walked up the alley. I watched him go until he turned onto Pacific Avenue.

I was devastated. Kiera was distraught. Emily came home later and we told her about the whole thing.

"At least he didn't shoot you."

"He was very hurt," I said. "And he's out of his mind."

The next morning at about five o'clock we woke up to the sound of four loud knocks on the door. I knew it was Shooky.

"Don't answer it," said Kiera.

"I have to."

We heard Emily's door open. "You guys hear that?"

I turned on the living room light and then the porch light and opened the door. He'd left an envelope addressed to me. I went out and looked down the alley, up and down Speedway, but he was gone. I took it inside and the three of us sat on the couch.

My only brother, I don't know what you think you're doing. You've done me wrong, man. I'm not like you. I do right by you. I'm sorry to have to say this, man, but you're way out of your league with that Irish cunt. You'll be dumped worse than me. I give it a month. And listen carefully dumbshit: I never want to see you or Kiera again. DON'T COME ANYWHERE NEAR ME. DON'T TRY TO "BE MY FRIEND." <u>IF YOU DO YOU'LL REGRET IT</u>. The damage is done. And though those who are betrayed do feel the treason sharply, yet the traitor stands in worse case of woe.

JAS

"Now I feel bad for him," said Emily. "He's so pathetic."

"I'm speechless," Kiera said, looking at me, starting to cry.

I felt something in me die that night, just as I felt it with Sarah. I thought that at that rate, at some point there'd be nothing of me left. I went to the kitchen and brought a large mixing bowl back to the couch. I struck a match, picked up the letter, set it on fire, and dropped it in the bowl. We watched it curl up and turn into black flakes of ash.

§

We never went back to sleep that morning. I went to Greta's and picked up the guitar and when I got back Kiera was at work. I called in sick again to K & L and this time it was for real.

I played a few songs for Kiera when she came home. At the end of the last song she took the guitar from me and set it aside.

"This has been a rough beginning for us," she said.

"I'm so sorry he called you those horrible names. I wanted to kill him."

"He's just a junkie now. It's pretty sad. So are you OK with this whole jealousy thing? I'm still scared."

"Yeah, baby. I'm OK. We're good. I promise." That wasn't true, but I did get over it eventually.

"I hope so."

After a minute she sat up and looked at me, her expression letting me know that she was trying to cheer us up.

"So let me understand something."

"Yeah?"

"He was gonna give you eight thousand dollars if you helped him try to get me back?"

"Yeah."

"And you turned him down."

"Yeah."

"I'm never letting you handle our finances."

Twenty-Four

On my eighteenth birthday we got married at the court-house in Santa Monica. Greta and Emily were there with us. It was a simple, sweet ceremony conducted by Judge Sylvia Kurbegov, who read to us from Rilke, the passage about us being willing to stand guard over each other's solitude. Then we all went out for pizza and beer.

Back then you would have had a hard time finding someone less suitable for marriage than me. Kiera and I were kids, but that's not the half of it. We were drawn together because we were, in our respective ways, exotic to each other. Kiera was the stable, sane, well-rounded college student from Ireland whose family owned a house in Dublin and a house at the ocean, whose father, she told me, was a successful lawyer, and whose whole life, with the notable exception of her mother's death and her sister's jealousy, had been free of strife. She was ambitious, full of promise, confident. In my most delusional, hallucinogenic sojourns into life's improbable possibilities, Kiera would never even have come into my most distant orbit, let alone *marry* me. But on the day we got married I was convinced, because I was still young and naïve, that the world had, for a long time, owed me an amount of happiness proportionate to the degree I'd suffered. So I believed — if you can imagine this — that through Kiera the universe was *paying me back*.

That delusion was all wonderful and good at the time, except the nature of my upbringing was such that my capacity to sustain a stable intimate relationship had been seriously compromised. Remember how I failed with Sarah. I had been unable to figure out how to love her until it was too late, and even then I'd killed her. I was genuinely afraid that Kiera would get tired of me — that was already out in the open. But I kept my paranoia hidden after that. I know now that I clung to her like one clings to a capsized kayak hurling down the rapids. But it's important to me, to my ego, to point out that mine was not a suffocating clinging. My clinginess was almost completely internalized, or at least that's what I made myself believe. In the same moment I was making Kiera laugh, feeding her a spoonful of strawberry ice cream, I might also be feeling total panic at the thought that she might leave me someday. In fact, it was most often in moments like that that my fear would most energetically assert itself.

It is perhaps the greatest of all ironies then that, to her, I was the answer to some of her most fundamental insecurities and fears. Her problems were rooted in whether she could break away from the heavy expectations imposed, in a loving but oppressive way, by Connor, her father, and even, in a weird way, by her sister Nora. This was the result of a long-cultivated, religiously induced obligation (e.g. honor thy father), and by extension, to her sister. Connor wanted her to move back to Ireland when she graduated and be a pious, devoted Irish woman who would marry a similarly pious and devoted husband and stay in Ireland forever.

Sometimes Kiera would express doubt about whether she'd really transcended the good girl role she'd assigned herself after her mother died. She'd asked me whether I thought she was deceiving herself. I'd remind her, with a very happy face, that at the very least she'd broken out of her Irish sexual repression quite deftly and demonstratively. She would usually smile, then make a face.

"I hate to disappoint my father," she said once. "He's not someone who's easy to disappoint, but when you do you kind of wear it around with you for a while like a fuckin' hairshirt."

We were driving up Highway 1 on a weekend trip to Big Sur. (We'd bought a cheap little VW bug with the money I got from Shooky.) Over the hills to the east puffy white clouds floated like cartoons, and there was nothing but blue sky over the ocean to the horizon. Another gorgeous day on one of the most beautiful coastal highways in the world.

"Won't he be happy you're happy?"

"Yes. Well, I don't know. You're gonna meet him soon and you'll know what I mean. There's nothing I can do about it except try harder to believe in myself."

I was driving, but I leaned over and gave her a quick kiss on the cheek. "I believe in you, baby. You're everything I think you are. You're a long list of synonyms for 'wonderful' and 'amazing' and 'woman.'"

"Oh my god, where did I *find* you?" She held my hand and we drove on, living the dream.

Twenty-Five

During Kiera's Christmas break from school, Connor paid our way to Dublin. He was as tough as any man in Ireland. Kiera told me on the flight over that he'd grown up on a sheep farm in County Mayo, south of Sligo, and had worked every day for fourteen years — since he was four — in all kinds of weather, never any time off except when he was at school. When he was eighteen he left the farm, went to Trinity College in Dublin, then law school, and succeeded in life far beyond his own expectations.

When I first saw him at the gate when we got off the plane I thought about how I'd heard that girls sometimes marry guys who are like their fathers. That couldn't have been further from the truth in my case. Connor was a big man, strong, intense, and not someone you'd ever want to try and con. He'd see right through you.

He shook my hand and said, "Hello, son. It's a pleasure to meet you." I expected his handshake to crush me, but he wasn't one of those insecure bastards who have to prove how manly they are.

"A pleasure to meet you too, sir."

He drove us straight out to Drumcliff, about a three- or four-hour drive on the wrong side of the highway.

All Kiera's childhood holidays and summer vacations were spent there. The Wild Atlantic Way is what they call that coastline. Brilliant. The house was on a hill overlooking the ocean, which was a mile or two away. It was a big old house made of stone and timber, renovated with all the usual modern conveniences, on an unnamed road with a giant oak tree on the other side. It was right smack in the middle of Yeats country, Ben Bulbin looming gloomily nearby on overcast days, on sunny days taking on a more cheerful character, a friendly green monster peppered with sheep. The Drumcliff house was one of those with ghosts in the walls and the rafters and stories to tell, stories you could feel even if you'd never hear them. In spite of, or because of, the house's mystical eccentricities, you felt as if you'd always belonged there; never did you want to go back to wherever it was you'd come from.

The trip was ostensibly meant as a Christmas/wedding present, but it was also a way for Connor and Nora to size up the situation. Nora was back living at home because her first marriage had just fallen apart. She greeted us at the door.

"Kiera, my darling. You're here! Happy Christmas," she said.

"Happy Christmas," Kiera said, looking at me as she hugged Nora and giving me a look that said don't worry about anything.

Nora was four years older than Kiera, a good twenty pounds underweight, with a ghostlike complexion that at night made her look like she had crawled out of a crypt.

"And you're Owen. Welcome to you too."

"Hello Nora," I said jovially. I yawned. "Oh, I'm sorry. I couldn't sleep on the plane."

"It's a ten-hour flight," said Kiera, as if to remind her.

"Yes, I know," she said. "So very stressful."

§

By that time, December 1971, The Troubles had shifted into high gear in Belfast and the country was mired in violent conflict. To the consternation of Kiera and especially of Connor, Nora was dead set against the unification of Ireland, claiming that Sinn Féin, the leftist political party, was a terrorist organization, and believed Northern Ireland should remain under British control forever. It was ludicrous. Connor prohibited political arguments in the house because, as he told Kiera in confidence and with a dash of humor, he didn't want to go to prison for murdering Nora.

It was clear that she'd taken an intense dislike to me. Much (if not all) of her revulsion arose from the sad truth that I had just become her brother-in-law. What she and Connor discovered was that Kiera had married a street urchin, for all intents and purposes orphaned, with no realistic prospects. What they didn't know would've caused them both to have heart attacks.

The day after we arrived and had taken some time to get settled, I sat reading the *Irish Times* — a very exotic moment for me — while Kiera and Connor played hearts. Nora took me aside and whispered, "Come into the kitchen." When we got there she said, "You're a nice boy, Owen, but I don't believe I'll ever see you again." A stew was gurgling on the stove. The hearty, wholesome, and appetizing smell was corrupted by Nora's perfume. It was that kind of heavy, dense, air-killing, old-lady perfume you smell in department stores. And Nora was only twenty-three!

"Why do you say that?" I smiled, immune.

"You're . . . well, there's something not right about you. I can feel it."

"What do you want to know? Just ask."

"I'm very intuitive; I don't need or want to know anything more than what I feel already. I can't put my finger on exactly what it is about you except to say that you're of a different . . . a different ilk than we are, we O'Kernaghans. You're not a good fit for my sister, and when she comes out of her delusional state of mind, she'll realize that too, and drop you like a hot potato. So enjoy yourself while you're here and then off you go."

I saw a bowl of peanuts on the counter and grabbed a few. I popped them into my mouth. "Nora, you don't know anything about anything."

"I know this: Kiera's description of you — who you are, where you're from, what you do — is lacking specificity. That's not like her."

"I don't know what she told you or didn't tell you. But you can ask me anything you want. Maybe I'll even tell you the truth."

"My father doesn't like you either," she said and walked out. "He's never been more disappointed in my sister."

Bullseye.

§

That night Connor brought me outside the house because he wanted to show me something. Kiera said later that while I was with him, Nora was in the house trying to convince her to annul our marriage. I don't know if Connor was in on that. It had snowed heavily overnight and he was bundled up in a brown bear coat, a black scarf, a knit brown cap that he told me Nora had made for him, and snow boots. I wore a Buddy Holly sweatshirt and a black overcoat Kiera and I found for two dollars at the thrift store in Venice.

Connor and I stood under the giant tree. It was almost dusk. The sky was clear and high, teasing the landscape with the first hint of the night's stars. Uneven trails of moonlight glittered on the winding snowy road.

"So what's this my daughter tells me about you wanting to be a musician?"

My daughter. Not Kiera. Just looking at Connor's face you began thinking of Genghis Khan. I was afraid of him after what Nora said.

"Well first, I *am* a musician. I've been playing guitar for years. But yes, getting paid for it is better than selling office supplies over the phone." I chuckled and hoped he would too. He didn't.

"Is that what you're doing for money?"

"Part time. That and playing guitar on the boardwalk."

"Fookin' Christ. What about college, boy?"

"I'm not ruling that out, sir. I just gotta give music a chance. I'm a songwriter. I sing the songs I write. A solo act kind of thing. I'm good at it."

"Not ruling it out. Shit. Don't you think you'd be a better musician if you went to college? Can you read music? Do you know music theory?"

"None of the Beatles could read music. Not even Paul."

"Oh my," he said. Now he chuckled, but not in a mean way. "Son, you must know that Lennon and McCartney are blessed with God-given talent that comes along in this world maybe once or twice in a hundred years."

That shut me up.

He pointed up at the tree, which lorded over everything within forty feet.

"You see this oak tree?"

"Yeah."

"It's maybe three hundred years old."

"Wow."

There was a long pause before he spoke again.

"My wife Aoibheann — Kiera's mum — never under-stood that tree."

I had no idea what he was talking about. My feet were freezing. I was wearing Converse All-Stars in two inches of snow.

"Do you think you understand it?"

"What?"

"The tree, boy."

Kiera had told me a lot about her father, but she never said anything about him being a mystic or a kook.

"I just met the tree, sir. So no, I don't." I was so intimi-dated that my mind slowed to a crawl. I felt that everything I said would be scrutinized and taken apart. I couldn't think. It was like having a teacher standing behind you watching you take a math test.

"That's the wisest thing you've said since you got here."

He looked at the tree a while longer.

"Would you have known that was an oak if I hadn't told you?"

"No. I can only identify a pine tree. That's about it. A palm tree too." I laughed idiotically. "Southern California, you know."

"How many of the one hundred seventy-five varieties of pine do you think you can identify?"

I stared at him like an imbecile. He was already very good at making me feel that way. "I don't know. Can we please go inside? My feet are freezing."

"I just have one more question, young man. You are my son-in-law now, and family means the world to me. So by virtue of Kiera you are welcome in my home. But you are likely mistaken if you think that you can support her as a songwriter. One in a million have the gift *and* the luck. I'm sorry, but I sincerely doubt you're one of them. Not because you don't have talent — I know nothing of your ability beyond what Kiera has told me, and she's in love with you, so there is that. It's sheer probability, son. The odds are stacked against you. Massively stacked against you. You need a back-up plan. I want you to think about that. What is your back-up plan if this doesn't work out?"

"Um —"

"Don't try to answer that now. Think it over; you obviously haven't. And I'd prefer that I have the last word in this conversation. If you don't come up with a back-up plan, and let me know soon what you've come up with, I'll have no choice but to modify my assessment of you. Kiera is brilliant; she is one of the smartest people I know. I don't imagine she would have married anyone who isn't her match in some important ways, even though the two of you getting married so quickly was reckless, to say the least. Excuse me for saying so, and nothing personal, but it was the stupidest decision I've ever seen her make. But I must assume that you are a smart and capable young man. Kiera is very precious to me, as you might imagine. Between you and me, she and I, we have always had something very special. Understand, I love Nora, couldn't love her more, even taking into consideration her terribly misguided view of what's happening in this country right now. But Kiera. Well. She's *Kiera*. I'm sure you of all people get what I mean. Now, you know her mum's been gone more than half her life?"

"Yes. I'm sorry."

"Thank you. The point I'm getting at is Kiera needs a husband who isn't off in dreamland, insisting on living out all the follies of youth. Son, if you don't start now getting something going that's more realistic, I will have no choice, my daughter's judgment notwithstanding, to consider you an idiot." He looked at me and smiled. His smile was at the same time challenging, cheerful, and sad. "Now let's go have a festive Christmas Eve, eh?" He turned and walked into the house.

§

Kiera and I cozied up in her bed that night. It was fun being there since it had been her room since she was a kid. "He's an enigma," she said, gently adjusting herself so I could lay my head on her shoulder. "I have no idea what he meant about the tree. My mum not understanding it. He never talked to me about that. But we don't have to know what it means. The important thing is that *he* does."

"He told me he'd think me an idiot if I don't make a back-up plan."

"He's a very practical man. But you know, he has his gentle side. He'd take me to work sometimes when I was little. Imagine this bulldog of a man going into some multimillion-dollar meeting with me dressed as Pipi Longstocking! He'd walk into the room with a rugged kind of sheep-farmer fearlessness that scared the shit out of everybody, especially those pasty boys in suits who couldn't tell a sheep from a goat. And all the while he'd be holding my hand. The first thing he'd do is set me up next to him with crayons and a coloring book. I am proud of him. He cares deeply for Nora and me, and probably secretly admires you for loving me like you do."

"If he's secretly admiring me he's doing an excellent good job of keeping it secret. Nora said he doesn't like me. And she said I wasn't 'up to the level' of you O'Kernaghans. That I'm not of your 'ilk'."

"She's a mean-spirited fool. Don't waste your time thinking about anything she says. It's all gonna work out. I love you. Now cuddle me closer and shush." We wrapped ourselves around each other and drifted off together.

§

Early on the morning we were to drive back to Dublin we took a short drive north to the tiny village of Mullaghmore. We stopped in a café and had a coffee and a scone, sitting at a table that looked out over the little harbor. The café was busy but all was quiet outside, it being cold and a Monday.

"We have to take a walk now," said Kiera when we finished. "I wanna show you where I go. It's where me and Da are in the picture."

She took me along a one-lane road that wrapped around the village, a walk that we would take at least once every time we came to Drumcliff. I remember that day so vividly. It was dramatic. The wind coming off the ocean was wild. Waves crashed into the rocky cliffs with reckless speed and intensity. The Wild Atlantic Way. I was wearing one of Connor's coats, warmer than mine but too big for me, which helped because Kiera could slide one of her gloved hands up my sleeve as we walked closely together. Between silences we talked about nothing important, listened to the manic waves, shared our affection for the sheep and love of the cows, all of whom seemed impervious to the weather. A magnificent castle was up ahead about a half a mile off the road.

"That's Classiebawn Castle," Kiera said. "It's only about one hundred years old, but it looks a lot older doesn't it?"

"It looks ancient. Like the home of the first Count Chocula."

"It does! It's magical. I always choose not to think of the fact that it's owned by this royal guy called Lord Mountbatten, who I know nothing about except that his name makes me believe he's got a stick up his ass the size of a fence post. I like to think of it in a more mysterious way. When I was a little girl I thought one day I might grow up and be a princess in that castle. That ended when I found out the amount of bullshit princesses have to put up with."

"That's my sweetie."

"This is my favorite walk in the world. We'll come back next Christmas too. That's what my da told me. He'll bring us over. He wouldn't have said that if he wasn't trying to like you."

"Far out. He's *trying* to like me. Oh good."

"Don't be that way. It's not you. He had this idea that I would marry some boring clown who wears bow ties or something. It'll take him some getting used to."

"I've gotta come up with some sort of a back-up plan to tell him about."

"Tell him you've decided to join the Irish Navy."

"I'm sure I can say that in a way that'll convince him."

"By the way, you can become an Irish citizen now if you want. And I can become an American. We could have dual citizenship."

"With seconds, and at ten paces. You choose the weapons."

"My god, that's an awful joke."

I laughed and lit us both cigarettes.

"I'm amazed that you can do that in this wind."

"Shooky taught me when we were about thirteen. And you'd be surprised at what else I can do in the wind," I said. I grabbed her ass.

"Easy boy." She took my hand away. "We have to wait until we get home."

We went back to the café for another coffee. I told her I had a dream about Shooky. "I dreamt that he OD'd and died."

"You mean he killed himself?"

"No. He just OD'd."

"I hope he's OK. That was so ugly. Such a terrible way for your friendship to end. And for him to be so obsessed with me was so weird. I'm so sorry all that happened."

"Me too. That dream was disturbing. Maybe he'll OD and survive it and that'll straighten him out."

"You know, sometimes dreams can be prophetic, kind of telepathically connected to something or someone at the moment you're dreaming, you know? In 1916 or 1917, something like that, my old cousin Brian Linney was fighting in the British Army in World War I. He'd gone missing for more than a year and was presumed dead. Nobody'd heard a word. Family legend has it that my da's aunt Colleen, my great-aunt and Brian's mum, woke up in the middle of the night and said to my great-uncle Edward, Brian's coming home tomorrow. I had a dream, she said, and I've got to get things ready. She got right up and started cleaning the house. Later in the morning she brought out her finest tablecloth, took out the special dishes, you know, did all the fancy stuff. Then she started cooking Brian's favorite stew, something she never did after he went missing. Meanwhile, Uncle Edward thought she'd gone loony. He was ready to call a priest, thinking maybe she was possessed (although that would have been a rather benign spirit). So, about three that afternoon somebody knocks on the door. My aunt shouts to Uncle Edward, 'It's Brian!' She opens the door — and it's him!"

"Wow! I've heard of stuff like that."

"The funny thing was, even though she knew this all along, she fainted." She laughed. "It's Ireland, you know. Things like that happen in other places but I think they happen more here. This is a mystical island. Lots of ghosts. When someone dies in a house the first thing you have to do is open the window to let the spirit out."

We walked back to the car. Kiera asked, "Do you want to be buried? Or would you rather be cremated? I guess that's something we should know about each other."

"I don't know. Ask me in sixty years."

"So it's my decision then? If God forbid something happens."

"Yep."

"I don't want it to be my decision."

I shrugged. "I don't know. And I don't want to talk about this anymore, OK? I don't want to ask you and I feel like I'll be obliged to."

"OK, never mind. Let's go home. I need some more quality cuddle time before the drive back to Dublin. Being here makes me miss my mum more."

Twenty-Six

Not long after returning from that first trip to Ireland we entered what Kiera called our Pygmalion period. We were walking on the beach again, where we always seemed to end up having our serious talks, heading over to Santa Monica to have an early dinner in an Indian restaurant we liked. It was slightly overcast, and the surfers seemed to love it. A couple dozen of them wearing dark wetsuits floated up and down on the swells like buoyant little raisins.

"For starters, O, you have to get your GED. You probably can't do anything without one except sell those stupid office supplies over the phone. You're too smart not to go back to school. You need a new job too. Greta got out of there and she makes decent pay at the record store. Maybe you can apply there."

"If I go to school will you spank me if I don't do my homework?"

"No, because that would mean you'd never do it."

"That's true."

"Can you *please* try to be serious for once?"

The next day I enrolled in Santa Monica Community College. It was the end of Christmas break and winter classes were just starting up. At first sitting in a classroom was torture, like being shackled to a dentist's chair and probed without Novocain. But I got used to it. I got a part-time job at McCabe's. They sold every kind of stringed instrument you can think of, and also had a little music school. I was at home there. I'd had no idea how bad it had been at K & L until I got out. I started playing out a lot and met some people.

The other Pygmalion challenge for Kiera during this era, equally important to her, was all about art. Being a film and literature major, she started taking me to the movies. I say "she started taking me" rather than "we went" because it was all her doing. The films were almost always foreign, usually European or Japanese.

And what did I care about foreign films? I hated the idea of subtitles. I thought people who went to movies with subtitles were there just to show everybody how bohemian they were, or maybe to prove they really knew how to read. The movies themselves had little to do with it. When I first saw Goddard's *Weekend* I felt like I'd been conned. Watching a massive traffic jam for *ten minutes?* Cannibalism? The movie makes absolutely no sense. I still don't like it. Goddard, mad at the world, mercilessly subjecting his audience to stupidity. Even Kiera hated it.

But the better movies meant so much to her. I realized early on I'd better give them a try, and the Fox Venice on Lincoln Boulevard, and the Nuart in Santa Monica, were close enough to make it easy.

The first film she took me to was at the Fox.

"You'll like this one," she said with an alarming level of enthusiasm. "It will please you, and pave the way for other, better movies to come."

It was Roger Vadim's *"And God Created Woman,"* starring the twenty-two year-old Brigitte Bardot, nude in the opening scene and a relentless lust inducer for the rest of the movie. Kiera always made us stay until the lights went up, and while the end credits crawled, I said, "Wow, if this is what these movies are like, sweet love, I'm your popcorn."

"Uh huh. See? I knew you'd like it. We're going to see *Rashomon* next week."

"Who's naked in that one?"

She laughed. "Sorry, baby. Nobody. It's a classic Japanese movie about the vagaries of truth and perception. You'll see on Friday night."

"It sounds awful."

"It sounds awful *now*. But just wait. It's an amazing film. See, you're my Eliza Doolittle, honey. Follow my lead and before long we'll knock the Fuckville Flats right out of you."

That was the first moment when her Pygmalion project was actually out in the open and I resented it.

"I don't *have* any Fuckville Flats in me, Kiera. I'm just not a movie snob."

She put her hand on mine, as if to soothe me. "You're a philistine, love. But it's not your fault."

"I am not! I read *From Here to Eternity* when I was in jail and I loved it. That's eight hundred and forty pages! What's the longest book *you* ever read?"

"I don't know, but that's truly amazing, love. Nobody reads books like that anymore."

When we got home I had to secretly look up "philistine."

We went to the movies all the time, and I slowly began to look forward to them. From one screening to the next I began to realize that it wasn't all pretentious bullshit. Bergman, Truffaut, Rohmer, Wertmüller, De Sica, Fellini, Varda, Kurosawa — these were a few of Kiera's spiritual guides, and they were to become mine. There were two reasons for my slow conversion. First, I didn't want her to be right about me being "Owen Doolittle," so I resisted seeing any value in them for as long as I could. And second, I never trusted religion, and film was, for her, a religion. She believed in its power.

She so wanted to open up the world for me through these films so we could share them, and eventually she succeeded. "This may sound cheesy," Kiera said one night as we walked out of the Nuart, weepy-eyed after seeing the *The Cranes Are Flying*, a moving, thought-provoking, Soviet anti-war film from the fifties. "It may sound Polly Anna, or whatever, but I mean, think of it, O. The people who made this beautiful movie, the actors, the writer, the director and so forth, they're supposed to be our sworn enemies! These are people that we're supposed to want to murder in a nuclear holocaust. We're supposed to hate them. I'd like somebody to tell me how anyone could hate or even *dislike* Tatiana Samoylova, and try to explain to me how she could be *anyone's* enemy!" She gave an unforgettable performance as Veronika, a young woman who is brokenhearted by the terrible losses she's suffered in the war.

"It's so painfully ironic," Kiera continued. "These wicked, evil devils, these mortal enemies of ours, make a movie about the ghastly human cost of war! Their film is a gift to the world. To me, films like this do more to bring people together than any fuckin' pope ever did. Organized religion, especially Christianity, turns people, turns nations, against each other. Look what's happening in Ireland right now. They say it's not a religious war, but you can't look at it without seeing Protestants on one side and Catholics on the other. And I agree with the Catholics, which is a first for me, not that I ever agreed with the Protestants either. There should be one Ireland for all of us.

"The sad thing about *The Cranes* is, like, how many Americans have seen it in the last fifteen years? Maybe a few hundred? And all of those people are in L.A., New York, or San Francisco. That's it. The rest of the country will never even know it exists. They'll never know the goodness of those people, and they'll go on thinking everybody in the Soviet Union is evil, inhumane, and wants to murder us too."

Kiera was never anywhere close to being a stuck-up-affected-berét-wearing-unwashed-Gauloises-smoking-pseudo-cinéaste bore. She loved Hollywood too. *Easter Parade* was a favorite. We saw *Enter the Dragon* three times. And when we spotted big-name actors around town, which happened a lot, she'd get overexcited. Once we stood in line behind Dustin Hoffman at an ice cream shop and she practically had a seizure. She was thrilled even when we ran into has-been TV stars. Gomer Pyle (Jim Nabors) sat two seats away from us when we saw *200 Motels* and she couldn't stop reminding me that he was there.

§

The spring and summer came and went, and life was easy, exciting, and wonderful. I never knew it could be like that. Once I asked Kiera, "Is this how most people live? A life without a major crisis every other day?" That's the way she grew up and that made me happy for her. Imagine if both of us were as fucked up as I was!

We started taking turns reading to each other every night, which we both loved. One day I went over to the bookstore looking for something new. Moonlight Wind handed me a book called *The Himalayas*.

"Remember that time I told you guys a little about the Himalayas? This is what I was talking about."

She opened it and flipped through a few pages. The pictures were astonishing. They moved something deep in me. These were more than just pretty mountains.

"I thought you might like to look at this. I can loan it to you for a couple of days, and if you decide you want it it's fifty cents."

"Wow, thank you. This is so far-out! You know what? I'll just buy it now. After talking to you that time, we've dreamed about going there."

"I know you will."

There was a book on the counter with a naked woman on the cover, sitting on a fancy chair in the shadows of an old-fashioned, fancy room. It was called *The Pearl*. Moonlight Wind saw me looking at it.

"What's that about?"

"*The Pearl* was an underground erotic magazine in England back in the 1800s. This book has all the editions. I don't think there are many copies around these days. The British government, hypocrites of course, shut it down for obscenity. I can loan it to you and Kiera if you like. It's *very* graphic," she said with a mischievous laugh. "Steinbeck's pearl was a real pearl. This one's a clitoris!" She handed it to me. "Bring it back in a couple of days?"

"Sure. Thanks!"

She'd become a friend of ours. Kiera and I had our little group. We spent a lot of time with Greta, and of course we lived with Emily. We hung out with Moonlight less often, but she was always fun to be with. She was married. One night when I was packing up to go home from busking on the boardwalk she came by.

"Owen, my husband manages Highway 61, and last night I told him about you." Highway 61 was a well-known singer-songwriter, blues, jazz café in West Hollywood. It was a step up from where I'd been playing. "He wants you to do an open mic. Three songs. Can you come Tuesday night?"

"Absolutely. Thanks so much! That's election night, isn't it?"

"Yes. A dark day for humanity because McGovern is going to get killed."

"I know. I know. Holy shit. We're going to have to get very drunk afterwards."

"Basil doesn't have a liquor license so we'll have to bring it in."

"How are we gonna survive another four years of Nixon?"

"With love for each other and for the world. Right?"

A pattern had emerged with the women who had come into my life. Sarah, Lorelai, Greta, Kiera, Emily, and now Moonlight Wind: they were all under the impression that I was worth something.

Kiera and I went to Highway 61 with Emily and Greta, who at that point still hadn't given up hope on Aaron, although she was getting very tired of the whole thing. I was nervous. This would be the first time I played for all of them at once. The place was packed with other songwriters and their friends. Everywhere you looked there was another guitar case. We sat with Moonlight Wind, who told us for the first time, after a glass of wine, that her real name was Jane.

"It's boring and dull and stupid and that's why I don't use it. *Jane?* It sounds like a guy from Tijuana saying 'chain'."

"I like it," I said.

"What about Janie?" Emily asked.

Moonlight Wind said, "Hmm. That might work someday."

"It could," said Kiera, "but I'm with you about 'Jane.'"

"I like the Tijuana thing. Why not call yourself 'Chain' emphasizing the 'ch'? It'd be far out because nobody's called that." That was Greta, of course. Everybody laughed, and for the rest of the night we called Moonlight Wind "Chain."

Moonlight Wind's husband Basil was a black guy from England, balding, with dark brown mutton-chop sideburns and a gold-hoop pirate earring in his left ear. He wore jeans and a rope for a belt. Like his wife, he had a friendly openness about him. It was as if he was determined to refuse to be cynical, committed to wake up every day and say fuck you to the oppressors and believe, in spite of it all, that nothing bad would ever happen to him or anyone he loved. I thanked him for inviting me.

"Moonlight knows talent. I'm happy to meet you and can't wait to hear you. No pressure! Excuse me." He went up to the little stage.

He made an announcement to the crowd.

"Hey everybody, can I have your attention please? As we all know, it's fuckin' election night in America. Before we start the music I'd like to have a collective moment of silence, a brief meditation, especially for the people Nixon and Kissinger are slaughtering in Vietnam and Cambodia, and on the streets of our country. We will overcome evil eventually, I think we all believe that, but tonight let's take a moment, eh? A moment for the world? Then we'll play and be happy we're all here, safe and surrounded by friends!"

You couldn't hear a thing in that café. A few cars drove by outside. The silence was profound and very moving. It didn't last long in real time, maybe a minute or two. When Basil ended the silence everybody spontaneously applauded, looking around the room, smiling. You couldn't have created a better atmosphere for my first open mic at Highway 61.

The first song I played I said, "This is dedicated to a friend of mine who knows who she is, and who she once was." I played Gerry Goffin's and Carole King's song, "Chains," but I always sang "chain" instead of "chains." *Chain, my baby's got me locked up in Chain....* Kiera and Moonlight Wind both laughed and rolled their eyes. I got the biggest laughs out of Greta and Emily.

The other two songs I played were mine, an up-tempo protest song called "Killinger" about Kissinger, and a ballad I wrote for Kiera called "Kiera." I got a good response from the audience. I kept coming back every Tuesday night for six weeks straight, playing covers and a few of my own songs. Finally Basil offered me a regular spot on Thursday nights, nine to eleven.

Over the next few months I was slowly becoming a minor success at Highway 61. I started to play gigs in other places and hanging out once or twice a week up in West Hollywood at the Troubadour, getting psyched up to play an amateur night. Back then, and even now, you don't fuck around at the Troubadour. You have to be ready and you have to be good.

I discovered I had a lot of songs in me. For every ten or twenty songs I wrote half were bad, but the others went over well. Meanwhile I was getting through school. When I enrolled in a class called "Six Moral Tales: Intro to the Cinema of Èric Rohmer," Kiera declared the Pygmalion era complete and successful.

Twenty-Seven

Those first two years we were married were by far the happiest and most stable of my life, and therefore of little interest beyond what I've just written, with one major exception. In January 1973 the draft ended. The Scribe's magnificent handiwork had provided me with a baseline level of confidence, a reasonable belief that the parasites wouldn't steal my life, and as a result I'd been able to avoid living waist-deep every day in the thick swamp of paranoia. But still, hearing the news that the draft was over was like a doctor telling you that your fatal malignant brain cancer had miraculously healed itself.

One early spring night, after playing my first amateur night at the Troubadour — which went *really* well — Kiera and I drove over to the Griffith Park Observatory. Neither one of us had ever been there. She would be graduating in May, and things were looking more promising for me all the time. I was ecstatic with what I'd just done. The bartender told me, "Make sure you come back." To me, that was like Dylan calling me up to ask if he could record one of my songs.

We stood with our arms around each other, looking out over the insane city, beautiful in its absurdity, the endlessness of it being almost a parody of itself.

"Crazy how things turn out, isn't it?" she asked.

"What do you mean?"

"We come from such different places and we met here, somehow. I mean, we met in Venice, which is different, but still. Out of all *this* we found each other."

"Yeah."

"You were fantastic tonight. You could make it anywhere. London. New York."

"Yeah? You think so?"

"Yeah. You know, I think maybe . . . ."

"What?"

"What do you think about us moving to New York after my graduation? I think everything I want is there."

I felt like she just slapped me. "Everything you want is there? Where did this come from?"

A full moon. Her face in a soft light. I tried to glean from her expression how serious she was and couldn't be sure.

"I got a phone call yesterday. I've been offered an amazing job there. I would have to start on July first, after graduation."

"You applied for a job in *New York* without telling me?"

"Well, not really. Amy and I were talking and she said her sister, Pauline Yasgur, who teaches at NYU, and is a publisher too, needs an assistant. She — Amy — picked up the phone and started dialing, and while the phone was ringing she whispered to me, with a big smile and bright eyes, 'Let's just see if the stars are aligned.'"

Amy Yasgur was her favorite writing professor. She was a weirdo of about fifty who wore kimonos and wigs and rectangular glasses, each lens about the size of a piece of Wrigley's Spearmint Gum.

"So I guess the stars were aligned then. But why you? There have to be a bunch of people who could be her assistant."

"Amy likes me. Through her I have an in. She thinks it would be a good opportunity. Actually, she thinks it would be an *excellent* opportunity. You gotta understand, O, Pauline Yasgur is like, *it* in the poetry world. And a job at NYU would be amazing. No more surfboards. And she *runs* Bananafish Books!"

"What's Bananafish Books?"

"It's a really well-known independent publishing house. She named it after a J.D. Salinger story called 'A Perfect Day for Bananafish.'"

"A perfect day for bananafish. That's sounds so *stupid*."

"Well, to *you*, I guess. A guy commits suicide." She looked away, then back at me. "My pay would be way better than Shark Attack, and you could find a job easy and we'd have enough for us to live on. We wouldn't need a car so we'd save that way too. And the music scene there is off the charts. I asked Pauline about it in the interview. She said Greenwich Village is like fuckin' Mecca for musicians. I mean, *Dylan* and *Hendrix* and about a million other people started there."

"How much better than Shark Attack?"

"A dollar more an hour. Forty bucks more a week."

"I can't believe you would do this to me. Things are finally going so well for me here."

"I'm not doing anything to you. I know the timing is bad, especially after how well things went tonight. I'm just asking what you think about moving. That doesn't mean we are moving. But I think you'd love New York, O. You'd *thrive* there."

"Oh come on, let's not bullshit around. You're asking me to leave L.A. You're asking me to throw everything away when I'm finally getting somewhere." She started to protest and I interrupted. "OK, no, wait. You're asking me to *think about* throwing everything away. Like there's a difference."

"Maybe it's the full moon that's getting us all riled up."

The full moon was a button in the sky that wasn't doing anybody any good.

"I'm not saying it's an easy decision," she said. "It's just that L.A. has played itself out for me. I'm graduating. I think I need a change. I grew up in Dublin, O."

"So what?"

"So Dublin is a city with history, with atmosphere, a city you can *live* in. New York has the same kind of gravitas. Everything is there. I do love our life in Venice, but something is happening to my soul here. You don't see guys with fake tans and women with fake tits driving around New York in fifty-thousand-dollar convertibles. I want to get out of here. I want to live in Manhattan and get into publishing. I want us to live a different life now."

All the time I'd known her I'd never seen such a look of yearning, of longing, of urgency on her face.

"You've obviously felt this way for a long time. I don't know why we haven't talked about it before."

"I don't know. I was getting restless but it didn't have a focus, you know what I mean? It feels like maybe it's now all falling into place. You know how it is. Sometimes your life can change just by turning a corner, or losing a key. Look what happened to us. Two minutes at Shark Attack and that was it."

"And I suppose after a few years, when things are hopping for me there, you'll want to leave New York and move back to Dublin."

"Is that a question?"

"I don't know. Is it?"

"You don't have to come with me right away, you know. I wish you would."

"Sounds like you've already made up your mind."

"No, I haven't. I don't mean it to sound like that."

"How else is 'you don't have to come with me right away' supposed to sound?"

We watched the lights of the city for a while. The longer we stood there the more pieces of my heart were left on that spot when we walked away.

"Let's go home," she said.

A couple of days later, after agreeing not to discuss it until we calmed down, I said, "Baby, listen. I love you more than anything in the world. But I can't go to New York. It's my future at stake. If I went to New York I'd resent the hell out of you for doing this to us. It would destroy everything. Fuck it all up forever."

"For 'doing this to us'? Tell me how you really feel, love. OK, that's it. Because the same goes for me. If I stay here I'll resent you for making me pass up this opportunity."

"Hey, you're the one. Everything was going so well until you decided to apply for a fucking job in New York without telling me. You put what's important to you above what's important to us."

"It was Amy. She pushed it. The whole thing gathered its own momentum. Yeah, I'm ultimately responsible, but you have to leave room for the mystical things that come along in life, the magic, things no one can explain. Your Good Samaritan, what was her name? Laurie?"

"Lorelai."

"Lorelai. She was one of them for you. I mean, obviously they're different. She rescued you from hell and this is just a job, except it's *not* just a job. You know what I mean, right?"

Kiera had two weeks to decide and time was running out. For days on end we argued, we cried, we each held our ground, and at one point we both decided in favor of the other. Finally, one night I went out for a pack of cigarettes I didn't need. I realized that I couldn't keep her from this. I was angry and confused, but I understood what was necessary. When I came back I said, "I think you're right. You should go. But I can't go with you."

We were both stunned. Something about this time was real, not just another argument or decision that went nowhere. We were so devoted to each other, and yet there we were. We made love. Sad love. Heartbreak love. Kiera cried.

"We're going to have to split up, aren't we?" she asked afterwards.

"I don't know."

She took my hand and put it against her cheek, kissed it, and gave it back to me. "If you change your mind and come, and I hope you do, it would be such a relief. I'm scared. I'm afraid that we won't be able to keep our marriage from dying. But I totally understand why you need to stay here. I admit I would do the same if I were you."

We had to wait three months, until the middle of June, for Kiera to leave. The wait was like a slow hanging. Emily and Greta were very sad that Kiera was leaving.

We saved everything we could for the move. The money from Shooky was long gone. Kiera worked as many extra hours as she could at Shark Attack. I asked for extra hours at work but didn't get them.

Kiera's graduation was a bittersweet moment for us, signaling the end as it did. Connor and Nora came over and stayed in a hotel in Westwood for the graduation celebration, and we had to pretend that everything was hunky-dory with us; we let them think we were both excited about moving to New York.

"Only a six-hour time difference for our phone calls," Connor said. "And New York to Dublin? The flight is over before you know it."

He'd declared to me at Christmas the year I went back to school, "Well, son. I think it's official. You're not an idiot after all." He didn't say it in jest. It was more like a decision he'd arrived at after a great deal of thought. We were drinking single-malt whiskey in the kitchen. There was nothing to do but laugh.

I was planning to drive to New York with Kiera to help her get settled. We were looking forward to the road trip. But the day before we were to leave, I got booked on a ten-day-cheapo-shoe-string-shitty-motel tour opening for a folk group called The Messengers, going north up the coast, Santa Barbara, Monterey, San Francisco, Santa Rosa, Ashland, Portland, Seattle, Bellingham. It was a big deal for me. My first tour.

When I told Kiera, she said, "Well, that's what I mean. Mystical things. I'm so happy for you and so proud of you! But I'm really sad that you're not going with me. But OK. Life sends messages. I'm supposed to go alone. This really tells the story, doesn't it, O?"

"I hope it doesn't tell the whole story."

At sunrise the next morning we made love one last time. It wasn't sad, but rather a powerful affirmation of our love for each other. We both knew the deep, abiding affection we were so overtly expressing that morning brought to light the painful awareness that in those very same moments we could be losing each other. We ate breakfast together although neither of us was hungry. The time came. We loaded her things into the car. Maxwell was staying with Emily and me. Kiera had been picking him up and holding him and kissing him off and on all morning. We tried our best to keep from crying but it was impossible. We wept like it was each other's funeral.

"What are we *doing?*" I said, holding her close.

"We'll do this long distance and see what happens," she said. "What other choice do we have?"

Twenty-Eight

The tour was fantastic for the one hour I played every night and the late-night partying with The Messengers, but the rest of the time I was preoccupied with my fear and anxiety about losing Kiera. I was pissed off that my first tour had to be like that.

By the time I got home I missed her so much it was almost beyond my comprehension. Long-distance calls were extremely expensive. We tried to keep our calls to an hour on Sunday evenings when the prices were cheapest, but that was impossible. Our phone bills were astronomical. We were already planning for me to visit, but the money we were spending on the phone calls was depleting the savings for the trip.

Since Emily had at least temporarily lost her best friend and I had, at least temporarily, lost my wife, we clung to each other. It's not that her need for Kiera was anything like mine, but they'd lived together for three years and did everything together. She and Greta and I became a trio. They came to some of my gigs and on other nights we'd hang around, get stoned, go up to the Troubadour or go to the movies.

Kiera was getting along great with Pauline, felt needed and appreciated, and lived in an attic room on the top floor of Pauline's somewhat dilapidated brownstone on West Eighty-Eighth Street. She was always taking Kiera around the city, to the theater and to the Museum of Modern Art, introducing her to all the magic of New York. "I just met Joan Didion!" Kiera told me about a month after she'd arrived.

I didn't know who she was, which made me feel even further away from her. "That's fantastic!" I said.

One night in early September Emily, Greta, and I were walking home after picking up some Chinese take-out and I was quietly, but evidently obviously, freaking out.

"Owen, what's the matter?" Greta asked. "You look preoccupied. You look like you need leeching." She'd been in a great mood lately. They'd made her manager of the record store, and more importantly she'd given up on Aaron and was going out with a guy she liked. I hadn't met him yet and I have no memory of him, so maybe I never did.

Emily looked at her quizzically. "What did you just say?"

"He looks like he needs bloodletting," Greta said. "It's supposed to be a joke. So kill me already. But I think I made my point."

"Kiera *loves* New York," I said. "She's meeting writers, going to parties, hanging out with Pauline Yasgur. I couldn't get her on the phone tonight. Our Sunday call, you know? There wasn't any answer."

"Oh, don't worry. Nothing's *happened* to her," Emily said.

"I'm not worried about that. I'm worried that she's met somebody else."

Greta looked at me funny. "You mean you guys have agreed to be faithful?"

"Of course they have," said Emily. "They're *married*."

"Owen, you never told me that you agreed to something as crazy as that."

"Don't listen to her. Kiera loves you. Remember that," Emily said.

"Yeah, but there are literally about ten thousand guys her age at NYU," Greta said.

"Greta, please!" Emily punched her gently in the arm.

"It's true. Let's face it."

"You're ruining my night," I said.

"Only because you're thinking about this all wrong. Monogamy is a fantasy under these conditions. Three thousand miles away from each other? You're a musician. You could get laid constantly if you wanted to."

"I don't want to."

"And neither does Kiera," said Emily.

"I know that too. I do," I said. "Except I don't."

"Look," Greta said. "You need to decide what you want more, your wife or what you're working for here."

"I don't think this is an either/or choice," Emily said. "There must be a way to work this out. Those guys are madly in love."

"Can we talk about something else?" I asked. "I don't want to wallow in this. We've got Chinese food. That's supposed to automatically be a good time."

Greta said, "You guys need to figure out an *exact date* as to when you're gonna live in the same city. If you don't know that, well, I mean, how realistic do you think this is?"

"Greta! Jesus fuck!" Emily's tone was one of surprise and outrage. We were at the house. "You're making Owen feel worse!"

"I'm sorry, I'm trying to help."

"Well, you're not."

Greta put her arm around me. "I'm sorry, Owen. It's the sad, brutal truth."

That night after she went home Emily and I sat up smoking a joint. I was down, full of fear. "I don't think I can hang on to her," I said. "To tell you the truth, I don't know why she married me."

Em was dressed for bed and so was I. She wore baggy shorts and an oversize, sleeveless Mr. Natural t-shirt and nothing on underneath. That night I was vulnerable, afraid of losing Kiera, and especially afraid in that moment of what I had to admit was my very real attraction to Em, which had been there from the beginning, albeit in a dormant, suppressed state, for obvious reasons. Now we were sitting close enough on the movie palace couch to easily hand the joint to each other. In spite of my best intentions, I tried to detect if she was feeling something too. Not that I would do anything about it, I told myself. I asked her if she wanted a supercharge.

"Oui, je suis toujours d'humeur à ça!" She laughed.

"What?"

"It's French."

"Duh."

"It means I'm always in the mood for that."

"Oh. Well *that* was a waste of time. You coulda just said it in English."

"I wanted to be sophisticated for a minute."

"I don't think sophisticated people like to smoke dope in their pajamas."

"Oh shut up, I'm not wearing pajamas. Donne-moi la supercharge maintenant s'il tu plait."

I wrapped part of a matchbook cover around the joint, put the burning end in my mouth. Emily leaned in to me. Our faces were two inches apart. I blew the smoke into her mouth. She looked into my eyes and she smiled. It felt like my whole body smiled back.

"Now let me give you one," she said, pretending it was all logistics now.

She sent a perfect stream of smoke into me and it was even more intense. We were about twenty seconds away from anything-can-happen. Emily moved back a little while we looked at each other.

"Kiera told me you're exactly what she needs, Owen. You're so different than anyone. Somewhere along the road you learned how to talk to women. You've lived a crazy life, which gives you a certain kind of romantic edginess. You're a great guitar player. You're an orphan. You've been in jail. For girls like us that's pretty exotic."

She deliberately didn't look at me when she said that. Instead she got up and went to the refrigerator. "You want a beer?"

I said I did. "How long ago did she tell you this? Two years? Maybe it's all worn off by now. Maybe that's why she left in the first place."

"She told me that the other day, actually. She was crying. She misses you more than you know." Emily handed me the beer and plopped down next to me. It took military discipline for me to avoid looking at the outline of her tits on Mr. Natural's happy face. But I've never been much of a rule-follower. I wanted to devour them. I began to internally panic. This time *I* moved back a few inches.

"Em, I have to tell you something."

"Yeah?"

She seemed to anticipate what I was going to say. The way she folded her hands in her lap.

"I'm just kind of reporting this as a fact, without any ulterior motive so don't read anything into it, OK? I'm so fucking attracted to you right now it's driving me a little crazy. So if I suddenly get up and leave the room, you'll know why."

She started reading the label on her can of Pabst Blue Ribbon. Without looking at me she said, "Me too. So if *I* do, now you'll know why. So we'll agree that we'll stay here and talk and neither of us better try to do something, right? Cheers on that?" She held up her beer to me.

"Cheers," I said, with the best intention, tapping my beer with hers.

We drank and then we kind of unintentionally slammed our beers down on the table at exactly the same instant, as if to emphasize our resolve. Little foam volcanoes erupted from both of them and then we both reached for the same cigarette at exactly the same time. That seemed to be the funniest thing either one of us had ever done in our lives. We laughed until we cried and we kissed once, a tiny, tiny, insignificant little meaningless nanosecond of a kiss that meant nothing, it meant nothing more than that we were housemates having a routine night of good conversation, helped along by a little beer and weed. And I would learn approximately one second later that when another insignificant, meaningless kiss with Emily was drawn out a bit longer, the two of us were in big trouble.

We stopped and she jumped up quickly and stood on the other side of the table. While she was doing that I backed up until I was sitting on the wall end of the arm of the couch. We looked at each other with a mix of confusion, fear, shame, and lust.

"Looks like Greta was right," I said.

"Jesus-H-Christ, Owen! One of us is gonna have to move out. Now that it's out in the open. It's a disaster. If we fuck we'll both lose Kiera. Even if we never said anything it would never be the same."

"I know. I'm sorry. I've been feeling this and denying it for a while now. I *love* Kiera. I'll move out. This place is suffocating me with memories anyway."

"I love her too. I'm the one who's sorry. I pretty much knew this was gonna happen too. I feel terrible." She came over and sat down next to me. "I'll say one thing." She took my hand, maybe to show me that we could still be close. "You're a dear friend, and that's all we'll ever be to each other."

"I totally agree."

A pause, looking into each other's eyes with all the conviction we could muster. And then we kissed. Gently. And then again. And again. And then we gave in to each other and made out with vigor. For about five minutes. It was delicious. When my hand, with a mind of its own, slipped under her t-shirt and began playing with her perfect tits, teasing and squeezing her nipples, which were wide awake now, perky and alert and ready for anything, she responded by biting my earlobe and scratching my bare back. That drove me crazy. I was now about one breath away from fucking her. And then we both leapt up off the couch and sort of screamed.

"OK, OK, OK, OK!" I said. "Holy shit."

Emily lit a cigarette and said, "I'm gonna call my cousin Lisa now and get the hell out of here."

"Good idea," I said. "Good idea for sure. And when you leave I'll have to toss one off. Otherwise I'll go insane."

"Don't think about me when you do."

"Don't think about me when *you* do."

"If we think of each other, just tonight, will that be cheating?"

"I don't know. I don't think so."

"Me neither."

Ten minutes later she was at the front door.

"Well, I'm outta here."

"You know, I feel guilty, and if I had to do it over again I wouldn't. But wow."

"Yeah, well. Damn. Life is sad sometimes. Let's not fool ourselves. One of us has to move. This will never work. I know I said that already. But I have to say it again."

"I think maybe Greta would move in here with you if you think that would work and she'd give me her apartment. She'd love to get out of that little place."

"Excellent idea. I gotta go now."

And she was out the door. I smoked a cigarette and tried to clear my mind. Fat chance. I jacked off thinking about her and then fell into a miserable guilt-ridden sleep on the couch.

The next day after I got off work and Em got out of school, we went over to Greta's. She suggested we go down to the beach. We walked to the boardwalk. I saw Warren in Shark Attack and we waved at each other. It was painful for me to walk by, which I did all the time, but now, knowing what I'd done the night before, it was worse. It changed the tenor of my memories, sullied them. Em and I looked at each other and I think we were feeling the same thing. Our awareness was heightened because we were still attracted to each other, probably more so now, and there wasn't a switch to turn it off.

"Let's sit for a minute," I said, dropping down on the sand when we got close to the water. The ocean was never anything but nourishment for me, but that day it didn't take.

"I have a proposition," I said to Greta. "How about you move into the house and take Emily's room, she'll move into my room, and I'll take your apartment?"

"She can take your room," Em said. "I don't have the time or the energy to move."

Greta looked at both of us and smiled. "Hmm. So what brought this on?" She said to me, "Why would you want to leave that sweet little house for my crappy apartment?"

"Because if I stay in the house, Emily and I won't be able to keep our hands off each other."

"Oh my baby Jesus! After that conversation last night? Did you guys fuck?"

"No. This is like the Cold War," said Emily. "Mutually assured destruction keeps the worst from happening. But we did fool around for a few rather intense and admittedly delightful minutes."

"You rascals. I hate to say I told you so. It's human nature. Monogamy is an insane concept to begin with, but in this situation? It's like trying to keep a fish from swimming. Emily, you're totally cool with having an ex-Mormon weirdo move in?"

"I have a thing for ex-Mormon weirdos. They're more liberal than atheists."

"And we're clean too. Owen, did you ever get in touch with Kiera? Last night you were kind of strung out. Oh, wait. You were kinda busy."

"Very funny. It was late anyway, and she's three hours ahead. I'll try tonight. I'll have to tell her about the switch."

"What are we gonna tell her about why you're moving out?" Emily asked.

"I don't want to lie."

"Owen, we *have* to lie."

"Why? If we tell her the truth it'll show her how devoted I am."

"It'll show her how *dumb* you are," said Greta. "There's something called the merciful lie, my dear friend. This is the time to tell one."

Emily said, "If you tell her I will *kill* you. And if you tell her, it will kill her too."

"OK, look. I'll tell her Greta needs a change and I need a place to myself. Too many memories, which is true."

"Much better," said Greta.

Emily nodded. "That's the story."

Part Four

September 1973 – February 1977

trust your heart
if the seas catch fire
(and live by love
though the stars walk backward)
   –E.E. Cummings

Twenty-Nine

After what happened with Emily I had to get to New York as soon as possible. I pawned my guitar — a Martin D-28 I'd bought, at cost, from work — and a week later I hopped on the red-eye. When I got off the plane at JFK Kiera was there at the gate, a divine vision that made me laugh and cry at the same time. I had never experienced a moment like that before. We held each other for an eon or two. The smell of her hair, the feel of her body so perfectly aligned with mine, the softness of her white cotton top, the passion and tenderness of her kisses; the sights and sounds of the airport disappeared, fading into nothing.

"What are we *doing?*" I whispered, her hair caressing my face. I would only be there for four days, going back on Sunday.

"I don't know," she said. "Let's not talk now."

When we got back to the house, Pauline had breakfast ready for us. I liked her immediately. She was not what I'd imagined. A short, plump woman with wild white hair, and, as Kiera put it later, a smile that had a history of overcoming things you don't smile about. She hugged me and kissed me on the cheek like she knew me.

"Oh my," she said. "Isn't it wonderful that we've finally met?"

"Yes, it is. Thank you for making Kiera feel so at home."

"Well, she didn't need *me* to make her feel at home. It's like she was born here. But thank you. Come have breakfast.

You must be starving." She served up scrambled eggs, bacon, homemade blueberry muffins, orange juice, and coffee.

Kiera said, "Pauline, you're amazing. Thank you!"

We sat down, a happy trio, and ate together. I couldn't take my eyes off of Kiera. She was glowing. New York had been very good for her. It scared me. It made me want to never leave her. We couldn't stop smiling at each other. Our knees were touching and it felt like foreplay.

"I've only seen the outside and the kitchen, but I love this house," I said.

The house, Pauline said, was built in 1901. "I bought it in 1951, when for some reason nobody understood the value of this neighborhood. We're half a block from Central Park! How could anyone not get that?"

After breakfast Pauline said, "Don't worry about helping to clean up. I'm sure you have a lot of catching up to do." We protested, but she insisted. We went up to Kiera's attic room, which was quite a bit bigger than it sounds. She had it set up much the same as she did on Breeze Avenue. The same bedspread, the picture with Connor at Mullaghmore, of Nora, and the one of her mother at the piano. Added to the pantheon were several pictures of the two of us. If you craned your neck out the one gabled window, which faced south and let in a decent amount of light, you could see the trees in the park. Across the street in a brownstone just like Pauline's was the International Student Center, a dorm and community hub for cash-strapped itinerant kids to hang out in, meet people, and have a place to sleep. Pauline said she loved seeing young people from all over the world coming and going on the block.

We made love, my precious Kiera and I, and slept some and made love again and talked until afternoon. Good things had been happening for both of us. She had just published a short story called "The Gift" in *Story* magazine. No small thing. It was autobiographical and a bit risky, about a girl who's jealous of her younger sister. The story is written from the jealous sister's point of view. The night before the morning the mother dies, she gives the younger sister a black onyx ring that the narrator wants badly. Things deteriorate after that.

As an older sister Nora was a braggart and, at times, cruel to Kiera. Her vitriol was rooted in jealousy. It was like an illness she suffered for which there is no cure. Their mum, like Connor, had openly adored Kiera, and when she died Nora was just twelve. She was robbed of any chance to show her mum that she was just as lovable. Nora taunted Kiera off and on for years, ridiculing her for, among other things, "copying Da's liberal politics" and wasting her life reading novels and poetry. Kiera's story explored all of that.

Nora had become so awful that when the time came for Kiera to go to college she told Connor she wanted to get as far away from her as she could. He agreed that UCLA was a good idea. It's so ironic that Nora played a huge part in inadvertently and blindly enriching my life far beyond what I ever could have imagined, by unknowingly helping Kiera get to Venice. I never got around to thanking her for that.

§

Later that September afternoon in New York, it was sunny and warm and Kiera and I were as happy as we had been on our best days in Venice. As much as it was exhilarating, as much as I was totally smitten and enthralled with my wife, it was confusing too. Why weren't we together? Why this crazy separation? Of course I knew the factual why but I didn't understand the "depth-of-soul why" or how we'd resolve it.

She asked me if I wanted to go to The Boathouse in Central Park and have coffee and dessert. "You'll love it. It's beautiful and there probably won't be many people there at this hour on a Thursday. If you want, we can rent a rowboat!"

She had a bike, and I borrowed Pauline's. We rode at a good pace down Central Park West, me following behind her, astonished at how much in love with her I was. Once again I flogged myself for being the world's biggest idiot. I'd forgotten the passion, the intensity, and most importantly, how we could simply be with each other. I should have at least come sooner and checked out the possibilities for myself. At a stoplight I said, "Hey, let's check out some music in the Village tonight! Who knows?"

"Yes!" she exclaimed. "We'll go to Folk City. You'll see what I've been telling you about! Yay!"

§

Philip T. Briggs, age 31, taxi driver, New York City Taxi and Limousine Commission hack license number 148437, medallion number 9H72, was driving his cab on East Ninety-Third Street when Professor Genevieve Stanton of Columbia University hailed him on the corner of Madison Avenue. She was late for a presentation she was giving on Jupiter's moons at the American Museum of Natural History. She told him she'd give him a big tip — double whatever was on the meter — if he could drop her off by three o'clock. Briggs promised he'd get her there on time.

He roared down Fifth Avenue, swerving in and out of lanes, getting ahead of a few cars only to be delayed by others. Then there was the M79 bus entering the Seventy-Ninth Street Transverse blocking Briggs' access for some unseen reason for two light changes. Professor Stanton made noises expressing frustration and Briggs was eager to make up for the delay. Once they were roaring through the Transverse they caught up with the bus. Professor Stanton encouraged Briggs to *pass* it — a dangerous move and about as illegal as you can get. Briggs agreed. His success was confirmed by the angry honking of the bus driver. Now as he flew through the park Professor Stanton relaxed a little. Briggs felt confident that he'd get her there on time.

As he rounded the last curve and drove up the little hill to Central Park West, the light turned red. Briggs was forty or fifty feet shy of the intersection. He gunned the engine and ran the light.

§

I saw him coming. He saw me and slammed on his brakes and went into a skid. Professor Stanton was thrown forward and bashed her head against the partition, an injury that would require an ambulance. I had no time to get out of the way. Absurdly, I held out my left hand as if it might stop Briggs' skidding taxi. I don't remember the actual impact. I think I heard Kiera screaming.

Thirty

Iwoke up many hours later in Roosevelt Hospital, heavily drugged and disoriented. Kiera was holding my right hand up to her cheek as I awoke, kissing it, tears falling, smiling through them at me as if things weren't that bad.

"Hi baby," she said.

"Hi."

I discovered a cast the length of my left arm, from the shoulder on down to the very tips of my fingers, except I couldn't see or feel them. My left leg was in a cast too. Some kind of something was wrapped around my ribs, making breathing a little difficult. I was in a lot of woozy pain.

"Did they amputate my hand?" I was only half joking.

"Yes," she said, forcing a smile. "But they were kind enough to give it to us. From now on we'll use it to wave at people and hitchhike."

"I love you. Thank you for that," I said. "What really happened?"

"You were hit by a taxi. You're in Roosevelt Hospital and they're taking good care of you." She kissed me on my forehead.

I fell asleep again. When I woke up it was dawn, Friday morning. Kiera was sitting in a chair next to me, asleep. I was so sedated I thought we were at home. I remembered where I was when I felt the heavy weight of the casts on my arm and leg. I would clue into reality then fade out.

"I missed you so much," she said when I woke up.

"Me too. I promise I'll come back soon."

She started crying. Then she laughed. "You're so high."

"Look at us," I said.

"I know. We'll find a way."

I looked at my arm cast, a white ghostly thing in the early morning light. Pain throbbed from every part of it. My leg was killing me. Kiera watched me quietly, not daring to say anything.

"So what's all this about?"

"You broke your leg in three places and you broke your hand. And you've got a couple of fractured ribs."

"I hope they're not the same as the ones from those Flatville cops."

"I don't know, baby."

She didn't say anything for a long time. Something was very wrong. Through the morphine fog it hit me.

"I'm not going back to L.A. on Sunday am I?"

She shook her head.

"What did the doctor say? How long will all this take?"

"The doctor's coming to talk to us this morning."

"Did he say anything?"

"He just said he'd be here."

"But how bad is it? They must have told you something."

"We'll get more information from the doctor. Soon."

"Kiera, how bad is it?"

"He'll be here around nine."

"How bad?"

"Please, love, I'm not the doctor."

"How bad?"

She did her best to hold back a cry but it didn't work. "Your hand was crushed."

"What do you mean 'crushed?'"

"The bones in all of your fingers are broken. Multiple breaks. Bad ones, O. I guess it's better you hear it from me. They don't think you'll be able to play guitar anymore." She kissed my good hand as if to thank it for still being there. "My sweet love. I'm so sorry."

I took another look at the cast. I looked at Kiera and out the window at the city. I couldn't speak. I was too shocked for tears. She caressed my hair and my good cheek — I would learn soon enough that most of the skin on my left cheek had been scraped off in the fall.

"Baby, I'm heartbroken for you," she said, summoning up strength. "I'll be here. You don't have to be brave, O. We'll get through this."

"How will we do that?"

"We just will."

I tried to smile at her so I wouldn't seem as pathetic as I felt. "I need more pain killers. Can you please ask them?"

"I'll go and tell the nurse." She left and came back quickly. "She's coming soon."

The doctor arrived on schedule. He introduced himself as Dr. Sutcliffe. He was about sixty-five, with a less than cheerful bedside manner. I appreciated that. Nothing worse than a fake jolly doctor when you're about to get terrible news.

"In layman's terms, Mr. Kilroy, your fingers and wrist have been shattered. After two or three more surgeries you might gain a little motion. But it will never be functional in the normal sense of the word. I'm sorry."

"How sure of this are you?" I asked. The nurse came in and stopped when she saw the doctor.

"No, it's OK," he said to her. "Go ahead."

She shot some more morphine into my IV. I felt the rush. The doctor could have told me the next step in my treatment was to behead me and I would have been OK with that.

"In answer to your question —"

"I'm sorry, what question?" I asked.

Kiera said, "You asked how sure the doctor is about your hand."

"Oh. Yeah."

He looked at Kiera, who must have told him at some point how devastating this news would be. She nodded.

"I'm as positive as I can be. It's possible that someday a team of geniuses will come up with a way to restore motion after an injury like yours, but right now, I'm sorry, the damage is far too extensive for any realistic expectation of a substantial recovery."

"That's just your opinion, isn't it? I mean, I'm a survivor, doctor. All my life I've survived all kinds of bad shit. Sorry for swearing."

"That's OK. And you most definitely *are* a survivor. By any measure it's a miracle you weren't killed. One of your ribs, the one that's broken — the other two are fractured — came within a quarter inch of puncturing the aorta near your heart. If it had, you probably would have bled to death before you got to the hospital."

"Oh my god!" Kiera started to cry.

I tried to feel lucky but never got there. "Wow."

"I'm so sorry, Mr. Kilroy. I know this is devastating news. We're going to have to keep you here for a while, so get some rest and I'll come back and check on you tomorrow."

"Thank you for not bullshitting me, Doc," I said.

"I'd never do that. See you tomorrow."

"I'm so sorry, baby," I said to Kiera. "I should have gotten out of the way." Before she could answer the morphine kicked in big time and I fell asleep.

§

When I woke up I didn't know where I was, or what time or day it was. Kiera was asleep in her chair. I tried to move my fingers and I couldn't even feel them. There was some writing on the cast. *"Trust your heart if the seas catch fire, live by love though the stars walk backward."* Love, your Kiera.

I read it over and over again.

"E.E. Cummings," she said, waking up.

I broke down and cried so hard my whole body hurt, especially my ribs. "You're so precious to me, you know that?"

She smiled. "I know. As you are to me."

"So guess what?" I said, smiling gamely when the grief subsided for the moment.

"Hmm?"

"Throw me the pen." She handed it to me. "At least I can still write." I navigated the topography of the cast carefully to make sure what I was writing wouldn't look like it was written by a first-grader.

"Kiera and O live in NYC."

"Yes, we do! Sometimes mystical things happen and they're awful," she said. "I don't know why this happened. But at least I know I'll never leave you again."

"We'll always be together now that I'm a cripple."

She laughed and I did too.

§

It's slow going, this work. As I write, my left hand, even years after the accident, doesn't always let me get very far. Too much typing, even with just the index finger, and the pain can be too much, so then I type with only my right hand. It's frustrating, still, but I've come to the conclusion that it may be a good thing to slow the tempo down anyway. This remembrance is for me, in my most vulnerable moments, fraught with peril.

§

Our lawyer deposed Philip T. Briggs and Professor Genevieve Stanton, and that's how we learned how the whole thing happened. Briggs sued Stanton for making him break the law. Stanton counter-sued for her injuries. Then Briggs disappeared. Nobody in his family knew where he went. We found out that he'd stolen the cab from his brother-in-law, who'd never reported it because, like me, he hated cops and wanted to keep the problem in the family.

There would be no money.

I couldn't work during that first year. We survived on nothing. Very soon after the accident Greta boxed up my stuff and sent it to us, along with a couple of care packages. Emily came to visit on her way to Paris. She was moving there to finish her doctorate at the Sorbonne. Any awkwardness with her was overshadowed by the predicament Kiera and I were in. It was wonderful to have her with us. Pauline loved her and wanted her to stay.

I was covered on Kiera's insurance from NYU, which helped a lot, but because medical insurance companies will suck the blood out of a transfusion if they think it will make them money, we were on the hook for twenty percent of the cost of the ambulance, the three surgical procedures over the next year, the surgeon and the anesthesiologist for each one of them, the three stays in the hospital, the drugs, the physical therapy, the follow-up care, and whatever other miscellaneous charges we had.

On one bill they wanted seventy-seven dollars and forty-two cents for "gauze." We had a good laugh over that one. In fact, after living in despair over this for months, we started finding the whole thing absurd. We laughed a lot as these bills kept coming in. There was nothing to do but laugh. It was our version of playing violins on the deck of the *Titanic*.

"Hey, check this out," I said one day, sitting on a bench in the park near Pauline's. I still couldn't walk very far.

"What?" Kiera was reading something for work.

"I think I figured out roughly how we can pay these medical bills. How much do we owe?"

She laughed. One of us always laughed when the other asked, "How much do we owe?" We asked it a lot. It became a thing. We'd found a way to enjoy ourselves in the face of the

Great American Health Care Fuck Job that is always claimed to be "the best in the world."

"We owe (we always started the answer with "We owe . . . ") sixty-three thousand two hundred nine dollars and seventy-one cents. But with the interest they're charging us, by tomorrow it will be one hundred fifty-seven thousand eight hundred thirty-four dollars and thirty-six cents."

That was our running joke. But after a while it stopped being funny.

Throughout the entire fiasco Kiera couldn't help but be stunned at the cruelty of it all. Coming from Ireland, a country with universal health care, she couldn't fathom how such a system was tolerated in this country, how it was that people protested the war, burned bras, and marched from Selma to Montgomery, but never took to the streets over being robbed by the medical industry. It didn't make any sense to her.

"America the beautiful, my ass," she said one particularly stressful day. "What a crock of shit that is. We should move to Ireland."

We filed for bankruptcy. Our credit was ruined and would be for the next seven years, but that was nothing compared to having to devote the rest of our lives trying to pay off those bloodsuckers. Connor and Nora never knew anything about this. They knew about the accident, of course, but we told them that we had everything under control, which we did, in our own way. It was never a question that we'd ask for help.

During that healing time I couldn't see the future, and I didn't really want or need to. It was all about recovery. Kiera was an angel throughout the nightmare, giving me the love and comfort that meant so much to me. But I was on my own when it came to searching for an identity that was more than just that of a young man who'd suddenly lost his music.

In the end my hand was "restored" such that I could hold a book, hold a door open for Kiera, and hold a steering wheel with my palm. I couldn't pick up a glass but I could hold a cigarette or a joint. I got a job driving a cab out of Dover garage down on Hudson Street in the Village.

Thirty-One

When my weekly treatments were over we moved out of Pauline's and rented a small one-bedroom apartment on MacDougal Street, a few doors down from The Kettle of Fish. It was a fifth-floor walk-up at the front of the building. By then I could take stairs without much pain. It just took me a while. Our two windows faced west and let in plenty of light, and gave us a view of the apartments across the street. We had old, well-worn hardwood floors that took little dips here and there, red brick walls, and a bathtub in the kitchen. The toilet flushed with a chain. We loved it. And we loved the neighborhood. We were thrilled to hear that Dylan had lived only a block away in one of those beautiful townhouses near Houston Street. It was the same house where A.J. Weberman, identified by some as a Yippie nutcase, rifled through his trash in hopes of discovering some kind of world-shattering revelation, like a Dylan version of the Shroud of Turin. Among other useless detritus, he found orange peels and empty jars of Ovaltine.

The Bleeker Street Cinema, which was the Village equivalent of the Fox Venice, was a couple of blocks away, and Knockin' on Kevin's Door, a little café which soon became our home away from home, was on East Tenth Street and Avenue A in the East Village. The café was cozy and warm in the fall and winter. People could play chess, Scrabble, Yahtzee, Operation, Life, or card games. Newspapers and long-out-ofprint hardcover books were scattered around helter-skelter, and the smell of coffee from the espresso machine ignited the wisdom, to whatever degree it existed, in everyone who came and stayed a while. In the spring and summer you could sit outside with an ice-coffee or an iced tea, reading, writing, and people-watching for hours. The door was always open because there was no air conditioning.

Kevin was a big, burly man of maybe forty (tattoos, leather vest, leather and silver bracelets, a skeleton ring). A gregarious socialist with a bizarre and provocative sense of humor, he was proud of the sign he'd hung behind the counter in a black ornate Gothic wooden frame. *SORRY, WE CUNT CONDONE PROFANITY AND FUCK OFF IF YOU DON'T LIKE IT.*

Frankie (western shirts with pearly snap buttons, Lee jeans, cowboy boots) was about twenty-five. He was Kevin's partner in the café and in life, and a fantastic bluegrass musician. Originally from rural Tennessee, he was born into a musical family and played guitar, banjo, and mandolin like he'd invented them. He'd come up to play the Clearwater Festival a few years ago and met Kevin, who was a volunteer backstage. "On paper" they were a peculiar couple. Nobody would guess the relationship would even get off the ground, let alone last. Frankie was a conservative, USA-loving, flag-waving, quasi-redneck with outlandish ideas that infuriated everybody. He believed people receiving welfare were thieves. Kevin believed that one of his most sacred duties in life was to transform Frankie into a rational human being. We all kind of put up with him, we loved him, wanted to kill him, wished he didn't like shooting guns. But man, could he play! And when he did your judgment disappeared; he shut everybody up. And he loved Kevin with every misguided molecule of his being. We became good friends with them.

Greta came to visit with her new boyfriend Kalish, a documentary filmmaker from Morocco. He had just finished a film about the characters on the Venice boardwalk. She was madly in love and moving with him to Tangier. We'd never seen her so happy. Kalish was a very charming, handsome guy with a great sense of humor. Kiera and I liked him. We spent three days showing them around the city and were sad to see them go. We all promised to keep in touch more often, but phone calls were out of the question and Kiera was the only letter writer among the three of us. Communication dropped off and eventually ended.

One April afternoon in 1976 Kiera and I were sitting in Washington Square Park people-watching, smoking a joint, marveling at how much we loved the city. As always, the park was full of boardwalk-like characters. Jugglers wearing Fool's hats, addicts nodding off on the grass under trees, old men playing chess with young guys most people would dismiss as thugs, little girls with Hula-Hoops, and an amazing fiddle player who was always there and always making good money. As we took it all in that day, a young Jamaican guy, maybe eighteen or so, walked by with a little kid riding on his neck. Kiera watched them until they were out of sight.

"I think it's time we had a baby," she said.

I was surprised to feel my body clench up, almost every muscle contracting. My bad hand hurt because I involuntarily tried to close it into a fist.

"Baby, we're broke. I'm a cab driver."

"My job pays OK. If that guy can do it, we can. Besides, we could let my da help. That'd be different."

"That guy might be carrying his nephew or his little brother."

"True. But that doesn't mean having a baby is the wrong idea for us. And think about it: if it's a boy we could name him Eddie Vincent Kilroy! We'd dress him in white shoes and a plaid jacket on his first day of school."

I laughed. "And as soon as he learned to read we'd get him a subscription to the Racing Form."

"When he gets older we'd find him a gun moll for a girl-friend. Somebody we'll call Floozy O'Flaherty. Does all that sound OK to you?"

When I stopped laughing I said, "The thing is, baby, I don't think having a kid is a good idea. I've got bad genes. Terrible genes. And what if he (or she) turned out to be like one of my parents? Or even worse, like both of them? We can't take a chance on that."

"So you've decided for both of us?"

"I'm basically a useless cripple, baby."

"Oh, shut up. I'm getting tired of this whole self-pity thing you're doing. You're not a useless cripple. You're just useless generally."

"There you go," I said, laughing.

"It's time for us to move on to the next adventure. That means Eddie Vincent Kilroy. Or if it's a girl, I don't know yet. I was thinking that we could name her after my mum."

What could I say to that? "That would be perfect."

"You think?"

"Definitely. But we can't do it. I could become an alco-holic."

"You think you turned your parents into alcoholics?"

"Maybe. Maybe not."

"I don't think that's what happened."

"I *have* been thinking about going back to school."

"I've been hoping you'd say that for a while now."

"Really?"

"Yeah. What are you thinking of studying?"

"Something that will make us rich."

"Like what?"

"I think I want to write. Shooky wanted to be a writer, and you write, and I can't play music anymore and I need something."

"That's a fabulous idea, baby. You've got tons of stories to tell. I can see you writing like Henry Miller. Somebody edgy. Just don't write about us, OK?"

"I'm not promising anything."

"Promise me you'll never leave me."

"Never in a gazillion years."

"Now promise me you'll think about us having a little one."

"I promise." I meant it.

§

The same day we sat in the park talking about having kids, maybe even the same hour, Connor died. He was at home in Dublin, complained of a severe headache, and collapsed. The cause of death was a subarachnoid hemorrhage, aka an aneurysm. It's sometimes described as a "balloon" on the artery, a miniature Hindenburg that bursts without warning, flooding the brain with blood, and in Connor's case, killing him within minutes. He was only fifty-five.

"The house feels like one of the walls has come down," Kiera said when we arrived in Drumcliff. "He's everywhere here, and yet everything is wrong." Another time she said, "When we have our little Eddie Vincent, he won't have any grandparents."

The funeral was attended by about ninety people from there, and many others who had driven over from Dublin. Connor was buried in the family plot with Kiera's mother. Nora put on a big show to convince everybody that she'd been the favorite daughter. ("Da and I spent so many wonderful, good times together while Kiera was so far away.") It was pathetic.

Her big idea for Kiera, expressed the night before over dinner, was that the two of them would be buried in the plot too. "The whole family reunited in death," she said.

Kiera said, "I don't think so. Owen and I have other plans."

§

Late in the afternoon after the funeral we drove up to Mullaghmore. We took our usual walk, Count Chocula's castle up ahead, the ocean calm that day, the spring weather very pleasant. Kiera stopped us and we stood looking out at the waves lapping up against a mini-shipwreck of rocks not far off the shore.

She said, "Love, if you survive me — if I end up going first — will you promise to bring me back here?"

"Baby, you're gonna outlive me by at least twenty years."

She smiled the brightest, most mischievous smile ever and said, "God, I *hope* so!"

"I bet you do."

"And as long as we're on the subject — and this is serious now, OK?"

"Yes, darling."

"It's sad to have to say, but if I should actually have the ignominious distinction of dying before you do, you mustn't let Nora have a hand in what happens to me. I want you to pour my ashes right out there in the ocean beyond the harbor. I want to be here where my da and me were together so many times when I was a little girl, and where you and I have had so many lovely quiet walks like we are now. Do whatever you feel you have to do to put me where I belong, OK?"

"Do we really need to talk about this now?"

"Yeah, I know, but these things come up, don't they? Look what just happened to my da. Just keep Nora out of it."

"Don't worry, my lovely. I know exactly how to solve this problem."

"How?"

"I'll make sure she dies first."

She laughed. "Excellent! Now, *finally*, I know I married the right guy."

§

Kiera and Connor had talked on the phone for a few minutes on most Sunday mornings, and for the first few days after we got back to New York she could do nothing but cry. The phone rang one morning a week after we got home, right around the time that he would have called. Kiera looked at me as if she thought it might somehow be him. She picked up and mouthed to me that it was Nora.

First, "Oh really? Wow! I hadn't thought of that." Then, "Yes, of course." Then, forcefully, "No. He's coming with me. No, no, no. He's coming with me, Nora. He's my husband. I'm sorry you're divorced again, but *I'm not*. We don't have any money so you have to book the flight and we'll pay you back. Call me with the details. OK, 'bye."

"What was that all about?"

"We're going back to Dublin. There's an inheritance. I don't know why but it never crossed my mind. Nora must've been working behind the scenes. She had to have known right away. She's a lawyer."

"Goddamn, baby. I wonder what that means."

She shrugged and then it came to her. "Oh my. The two houses. I think Nora and I might be getting the two houses."

§

We sat down in the Dublin office of Connor's estate lawyer, Seamus Hart. He was a pleasant older man wearing an expensive gray pinstripe suit, one of those that has a sort of sheen to it and under the right conditions seems to emit its own light. His shirt looked so soft and so blue it made you want to swim in it. He had a smile in his eyes that seemed genuine. At the same time an unnamable, darker quality lurked underneath, a little on the grim side. He held the will as if it were something rare and precious, like one of the few surviving copies of the Magna Carta.

"There are a couple of preliminary pages I feel obliged to read before we get down to the nitty-gritty," he said.

We'd been drinking beer at lunch and I excused myself to use the restroom while he started reading the legal mumbo-jumbo. As I came back in I heard Kiera gasp and Nora shriek. Both of them froze and the room was quiet, but only for a second or two. They looked at each other and started crying and leaned over and hugged and cried some more. I hadn't heard what was said. I turned to Seamus Hart and shrugged. "Mr. Kilroy," he beamed, as if he were presenting me with a Golden Globe award, "your wife has just become a very wealthy woman."

"What?"

Kiera nodded, stood up and came to me and hugged me with her customary strength and intensity, and kissed me hard on the mouth and looked deep into me with those dark eyes that sparkled through her tears.

"Da left Nora and me *eleven million pounds*. I haven't a clue how this is possible."

"*What?*" I think I shouted it.

"I know. I know."

"I can't even comprehend this," I said.

Kiera leaned in to me and whispered in my ear. "It means we can have Eddie Vincent."

Hart said to Nora and Kiera, "Eleven million seven-hundred forty-seven thousand pounds to be precise. Your father started out with the farm he inherited from your grandparents, which over the years increased in value quite substantially. And of course he made an excellent living. He invested wisely, but he was more than an ordinary investor. He was, if you don't mind the understatement, *savvy*. And if I may say, for the last twenty years I've followed his advice. Forgive me for boasting — I don't mean to — but I've done very, very well.

"It will be helpful," Hart said to Kiera and me, "since you live in the States, for me to tell you that at least at today's exchange rate — 2.35 dollars to the pound — your half — five million eight hundred seventy-three thousand five hundred pounds — equals," and he consulted a small yellow pad, "two million four hundred ninety-nine thousand, three hundred sixty-one dollars and seventy cents." He tore the page out and handed it to Kiera.

"I'd rather have him back," Kiera cried.

"Me too," said Nora. They hugged.

I've thought about that moment. I don't know if I really did want him back. He didn't like me much. But for Kiera's sake I tried to.

Hart went back to his desk. "And then there are also the houses — the one here in town, and the house in Drumcliff. The two of you share ownership."

"The house here too? We share?" Nora asked. Kiera shot her a look. Seamus Hart seemed slightly taken aback, but he tried to hide it by smiling.

"Yes." He paused for a few seconds. "Your father understood that you might feel you have a greater interest in the house since you live in it and have for most of the last few years. But he was clear: it goes to both of you."

Nora gave Kiera a perfunctory smile. "That's fine."

Hart said, "Now keep in mind that a significant portion of your father's estate isn't in cash, but rather draws an income. He's put together quite a complex portfolio. So we can talk about how to make that work."

"How much cash is there now?" Kiera asked. "I'm embarrassed to say we're totally broke."

"You read my mind," he said. He took two envelopes from a drawer in his desk and handed one to her, the other to Nora.

Kiera looked at me, her hands trembling. "Should I open it now?"

I could feel Nora's eyes on me. "It might be a good idea in case you have questions for Mr. Hart," I said.

She took out a Bank of Ireland check made out to her for three hundred twenty-three thousand pounds.

"This is unreal," she said. She started crying again.

Hart said, looking at his notepad, "Again, at today's exchange rate, that's one hundred thirty-seven thousand four hundred forty-six dollars."

"Oh Daddy," Kiera said.

Nora looked at me. If looks could kill.

Hart said to Kiera, "I'll help you get that wired into your New York account. You'll need to retain an accountant and a financial advisor as soon as you get back."

Kiera said, "OK. Thanks so much, Mr. Hart. Can you please keep this check for me? We'll come back tomorrow if that's OK. I need a whiskey very badly and it's best I don't carry this around."

"Of course." He took the check back. "Just tell Alice on your way out you'll come 'round tomorrow. She'll understand."

"Thanks so much."

Kiera and Nora walked together to the nearest pub as if they were already drunk. They held on to each other the whole way, talking, laughing, crying. They asked each other how could they not have known? I walked several paces behind them like a Geisha. Once in the bar — I remember nothing except a blur of people and the three of us in our chrysalis, contemplating our new lives — we downed quite a few shots in quite a short time. Kiera and Nora continued streaming seamlessly from ecstasy to mourning and everything in between. I was thrilled but scared too. It was creeping up on me just how big it actually was. And I was aware of the dynamics involved and hyper-aware that Nora was too. This was their gift, not mine. Kiera and I held hands under the table, each of us squeezing from time to time, the kind of squeezing that means, "hold on." She got up and wobbled to the bathroom.

Nora and I sat there for a while, my mind in a peculiar state of jubilant confusion. She broke the prolonged silence with a bitter smile and said, "Well, well. So you're rich now,

Owen, and you've done fuck-all to deserve it. A real working class hero, you are. My da was right about you."

"What do you mean?"

"He thought you were *nothing*."

"Oh, piss off."

Kiera banged on the table. I didn't realize she'd come back.

"What's the matter with the two of you? Here we are with this incredible, unexpected gift and you're fighting? Over what?"

I looked at Nora and said, "Nothing worth our time talking about."

"I'm overwhelmed," Kiera said as she sat down. "This isn't real, is it? What the hell does a person do with money like this?"

"Grow up," said Nora. "You'll figure it out."

"Leave her the fuck alone, Nora."

"We'll give lots of it away," Kiera said.

"Yeah," Nora said, "go ahead and give Da's money away. That's just fuckin' precious."

Kiera grabbed her shoulder bag and said, "I've never understood why you're so bitter."

"I bet even now he won't agree to have children."

"I bet you're wrong."

I felt a sting then. Kiera'd been talking to her about it. I snarled at Nora, hopped off my stool, and Kiera and I booked ourselves into a hotel rather than go back to the house.

As we lay snuggled up in bed, which is something we did all the time, Kiera said, "You know that book Moonlight Wind gave us about the Himalayas?"

"Yeah."

"Let's make it real. Let's go to Nepal, take a break, and try to get some perspective." A week later we were in Kathmandu.

Thirty-Two

"It's fun to be cold," someone said. Kiera and I were eating dinner in a restaurant crowded with trekkers, some just returning from the mountains, others, like us, gearing up for going. Kiera had just said that it would be freezing at night in Gokyo, where you stay when you're at the Everest Base Camp — an altitude of seventeen thousand feet.

It was a woman sitting at the next table who'd spoken. She had a French accent. She was about fifty, with long graying hair, intense, curious, light brown eyes, and a face that had seen its share of high-altitude winds.

Kiera said, "Excuse me?"

"It's fun to be cold." The woman stated this as an irrefutable fact.

"Why is it fun to be cold?" Kiera asked.

"First, I have to say — and forgive me if you know this — the mountain should not be called Everest. The Nepali name is Sagarmatha. The Tibetan name is Chomolungma. Take your choice, but don't call it Everest. It will make a big difference in the way you see and experience the mountain, believe me. George Everest was a British government employee, a retired surveyor who'd spent time measuring the height of the Himalayan peaks, and even he didn't want the mountain to be named after him. Some lickspittle idiot decided it was a good idea. British imperialism at its worst.

"Anyway. It is cold? Yes. You'll be sleeping — if you can sleep — at an altitude higher than most of the mountains in the world. So what? It's fun. Look where you are! Some people can't breathe well. They get altitude sickness and have to go to a lower altitude. Be very careful to take your time and acclimatize to stay out of danger. Go up slowly. You first fly to Lukla. It saves many days of boring trekking through the lowlands. It's the most dangerous airport in the world, with just a tiny dirt runway perched on the side of a mountain. Part of the adventure. But you make it there and start your trek up to a village. Namche Bazaar. Stay at least two days. You'll meet people, some on the way up, others on the way down. They'll help you figure things out. You get to Gokyo and find yourself in one of the most mystical, misunderstood places on the planet, a place only a tiny fraction of people at any point in history have ever seen. The Sherpas are full of welcome. Amazing human beings. So is it fun to be cold? Yes, it is a fact."

"That sounds very inspiring," I said, "but maybe people in France have a different definition of 'fun' than we do?"

"What difference does the definition make? You either experience the Himalayas fully or you stay in Kathmandu in safety and comfort. And if I may be bold, if you make the second choice you might want to ask yourself why you came to Nepal in the first place."

I didn't know what to say. She finished whatever it was she was drinking and added, "Be careful of your assumptions. I'm not French and I don't live in France. I'm Swiss. From Neuchâtel. You should visit someday. It's a beautiful city."

"Oh, I'm sorry."

"It's OK."

Kiera and I looked at each other, a little embarrassed. She said, a little too defensively, "Well, I just want to say that it's not like we're not going. It's just that I don't like being cold, that's all."

"Good," said the woman. "I wish you a wonderful trek. And I admit, it may not be fun for you to be cold, but it's better than *not* being cold. You understand? Bonne chance. Au revoir," she said, and left, waving at a few people at a nearby table on the way out.

"She acts like we're *climbing* the goddamn mountain."

"We came to the right place," said Kiera. "We needed to hear all that."

§

The flight into Lukla was scary and made the possibility of dying from altitude sickness on the trail seem pedestrian by comparison. The pilot skillfully navigated through a maze of mountains until, after about half an hour or so, I saw the airstrip — a band-aid on the edge of a cliff. The landing was terrifying. If the pilot was just a little short, we'd smash straight into the cliffside and our crushed bodies would drop two-thousand feet into the Dudh Khosi River; if he came in too fast we'd smash into the wall of rock at the back end of the unpaved runway.

There were five of us on the flight and as soon as we got off the plane and put our backpacks on we found the trail-head and started out. The other three zoomed by us. One thing that's generally true of having a permanent limp is that you find a rhythm you can follow all the time and that's how you get around relatively easily. But on the trail I had trouble. I'd practiced on little hikes around Kathmandu, but the persistent changing topography of the trail required constant adjustment.

The trek to Namche Bazaar was the most difficult thing I'd ever done. On our second or third day we were faced with a two-thousand-foot elevation gain on a long, steep trail that climbs up to the beautiful little village. Perched on the side of a mountain, Namche serves as a kind of crossroads for local commerce, for trekkers heading to Sagarmatha or coming back down from there, and as a place to rest no matter who you are or where you're from. We stayed there for three very happy days before we were ready to continue. Of course the higher we got the thinner the air became, and by the time we walked into Gokyo a couple of days later (we stayed the night at a small guest house along the way) my neck was aching from having spent the last few days looking down at the trial, careful not to trip, and then up at the mind-blowing views of the tallest mountains in the world. The trek on that last day required us to rest every ten steps because the air was so thin. Ten steps, rest, breathe, drink water, try to slow down the confused heart; ten steps, rest, breathe, drink water, try to slow down the confused heart.

§

You don't have a good view of Sagarmatha from Gokyo, so you hike to Kala Patthar, which you might call a huge pile of rocks, from the top of which you can clearly see the mountain. But there's so much more to it than that one mountain. Once there, you are liable to start believing in God. You find yourself cradled in an embrace of a formidable, exalted beauty you can't find anywhere else. You are in the humbling presence of giants, most, in our opinion, more beautiful than Sagarmatha, which looked dark and hard, while the others, including Lhotse and Nuptse, both white with snow, and Ama Dablam with its sharp snowy peak, seemingly gentle and not as narcissistic.

Getting there was a test of fortitude and determination. We had to hike as far up into the Himalayas as we could to leave that money and the sudden complexity of our new lives behind for a while. We needed to put actual space, geographic space, between us and whatever decisions we were now able (and obligated) to make. We wanted to be careful, not because we were afraid of losing it but because we were afraid of what it might turn us into. So many rich people were heartless. And we knew then, standing there facing what we called, somewhat ironically, the "miracle of God's creation," that the place we'd chosen to go was as spiritually cleansing as anywhere on earth. It was just like Moonlight Wind had said, except more so.

The freezing wind cut through our clothes but neither of us were bothered much by it. After five or ten minutes taking it all in, we felt each other shivering. Simultaneously we said to each other, "It's fun to be cold," and laughed even though we could hardly breathe.

People around us were sharing our sense of awe, I think not only because of where we were all standing but also acknowledging how we all got there. We'd met some of them on the trail over the last week. A feeling of fellowship was in the air; I believe all of us knew that we were living a moment none of us would ever take for granted or forget. Kiera and I felt in our bodies all the hours and days we'd put in to get there, all the miles behind us, all the blisters and bad food and the magic of villages we knew nothing about, glimpses of the massive peaks in the morning, white shark teeth cutting into the deep blue sky, the peaks shrouded in the afternoon by clouds and mist, the Babel of people we encountered from five continents, and the awareness in both of us that we were where we belonged for the first time in recent memory. And standing there with those giants around us, we looked into our camera held steadily enough by a guy named Geza, a Romanian trekker with a white beard who said he'd arrived yesterday, and when he snapped the picture it came at a time when any animosity, resentments, jealousy, fear that may have accumulated over time, slipped away in the face of the mystic spirit of those mountains. We were tired and dirty and looked like hell, but oh man, were we beautiful.

"I hope we never forget how lucky we are, O. Not only that we have this money, that we can travel, but most important to me is that we found each other. Nothing matters more to me."

"I'm still madly in love with you."

"We're going to do a lot of great things together."

I thought for a minute about what that might mean and then it came to me, clear as any thought I've had before or since.

I've learned that you can experience rare, extraordinary moments of clarity if you're open to them, in which ideas, insights, premonitions, answers to long-misunderstood mysteries come to you fully formed, crystallized, present, and available in a way that's beyond thinking. Those moments are gifts that shouldn't be ignored.

"It's time, don't you think?" I said.

"You want to go get some tea? Me too, but I'd like to stay a little longer."

"I mean, now we're gonna be OK. More than OK. So it's *time*, right?"

"O, are you serious? Really, really, really serious?" She hugged me so hard it almost knocked us over.

"Yeah, baby. I'm serious!"

"Then let's go make the baby right now," she whispered.

I laughed. "Where?"

"Good question. I suppose we might kill ourselves, what with the thin air and the insane, racing heartbeats."

"I can think of worse ways to die."

We laughed and kissed and held each other tight, which warmed us up just a little bit. It was not really fun to be cold, but what the Swiss woman said was true. It was better than being not cold.

§

The trek was like stepping through a portal. Those blissful moments of transformation faded eventually, as these things tend to do, yet their echo remained.

Connor's money scared us; it smothered us with undreamt-of possibilities. I can imagine someone asking how anyone but an idiot could inherit a huge sum of money and experience anything other than bliss. The difference for us was how to manage the responsibility. Wealth is not wealth in a vacuum, it's wealth in a world full of people who've lost everything. That's no great insight, but it's an abstract notion until you have enough to make a difference, and then it becomes a moral issue. During those lonely nights in the Hotel Rialto I used to think that if I ever became rich and famous I would owe it to everyone suffering from poverty to live my life at the apex of happiness. Living any other way would be like shitting on them.

But then the question "what is happiness" comes ambling along in all its inimitable, feigned innocence, poking at you, demanding answers, making you second-guess everything you were content to be ignorant about before. In Kathmandu before the trek, walking in a side street near Durbar Square, we came across filthy, broken men with no teeth and nothing but the ragged clothes on their backs. There was one man so far beyond hope that giving him money was almost worse than not giving him anything, because it would sustain his life a little longer and thus his misery. We walked away, stricken. We had the money, the power, to make the rest of their lives bearable. More than bearable. Per capita income in Nepal was, and is, about $300 a year. But what were we to do? It was a deeply troubling realization, confusing, and a big drag. But it was also enlightening. We came up with a theory that we thought might explain why so many rich people tend to be so heartless when it comes to helping the poor. The root of their miserliness is cowardice. When you've done nothing, you avoid having to ask yourself whether you've done enough.

"We're so lucky," Kiera said. "Do you think that someday we can know that there's such a thing as a lasting happiness without guilt?"

"Shooky once said, 'Anybody who's lucky and doesn't know it in the end, isn't.' We have to remember we're lucky and try to see the rest as something we just have to figure out as we go."

Thirty-Three

Flush with the inheritance, we bought a three-bedroom ground floor apartment on Charles Street in Greenwich Village. I still live there, and I'll go back when I'm done here. It has a working fireplace, three bedrooms, air conditioning, and a garden big enough to host a party. Kiera reserved the smallest bedroom for the baby we were yet to conceive. She said, "The tiny one will come when he or she is ready." In the meantime we'd reached a kind of spiritual depth in our marriage we hadn't known possible. We spent so much time together! Of course I'd quit my taxi driving job, but she kept working for Pauline at NYU and volunteering at Bananafish.

Now that I literally had nothing but time to do whatever I wanted — something I'd dreamed about when I was playing music in L.A. — the second wave of grief about my withered hand came over me and it was stronger, and in many ways more debilitating than the first. Early on it had been more physical pain than existential, and I still held out hope for a miracle. When that faded I lapsed into a grudging acceptance. Now I felt I had nothing to do, nothing to offer. I sank deeper into a depression and gave up on the idea of writing. I convinced myself I'd be terrible at it. I tried to keep Shooky's aphorism in mind but often I couldn't live up to it. Meanwhile Kiera was thriving, and she was beginning to get really annoyed with me.

One night she laid down the law. "You either start writing something here on your own, or you go back to school, or you open a pickle store, or you do *something*. See a therapist. You're driving me insane. And I don't want to conceive our child with bummed-out sperm. It won't be good for the baby."

"But I'm *very* cheerful when we're fucking."

"Yeah, but you're depressed during the hours before, which means all your little sperm guys are lying in there feeling sorry for themselves."

"So do you want to stop trying?" I said, with more than a trace of anger.

"Of course not. I'm only half-kidding. But for god's sake, O, *do* something. What happened with going back to school?"

"I don't know. I will eventually."

"I hope so. It'll be good for you and for us."

"I went to that shrink for a while but I didn't like it. I felt too much like a freak."

"Fine. I understand," Kiera said. "So here's an idea. For a start, look for more places we can give money to. Set a goal. Ten charities that especially need help. We'll give a thousand dollars to each one. That'll make you feel better and it'll help people."

She was a genius.

§

She and Pauline created new opportunities for writers at Bananafish. Kiera created a subdivision called O'Books (as a smile to me and a nod to Ireland) that published limited edition fiction and non-fiction. She also started a monthly literary magazine she called *Breeze Avenue*.

We were invited to a poetry reading that one of Pauline's friends was putting on at a bookstore on the Upper West Side, one of those things we had to go to. We loved poetry, but this was like taking a strong sedative with a cocktail. The misery had nothing to do with the poet's talent. Her writing was quite good. The problem was the typical bullshit poet presentation: poet-standing-at-podium-speaking-in-traditional-weird-poet-voice-that-sounds-fake-and-sounds-like-every-other-poet. And then the odd, deeply reverent silence of the audience after the end of each poem. Kiera spontaneously came up with a name for readings like that: Bad Church.

"Nothing can make the brain atrophy more quickly," she said, "than Bad Church."

She decided to hold poetry events that actually got people involved. She held the events in a gallery space, and they always featured three poets. Their poems would be printed on high quality paper, in whatever color and font the poet chose, and placed randomly on the walls of the gallery. The poets were never allowed to stand at a podium. They were asked (actually, required) to memorize three of their poems and recite them to the room at various intervals. There was no schedule to refer to as to who would read what, and when.

Everyone was given a number when they entered and asked to keep it in a safe place. They were not told why, only that it was important. About halfway through the event three numbers were called at random, and the people holding those numbers would be asked to choose any poem on the wall and, in half an hour, if they felt like it, read it to everyone and explain what drew them to that piece. (If they declined they were asked to find somebody willing.) And they were asked to confer with the other readers to avoid two people reading the same poem. I went to these events with Kiera all the time. They created interest and energy and curiosity about poetry and the poets loved it. They sold more books. In essence, Kiera took the Bad Church out of poetry and offered it in an environment in which people could actually enjoy it. She was very successful.

§

Working on the charities helped a lot. I took my time; there were so many people out there who needed help. I focused on children's charities, and left-wing political publications and organizations. I also tried volunteering at Spofford, the juvy jail, but because of my gimpy hand and bad leg I didn't make the cut. When I asked what the hell that had to do with anything, a woman guard in a sergeant's uniform at the desk said, "You're what we call 'vulnerable.'"

I decided to try to write a short story about it. Kiera was thrilled.

"You're coming alive! I can't wait to read it!"

"It'll probably suck."

"It might. And it might not. Writing is all about *writing*. Keep at it and the good stuff comes."

It was the best I'd felt in a while. I put my arms around her, grabbed her ass, and took a bite out of her neck. "So let's go make the good stuff come."

She grabbed my ass too. "Let's go make Eddie Vincent, you nasty boy."

§

One uncharacteristically mild afternoon in January 1977, we were sitting bundled up in our backyard, drinking hot toddies. It was the first time we had nothing at all to do in what felt like weeks. I was busy writing and volunteering at the Jefferson Library, and Kiera was always running around doing something. It was a Saturday, and tomorrow was free too. We'd finally landed.

"I was thinking that it's time we go to Ireland," she said. "In two or three weeks maybe? We haven't been since we were there last. What do you think?"

"You're getting pretty tipsy there, kid. 'We haven't been since we were there last?'"

She laughed. "My brain. Geez. That's why I need a break. I was thinking I can go first and see Nora — we need to keep

265

you two away from each other, and even though I'm not exactly keen on seeing her either, I should. And then you can come and we'll go to Drumcliff for ten days or something. Without Nora of course. What do you think?"

"It'll be February."

"I know. But it's the only time I'm gonna be able to get away for a while. We'll be so cozy. Just the two of us with the fireplace and the books. No TV. And I think we're gonna make the baby in Drumcliff. I just have a feeling."

I had never been more in love with her. Things just kept getting better. "OK. We'll wear layers. Let's go!"

Thirty-Four

The morning she was to leave for Dublin we were both in great moods, talking and joking around, looking forward to going back to Ireland, anticipating the treat of having the Drumcliff house to ourselves.

"Hmm," she said, crossing her arms, looking at her suitcase. "It would take a large hippopotamus to sit on that and get it closed." It was full of books and poetry submissions that she was going to look over in addition to everything else. "I can leave a few things. But what?"

"You're taking a library with you, baby. I can take a few of those books with me."

"But I never know what I'm gonna be in the mood to read."

"Yeah, I know. But you're only gonna be there a week before I come over."

"I can take these out." She removed a red turtleneck sweater and a pair of black jeans, carefully rearranging the space she'd just created.

"No, take the black jeans! You're so fuckable in 'em it drives me insane. The red sweater too. Goddamn. I *love* you in them!"

"OK, OK, but that's not helping, O. Now let's focus." She kissed me. "Maybe I will let you take a few books. And I can leave the shawl." She lifted it out of the suitcase.

"Now you're talking."

"Oh my fucking god!"

I thought she'd forgotten something, or was reacting to something about the suitcase, but then her eyes widened and shut and she grabbed her head with both hands as if to protect it from itself. She fell hard onto the red-gold kilim we kept in front of the closet. "Oh my god, O!" She opened her eyes and looked at me, stunned, aghast at the pain. "My head! What's happening? Oh shit, it's so bad. Call 9-1-1!"

I called and yelled at the operator, who when she took our address sounded distracted and indifferent, as though I was calling to order a pizza. "Get a fuckin' ambulance here *now!*"

I ran to get ibuprofhen, which is like running for a water pistol to put out a house fire, but it's all we had. She took four and threw up. "I'm so scared," she said, crying, looking up at me. I have never felt so helpless and afraid. I held her in my arms and stroked her tenderly. "You're gonna be OK, my love. They'll know what to do at the hospital. I've got you, you're safe." Just before she lost consciousness she said, *"It's getting worse, O. It's getting worse, it's getting so much worse."*

The ambulance was cold and metallic and reeked of nothing but bad, bad things. It was like a jail on wheels in the sense that just by virtue of being inside it nothing good could possibly be happening. The medic was working on Kiera with an alarming degree of intensity, while the driver was hauling ass to St. Vincent's, which was about a two-minute drive away. Kiera was still unconscious and not responding. In my own vortex of fear I kept asking the medic if she was going to be all right and I kept hearing answers like "we're doing our best" and "it's best if you stay quiet and let us handle this," and why wasn't I hearing "yes, she'll be fine, she just needs X, Y or Z?" It was just as we pulled up to the hospital, the only moment I was free to be next to her before they flew that gurney out the back door, that I was able to take her hand. I watched the medics run full speed into the emergency entrance. I ran after them. And just like on TV, they bulldozed her under the terrible bright unfriendly unnerving hospital lights straight through a pair of double doors, beyond which I was not allowed to pass.

§

St. Vincent's stark waiting room. The *faux* cheerful motel-like walls, witnesses to thousands of hours of anxiety and misery, whispered sorrowful things. Every moment of accumulated sorrow, guilt, resignation and pain that those walls had absorbed over the years choked me and whoever else might have had the misfortune to be there with me that morning.

Time was glacial. After I don't know how many minutes or hours, a doctor walked toward me, her steps echoing in the somber hallway, her face already conveying the impossible. The doctor was a pleasant, well-intentioned woman, young, grave and serious in that moment, of course. She had dyed red hair with black streaks, reminding me of Sarah — her style an indicator, Kiera would have said, that she probably had an interesting life outside the hospital. She wore two small sapphire earrings in each ear, just like Kiera. In a flight of irrationality, I even wondered if they *were* Kiera's. I'd given her the earrings on the most recent anniversary of our first walk together, when she'd given me the surfboard key chain and I gave her that silly piece of driftwood. Both were on our bedroom wall in a little frame. The doctor brought me with her into a comparatively pleasant private room with a couch and two chairs. She asked me to sit down. I couldn't.

"Just tell me," I said. "Please."

"Your wife has passed away," she said. "I'm so very sorry."

§

Kiera Anne O'Kernaghan. June 9, 1951, 2:09 am GMT – February 17th, 1977. 10:44 am EST. She lived for twenty-five years, nine months, and twenty-three days.

§

Like Connor, it was an aneurism. The minute it happened she'd had no chance.

I couldn't speak. I couldn't cry. The doctor — I never got her name — put her hand on my shoulder. Her touch was warm and confident and human, and although it was there for a mere four or five seconds it was long enough to make me want it there forever and I actually felt sad — a different, lighter kind of sadness — when she took it away.

"Kiera is only *twenty-five!*" I said finally. "Her father died at fifty-five of the same thing. How could this happen *now?*"

"Sometimes these things are hereditary," she said. "It's possible, perhaps even likely. There's no way to know for sure. This could have happened at any time. I'm so very sorry for your loss."

"Did she suffer much?" I began to weep, looking down at my shoes. "She was in such incredible pain."

"She wouldn't have felt anything once she lost consciousness. My understanding is that happened soon after it began, is that right?"

"I'd say within a minute or two of when she fell on the floor."

"I see." The doctor hesitated, and then said, "There's something else. Something more I have to ask you."

I looked up at her and wiped away my tears. "Yes?"

"Did you know your wife was pregnant?"

"*What?* Oh, fucking Christ." That sent me into spasms of grief like I'd never experienced before. "But wait. That can't be true. She would have told me. She couldn't have been pregnant."

"She probably didn't know herself. Or maybe she was waiting to be sure. It was probably only four to five weeks. There's no way I could not tell you. I'm so sorry."

I collapsed back into a chair with no give to it. I stopped breathing. The room seemed to be swirling around me as if

I were falling a long, long way down into something dark I'd never escape from.

"Mr. Kilroy, take a breath. Take a breath."

I couldn't.

"Mr. Kilroy, please."

"Yes, of course I'm breathing. I'm sorry for swearing."

"Of course you don't have to apologize."

"She *didn't* know. She would have been so *happy* if she knew, she would have told me right away. Doctor, I want the baby — I'll call it a baby, can I do that? OK? I'm aware of the whole conservative thing and I don't agree with it, OK? I'm just saying I want the baby to be with her, to be cremated with her. I hope to god you haven't done anything with —"

"Don't worry. Nothing's happened. It's — we didn't do anything. We discovered she was pregnant in a blood test. Then we did an ultrasound. There wasn't anything we could do."

"My whole life just ended. She was everything to me."

"I'll call in a grief counselor for you."

"No, no, no. I'm an expert on grief. Really."

She sat with me for a while and finally asked me if I was ready to see Kiera.

I instantly knew I wouldn't. "No thank you. I can't have that be my last memory of her. Seeing her taken away out of the ambulance was bad enough."

"I understand completely." She opened the door.

"I have to stay here for a moment longer, please."

"Of course."

"She was in so much pain!"

"Remember, she lost consciousness quickly, so she didn't feel it for long."

She stood back as I cried again. I cried as hard as I've ever cried in my life. I stared at the floor. I stared at the square tiles, looking for variations. I was empty. My head and heart had left me.

A short while later she came back and asked me, gently, if I was ready to meet with an administrator and fill out some paperwork. In a weary, disoriented daze, I signed for Kiera's body to be picked up by the mortician.

For all I know I was out of my mind when I left the hospital, lost for hours or more, falling in the street like an addict on the tail end of a last fix, picking myself up, only to fall again. I was in a state of grief so deep it was psychosis.

Part Five

February 1977 – August 1979

I believe that I am in hell. Therefore I am.
    – Arthur Rimbaud

Thirty-Five

I stood paralyzed in the middle of our bedroom, confronted by audacious silence. In that room our lives were incarnated in *things*, objects we'd accumulated from our travels all over the world, gifts we'd given to each other. In our life together we had everything any couple could ask for. We were affectionate, tender, raunchy, playful, happy, always sweethearts, and always *real*. We survived the Shooky catastrophe, our separation and my accident, and the usual ups and downs that couples go through. She taught me to live in the world more than in my head, to believe in myself when I was convinced I'd die someday as a lonely man in an old roach-infested New York hotel. And in the end, we'd made a baby together. In the end we were just as much in love as we were in the house on Breeze Avenue. I'm not a religious man by any stretch, but Kiera and I knew we were blessed. We knew it from the very beginning and we knew it at the very end.

I felt panic coming on. I knew that if I stood still or sat down I would crumble. The first thing I did was unpack her suitcase, in a trance, putting every last thing back. I didn't know where some of it was supposed to go so I made up places, just as long as it was all put away. I cleaned up the carpet where she fell and threw up the ibuprofen. I washed the dishes. I threw away the clothes I was wearing, knowing, suddenly and with absolute certainty, that I could never wear them again.

And then there was the call to Nora, looming ominously ahead of me like an execution date. How do you make a call like that? Kiera was all Nora had. Over a period of about two hours I told myself thirty or forty times that it would be wrong to wait even another minute.

Finally.

"Nora?"

"Owen? What's going on? Where's Kiera? I went to the airport, her flight arrived and she wasn't on it. I've called a hundred times. I've been frantic."

"I'm really sorry."

"Let me speak to my sister."

I discovered that I couldn't speak, could not get a single word out.

"Owen, are you still there? Owen?"

I began to cry, holding the phone as far away from myself as possible lest she hear me. She said my name a couple of more times. She said "asshole" and hung up. A moment later she called.

"What is going on, Owen? Have you *done something* to my sister?"

"No," I said in a monotone. "I'm sorry I have to tell you Nora, Kiera's gone. She's . . . *gone*." Hearing myself saying those strange words. Unfathomable.

"Gone? You mean she's coming on a later flight?" On top of her voice, the desperate effort to not know what she must have known instantly.

"I mean she's gone, Nora. A brain hemorrhage, an aneurysm. Just like your da. She died here, with me, just this morning."

There was silence. Then, "Kiera is dead? She *died?*"

I told her everything. She didn't cry; that would surely come later. She was silent again, then shifted into her I'm-in-control mode, her lifelong way of coping with stress and adversity.

"I want to speak to the doctor. What's his name?"

"It's a woman. I didn't get her name. I was too much in shock."

"I understand. I can't imagine what this must be like for you."

"It's horrible." She didn't have any idea. I would never tell her that Kiera was pregnant.

"Yes. Well, I'd like you to call the hospital and get the doctor's contact information. Will you do that immediately?"

"Yes, of course." I knew I wouldn't and never did. "Look, I want you to know that I'm taking care of everything, so you don't have to worry."

"What does that mean?"

"I mean, when everything is . . . . When Kiera's ashes . . . ." I took a breath. "I'll be coming over. Kiera wanted me to bring her back and I promised her I would. I know she wouldn't want me to wait. She wouldn't want to sit in a carafe on a fucking shelf."

"She asked you that *today* and you didn't let me speak to her?"

"She told me that in Mullaghmore after your da's funeral."

"You are *not* bringing her," she said very quietly, in a tone of voice that was worse than if she'd screamed it. "I'll fly to New York and *I'll* bring my sister home. She'll be interred in our family plot with our mum and da. Of course, you will come over, but you'll come by yourself. So that's settled. I'll be expecting the doctor's contact information within the hour."

She started to hang up but I stopped her.

"Nora, wait!"

"You have something else to say."

"Yes, I do. Don't bother coming. There's no way in a million years I'm letting you try to take her from me. I'm telling you: if you come, I won't see you. Look. We both just lost the most important person in the world to us. Let's try to get through this together."

"You're an appalling human being." I heard her taking a breath and when she exhaled it came out in little gasps. "I'll tell you *this*," she said, her voice trembling. "My sister was more my sister than she was your wife. Don't you ever forget it."

I let that go. I have no clear memory of how I spent the rest of that day. I do remember that I smoked the rest of our stash of weed and downed quite a bit of whiskey, but I remember that only because the next day I saw that everything was gone.

I called Pauline and she came over with a couple of our friends and they stayed with me the next few days. The only thing I remember is that I was worried about how I was going to manage to get Kiera's ashes into the waters off of Mullaghmore.

I called our financial advisor, Linda, a brilliant woman who'd been working with money for thirty-odd years or something. She'd been with us from the first days of the windfall. She'd become like a loving aunt to us. We'd liked her immediately, although at first she intimidated us, unintentionally, I *think*. Her default, baseline facial expression was (and still is to people she doesn't know), "I'll be nice to you, but don't you dare fuck with me." Linda has silvery-white hair that she wears long, parted down the middle, and when she wears black, which seems to be most of the time, the contrast is brilliant.

I told her the terrible news and said I'd decided to give all of the money away to all of the charities we support, that I was going to sell the apartment on Charles Street, quit claim my interest in the houses to Nora, and say goodbye to every comfort I'd come to know through that inheritance. Given the guilt I felt about having done "fuck-all to deserve" the money, as Nora had said, I conceded that she was right, and so giving everything away was the only thing left to do.

After expressing her shock and sorrow and heartbreak and taking a moment to absorb the news, Linda said, "You're not in your right mind, Owen. I understand that. You're suffering so much and I'm so sorry. But don't let your grief lead you to recklessness," she said. "That would be, in a word, and with all due respect, stupid. Kiera wouldn't want that for you." I fought her on it. She told me to think more about what Kiera would want and call her the next day. At the end of the conversation she said, "Have you thought about a memorial service of some kind? I'd like to be there."

"I'll arrange it when I get back from Ireland, and of course I'll let you know."

Thirty-Six

A week after Kiera died I walked with her onto the plane for Dublin. She was in a purple ceramic urn. I held her in my arms as if she were my life preserver. The irony didn't escape me. I knew that once this was over I'd be lost forever. I was emotionally and physically exhausted.

I drove out of Dublin in as sad and miserable a state of mind as I'd ever been. I've lost Ireland too now, I thought. As much as I'd come to love it, without Kiera it meant nothing. Being there was a bad dream, a blur, a riot of unwanted emotion. I took a room with a kitchenette at the Strandhill in Sligo so I could be close to the ocean, and so I could make a little food for myself if I didn't want to see people. The room was a perfect place to grieve alone. The light coming through the two west-facing windows was soft and comforting, that kind of mid-to-late afternoon Sligo winter sky that could make you feel like nothing in the world would be better than to curl up with a book and read until you fell asleep. I lay down for an hour and couldn't feel anything.

Nora had had a week to come to a boil. She answered the phone and knew it was me. She characteristically started off with fake kindness: "Hello, Owen. How was the flight?" "Oh, you must be tired then." "That doesn't sound bad at all." "It's good it's not raining. That would have made the drive more stressful in your condition." "You've been through a great deal." And then the shift: "Of course, Kiera was my sister and I've known her all her life. About two *decades* longer than you." "I have everything arranged."

She told me that she'd scheduled the funeral at the cemetery and a memorial for Saturday afternoon at the house. "Many, many people here loved Kiera. You probably don't know any of them. I want you to bring the urn here today and I'll keep it safe. We'll have the funeral, a short ceremony there, and then you can go home."

"OK, that sounds good. I'll be there soon. It's all going to be fine. We can do it all your way, Nora. I'm sorry I was unpleasant in New York. My emotions were spinning out of control. You can imagine."

"Yes, I surely can. Well, this is a positive turn of events. I'm so glad you see that I know what's best for my sister. Whatever she might have told you she wanted, well, come on. I'm sure she was just going off on another one of her tangents."

"I'm sure you're right about that. Oh, and Nora?"

"Yes?"

"This *is* a bit awkward, but we should decide on a time to talk about what we're going to do with the houses."

"What do you mean?"

"Well, I own Kiera's half of the Drumcliff house and the house in Dublin."

"Don't try to get cute with me, Owen. My lawyer, Seamus Hart, is a phone call away."

"Seamus Hart likes me. You can ask him to help buy me out at whatever the market rate is for the two houses."

"Don't you try to fuck me over, Owen. If you do I'll see to it that you'll regret ever having had the thought."

"What are you gonna do? Make me *marry* you?"

"That's not funny."

"We're gonna be seeing each other soon. Let's agree on a cease fire."

"A 'cease fire.' We're not playing Army. This is real life."

"You know what I mean."

She grunted and hung up.

I opened my suitcase and took out a large square sheet of pliable plastic and laid it out flat on the bed. I was relieved to find that the bag of soil, sand, and little bone-colored rocks I'd bought at the garden store on Sixth Avenue hadn't broken open on the flight over. I lifted it out and placed it on the plastic. The second urn waited patiently, intact and ready for what came next. It was an identical shape to the purple one, except that it was a creamy off-white, with hand-painted wildflowers all around it. I slowly filled a large plastic bag, a bag the same size as the one Kiera's ashes were in, with the garden soil and a smattering of the little rocks. It spilled all over the plastic sheet in the process. I put the bag in the urn, filling it a little more once it was in there, until the weights of the two urns were the same. I sealed the second one with crazy glue and left both of them in the room while I went down and had a couple of Bushmills at the bar. It was my last chance to change my mind.

I drove out to Drumcliff and presented Nora with the counterfeit urn. She complimented my choice. She held it tenderly and brought it into the living room and placed it on a table she'd prepared. There were candles on both sides, and two pictures of Kiera, one taken when she was a child. I'd seen it before. She was hugging their little puppy Boing-Boing, and smiling with the kind of happiness available only to children with loving parents. She wore a little red dress, a white coat, and black shoes. The other picture was taken at Nora's second wedding. Kiera had hated it. Her shoe had come off while she was dancing with Connor and in the picture she struck an awkward and unflattering pose.

"Why, of all the pictures you have of Kiera, did you pick that one?" I asked. "You know she didn't like it."

"It's not just of her. My da's in it too."

Seeing the fake urn on that table, in the middle of the living room of Connor's house, the house Kiera had spent every holiday in, the house where we'd spent almost every Christmas even after Connor died, made me dizzy with guilt, just for a moment, in spite of my firm commitment. There was no taking it back now.

§

The next day I drove out to Mullaghmore and took Kiera one last time on our walk.

During our annual Christmas visit the walk would always be cold and intense with the wind coming in off the ocean. Sometimes Ben Bulbin would be covered with snow, looking like a giant, cresting wave. It was that way this time. I carried Kiera in my arms, hugging her to me. I stopped at the curve in the road, the part of the walk closest to the castle, where she'd pointed to where she wanted her ashes to go. I looked out at the waves now, waves that were alive with anticipation, waiting for her.

"OK, love," I said.

When we reached the little village harbor, I looked for someone willing to take us out. It had to be the right person, someone I felt comfortable with, who didn't mind me spreading Kiera's ashes. A young guy named Gavin had a little trawler. He was very much the sea-going type, bundled up, long hair billowing out from under his blue knit cap, tattoos visible on his neck and hands, and a look in his eyes that made you believe you'd be safe with him. I told him I wanted to pour Kiera's ashes into the ocean about a half-mile or a little more off the coast.

"Oh, I'm sorry for your loss, man. That's a relatively quick trip. But if you want to go we have to go now, my friend. There's a storm coming. It's not due for a while, but still."

I offered him a hundred pounds. We were both very cold and I wanted to seal the deal quickly.

He shook his head. "I'll give you fifty back then. This is nothing for me. There won't be anything else happening today. I'm glad to help."

As he got everything ready he asked, "It's just you, is it? She had no other family?"

"Not today. I'm here from New York."

"I see. She was a New Yorker then too, eh?"

"Yeah. But she was born in Sligo. She loved Mullaghmore. We both did."

"It's a special place, that's for sure."

The boat was called *Hooligan*. That seemed perfect somehow. The wind was loud and the engine was louder, so we rode out in silence. The waters were alive and wild and I took a lot of spray on the way out. I clung tight to Kiera, snug under my left arm because my hand was useless, and held on to the boat. I talked to her quietly, describing it all to her. With each new splash on the bow it was all becoming more and more real to me. I was vividly, acutely, *alive*; all of my senses were at their highest point of reactivity, which I thought was both poignant and sadly ironic. The rocking of the boat on the waves, the salt air mixed with the exhaust and the briny smell of the ocean, my darling in my arms, my pants wet against my legs, my face wet with the taste of saltwater, all of this rooted my emotions in the present. But there were moments, too, when I was lost in the fog of disbelief. How could it possibly be that only a few days ago we were talking about maybe having two kids? And now?

Count Chocula's castle looked like a child's toy from where we were. No other boats were on the water. The wind was blowing in from the west, and out on the horizon the storm clouds loomed. The sunlight, filtered through the clouds, spread in silvery diagonal beams across the water. It was about as beautiful as it could be on a cold February afternoon.

I thought I'd be weeping by this time but I wasn't, perhaps because so much of my focus was on not dropping Kiera and not falling out of the boat. Every now and then I'd turn around and see Gavin, determined, competent, nodding to me, as if to say, it's gonna be OK, man.

He slowed the boat down and put it in neutral, which lowered the volume quite a bit. "It's too dangerous to go any further with those clouds where they are."

"This is perfect," I said.

"OK." He shut the engine off. Now the only sounds were waves slapping up against the boat, the wind, and the creaking of the wood. I looked at the whitecaps breaking in the distance and all around us, and at the water just below me. That's when it really hit me, full on, that *this* was where Kiera was going. Gavin came out of the cabin with a bottle of Tullamore Dew. The boat was bouncing with a great deal of agitation.

"Take a healthy drink," he said.

"Thank you." I took the bottle and swallowed a mouthful. Tears were starting to come. The whiskey lit a lantern inside me, kept me warm. "May I pour one over the side for my wife? She'd like that."

"What's her name?"

"Kiera."

"Absolutely. Pour one for Kiera."

"Would you mind holding her?"

Gavin smiled. "I'd be honored."

I gave him the urn.

"Here you go, baby. Here's to us and to the baby we made."

I poured a healthy splash of the whiskey into the water and started crying quietly. He handed her back to me.

"I'll go inside so you can be alone."

"Thank you so much."

I opened the urn. I took a moment to try and will time to go backwards, to give me another chance to live a life with her, this time doing it right, being a better, stronger person, a better friend, more compassionate, a better listener, a better lover, a funnier husband, a man not haunted by trauma. I took that moment, as I held her in my arms for the last time, to ask the gods to give me one more chance.

Handful by handful, I gave Kiera and our precious microscopic baby-to-be to the Mullaghmore ocean. Powder and dust and bone. One handful after another, into the water they went. The ocean welcomed them. Parts of them flew away in the wind. The boat started bouncing with greater force. I watched, fascinated, as my love became the rising waves, even the tiniest flakes of her spreading and disappearing into the waters like the clouds that were moving in the high wind across the sky.

I had some left on my hand when the last went in and so I kissed it. It was almost like tasting sand at the beach. Maybe the beach in Venice. I had one more thing I had to do. This had started as one of Kiera's jokes when once we talked in greater detail about what to do when we died, and then it became part of the ritual she wanted. Very, very quietly, hoping Gavin wouldn't hear me, I began to sing:

"I'd like to be under the sea, in an octopus's garden in the shade.

We would be warm, below the storm, in our little hideaway beneath the waves . . . ."

I cried through it, tears of pain and joy and the deepest gratitude.

"Sorry, Owen. I have to ask, are you almost ready?" Gavin said. "We've only got a few more minutes."

I didn't turn around to look. "Yes, almost. Thank you." Then I laughed.

"Sorry, baby, I have to finish early. Only you would have me singing that song, and only you would have me singing it with a gale storm on its way, threatening my life."

Gavin started up and we headed back, having to tack in because the wind had gotten so strong and the waves so high. I stood at the back of the boat looking behind us, taking in as many of the waves as I could. They rose and fell and showed their salty foam to me to make it easy for me to see her.

When we got to the dock, Gavin took out the whiskey and two glasses and said, "Let's have one together." He poured us each a shot. "You're a good man. I can see that you loved her a great deal."

"Yes."

"I'm lucky like you, Owen. I adore my wife."

"What's her name?"

"Valeri."

"Here's to you both," I said.

"And to you and Kiera," he said.

We raised our glasses and drank. I could barely thank him without breaking down. Gavin was one of those people whose kindness calls upon you to believe that there's always goodness in the world somewhere, even in your darkest moments, even when you've lost hope.

About twenty minutes later as I was driving to my hotel, the storm hit. It gave me an excuse not to go to Nora's. I went to bed a little more at peace that night knowing Kiera was happy.

§

I can't pretend it wasn't strange at the memorial. People were there who I'd never met, but I knew most of them. Like at Connor's funeral, quite a few had driven over from Dublin. Everyone was very kind. I kept looking at the white urn. If anybody had known Kiera wasn't really in it, god knows what might have happened. But I was happy and proud that I'd carried out her wishes, carried them out to the letter. The way people were regarding it with such loving devotion and respect made me feel happy for her. Those people really loved her. And as they stood before it, some touching it softly, others closing their eyes and praying over it, everyone in the room walking by it several times throughout the course of the morning, it made me think. When a forgery of a Rembrandt is perfect, people respond to it as if it's the real thing. Their ignorance of the truth allows them to experience it as the real thing because, subjectively, it is the real thing until they find out otherwise, in which case the pleasure they'd gotten from the experience is replaced by outrage. In this case, nobody in that room would ever have any way of knowing that Kiera's ashes weren't in the urn. Any hint of guilt I still felt evaporated. I was depriving them of nothing.

A lot of people attended the gravesite ceremony. It was very crowded around the grave. People read poems. Some spoke about things they'd done with Kiera. Some cried quietly and said nothing. It was beautiful. There was nobody from a church. Nora spoke at some length about her life-long devotion to her sister, even congratulating herself at one point (in so many words) about how she'd helped her da "raise" Kiera after their mother died. When I heard that I wanted nothing more than to bash Nora's head in and kick her until she fell, unconscious, into that hole in the ground. Kiera would have thought that was going a bit too far, but I didn't.

When Nora was done she asked me, because she was obliged to, if I wanted to say anything.

"I thank you all so much for being here. I know Kiera loved all of you. She's looking down at all of us and smiling. We can know that because the sun is shining today. She's with us. I know that. And I know that when we walk the streets of Dublin or New York, when we walk through Drumcliff or Sligo, when we look up at Ben Bulbin, when we gaze out at the ocean off of Mullaghmore," I said, now having to hold back real tears, "my precious wife, your precious friend, your beloved sister," I said, nodding to Nora in an unplanned moment of forgiveness, "will be there with us all, always. Again, I thank you, and yes, Kiera thanks you all so much for all the love and kindness you've given her today and all the fun you've had with her throughout her life."

We came to the moment when the urn was placed in a wooden box and lowered into a space in the grave next to Aoibheann's and Connor's caskets. Even though I knew that it contained nothing but what I had brought over from a garden supply store on Sixth Avenue and Twenty-Eighth Street, I found myself becoming emotional again. A quiet, soulful cry came up from deep within me, its source being the loss, but also a cry mixed with joy, too, because Kiera wasn't there, in the cold ground, but free, out in the ocean where she belonged.

§

Before I left for the airport, Nora stopped me in the parking lot.

"I want to talk to you about the two houses. I don't feel comfortable with you inheriting them."

"That's the way it worked out, isn't it. There's nothing Seamus can do about this. You can try to buy me out if you want."

"I'll offer you what *you're* worth, not the houses, which means don't expect much. You'll be hearing from me."

"You claim to love Kiera. You gave all these people, all of her friends, this pack of lies about how you raised her when the fact is you were often terrible. Abusive. Maybe it's about time you showed Kiera some real respect."

"By acknowledging you as someone worthy of her? Don't be silly." She put her hand on my arm. "Why don't you use some of that money of yours and take your mind off her. I'm sure you'll think of something."

"You know, Kiera thought one possible reason for your bitterness was that maybe you'd suffered a serious brain injury that she'd never been told about. She preferred that explanation over other, darker explanations because it would mean your pathetic and ineffectual meanness wasn't entirely your fault."

That was a lie I enjoyed telling her. But it didn't have any impact.

"Piss off, Owen. For a lucky man who deserves nothing you certainly are full of yourself."

"I'd rather be full of myself than full of bullshit like you, Nora."

We got in our cars and I immediately felt bad, and even worse, stupid, because I'd acted like a kid fighting in a school-yard. Kiera always wanted me to take the high road. I'd never see Nora again. That was the last thing I'd ever say to her. I pulled up next to her and rolled down the window to apologize. I had nothing to lose by doing so, and Kiera would have wanted me to. Nora must have thought I was going to insult her again because she roared off without a second look.

Thirty-Seven

I did have a party for Kiera at the apartment. I say "party" because she would have killed me if I called it a memorial. We'd lost track of Greta. The last letter Kiera had written to Tangier came back undeliverable. I tried to reach Emily in Paris but didn't hear back until a week too late. She'd been without a phone due to a mistake by the phone company. Her payments for the last three months had been applied to someone else's account.

She was so stunned by the news of Kiera's death that she couldn't speak. It was like my phone call with Nora when I had experienced the same thing. When she finally stopped crying she said, "This is the worst thing I've ever heard." We tried talking for a while to catch up but it was impossible. We were too distraught. We promised to meet next time she came through New York or I went to Paris, and we've made a point to keep in touch. Writing this now makes me want to call her.

I spoke to Moonlight Wind's (Janie's) husband Basil, and he gave me the number to the bookshop (I'd lost it). She answered the phone in her customary sweet way and she was surprised to hear from me. I invited her and Basil to New York for the memorial.

"Basil can't make it but I can," Janie said. "I'm so so so so sorry, Owen. She was a beautiful soul and she'll always be with you. With all of us. I'd love to come. But it would be just me."

"That's OK. I feel like an idiot for not keeping in touch. We've missed you."

"Well, there's that Dylan line: *friends will arise, friends will disappear*. But we're reappearing to each other, so good. Basil and I are moving to Hawaii in June. The owner is selling the bookstore and Basil is tired of L.A. I'll make sure you know where we are. You'll have to come visit. How are you holding up?"

"To be honest, I'm not. I'm a wreck. I feel so fucking lost, Janie. I like calling you Janie, by the way."

"I like hearing it. It's nice."

"I'm totally fucked. I don't know who I am or what to do. I'm realizing that Kiera was a huge part of who I was and now there's this void, this emptiness that's taken the life from me. It's good I have something to do now, getting people together."

"I understand. Especially for you, with your history and all. It's horrible, Owen, but it'll get better. 'Time heals' and all that."

"Thank you. You can stay with me when you come out. We have a second bedroom. I'll pay your way, and I insist. We came into some money and I'd like to be able to do that. It would mean a lot to me."

She agreed. One of the wonderful things about her is she has absolutely no pretense about anything. I had the money to fly her out, so yes, thank you!

I felt good about the party day. The apartment was crowded with our New York friends, and Janie was a delight to be around. Kiera would have been shocked at how I'd pulled the thing off, but the truth was Pauline did most of it. I made sure to tell her that I'd continue to support Bananafish, and we discussed producing an issue of *Breeze Avenue* in tribute to Kiera.

At the end of the day I thought of Shooky again, as Kiera and I had from time to time, and in spite of the way things ended with him I wished I had a way of letting him know. But then again, why do that to him? In a way not telling him would be like burying the fake urn. On the other hand it may do nothing but harm, seeing me and knowing she's gone. In any case, I had no idea where he was. Kiera and I felt a continuing sense of loss over that whole debacle. The feelings would come and go, sometimes with months in between. Now I had too much time to think. Janie stayed a couple of extra days, and it helped to have her there and not be left alone yet.

In the days that followed, when everyone had gone and the phone stopped ringing and people stopped dropping by with food, I was crippled with grief. How was I to be worthy of surviving Kiera? How was I supposed to fill every hour of every miserable day for the rest of my life? I had to do *something*.

I cleaned again. I cleaned like I'd never cleaned before. It took all day and all night. As best I could with my crippled hand I scrubbed, vacuumed, swept, mopped, polished, recycled, threw things away, moved furniture, washed clothes — even clean ones — flossed, took a shower. Anything to keep from being in our apartment with nothing to do. And so by dawn the place looked strange, like somebody else lived there, because Kiera and I preferred a certain amount of disorder. Or maybe we were just lazy. I got stoned, took a couple of Valium, and still couldn't settle down. I finally fell asleep in an astoundingly comfortable overstuffed chair we'd found forlorn and discarded in front of a townhouse on East Sixty-Fourth Street. We called it the Fat Elvis Chair because if fat Elvis had owned it he would have sat in it until he died. When I woke up two hours later I was on the floor in the hallway with no idea how I got there.

In the early morning light I found the black onyx ring Kiera's mother had given her all those years ago, and her sapphire earrings next to it. They had not been there when I'd started. I believed that she had sent them to me, precious mementos to be added to all the others. She'd made them materialize somehow, travel, using some kind of kinetic power available only to the dead. I took the surfboard key-chain from its frame and strung it into a necklace, together with the ring, and put it on.

§

I called Emily and we talked for a long time about our days in Venice, about her time with Kiera before I knew them, about the night we almost went over the edge together, and about her life in Paris, which she said was exhilarating and challenging and stressful but, she emphasized, "There's no place I'd rather be." We agreed to keep in touch and I think we'll want to do that. I told her I was sending her a gift from Kiera and from me, and the next day the sapphire earrings were on their way.

Yahweh, our godlike black and white Tuxedo cat, who we'd rescued in an alley off of Grand Street, missed Kiera badly. He went through a period of lethargy — what I would call cat depression. No interest in food, toys, in killing and destroying lesser beings. He and I clung to each other as if we were holed up in an igloo. I finally ended up going to a "grief counselor." I paid one hundred and ninety dollars to cry in front him. He was a Buddhist. The sole insight he offered was that life is impermanence; all things arise and pass away. He wasn't entirely lacking in compassion. He was just an idiot.

§

Of all the twisted things my parents did to me, nothing was worse than putting me in the hands of Christians. People who thought it was a good idea to teach me all about heaven and hell. Like most, or probably all, young children who are taught the appalling idea of eternal damnation, I was profoundly traumatized by the descriptions. Equally upsetting in a very different way was the deep-rooted anxiety I experienced when I thought of heaven.

Even as a child I recognized that who gets into heaven and who doesn't is a decision made by the same God who, in a series of crybaby temper tantrums as yet unmatched in history, destroyed Old Testament civilizations whenever he perceived himself to be underappreciated. This age-old realization comes to each person in its own way and in its own time, and it came to me when I was eight.

Even in the beginning, knowing all things, God had to have grasped the magnitude of his problem. People were going to have a lot of trouble loving the neighborhood bully. Nobody wants to love somebody by *force*. As Nietzsche said, "I cannot believe in a God who wants to be praised all the time." The requirement that he be loved unconditionally even when he acts like Godzilla (no pun intended) has stood in the way of discerning minds for thousands of years.

But he came up with a brilliant solution: in a *quid pro quo* lacking any subtly or finesse, he offered people a way to cheat death in exchange for their undying love. He would promise them an eternal, happy life, free of pain and sorrow, as long as their love for him would be as resolute and everlasting as the orbit of the moon — no matter what he did, or what calamities he allowed to happen on Earth. In this exchange, God ingeniously gave himself permission to continue to be the most dangerous narcissist who ever existed, while still receiving the ceaseless adoration he so coveted from the people he conned.

It is at least possible (and as I write this I'm in a miserable, cynical mood) that if you go to heaven you believe, for the first five or six hundred years, that your eternal life will be nothing but blissful. But soon you'll come to understand, either through an epiphany (heh heh), or by somebody who's been there longer telling you, that the hundreds of years you've just experienced are a mere blink compared with the endless number of hours you'll have to find a way to fill in the eons that lie ahead. When the realization hits you that time in heaven passes just as slowly as it does in hell, you realize you've been had. God, it turns out, has betrayed you. But what would his reason be for inflicting such pain? He's God. He doesn't need a reason.

He's known all along that heaven is nothing more than a monotonous crawl, a banal torment devoid of any challenge, an eternal life in which you get everything you want whenever you want it, which is fun at first, but which inevitably leads you to want to kill yourself. Human beings need to want, we need to work towards a goal, we need to experience loss and disappointment now and then. But suicide is the one thing God denies you because you're already dead and you can't die twice. All this is his ultimate expression of contempt for those who have blindly fallen for his absurd promise. In the end heaven is hell. And it's not just the oppressive claustrophobia of infinity that burdens you from moment to moment. It's the terrible fact that things will only get worse if God finds out you don't love him anymore.

The moment Kiera died, infinity was no longer an abstraction to me, no longer a thought experiment about a sadistic God. This was looking down the wrong end of a telescope. I was twenty-four. I could end up living another sixty years. Maybe more. The brutal slog of living the rest of my life without her was inconceivable.

§

One morning I woke up to a massive panic attack. I thought I was going to die, that my heart was going to give out, and for a minute I thought, "Good." But I ran to the emergency room at St. Vincent's. I walked inside and saw myself back on that morning pacing in the waiting room, going crazy with anticipation and grief; I saw the doctor coming down the hallway, her gaze fixed on me; I saw the room the doctor took me into. I relived the hollow, sick feeling that came over me when she told me Kiera was dead. That emergency room was the worst place I could have gone. I ran out and kept running until I collapsed, exhausted, somewhere along the Hudson River. When I woke up it was dark and cold and a hopelessness permeated the city, but I believed only I could feel it.

In the next few weeks I had more panic attacks. I began to think of suicide. It would work like nothing else. Sarah had known that. I could give everything away like I'd thought of before, but this time I wouldn't ask Linda. I could just get a lawyer to write up a will and mail it to her the day I killed myself, like Sarah had mailed her letter to me.

I managed to convince my doctor to give me a prescription for Nembutal and anti-depressants. They helped a little, but many mornings I woke up in some strange part of the apartment not knowing how I got there. Of course having the Nembutal was like having a loaded gun sitting on the kitchen counter. I was tempted. Every day I was tempted.

One morning about four o'clock I woke up, staggered into Kiera's study, grabbed a pen from her desk and wrote *most people are worse off than you*. I didn't remember that when I woke up and didn't see the note for a couple of days. I avoided going in that room unless I had no other choice. When I saw it at first I was stunned. Kiera had written it to me. I recognized her handwriting. When I looked at it again it was my handwriting. But the note provided the answer I needed.

Thirty-Eight

Isublet the apartment and spent the next two years moving from place to place, seeking out people who were far worse off than I'll ever be. Before I left, I took copies of my driver's license and passport to Linda just in case I was robbed. Pauline agreed to take Yahweh while I was gone. I told them I just needed to "get away for a while." I went to the poorest places in the world, deliberately making myself come face to face with the most extreme depths of human misery. I stayed in the worst hotels and hardly ate anything at all. I "enjoyed" the famine in Ethiopia. It made me feel better. At least I wasn't starving. I expressed gratitude to the cosmos for allowing me to spend time in the horror of Karachi's shantytowns. The decrepit smells coming from inside the tin huts and cardboard houses, garbage rotting everywhere, and the toilets — really no more than buckets of shit — made me feel better.

I spent some time with a dead man I met in a back alley in Jakarta. I was wandering around one night and followed the stench. By that time I knew quite well what death smelled like. The stink that hangs over a corpse and everything around it makes you gag. We deny death in America. We hide from it and when it comes it's a shock, as it was for me with both Sarah and Kiera. But for the people I met during my depraved odyssey into human pain, death was a nosey next-door neighbor ready to come visit at any time, without an appointment.

It was impossible to know anything about that dead man's life, only that it had ended brutally. Several dogs were fighting viciously over his intestines. His face was missing. I knew he was a man only because of his clothes. His was the worst smell of death I'd ever encountered because of what the dogs were doing. I spent the next hour throwing up on the way back to my hotel. But it still made me feel better. At least I wasn't him. Not long after that when I was up in Bangladesh, I mistook a woman's leg for the root of a banyan tree. She was suffering from a case of elephantitis that was so bad she couldn't move. Her leg was too heavy to lift. There was no way she would ever get up off the ground. I felt better then too.

Two years of this! I could go on and on. It all made me feel better. I wandered around the places where filmmakers shoot television documentaries to show the world bloated babies with flies crawling around their eyes. That sort of thing. I soaked up the real. I never stayed very long in any one place except Calcutta, where I spent the last four months of my time traveling, because of its staggering variety of human pain, its proximity to Bangladesh, and, unbeknownst to me at the time, the toll my emotional and physical exhaustion was taking. But I spent my days and nights deep in the jungles of self-deception, denying that any of the previous twenty months had taken any toll on me at all.

Don't think that when I say all of this made me feel better I didn't try and do something about it. I would give all of these people money; I would help them in whatever way I could, whether I was sticking around for a while or passing through. My ability to pitch in was limited with my hand being what it is. I'm ashamed to admit that when I found a way to give some help to whichever humanitarian agency was present, which usually involved some person-to-person contact with the afflicted population, I experienced a perverse pleasure experiencing someone's misery up close. Its proximity had a greater impact. That's when I felt best. Most of the time my help never really amounted to more than me

donating money. I probably gave away ten or fifteen thousand dollars over the time I was out there, all to individuals
who may have been incapable of improving their own lives,
like the man Kiera and I came across in Kathmandu. I'd send
a wire to Linda and have her take care of the details as to
how to get the money to people. I have to admit that all of
that made me feel better too, but not so that it made any real
difference. If I were really a good person I'd spend my life volunteering in Vietnamese orphanages.

Thirty-Nine

L ast September I left Calcutta. I needed a change. I took a train third class to Varanasi — the holiest city in the Hindu religion. Pilgrims travel there from places far and wide throughout India. To make it to Varanasi is a spiritual milestone of profound significance. People go to bathe and purify themselves in the holy waters of the Ganges River, and people go there to die.

I checked into a disgusting little hovel in the Old City called the Hotel Indra on a street that smelled of curry, garam masala, and piss. The monsoon season was not yet over and the street was ripe with rain-soaked filth. It was only about noon and the hotel already felt like an oven. My room was small, with cement walls and a tiny window overlooking the back of a restaurant, with flies buzzing around several open garbage cans. I had developed a talent for finding the worst places to stay.

I was eager to watch the cremations on the banks of the river. I walked into the crowded streets. My state of mind was brittle. I felt exhausted and anxious. All the traveling I'd done and the accumulation of human horrors I'd witnessed were wearing me out, and it was then, walking to the cremation ghats, that I first felt the weight of it all. I knew that I was having another bad day and that seeing the dead burn would likely make me feel better. But I also knew that things had begun to shift. The brutal sun seared its way through my skull and the skulls of everyone around me. It was more than oppressive. It felt deadly.

Bodies are burned on wooden funeral pyres. According to Hindu belief, to be cremated on the banks of the Ganges in Varanasi is a means of releasing the person from samsara, the miserable cycle of life and death. The cremation ghats — sacred spots on the riverbank — are busy all the time, the endless numbers of the dead coming without interruption all day every day. I couldn't wait to see them.

Varanasi is an ancient city, built little by little over more than three thousand years, and the streets near the river are laid out helter-skelter; you may think you're going in one direction and find out you're going in another. I looked for a way down to the ghats, and after several frustrating dead ends I came upon the entrance to a narrow alley. I looked over the heads of people sitting on the ground on both sides of the little walkway and saw boats on the river. I took a step forward but had to swerve around a woman sitting against the wall whose arm bumped my leg, and that's when I really looked at the people for the first time and saw that they were all lepers. Twenty, maybe twenty-five of them. A gauntlet of lepers — men and women of indeterminate ages, all on the verge of starvation — sitting there staring at me with hollow, sunken eyes. There was no choice but to walk past them to get to the river. All of them started moaning — imagine the low, mournful tones of twenty-odd lepers slowly dying together, and leaning toward me, even those furthest away, holding out fingerless hands, their flat, stub-like palms the place they begged me to put coins. It was loud and overwhelming. It was as if they'd been waiting all their lives for somebody, anybody, to walk into that alley and finally, *finally* . . . .

I'd seen lepers before but this was different. So many all at once in such a small, narrow space. But mostly it was the way they sounded and the way they looked at me, eyes popping out of skeleton sockets, the dreadful expressions on their disfigured faces — most without noses — physically knocking me back a step with the magnitude of their need and desperation and hopelessness and despair.

They would be grateful for anything I could give them. A morsel of food. A rupee. A *paisa*. (The exchange rate was twelve rupees to the dollar, and there are one hundred paisa in a rupee. Imagine.) Of all the myriad encounters with human suffering I'd had, of all those moments when I walked away from others' pain feeling better, I wasn't prepared for this. Nothing could top what I was seeing in that moment. According to the way I'd lived my life for two years, the sight and sounds of these poor sufferers should have made me feel better for weeks. They surely lived in that alley, dragging themselves down to the river when they had to piss and defecate. Or maybe they stayed where they were. The smell in the alley was terrible but I couldn't parse out all the elements in it and didn't want to. There was nothing left in life for these poor people but to wait to die. There was no hope. I was shattered. I found myself unable to walk any further. A panic attack was just moments away. And then it hit me hard — the way they were all moaning, thrusting their palms out at me, the woman closest to me persistently bumping my leg with her stump of a hand, looking at me, looking through me, her need was so great — I suddenly understood that I was dead wrong about them not having any hope. *Their hope was me.*

I was shaking as I reached into my pocket for money. I didn't have much with me, maybe five or six rupees. I never carried much; I'd been basically starving myself. The panic came. There were so many of them and I didn't have enough. I couldn't breathe. A cruel voice in my head asked, *"What's the matter? Don't these people make you feel better?"*

I handed a rupee to the woman, smiling now with rotten teeth and devastating gratitude, moaning some kind of thanks, sounds that tore me to pieces. The rest saw me giving her the money and they all started groaning louder. I quickly handed out the other five rupees. Most of it might have landed on the ground. I might even have just thrown it down. I don't remember. By then I was in a full-blown panic attack.

I stood with empty hands looking at those who didn't even get a paisa from me. I knew they couldn't understand me, but I said, "I'm so sorry. I wish . . . I promise you I don't feel better about any of this."

I'd finally hit a wall. I'd become human again and was filled with self-hatred. I turned and ran, and found another way down to the river. All the horrors that I'd seen came rushing back to me, all of them sought out so I could make myself feel better about losing my wealthy, white, Irish wife! How pathetic and repulsive. Everywhere I'd gone I'd seen suffering children; many were dying. Now I hated myself for deriving a macabre and freakish pleasure out of the fact that I was not one of those kids. My childhood had been bad but the children I saw who were starving to death — well, how could any person worthy of anything good on this earth derive any pleasure from seeing them? I wanted to die. I was sick to my stomach about how thrilled I was not to be one of those lepers, or any of the other unimaginably destitute people I'd seen.

I'd made a colossal mistake. A mistake that had been made possible only because of the money I'd inherited from Kiera, money that allowed me to travel the world feeling sorry for myself. I was totally humiliated, even knowing that nobody who knew where I was knew the real reason I was there. The one answer — the last possible answer — I'd come up with to recover from the emptiness, the loneliness, the futility of life without Kiera was to initiate an immoral, repugnant, and wicked exercise in exploitation of the poor. The shame I felt was fatal. Any remaining hope I might have had for a life I could be proud of evaporated. I had never been a saint, but I had at least thought of myself as a reasonably decent man. Not anymore.

I walked back to the hotel and took exactly fourteen Nembutals in honor of Sarah, and wrote a note to the proprietors for the inconvenience of having to deal with the fact that I was leaving everything I owned behind. I went back down to the river with nothing to identify myself. That was really the point; I was nothing and nobody. I sat on the riverbank next to a funeral pyre upon which a body, wrapped in white linen, festooned with flowers, was laid out. Soon flames, growing larger and larger, were dancing in the wind off the river. As my Nembutals started to take effect, I hoped, by my death on the Ganges, that I might never have to come back to this world.

The man working the fire, unsatisfied a few minutes later with the way the body was burning, struck a smashing blow to the now-visible blackened head with a club. The head broke open, parts of bone shooting out in all directions, and with the rush of oxygen now coming into it, I heard the accelerated hiss and snap of the fire accompanied by the roar of higher flames. It was a frightening thing to see.

I looked at the sky through the rising smoke as I felt myself dying. A giant monsoon storm cloud was overhead. I understood then why the man working the fire was so intent on speeding up the burning. There was about to be a deluge.

"Forgive me, Kiera. You've gotta give me a break about this. I've tried. There just isn't enough left. You took the best of me with you."

My little speech felt empty and stupid. The power of the drugs really started to kick in. I was now sitting on the steps of the ghat, the river only two or three feet from me. The water didn't look holy, it looked dirty. I reached down and put my left hand in the water, thinking maybe by Hindu magic it would be restored to normal. That would be interesting. The water was lukewarm. I couldn't feel any sign of a current. The water was stagnant and useless. The water wasn't holy for me, but then, I thought, why would it be? The water knew I deserved nothing.

The head, now in pieces, burned faster, as did the rest of the body of whoever that had been only so many hours before, or maybe as much as a day before. Another body was burning on a pyre a little further away, and it was further along, but this one, the one nearest me without the head, was the one I wanted to be.

Forty

My eyes opened onto a dark room that smelled terrible — unwashed humans and mold, if mold can grow in such surroundings, and if it wasn't mold I didn't care to know what it was. I had a band on my crippled wrist but it was too dark to read it. An IV tube was stuck into the back of my other hand. I wore a flimsy hospital gown that was wet with sweat. As I emerged slowly into consciousness I wondered why it was so hot in the middle of the night. I looked around and couldn't see my clothes. I wanted to check the time but I remembered I'd left my watch at the hotel with everything else.

How did I get here? The silence in the room made me think everyone was asleep but when my eyes adjusted I sat up and could see that all of my roommates were awake, staring into space. I looked at my wristband again and this time I could just make out the words: "Name and Date of Birth Unknown. Admit: 30 August 1979." Was this the place reserved for those who failed at suicide, all of us stunned and depressed at our ineptness?

I asked myself if I was glad to be alive. No response. I imagined Kiera looking down on me in that sad, sad room. Nothing was worse to me than disappointing her. I just didn't know if she was disappointed that I'd tried or that I'd failed. I had to pee very badly. I stood up and fell back onto the bed. A nurse appeared out of the shadows and escorted me to the bathroom, my IV pole dragging along behind me as if it were a reluctant dog on a leash.

"You must be careful," the nurse said.

My throat was sore (I know now that was a side benefit of having my stomach pumped) and I wanted to ask for water but didn't. I was afraid of menacing bacteria.

"Where am I?"

"In a hospital. The electricity is out, which is why we have to walk in the dark."

"What is that room I'm in? It smells terrible."

"It's the room for the poorest."

I went into the bathroom and when I came out the nurse was standing there waiting for me. She wore a light-blue uniform and a matching nurse hat.

"The administrator would like to see you now if you feel up to it. She'd like to know who you are."

"Now?"

"Yes, please."

"Isn't it the middle of the night?"

She looked at her watch. "It's just past ten-thirty on Wednesday morning."

"How long have I been here?"

She took my wrist in her hand and read the admission date. "You arrived Sunday."

"How bad was I?"

"It was my day off. Where are you from?"

I already felt disoriented, woozy, and off balance, but hearing that I'd been there three days made it worse. "I come from nowhere. I don't think I can walk very far," I said.

She went and got a wheelchair. The office of the administrator was on the same floor. It felt like a long way. The nurse said nothing as she guided me down the corridor, which was lighted by some means I didn't understand and didn't care about anyway. It was eerily quiet for a weekday morning. The prevailing smell now was vinegar and soap. I entered the outer office feeling self-conscious and embarrassed in the wheelchair, the flimsy gown lifted above my knees, the IV pole awkwardly banging against the doorframe. I took no semblance of dignity with me into that room.

The nurse knocked on the administrator's door. "The unknown patient, Dr. Shukla."

"Bring him in, Ms. Adani," I heard her say.

Once again, my nemesis the IV pole created new navigational problems that were harder to solve than they seemed at first. Finally I sat opposite an attractive woman of about forty, wearing a white blouse and a barely visible gold heart necklace with the most delicate chain you've ever seen, the links so tiny they were almost invisible. She wore elegant tortoiseshell glasses and kept her long dark hair pinned back. Her eyes were dark and intense, not suspicious, but curious in a way that gave me the impression she might be very annoying and inquisitive. Still, she appeared quite relaxed, and she'd created an atmosphere in the office that, with a lot of help from the morning light shining through her tall, wide window and the profusion of plants, made me feel a bit less anxious. Her white doctor coat hung on a hook on the wall, a stethoscope peeking out of a pocket.

"I'm Dr. Sarojini Shukla. And you?"

"Owen Kilroy."

"Ah, Mr. Kilroy. It's good to know you have a name."

"Yes, I guess so."

"I'm sorry, we had to go through your clothes to see if there was a way to identify you. The only thing we found was this." She opened a drawer and handed me a small paper bag with "Unknown Patient" written on it. Inside was my necklace with the surfboard keychain and Keira's ring. It was the only thing I'd taken with me on my way out to die.

"Thank you."

"Why this and nothing else?"

"They're the most precious things in the world to me." I took a moment to hold them, to feel the familiar wood and metal and stone, and then put the necklace on.

"Do you want to tell me more about that?"

"No. Sorry."

"I understand." She told the nurse she could go. To me she said, "You know you came within a hair's breadth of succeeding in your suicide attempt."

"How did I not succeed? I took fourteen Nembutals."

"Maybe you have good karma," she said cheerfully.

"Or bad karma."

"Oh, come on now, you don't really mean to tell me you're not happy to be here in this beautiful, state-of-the-art hospital?" She laughed. She made me laugh a little.

"What's up with this place?"

"It's run by the government."

"Oh."

"You're here because you had no identification on you. You're an American?"

I nodded.

"Where from?"

"New York City."

"Ah. I went to medical school at Columbia and did my residence at Mount Sinai. So you'll understand then, what I mean when I say this is the Potter's Field of Varanasi's hospitals."

"Yes. How did I get here?"

"I believe a tourist found you. Where are your belongings?"

"I left my things at a hotel in the Old City. I gave everything away."

"I see. When you say everything?"

"Clothes, watch, wallet, money, passport. Everything."

"You weren't messing around."

"No, I wanted to die, no doubt about that, Doctor."

"All of your things will be long gone by now. Can you give me your date of birth please?"

"October 9, 1952."

"You'll be all of twenty-seven next month. A very young man."

I said nothing.

"One of the things we need to take care of is your bill. It's not much by American standards. Can you have someone send you funds?"

"Yes. But assuming I decide to stay alive, which is still up in the air, I'll need to get a new passport before I can pick any money up, won't I?"

"I don't know. I suppose that's true. If so, you'll need to get to either Calcutta or Delhi."

I began to feel dizzy. The thought of getting on another train was exhausting. I was dying of thirst and afraid of the water. I'd met people who drank the water in India and were sick for weeks, sometimes months.

"Do you have any bottled water?"

She called for the nurse to get me one.

"So you have money to pay your bill, then?"

"Oh yes. You know, I'm so tired. If you have a room, do you mind if I stay a couple more days? I'm weak and very depressed. But I can't stay in there," I said, gesturing toward the room I'd been in.

"Forgive me, I have no reason not to trust you, but I have a concern: if you stay here and kill yourself, it would be most unfortunate. I would feel like I failed you. And then there's the problem of the hospital not getting paid."

"Isn't that really the same problem?"

"What do you think?"

"Since this is a government hospital I think you don't care as much about getting paid as you do about making me feel I need to pay you, so I won't want to kill myself while that important, unfinished task is still hanging over my head."

"Very good. You are lucid."

A man brought in the water and I drank almost all of it.

"I have an idea," I said. "If I can call New York, I can have the money wired to you directly. I mean, you'd have to be the one to claim it. Is that possible?"

She sighed, sounding a little frustrated. "That sounds like the only way that makes sense. I don't know what time it is in New York."

"I'm really sorry this is so inconvenient for you."

She called for a Ms. Ramasastry and when she came in, an older woman whose very presence suggested competence, Dr. Shukla asked her to find out the time difference. When she left, the doctor asked, "Now, would you care to share with me why you tried killing yourself?"

"No, I don't think so. Nothing personal. The thing is, I don't know you, and obviously this was the deepest kind of private decision."

"Do you feel *any* relief that you survived?"

"Unfortunately, surviving seems to be the one thing I'm good at."

"But?"

"Sitting here with you is pleasant, even while being filthy and wearing this horrible gown. You're a nice doctor. If I keep my focus on you and me in this room, then to be honest, the answer is yes, I feel some relief. But if I think about what's waiting for me outside your door, the answer is no. Quite the opposite."

"Fair enough."

Ms. Ramasastry returned with the information. "We are twelve and a half hours ahead of New York."

"Fantastic!" the doctor said. "Thank you."

"My pleasure," Ms. Ramasastry said.

"I don't know what I'd do without her," the doctor said, holding her gaze on the door that Ms. Ramasastry just closed. "She's going to retire soon and it puts me in a bit of a panic."

"It must be a big job running a place like this."

"It is. But I feel like I'm doing something here that wouldn't be as valuable in other places. Most people here have nothing."

"I really admire that."

"Thank you." She looked at me in a way that set up a new, more personal dynamic.

"There's a lot of good in this world, Mr. Kilroy."

"Yes, I know."

"What time should it be in New York when you call?"

"I think about ten in the morning would be a good bet."

She checked her watch. "We'll arrange for you to call tonight at eleven-thirty then."

"OK, thank you."

"In New York I worked in the emergency room for a year as part of my residency. Some of the things I saw there were beyond description. Gunshot wounds, knife wounds, overdoses, heart attacks, car crash victims, you name it. Do you mind me asking what happened to your hand?"

"Funny, it's exactly what you're talking about. I was riding a bike with my wife on Central Park West and got hit by a taxi. I went to the emergency room at Roosevelt."

"That's awful. I'm sorry. The reason I'm asking you — telling you about my experience — is because some of those gunshot wounds were self-inflicted, as were some knife wounds. Believe it or not, considering all the options, some people still stab themselves. And of course some used your method of choice, which is the easiest and therefore the most popular: overdosing. And I want to tell you something about all of the serious attempted suicides I've seen. I say serious because I'm not talking about people who just want attention, I mean people like you who really did want to die. Every one of them that I spoke to afterwards were happy they survived. And I think deep down you probably are too. Don't you think it would be a good idea to call your wife and let her know you're OK?"

Even people as kind and well-meaning as she was make mistakes that hurt, although I couldn't blame her. She was looking at my wedding ring, which I had never taken off.

"I tried to commit suicide, Doctor, because my wife died suddenly of a brain hemorrhage. The ring in the bag was one Kiera wore all her life. The keychain was a gift she gave me the first time we took a walk together. We were just kids then. She was only twenty-five and pregnant with our first child when she died two years ago. I couldn't get over it. I can't get over it. I've been wandering around without hope. I feel like I'm nothing without her, and I know how pathetic that sounds, but what can I say? She changed my life in more ways than I can count. I was nothing before I met her and I'm sure that has a lot to do with it." I didn't want to give her the whole seeing-human-suffering story. That was even more pathetic.

"Tell me a little about her."

"I don't want to take too much of your time."

"I run this place. I can do what I want." She smiled proudly. "How long have you been in India?"

"A long time."

"Then you must be well-acquainted with Indian bureaucracy and its infamous inefficiencies."

"Oh yes."

"Here's the thing: when I choose to be, *I* am that inefficiency. Whatever else I'm supposed to do today can wait."

I laughed. Really. I hadn't thought that was possible. I ended up telling her the whole story. She sat and listened and asked good questions. I cried a few times.

"There were times soon after she died when I was strung out on grief and Valium, unable to even feed myself, and I couldn't distinguish between whether a memory I was having was one of my own or a dream-hybrid from one of the foreign films she took me to. It was quite weird. She was a film major and so wanted me to like those movies. And after a while I did.

"My memory crisis didn't last very long in chronological time, maybe a couple of weeks. But in 'grief-time,' I experienced abysmal suffering. Kiera's death caused me more dissociation from reality, more emotional disintegration, and far more internal chaos than I ever could have imagined. It was only after time passed and a hint of clarity returned that I could count on guessing correctly where a memory had come from. Not whether it was accurate, but what its origin was. That was really important to me.

"I learned much too late the value of not resisting. As the episodes came to an end I actually began to miss them. I came to understand that each one of those crazy delusions, longer and more complex than ordinary dreams and invariably ending in loneliness and isolation, had at least allowed me to spend just a little more time with her. But the thing is, had I been aware that all that was a sort of gift I would have tried to force them and then they would have disappeared sooner. I don't know what else to say."

"That's remarkable, and obviously very painful. When you get back to New York you might want to find a Jungian psychologist to help you understand these dreams."

"Yeah, that would be helpful."

By the end of the conversation I was tapped out, but something in me had shifted. I was permitting myself to see and accept a stranger's goodness and genuine human compassion. And this almost completely against my will, my persistent drive to obliterate myself.

"Of course I'll pay to stay a couple of more days, Doctor, if you can find a room for me. I just can't stay where I am. It's too depressing."

"I'll have Ms. Adani find you one."

"I have money. I'll pay double."

"And I will accept your offer. That's very kind of you. Tell me, are you familiar with the French writer Georges Bernanos? I've read a couple of his novels. He was kind of a mystic, a sort of poet. I ask because I feel I need to address your fears, not that I'm a psychologist. I like you, Mr. Kilroy, and I don't want you to kill yourself. And especially not in my hospital!"

"OK. As for the writer, an old friend of mine studied French literature and she may have mentioned him. The name rings a bell."

"He said, *'Hope is a risk that must be run.'* I don't mean to be pedantic, and I suppose that's how this is coming off anyway, and if so, my apologies. But you might want to take heed of that. What do you plan to do now?"

"I don't know what I'm going to do. I don't even know whether I'm going to go on living. I don't say that for sympathy. It's just a fact. I'm about as lost as anyone can be."

"Don't you think your wife would want you to go on living?"

"I don't know."

"We've known each other for a very short time, Mr. Kilroy, but I think you do. From what you told me about Kiera and the kind of person she was, I think you know very well in your heart that she'd want you get over her death and move on."

After more conversations with Dr. Shukla over the next two days, in which she continuously reminded me through her humor, charm, and wisdom, that things can get better, I felt strong enough to leave the hospital. After I reassured Linda that I'd suffered nothing more serious than a mild bout of dysentery she sent the money directly to Dr. Shulka, along with a copy of my passport, driver's license, and plenty more cash for me to get to Delhi and back to New York.

Before I left for the station to catch the night train to Delhi, I brought a gift to Dr. Shukla's office, unsure whether she'd be there. It was an expertly crafted bronze statue of Avalokitesvara. When she unwrapped it she was speechless for a second, looking at it, then at me.

"Oh my. I don't know what to say."

"As I'm sure you know, Avalokitesvara is the bodhisattva of compassion, the 'Hearer of the Cries of the World,'" I said. "You've done that for me and for so many others."

"Mr. Kilroy, this is beautiful. I'll treasure this. I'm so glad I could help. Thank you so much." She put it in a prominent place, on the table near the window. "When this place drives me crazy, he can hear my cries too."

We shook hands like friends.

"You have everything? Copies of your ID and so forth?"

"Yes."

"Good luck. Have a safe journey. And umm . . . one last piece of pedantry? Is that OK? Can I take a parting shot?"

"Oh boy, here we go again," I said, joking.

"This is a pretty famous and therefore overused quote from Joseph Campbell, who's become something of a pop-cultural cliché ever since *Star Wars* came out. You know of him?"

"I've heard of him."

"Well, this is worth hearing in your situation, I think, if I may be so presumptuous. He wrote, *'The cave you fear to enter holds the treasure you seek.'*"

I felt threatened by the truth of that. "It wasn't presumptuous. I think it's a powerful statement; a little too much for me right now, to be honest. Kind of overwhelming. Can you write it down for me? Then I'll have it to think about."

"Not only will I write it down, I'll write it as a prescription." She took a prescription form from a desk drawer, wrote it out, and signed it. "*The cave you fear to enter holds the treasure you seek.* Read twice a day or as needed until happy."

Part Six

June 1980 – July 1980

Even the losers get lucky sometimes.
– Tom Petty

Forty-One

All that was ten months ago. It's now June 1980 and I write in the old house I rented outside of Montauk, on the end of the Long Island peninsula. I've had Dr. Shukla's prescription taped on the table in front of me since I started writing here last October. Now I've caught up with myself. These last months have been painful reliving it all, but Yahweh and I, we've gotten through it (now he's out in the yard, stalking seagulls, thrilled that it's summer), but I'm not sure what good any of it has done. When I came back to New York in September of last year, twenty pounds underweight, depressed after my suicide attempt, confused about almost everything, I spent a week or so restless, doing nothing, which was making me crazy. Nothing felt right. I still wasn't sure why I was alive and why Kiera and Sarah weren't. I said nothing about any of this when I met with Linda. We went over money issues, reviewing Kiera's and my charities, and now I added annual donations to Dr. Shulka's hospital and orphanage.

Nora had twice sent an offer to buy me out while I was gone. She undercut both the houses' value significantly, especially the one in Dublin. This came as no surprise. I'd told Linda that if Nora sent over an offer while I was gone, to ignore anything that was below a certain figure. So that was that. I wrote Nora a letter telling her that she either make a reasonable offer or I was going to donate my half of both houses to Sinn Féin.

She responded with a letter full of vicious insults, telling me how I was 'defiling' Kiera's memory. But in the final paragraph, after she'd shat all over herself, she made me an offer that I could accept. I donated all of the money to medical research on brain aneurisms.

I had lunch with Pauline, saw a few friends. But there was still that void. After a couple of weeks of this I knew I had to leave the Village again where our ghosts, Kiera's and mine, were still around every corner. I heard that this house was for rent from a real estate agent and Yahweh and I moved in about a week later.

§

Last night I felt empty again, unfinished, incomplete. I dreamt that Kiera and I had locked ourselves inside the house on Breeze Avenue. We boarded up all the windows, nailed the front and back doors shut and barricaded them with furniture. We painted the walls black in every room. It was hard work. Finally, exhausted, we sat down on the big red velvet movie couch to rest. It was so dark we couldn't see each other anymore. "You have to stop hiding," she said, sitting there in the dark, holding my hand. "Only if you stop hiding will we be able to get out."

I've had hundreds of dreams of Kiera since she died and I always try to remember details but most of the time I can't. The dreams are usually just the back end of a gust of wind by the time I'm awake enough to try and write them down. Her presence is always still there, but untouchable. But in this one she gave me a message. *She's* stuck too? I'm somehow keeping her from being where she should be? Is that possible? If I let her go will she stop appearing in all those shop windows on Bleeker Street?

The thought of going back to Venice, to Breeze Avenue, to our beach, to Santa Monica where we got married, to experience all those memories fills me with anxiety. Haven't I exorcised enough demons by writing all of this? But all of this has been in my head, I remind myself. There's nothing *real* about it, nothing *physical*. Nothing tactile or somatic. With this writing finished, and nothing left to say about the past, I have to go to back to California. Not as a walk down memory lane, but as a reconnaissance.

Forty-Two

The house on Breeze Avenue looks the same, too much sun and too much salt air and not enough attention, yet cozy and welcoming and, in a way, still and always ours. Up until the move to New York, Kiera and I were so happy here. Passionate, playful, exuberant. She saw me as I am, as I never knew I could be; she truly loved me, possibly only the second person who ever had. I remember we'd joke that if there was a God who, for some fiendish reason, set a limit to the aggregate amount of happiness allotted to people in this world, by some cosmic blunder he had given us far more than our share. We'd laugh and wonder what price we'd have to pay for that. Now I know all too well.

I see us, two happy kids in love the first time she took me home; I see us weeping the morning she left for New York; I see myself, confused and lonely the day I moved out and Greta moved in because Emily and I came so close to ruining everything. I see Shooky leaving in a rage and his letter on the porch the next morning. *Don't come anywhere near me. Don't try to be my friend. If you do you'll regret it.* Catastrophe. All of our ghosts are here. I want to go inside. I open the gate and walk to the porch and knock on the door. I hope someone is there as much as I hope there isn't.

The house is quiet. I take a last look and walk the block to the boardwalk, festive and alive and vibrant as ever. I go back to Shark Attack. Warren isn't there but it looks the same. A young bald guy asks me if I need any help. I want to tell him I need lots of help but none that he can give me, so I tell him I'm just looking. He wanders away and I walk over by the surfboards to stand in the spot where Kiera and I first looked into each other's eyes. I close my eyes and there she is again, alive and lovely as ever. I don't feel like crying; I'm beyond that in this moment. The two of us are still here and everything about it is good. The vision shifts and I watch myself leave the store after having just met her, floating out, heading up the street to Greta's in a wistful, euphoric high.

Now I follow Kiera's and my footsteps and walk down to the beach and sit for a while at the spot I think is probably right where she gave me the key chain and I gave her the driftwood. It might well be the same place I frolicked in the waves that first jubilant day I got to Venice. It is a Tuesday morning. Almost no one is around. I feel the emotion welling up and I finally break down. I'd thought cathartic crying was over, but today, sitting in that hallowed place, I am shaken to the core by the memories. There was no earthly reason why the first time I heard Kiera's voice I knew what I knew. I had no justification for believing it. I had every reason to disbelieve it. Nevertheless, at that moment I knew my life had changed. There is no explanation for things like that, but they happen to people all the time.

Harold and Maude was one of our favorite movies. We must have seen it a couple of times in L.A. and at least a couple of times at the Bleeker Street Cinema. She saw it first with Emily. I remember so clearly her coming home and telling me about it. One scene in particular wowed her.

"It's a *fantastic* movie, O. We have to go back and see it together. It's a romance between Harold, a 20-year-old, unbelievably lonely, alienated, astoundingly rich guy with a nut for a mother, and Maude, a 79-year-old woman with an amazing spirit who lives in a caboose. They fall in love. It's a lovely relationship. By the way, the soundtrack is unbelievably perfect. Cat Stevens. Anyway, Harold gives her a gift one time while they're sitting by the ocean, I forget what, it doesn't matter. It's a very meaningful gift; she's very touched by it. And then, to Harold's complete shock, she throws it way out into the water. He looks at her, baffled and a little hurt. But she turns to him and says, 'So I'll always know where it is.' Isn't that wonderful? I think it's a beautiful idea."

I understand more fully why I came to Venice. There are other reasons too, but this, I know now, is the most important. I take off my necklace and slip the surfboard keychain off and then close the clasp to keep Keira's ring safe. I put the necklace back on and take a long look around and see nobody nearby. I close my eyes and meditate for a few minutes. I take off all of my clothes so as to have nothing between me and fully experiencing this moment, and walk naked into the surf, clutching the key chain so I won't drop it, the same way I held on to Kiera when Gavin drove the *Hooligan* out into the choppy waters off of Mullaghmore. The saltwater washes over me as it did the first day I got here from the bus station and it's cold and bracing and full of power and fortitude. I dive in and swim out as far as I can. The surf bounces me around, the swells lifting me up and letting me down and when breakers come I dive through them. The sun is warm on my back. Kiera would call this a glorious morning. I take it all in, treading water. I wonder if by now Kiera's ashes and the ashes of who would have been our child have made it here from Mullaghmore. The possibility washes over me and makes me feel connected.

"I can feel you with me, Kiera," I whisper. "You of all people will know why I'm doing this. Your gift will always be sacred to me. I told you I had no keys to put on it. And the key turned out to be you."

I kiss the key chain just as I did the day she gave it to me, and then throw it as far out as I can. "So I'll always know where it is." I wait a little longer. It feels so good to be here, so right. I swim back to shore feeling a profound sense of loss, but at the same time I feel lighter.

There are a few more people on the beach now and there's nothing I can do except walk out of the ocean as I am, and they'll just have to find a way to cope with it. But nobody cares. This is Venice. I put on my clothes, sand in everything everywhere, and looking back at where I just was, I walk closer to the water and stop and watch the sun behind me cast a long shadow that is swallowed up by the kiss of a wave.

Forty-Three

Like our house, Greta's building looks exactly the same. I can't decide whether it bothers me or is a source of comfort that nothing in Venice appears to have changed very much. It feels like I've been away for a lifetime but after all, it's only been a few years. I stand between the two doors in the entranceway and the first thing I notice is her mailbox, which in the end never held the letter she'd longed for from Aaron in Vietnam. I watch the two of us rushing into the building after I'd first met Kiera, Greta insisting I tell her "everything" as we climbed the stairs.

The outside door opens aggressively behind me.

"Is there something you want?" The voice is angry and threatening.

I turn around. A fucking cop. Acne scars. Buzz cut. Mirror shades. Cliché city. A mustache that for some reason reminds me of a fence I once saw when Kiera and I were walking along a sandy trail that led to a rocky beach on Martha's Vineyard. Dark wooden slats held together with wire, traces of light coming through, creating cool-looking slanted shadows. I'm surprised at the incongruous, bizarre association. Maybe I've taken too many drugs in my life.

He's in uniform and smells of cheap cologne. It makes me feel sick.

"No, my friend used to live here."

"If she *lived* here why are you peeking through my door?"

My deep-seated and never-very-dormant cop hatred is already percolating.

"Look, officer. I'm not doing anything wrong, OK?"

"Let me see some identification." He's so huge there might as well be a tank blocking my way out.

"I don't have to show you anything. Please step aside so I can be on my way."

Bad idea. He slams me up against the door, kicks my legs out behind me, tells me to be still, searches me with disrespect and malice, grabs my wallet out of my back pocket, takes out my driver's license and reads it aloud.

"What you doin' in L.A., Mr. Kilroy? Why the fuck are you peeking into my building?"

You can easily imagine what my response would have been ten years ago. But all that I've felt in the last couple of hours, and my liberating *Harold and Maude* ritual just now, and the still-nagging feeling that my life has no present except in so far as it is a means, or a conduit, to communicate with the past, and all the grief and wonder and gratitude that I've felt over the months-long writing process, knowing I'd once had it so good, all of it makes this ludicrous person, this mindless buffoon, completely superfluous to everything in the world that matters to me. He might as well be a tree stump in a forgotten forest.

I speak then to who, in a better world, he might have been: a good man with a brain. I haven't made this choice consciously. I'm not capable of that kind of thinking. I just watch myself talk to him.

"I used to live with my wife over on Breeze Avenue. I met her over there at Shark Attack. She died of a brain aneurysm two years ago. She was only twenty-five. My friend Greta, my best friend, lived in this building on the third floor in apartment 307. I was just re-living the day — the day I first met my wife. Kiera Anne O'Kernaghan was her name. Is her name. The love of my life. Greta was with me. We came here right afterwards. I was all excited. I was in love. It was one of the most extraordinary moments of my life. So now, today, I was here remembering how Greta and I ran up the steps, me telling her what I said and what Kiera said and all the amazing stuff I was feeling that day. That's when you came in. That's why I'm here."

This completely disarms him. The poor sap doesn't know what to do. After thinking it over, trying his best to cope with a moment of real human feeling, he hands me my wallet. "I live here. This is *my* building. Your walk down memory lane isn't going to end well if you keep peeping through windows."

I don't tell him to fuck off until I'm safely in my rental car driving away, and when I do I scream it.

§

I go back to the hotel and shower and a couple hours later I'm on the freeway. With the morning rush hour over, long-distance truckers make up most of the traffic, solitary men who can't or won't stop moving. There was a story in the paper recently about a trucker who had a wife and kids in two cities. Neither family knew about the other. Imagine. Some guys can't even get a date.

After lunch in Barstow I turn east and drive, mile for mile, back through the years. Kiera had wanted me to take her to Rockville Flats so she could see it, but I wouldn't. I couldn't face it. She asked a few times, the last time being just before she left for New York, when things were generally pretty fucked up for us. I now think she was making an effort to get closer by going there and seeing where all the shit went down for me, the way our trips to Ireland had brought us closer. But I didn't understand that then.

"Come on, O. It's probably my last chance to see it for a long time!" We were at the Fairfax farmer's market in L.A., picking out berries for a pie she was going to make. A day that should have been fun. I have no recollection of how Rockville Flats had come up.

I got angry. It was one of my worst moments, one I've always regretted.

"How many fucking times do I have to tell you no? I'm not taking you there. I'm not going back to that hellhole, ever, do you understand me? Why can't you get that through your head? I never want to see it again. Got it?"

Nothing can turn you into a bigger asshole than fear.

She told me to fuck off and, like a child, said, "I don't wanna go anyway." She grabbed two little baskets of raspberries and stormed off.

§

Signs of human life begin to wane on the drive east. The desert takes over. The sky is as big as it can be, a washed-out blue. Only a few cars are on the road. The landscape is like a blank canvas, there to reflect whatever you project on to it. I project the faces of the people I'd known.

Passing the concrete "Welcome to Rockville Flats" sign on the edge of town, I can feel anxiety start to take hold. What a fucking hell-hole. After some time driving through the nothingness, I turn down my street and pull up in front of the house. The lawn is brown. Dead. I don't know how long mom stayed. The thought occurs to me that maybe she's still there. Wouldn't that be something? But no, I bet she sold my Hummingbird and left. I walk up to the door and knock. Nothing. I start to knock again and the door suddenly opens. A tiny Vietnamese woman with silver hair and a hearing aid the size of a See's candy looks at me with deep suspicion.

"You're not Tuan."

"No ma'am, I'm not. I'm sorry to bother you," I say with as much kindness in my voice as possible, peering over her head to look inside. Her couch is in the same place ours was. There's nowhere else to put one in that room. The little hallway is dark, but I can see the door to my room is open. Suddenly something comes to me, something I hadn't thought of. Something I'd forgotten. I could feel my heart pound harder, faster.

"I stopped by because I used to live here a long time ago. I just want to take a quick look. I think I left something in the closet of that room. Under the floor."

"You can't come inside. I don't know you. You're not Tuan."

I smell something cooking in the kitchen. Food she's making for Tuan.

"It'll just take a second. Please?"

"No. Please go." She closes the door.

But now I know I can't go. I sprint to the car and grab my wallet from my jacket pocket and take out a hundred-dollar bill.

"Ma'am, I have money for you. A hundred dollars," I say as I knock again.

"Why you come back? I told you, you no come in," she says through the chained door.

"I have money for you. I have money for you. A lot of money for you." I hold up the bill. "This is for you. Just let me in for five minutes to check. Please."

I watch her thinking. I reach into the doorway to get that bill as close to her as I can. She takes it.

"OK, five minutes."

My room is set up with a sewing machine, an overstuffed chair, and a TV. There's a new blue shag carpet. I open the closet. I have to move a broken fan, a box full of shoes, and another big box.

"You be careful," the woman says.

"Don't worry, I will." I slowly take everything out, placing it near her on the floor. It's not easy with my left hand, but I manage. Now the closet is empty. She stands there holding the money.

"Hurry," she says.

"One more minute," I say, and now I get down on my hands and knees and crawl over to the corner of the closet furthest from the door. It's cramped in there but it doesn't matter. I haven't grown any bigger than I was. I take a deep breath and slip my fingers into the crack between the last floorboard and the wall. It resists. I try again and there's a little give. I pull harder and then harder still and finally it lifts. I slide my fingers into the space as far as I can, feeling along the rough edges of the old wood. And then there it is. The envelope. I lift it out carefully, as if the paper might crumble to dust.

The woman says, "You hurry up," but this time I ignore her.

I carefully remove the single blue page with the silver ink and Sarah's unmistakable handwriting. It was tucked in snugly, as if it's been resting there for years in its cozy way, waiting for me to come back. I read it quickly, as if to reassure myself that I'm not mistaken. It's the saddest letter in the world, but it's beautiful. A rush of emotion passes through me, a wave of lost love and sadness rekindled, revisited, and on top of that, gratitude. I never thought I'd see it again.

I show the woman the envelope. "This is it. Thank you so much."

"OK. Good for you. Now you go."

In the car I read it again and feel it and smell it (sadly it smells like dust) and hold it and look at the shooting star that was her return address and read it again.

§

The cemetery is the only place in Rockville Flats where there are trees you can believe in. I stop at a flower shop nearby and take my time looking for the right arrangement. I decide on one with four different kinds of dahlias, all different colors. They come with a simple, sturdy vase.

The man who works there says, "There are faucets around the cemetery. Don't fill it more than three quarters. The flowers will last longer." I thank him.

I don't know how to find Sarah. I'd been so stoned the morning of her funeral. I walk all over the place reading headstones, many with pictures on them, most everybody smiling ironically, as if happy to finally be at rest. And then I remember her trees. At the far edge, up the hill near a little dry creek, there's a row of tall, regal Italian cypresses lining the west side. One tree is slightly smaller than the rest.

Sarah's on the edge of a little hill. She must be warm in the embrace of the morning sun when the dawn breaks, and shaded by the trees in the afternoon, protected from the hot desert winds. The headstone wasn't there on the day of her funeral, just the grave, the white casket with the gold handles, the piles of dirt. There's a headstone now with her picture. She's smiling at the camera, the look on her face hinting of a secret she might have been carrying around that day. That enigmatic, mysterious light in her eyes shines through, even under the thin film of dust that has accumulated. I use water from the vase to clean it off. She comes back to life, becomes so much more vivid. The picture was taken in a moment when she trusted whoever was taking it, on a day when her hair was dyed in wild streaks of red, blue, and black. To my astonishment, her parents had chosen that picture out of god knows how many others they must've had. Sarah had struggled and fought with them endlessly over how she dressed and what she did with her hair. But in the end they'd finally let her be herself.

The inscription is simple and heartbreaking.

Sarah Veronica Dreiser
December 12, 1954 – July 23, 1970
Beloved daughter of Stan and Rita Dreiser,
Beloved sister of Penelope.

"The sun is up, the sky is blue,
it's beautiful and so are you."

They even had those lyrics inscribed from "Dear Prudence," her favorite song. I wonder if she knew they knew that about her.

"I brought you dahlias," I say out loud. I place the vase in the holder next to the headstone and make sure it won't tip over. I kneel down and kiss her. I run my hands over her name, as if I were caressing her, soothing her.

"I'm so sorry it's taken me so long to come back." I take the letter out again and read it out loud to her. "I'll never forgive myself for giving you those pills," I say. "I don't care how many times you've come to me in dreams and told me I need to."

I hear her implore me to let it go.

"But so many years are lost, Sarah. I've missed you so much. I was so pissed at you, but I was more pissed at myself. What was I thinking? What can you tell me about where you've gone? I tried to follow you there, you know. Of course you know. I still can't make any sense out of why you're gone and why Kiera's gone too, and I'm still here. You're both better people than me."

"Stop feeling sorry for yourself. You're driving me crazy. And you're probably driving Kiera crazy."

"You wanna smoke a joint?"

"Fire it up. You're still my angel."

I take the first hit and then put it to her lips and give her a drag. We smoke like that until I place the roach next to the flower vase. I slept so little last night, the weed makes me sleepy and I let myself drop off. Sarah holds me. I am comforted. I lay there with her, watching the small cypress tree lean into the taller one. I am exactly where I'm supposed to be. I look at Sarah and feel such gratitude, not just because we are together again for a little while but for the time we had. She was the first to see the soul in me, the first to show it to me and convince me it was real. She was the first person who ever really loved me. If not for her I never could have been with Kiera. I wouldn't have thought enough of myself. That may be a contradiction to me telling Dr. Shukla that I was nothing then. I don't care.

With as much presence of mind as I can I open myself up to the feel of this cemetery. It is the prettiest green place within a hundred miles. I think about what Sarah must have been like as a little kid. Stubborn, determined, madly in love with animals, lording it over Penelope and being an overall pain in the ass, independent to the point that her parents were probably already concerned, even when she was only seven or eight, about how to rein her in later on down the road.

After sitting quietly on the grave for a while longer, thinking, remembering, listening to the snip-snip-snip of the gardener's shears down the hill as he trims hedges, I know it's time to go.

"You know that to see me you don't have to come here," she says.

"I know that now. I still love you, you know, and I always will."

I kiss her goodbye, touching all the letters of her name one more time. "See you in the next world, Sarah Veronica Dreiser. Don't be late." I walk down to the car, turning around only once to look back. I blow her a kiss like I did the last time we saw each other.

I drive by her house, tempted to confess to her parents that I'm the one who gave her the pills, but I immediately reject the idea as reckless and stupid.

Shooky's house is a few short blocks away. The house is painted a mild shade of green now. It was red and white back then. There's an old brown pick-up truck in the driveway, its cargo bed holding some kind of big oily machine. The garage door is open and an old man is sawing a piece of plywood balanced on two sawhorses. He turns and looks at me. I wave. He keeps his eye on me for a minute, nods slightly, and goes back to his work. I wonder what ever happened to Shooky's mom and Stacey. People disappear. That's what happens.

§

I drive over to Rockville Flats Boulevard and park the car, get out, hop the fence, and take the walk out to Manderley. I can still see Shooky there waiting for me on that last day, raising his fist in victory. We spent thousands of hours here and every one of them saved us from going crazy. On the edge of the ravine I watch three hawks play in the wind. For a long time I stand with my eyes closed, feeling the warm air embrace me, just as it had the night Sarah and I made love in this place. The wind blows like it wants to gently send the past on its way, while at the same time the ghosts of Shooky and me smoke hash and dream of Venice. I put my hands flat on the spot where Sarah and I made love. Its gravity embraces me. I look way over to the other side of the ravine where Officer Lloyd pussied out of killing me. There might as well be a headstone over there too, memorializing the death of my first life. In honor of Shooky and me, I light a second joint. Gazing to the horizon out west, I let the magnificent view flow into me as if I'd never denied any of it.

Shooky and I had wanted so badly to escape, and we were right. There had been nothing for us here. There was nothing left to feel or to know then. But I understand now that the pain I'd suffered was only a part of it. All the rest still belongs to me. Not everything need be lost in this life. It surprises me to remember that I'd spent much of my time in Rockville Flats laughing, and what did it matter that I was always high when I did?

I put out the joint, leaving half of it unsmoked as a kind of offering to the gods. I don't pray to the gods often — I've found them to be unreliable — but sometimes they come through. I say a silent prayer for Kiera and Sarah and Shooky and me, and then include my mother and father. Those two might still be out there in the world somewhere, waking up every day, facing the struggle. Or perhaps theirs is finally over. I'll probably never know. I forgive them, ask that they be kept safe, and say my last goodbye of the day.

Forty-Four

The next day I say to myself as I sit and eat a hot dog on the Pier where Greta and I used to hang out, "Thank fucking God I didn't die." The hot dog tasted that good. Later as I drive up Santa Monica Boulevard to stop by the Nuart, I see a small shop called Shook's Books. This I am not prepared for. It adds another layer to the whole reconnaissance. I don't want to drive by so I make a turn and avoid it.

I screech to a stop near the first payphone I see, grab the phone book, and flip through the white pages. I find the page: there's a Jack Shook, a Jade Shook, a Jake Shook, a James, Jasper, Jennifer, Jeremy, three Johns, and a Judy. No Jason. I slow myself down and check again. OK. I look up Shook's Books in the yellow pages. 213-445-7171.

Now what do I do? This is not what I came here for. I betrayed him. My huge lie of omission was about the worst thing I've ever done. Such a terrible ending. He warned me to stay away. How do I know the store is his anyway, I ask myself. How do I know that it doesn't belong to one of the other Shooks I just found in the phonebook? And those were just the Js!

I loved Shooky, and all these years I've carried that moment with me when he handed me Kiera's picture and asked me to help him get her back. I was a fucking coward. That was a colossal betrayal. A devastating lie. I should have told him then, face to face. Now I have to try to make it right. If he turned his life around it would make all the sense in the world that he would open a bookstore. All the drug money he made would pay for it. I call the store and a woman answers and tells me they close at ten. If Shooky answered I would have recognized his voice and hung up.

About fifteen minutes before closing time I park across the street. I'm like a cop on a stakeout. I can't see inside. That would be too close, a guy in a car staring into the store. It's dark and the other shops on the street are either closed or closing. My heart is beating fast. I'm so nervous. I've thought about this moment for years.

I see the lights go out in the store. A longhaired guy comes out wearing a white shirt, a vest (but not red), and black jeans. I think I should drive away. Why stir up his feelings for Kiera and then tell him she died? Why do that? Now I'm convinced that I'm doing the wrong thing. Leave him alone, I tell myself. But no. Give the reconciliation a chance. Why not do *that?* It could be such a good thing. I can only see him from the back. He's locking the door, checking it to make sure it's secure, puts the key in his pocket, and then starts walking. I roll down the window and am about to shout to him when a streetlight reveals his face. It's not Shooky. The guy keeps walking and I adjust the angle of the side mirror to watch him but it doesn't turn that far, so I just turn and watch him walk a long way down the street until he disappears around a corner.

I immediately feel deflated, and it takes some time for my heart to slow down. I think I should come back tomorrow night, or call in the morning, or just walk into the store and see him. But then as I finally calm down and look at the sign over the store, I say out loud, "I hope it's Shooky's, and not just for my sake. It would probably mean he's found some peace."

Wait a minute. Did I just say "not just for my sake?" Holy Christ. It hits me hard: this whole plan really isn't for his sake at all. In fact, in the end it really has nothing, or very little, to do with him. This is like what I did traveling around looking for pain for two years. Fuck. I think I understand now that this is all about *me* making *myself* feel better regardless of how it might affect him. I was going to use Shooky to try and assuage myself of guilt, whether seeing me and telling him about Kiera would be good for him or not. What is the *matter?* Am I really that self-centered? But is it a true benevolent act, a genuine act of courage to leave him alone, or another act of cowardice, a 'noble' choice that is really one made to avoid shame? I honestly can't tell whether I'm a pussy or a better person as I drive away. I know right away that's a question I'll struggle with from now on. Maybe we'll see each other again at some point. I drive back to my hotel and head straight for the bar and order a double shot of Tullamore Dew, neat.

Forty-Five

A week later I'm back in New York, on my way out the door when I get a phone call. It's John Kavanaugh, a private investigator I hired the day I got back, leaving a message on my answering machine.

"Hello, Mr. Kilroy. This is John Kavanagh. I have some information for you. Please give me a call —"

I pick up the phone. "Hello Mr. Kavanagh. I was just on my way out. I'm glad I caught you. What's up?"

"We've found Greta Dietrich."

"That's fantastic! Wow, that didn't take long."

"She lives in London, working in a store called Spinning Web Records. She left Tangier five years ago, married a Brit, a fellow named Ainsworth, and divorced him three years later. No children. She holds dual citizenship, UK and the United States. All in all it looks good, meaning she's probably not someone you'd want to avoid meeting."

"How did you find her in a week?"

"This is what I do. I'm good at it."

"Yes, you are."

"She married Ainsworth in Tangier, and because he's a Brit it made it easier to find them in London. After that it was a piece of cake. I haven't spoken to her. But I have absolute confirmation from our London office that it's Ms. Dietrich. If you'd like to come up I'll give you a copy of the file. I have all of her contact information. Phone, home address, and of course the address of the shop."

"Thanks. That is so cool! What time do you close?"

"Normally we close at six, but tomorrow's the Fourth of July so we're closing at noon today."

"You're a stud, Mr. Kavanagh. I'll be there."

"I'm happy you're happy, Mr. Kilroy."

§

I call Greta at three in the afternoon my time, not expecting her to be home at eight on a Friday night in London but I have to try. I'm nervous and I'm not sure why.

"Hello?"

"Greta?"

"Who is this?"

"It's Eddie Vincent calling from New York City."

A gasp. "Oh my god! Owen!"

We talk mainly about Kiera, what the last few years of her life — our life — had been like. After she cries and gets past the initial shock she says, "You guys made it. You stayed together. You actually *lived* 'till death do you part.' That's wonderful. It's unspeakably awful that she's gone, but at least in that way I'm happy for you."

"If that's what 'till death do us part' means, I think I'd trade that in for 'till divorce do us part,' any day. At least she'd still be around, even if we hated each other."

"Yeah. But she died in your arms, Owen. In her last moments you were together. Whatever bullshit you went through during your ups and downs over the years didn't matter at all, did it? It was superfluous in the end, to who you always were to each other. She needed your help, you took care of her, and she was looking into your eyes, need-ing your love, telling you how much it hurt when she passed away. Couples dream of dying in each other's arms. It makes me cry thinking about it."

She actually starts crying again and goddamn it I do too.

"Greta, I've missed you. How *are* you?"

"How the hell did you find me?"

"Believe it or not, I hired a private detective."

"Wow! Do I owe you money?"

I laugh. It's so good to talk to her.

"So how am I? The short version: decent apartment, decent job. Can we talk tomorrow? I don't even know why I answered the phone but I'm super happy I did. I have a friend here and we're watching a movie."

"What movie?"

"*Some Like it Hot*. I've seen it a bunch of times. Never gets old."

"I love that movie. So let's set up a time. I have all day tomorrow."

We agree on me calling the same time. It feels like it takes forever to get to three o'clock.

§

"Kalish turned out to be gay," she tells me. "It killed me, but I was happy for him when he finally came out. It's harder for a Muslim guy to admit he's gay than it is for a Mormon. We're still friends. He's still in Tangier, making docs."

I fill her in on the inheritance, and the highlights (aka lowlights) of my life after Kiera died.

"Suicide. Wow. I've been down but never that far. Well, I'm glad you pulled yourself out of that."

"I don't think I could've done it without that doctor."

"OK, look. We need to see each other," I say about an hour later. "Do you have any time off coming up? It would be great if you could come over and hang out. Stay as long as you want. Then we can really catch up. We — or I — have a nice apartment with a second bedroom. I'll pay your way over."

"Thank you, but I'll pay my own way. I'd have to. It's kind of a dignity thing."

"Look, I get the whole dignity thing. But listen, I've got a lot of money. And one thing I've learned through all of this, and it's taken me years, is that there's a certain amount of grace in accepting the good things that come to you, even if they come as the result of a catastrophe."

"Well," she says after a pause, "coming over there to see you would *rock*."

"When I got back to New York from Venice it suddenly hit me that I could hire Dick Tracy to go find you. Yesterday when I heard your voice I was like, what am I, an idiot for losing touch with you?"

"I know what you mean. My life just got a fuck of a lot more wonderful when I heard your voice. So Owen, what are you gonna do now? You've got a ton of time on your hands, more than most people. You can't just sit around. You've gotta find something meaningful to do. There's a lot of years left, man."

"Funny, I just thought the same thing. I just finished writing this epic about my life. I'm emotionally tapped-the-fuck-out. I don't know what to do, but you know what?"

"Yeah?"

"I'll find something. Something with music probably. But for the first time in my life I'm OK with not knowing anything. It'll come to me. I'm positive about that."

"That's an OK place to be for now. I think so anyway."

The next morning she calls and tells me she can stay all of September. I hang up and do a little dance. A lame, cripple dance, but a dance nonetheless.

"Yahweh, I have news! Greta's coming!" He's groggy, taking up all of his half of the couch, ready to crash. "Things are happening, man!" He nods, smiles, and falls asleep.

Forty-Six

I've avoided going over to Knockin' on Kevin's Door since Kiera died. I lost touch with Kevin and Frankie after the memorial party (as I did with everybody except Linda). But today I feel ready to reclaim the café for myself and to resume the friendship with them if I can. I think they must understand why I disappeared, or they will when I explain it to them.

I think maybe I'm on the wrong block, but no, I've been here hundreds of times. I know the view of the park across the street as well as I know my own backyard. The café is gone! I can barely admit to myself that I'm somewhat relieved not to have to face the onslaught of memories that would have hit me when I walked through the door, but Kevin and Frankie? Where are they? What happened?

Kevin's is now a children's clothing boutique with no discernable name. In the window you see a display consisting of a single pair of blue leather baby shoes perched on a white marble pedestal. As soon as I step inside I think I can smell Frankie's espresso in the air, in fact I'm sure of it, and I think to myself again that the past doesn't always have to be completely lost, does it? I savor all those years in one deep breath. I look for signs of anything else that might have survived but can find nothing on a quick glance around. There are only a few items on hangers in each separate little section. Four or five pairs of pants, three shirts on a waist-high display table, two or three pairs of shoes on a shelf. A little glass desk, its top as clean and devoid of clutter as the mind of a Buddha, occupies a corner by the window.

The lone saleswoman, who I must confess is just finishing a little porcelain cup of espresso, greets me with a pleasant hello and a smile. She looks to be my age, very pretty in a former-Upper-East-Side debutante sort of way, with wavy red hair, cute glasses, wearing a dress she might call "Tahoe" instead of blue. A minute or two later I see that she has beautiful hands, fingers elegantly harboring silver rings with small stones. I think I see coral, turquoise, lapis lazuli. A tiny silver band has captured one thumb. No wedding ring. I wonder why I notice that. It takes me off guard, makes me feel a stir. Her nails are painted red, a shade that complements her hair. She wears heels that match the dress; her legs are fine-tuned, no-nonsense legs that look up at me and say, *"Excuse me, do you have a question?"* Her smile is as fake as the smile on a divorce lawyer. It was not a rare occurrence to spot women like her on Madison Avenue, but to find her in the East Village, in a boutique like this, shocks me into realizing how long I've been hibernating.

Just for the hell of it I pick up a purple sweater on a glittery silver hanger, a sweater that would be too small for anyone over two. I examine it as if I were looking for lice.

"It's flawless," she says. "Made by hand in Wales on a nineteenth-century loom." She steps closer and reaches out to touch the fabric. A hint of perfume — gardenia and peach? — is just subtle enough to make me want to lean in closer and find its source.

"The artist is Dafina Wilde, who is a genius at creating innovative organic clothing for children."

"Organic clothing for children."

She nods.

I look at the price. Ninety-six dollars. I make an involuntary sound, something like a breath burp. She sighs quietly. I look at a couple more sweaters.

"These are Cruella De Vil as well?"

"Dafina Wilde. Yes. Made from organic sheep wool from the Moors."

"Organic sheep."

I walk around touching things. There isn't much there. I pick up a pair of shoes identical to the ones in the window. The leather feels good, very soft, probably very comfortable on a three-year-old.

I pinch the pair by the tops, holding them up. They are quite a bit heavier than you'd think, which seems odd to me. "Who's the shoe artist?"

"That one I'd have to look up. One of those Italian artists who goes by one name."

"You mean like Michelangelo?"

She laughs. "Something like that." She walks over to the desk and grabs a notebook. I wait as she flips through it with a kind of urgency, like someone rifling through the yellow pages trying to find a plumber before the kitchen floods.

"Romolini."

"Aha! Of course!" And of course I have no idea who that is. I look at the price of the shoes. One hundred seventy-nine dollars. "Holy shit!"

She sighs dramatically and leans back on the little desk. "I know —"

I interrupt her. "I'm sorry. I didn't mean to swear — it was involuntary." I put down the shoe.

She sighs again, this time making sure I hear it, and shrugs demonstratively. "Oh, you don't have to apologize." She walks to the pedestal, picks up a shoe. She pauses for five or six seconds. "You know what? I *know*. I know what you're thinking."

"You do?"

"You're thinking this whole place is one colossal rip-off. Which I totally get why."

"Why would you think I would think that?"

"I can just tell."

"What do *you* think of this place?"

"Shit. Do you know Candice?"

"Who's Candice?"

"She owns this shop."

"Two friends of mine leased this space when it was a café. I finally came over to see what it's like now."

She puts the shoe down, a look of trepidation on her face. "Look, if you really are friends with Candice just tell me and I'll walk back over there and die." She gestures to the little desk.

"I told you I don't know her. Don't worry."

"You didn't say that. You told me your friends had this place when it was a café." She says none of this with any trace of paranoia.

"Look. I should go. I don't know Candice. And from what I gather I'm really sorry you do." I take a couple of steps toward the door.

"I apologize. I . . . I should never have gotten into this."

"This conversation or this job?"

She smiles. "Both. Nothing personal."

"What happened? Did you lose a bet?"

She looks away, thinking. I believe I can tell she's dying to talk to someone and whether it will be me is still an open question. Then she says with a self-effacing smile, "I have a B.A. in Philosophy. So you see, here's where *that* plane landed."

"That's about as useful as having a degree in that Nazi thing, the one where they measured heads."

"I know. But I loved it. And here I am, the 'would-you-like-shoes-with-that' cliché."

I'd completely misjudged her, and my attraction to her immediately kicks in retroactively, with full force, from the moment she first said hello. "If it makes you feel any better, I have a Ph.D. in Failure. Graduated with honors, *summa cum laude*. Bit of a paradox there, I know."

"Congratulations. I guess."

Now I'm nervous and alive and start walking slowly around the store. Everything about her. Damn. "So Candice knows these . . . what? I don't know what to call them. These organic clothing farmers?"

"You know, I don't even know if Dafina Wilde is real. *I've* never met her. The nineteenth-century loom, the sheep on the Moors? Really?" She stops and laughs at herself, then points at the purple sweater. "For all I know that fucking thing was made by a couple of eight-year-olds in Shanghai."

I laugh and walk over to it again, a little self-conscious of my limp, and spin it around. "What's Candice like? A petty tyrant?"

"Not completely. You'd think she would be, owning a place like this, wouldn't you? But she's not the monster I've inadvertently conjured up for you. The job isn't so bad in some ways. She does make me wear these oddly-out-of-place cocktail party clothes, and I don't understand why, but it's really kind of fun dressing up. I don't have to do much. All her limits and restrictions give me plenty of free time. I'm not allowed to put more than two pairs of shoes within six inches of each other. I can't create outfits. I can't make a display with, say, a shirt, pants and shoes that go together. Her idea is to let parents express their creativity by buying this crap. That's why I'm required to use the word 'artist' when I talk about the people who supposedly make these things. She wants to promote the idea, through what she perceives to be a clever strategy of non-promotion, that picking out outfits for a toddler in here is an act of artistic expression."

"It's an expression of something, but I'm not sure what."

"It's an expression of stupid."

She lights up, happy she's made me laugh again.

"I want to ask you something," I say, feeling light and reckless. "Do you know how the more mass something has, the more it's subject to gravity? For example, the moon. If it was smaller it would float away."

"It would? That doesn't sound right to me."

"I overheard Carl Sagan say that one night at the White Horse. It snowed the day before and his shoes were all wet from the sludge."

"You know why I don't believe you?"

"Because you're smart?"

"No. Because Carl Sagan winters in Barbados with my Aunt Trudy. She's his mistress. They've had sex billions and billions of times."

I find that so hilarious I laugh until tears come, and she starts laughing too, and the two of us can't stop. I haven't laughed like that in eons. Then there's that moment when we resurface and understand that we've shared something strangers don't encounter very often. A few seconds of self-consciousness wash over me. Her too, I think.

"*Anyway*," I say after recovering, "what I'm getting at — wait. OK, would you pick up that pair of shoes?" I point to the blue pair on the pillar.

She picks one up.

"No, both of them, with one hand."

She does.

"How do they feel?"

"They feel like a pair of toddler shoes."

"Yeah, but how do they *feel?*"

"They're kind of heavy, actually."

"Exactly!"

"So?"

"How many pairs of these have you sold? And before you answer, if you sold just one shoe, like to the parent of a one-legged kid or something, that only counts as half."

"I only sell them in pairs, even if the kid has only one foot. I mean, what the hell am I supposed to do with the *other* shoe?" She looks at me in mock-befuddlement. Her expression is cute and funny as hell.

"I don't know. Grow a potato in it."

"Maybe plant some organic crabgrass seeds from the organic part of the Moors."

"If you keep me laughing I can't get to the point. So how many sales?"

"I haven't worked here very long."

"Should I take that as a 'I haven't sold any so don't ask me again'?'"

"What the hell are you driving at?" She tries to keep herself from laughing and barely succeeds.

"What I'm saying is you need all the help you can get selling three-million-dollar shoes for a kid who —"

"— for a kid who will grow out of them in a week. I know." She swings the shoes back and forth. "Can I put them down now?"

"Oh, yeah. Sorry."

"It's been a slow day, and this is quite unexpected." She laughs quietly, saying that almost to herself as she puts the shoes back.

"I *think* that Mr. Romoletti —"

"There's no 'mister.' Just 'Romolini.'"

"Ah. Well, we mustn't forget his assistant, Rigatoni."

"Or his mentor, Mussolini."

That brings a chuckle from both of us.

"So here's the theory: I *think* Signore Romolini — wait. Is using 'signore' verboten, too, or is he OK with that since it's Italian?"

"I'm pretty sure it's verboten."

"OK, then. The theory is that Romolini made these shoes heavier so as to give the earth's gravitational pull sufficient force to *draw each individual shoe earthward,* to keep the unwitting little shoe-wearing bastard grounded, to prevent the little thug from climbing on things or even running very fast. What I mean is, if you want to *sell* these things, you have to call them *Gravity Shoes* — a name and an explanation for why they're so goddamned expensive."

"Gravity shoes?"

"I think it's worth a try."

"That's as cockamamie an idea as some of the other stuff I have to say about these clothes."

"Well, this is one wacky shop."

"Did you notice," she says after an awkward pause, during which I pretend to gauge whether a tiny green shirt is my style (what has come over me?), "there's no open-and-closed sign? And no shop hours printed on the door?"

I put the shirt down. "No, I didn't. But yeah."

"See, the idea is, if you're a hip neighborhood parent, you'll just *know* when we're open. Kind of like you'd just know where the latest secret after-hours club is. Candice treats this place like that. Sometimes I get the impression that she might be making a very elaborate joke, an ironic comment on the neighborhood. If that's true it's hilarious."

"It is."

"Except it's my job to spew the garbage. As you know," she adds self-consciously.

"If it makes you feel any better, you weren't very good at it."

"Well, you are a terrible customer. You're not supposed to disbelieve me."

I stand there for a minute feeling very self-conscious of the fact that I am lusting after her, wondering if she can tell. More than that, or at least equal to that, I *like* her; I'm totally charmed by her. And I am acutely aware that all this is happening in the middle of Kevin's, in the exact space Kiera and I must have stood hundreds of times. But that awareness doesn't feel constraining like it might have before. Now it feels like continuity.

"Well, I have to get on with my life now that this mystery is solved." I tell myself to leave before I blow the vibe.

"I'm glad you came in. Was it a nice café?"

"One of a kind."

She looks around the space. "I can imagine. Cozy."

"So," I say, my good hand on the door, "if I meet somebody looking for a three hundred dollar pair of baby socks made in Lisbon from a Portuguese chicken on a fifteenth-century ox cart, I'll send her over. And who knows? It might even be me."

She smiles and moves a red pair of shoes two or three inches away from a pink pair of shoes. She adjusts the shoelace on one of them. "Drop by anytime," she says, still focused on the shoelace. "We're getting very rare organic rhino moccasins in soon."

"Those'll be at least ten or twenty thousand dollars a pair. How're you gonna sell 'em?"

"Don't worry, they'll fly outta here like fruit bats."

That makes me laugh. Again.

"So," she says, "if you're hip you'll just *know* when I'm here. And if you're not, you might guess that I usually work the tedious and boring weekday afternoons."

"I used to be hip. Now I'm a drunkard."

She looks me over. "You are not!"

"Bogart says that to a Nazi in *Casablanca*. The drunkard part."

"Thank you for sharing that with me. I feel special." She smiles ironically.

I'm still holding the door and it's beginning to feel awkward.

"To tell you the truth I have no idea why I said that."

"You said it because it's funny. To me at least. The kind of funny where it's funny but you don't laugh."

"Well, that's all that matters. To me at least. So . . . my name is Owen. It's been great meeting you. You're a marginally fun person to be around."

"Madeleine. Nice meeting you too. And you're a quasi-marginally fun person to be around."

"Between the two of us we're almost one whole fun person."

"A few more shoe jokes and we might've gotten there."

We both laugh again and I'm on the verge of asking her out. I want to tell her that I like her a lot, but I haven't got a belly full of wine, as Paul would say. Instead I just wave and smile, she waves back and smiles, we hold each other's gaze for an extra breath, and I'm on my way.

I walk home embracing powerfully invasive thoughts. Every two hundred feet another fantasy, one more vivid than the next. I have to stop for ice cream to calm myself down. I pay close attention to a voice that keeps saying, "Kiera would want you to." But I pay more attention to another voice that says, "*I* want to."

§

Three days later on a gorgeous sunny afternoon I'm walking over to see Madeleine, having made a promise to myself before I left the apartment that no matter what, I won't chicken out and turn back. On the way over my heart beats like I'm trekking in the Himalayas. I can't slow it down. The emotional altitude is pretty fucking high and gets more intense with every block. But it's a good intense. I'm alive. At last, as I turn from East Tenth Street onto Avenue A, I can already see the storefront with the door propped open, and I feel, at least for the moment, the radical insurgency of hope.

THE END

Acknowledgements

Owen Kilroy was born during a conversation I had with my friend Doug Mora some years ago on a December night in Seattle. We spoke over whiskeys in a neighborhood bar, having just come from seeing the stunning film, Shame. I don't remember what we talked about except that given the nature of the movie, it must have been about pain and loss and heartache and misery and what a great actress Carey Mulligan is. It must have been about how the past can shape a life, about identity and resilience and hope, or the absence of any of those. For whatever reason, I walked out of Ten Mercer that night with an early incarnation of Owen in my mind. And speaking of resilience, as I wrote the novel on and off over the years, Doug read countless drafts, and portions of drafts, and revisions of revisions of revisions, and talked through ideas with me, and was always there when I asked him to read something new. His comments and encouragement and unwavering support throughout all of it were invaluable. For all of that and for his friendship I am eternally grateful.

Extra-special thanks to my daughter Nicole for wandering around Ireland with me looking for where Kiera might be from, and finally finding her in Drumcliff and Mullaghmore. If not for Nicole reminding me to keep driving on the "wrong" side of the road, especially on the roundabouts, this book may never have been written.

I am deeply indebted to Joe Rutte, whose belief in me actually increased the more he learned about the many crazy, reckless, colossal mistakes I've made in this life. His impact on me and on this book has been immeasurable.

Many thanks to editor Marlene Adelstein, who worked with me over many months to help shape the manuscript into a viable piece of work, convincing me, after a Herculean effort, to cut sixteen thousand words that I believed were essential. I was wrong.

And thanks to Joyce Yarrow, whose comments on this manuscript, and whose decades-long support, have been extremely helpful and inspiring.

Other readers for whose time and effort I am so immeasurably grateful are Peter Melocco, Scott Palmer, Suzanne DeLacey, Kris Emanuel, Sarah Green, Jennifer McIntyre, and Rachel Forde.

Thanks so very much to Kerry Eielsen and John Fanning for my unforgettable time at the La Muse Writers Retreat in France (and to Sarah, Nicola, and Nell!), to Justin Ahren at the Martha's Vineyard Writers Retreat, and to Preston Browning at the Wellspring House Writers Residency.

I owe Michelle Latiolais and Ron Carlson a huge thank you for admitting me into the UC Irvine MFA program based on an early chapter of this book. I will always deeply regret that I was unable to attend. Their decision to recognize me as a writer worthy of their time and attention meant, and means, so much to me.

Finally, I am so thrilled and so grateful to Lou Aronica for inviting me with open arms into the Story Plant world, and to Allison Maretti for her patience, understanding, and expertise in preparing EG for its launch.

About The Author

Peter Marlton is the pseudonym for Pete MacDonald, who has discovered that writing fiction under another name can be psychologically and artistically liberating—it somehow skirts, without wholly avoiding, the imposter syndrome. Stories and essays published as Pete MacDonald have appeared in The New York Times, The Battered Suitcase (a novella), Inkwell Journal, Barrellhouse Magazine, and others. His original screenplay was a finalist in the Austin Screenwriting Competition. More info is available at www.petermarlton.com.

Reading Group Questions

1. Why did Owen feel the need to write? What did it do or not do for him? Have you ever felt the need or the desire to do write about your life?

2. Why did Owen hate the police? What are your thoughts on how cops deal with juveniles?

3. How did you feel about Owen's and Shooky's drug dealing?

4. Was Owen's mother a character you found yourself judging? Why? What about his father?

5. Should Owen be held responsible for Sarah's death?

6. Did Sarah's suicide effect you? If so, how?

7. What did you think of the prison characters: Grandma and Bodean? Did they have their hands full with all those kids?

8. When Wesley blew up Bodean's truck did you see that as positive under the circumstances, negative, or a little of both?

9. The Good Samaritan in the novel took a huge risk. She broke the law as a way of honoring the memory of her brother. Are laws and morals the same thing?

10. Greta and Owen become close friends very quickly. How and why?

11. What did you think of their friendship as it developed?

12. Owen met Kiera, fell madly in love with her, and knew she had strong feelings for him, yet while she was in San Francisco with Nora he made another porn film with Greta. Did that bother you even though he was fulfilling a promise to Greta?

13. Kiera invited Owen to move in with her very quickly, mentioning her mother's death as part of her motivation. (Carpe diem.) Do you think Kiera had a premonition that she would die young like her mother?

14. Did Kiera "save" Owen by loving him and "teaching" him about art?

15. What did you make of Shooky and Kiera's relationship?

16. When Owen was faced with the opportunity to tell Shooky that he and Kiera were together, he didn't. Was that the right thing to do?

17. Why did Kiera keep Owen's history a secret from Nora and her father? Why not be honest? Was it strength or weakness to do that or something else?

18. Was Owen's attraction to Emily something he and Kiera should have talked about?

19. What about Emily's attraction to Owen? Same question.

20. What would have happened if Owen and Emily had had sex the night they kissed? Would it really have been so bad?

21. Kiera believed in fate, and signs, and Celtic mysticism. Did Owen?

22. There are many women in this novel, all of whom had an impact on Owen. His mother, Officer Beatrice Walls, Grandma, the Good Samaritan, Moonlight Wind, Greta, Kiera, Emily, Nora, Dr. Sarojini Shukla, and Madeleine. What part do they play, if any, in Owen learning to grow up?

23. How did the inheritance impact Kiera and Owen (besides making them rich)?

24. Did Kiera know she was pregnant? If so why hadn't she told Owen?

25. The novel has several instances of deception, lies, lies by omission, and betrayal. One of these is Owen giving Nora a fake urn to bury. Was that wrong? Should he have stood up to her, told her the truth, and insisted on honoring Kiera's wishes?

26. Owen falls apart after Kiera dies. Is he a weak character?

27. Was it weakness that led him to attempt suicide?

28. Why did he "let himself" be comforted and guided by Dr. Shukla?

29. Did Owen have an ongoing relationship of some kind with Sarah over the years covered on the book?

30. When he visited Sarah's grave he saw that her parents chose a picture of her with hair that they hated. Was that too little too late?

31. Should Owen have tried harder to find out if Shook's Books belonged to Shooky?

32. Do you think Owen and Madeleine become a couple? Why? Why not?

33. What do you think the next ten years of Owen's life might be like?

34. If this book were made into a film who would you cast as Owen? Shooky? Greta? Kiera?